EST
1637

IN VITAM MORTEM

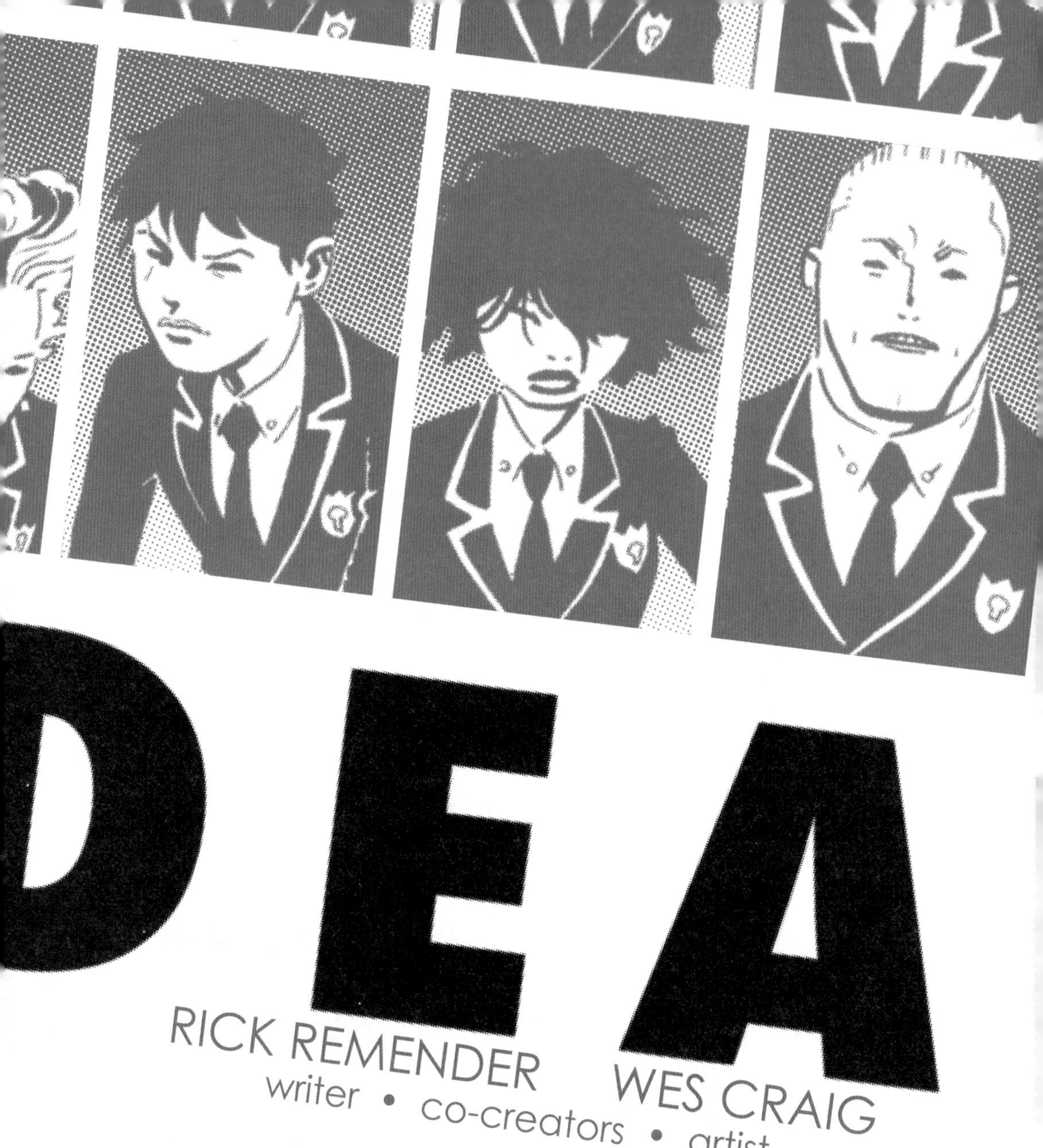

DEA

RICK REMENDER writer • co-creators • artist WES CRAIG

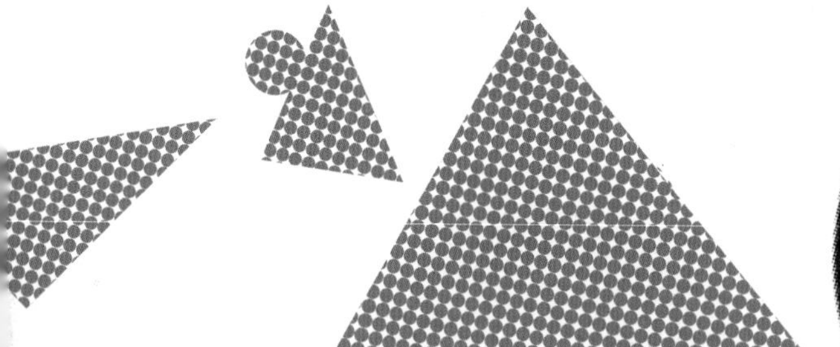

C

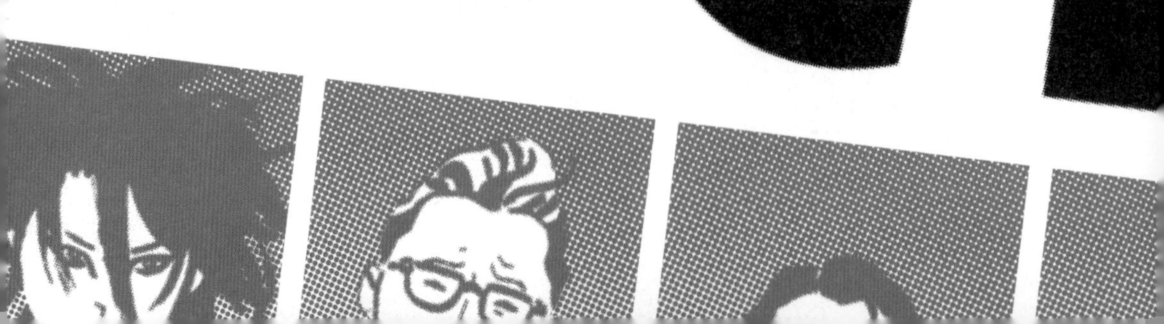

DLY ASS

LEE LOUGHRIDGE
colorist

RUS WOOTON
letterer • logo design

IMAGE COMICS, INC.

Robert Kirkman • Chief Operating Officer
Erik Larsen • Chief Financial Officer
Todd McFarlane • President
Marc Silvestri • Chief Executive Officer
Jim Valentino • Vice President

Eric Stephenson • Publisher / Chief Creative Officer
Nicole Lapalme • Vice President of Finance
Leanna Caunter • Accounting Analyst
Sue Korpela • Accounting & HR Manager
Matt Parkinson • Vice President of Sales & Publishing Planning
Lorelei Bunjes • Vice President of Digital Strategy
Dirk Wood • Vice President of International Sales & Licensing
Ryan Brewer • International Sales & Licensing Manager
Alex Cox • Director of Direct Market Sales
Chloe Ramos • Book Market & Library Sales Manager
Emilio Bautista • Digital Sales Coordinator
Jon Schlaffman • Specialty Sales Coordinator
Kat Salazar • Vice President of PR & Marketing
Deanna Phelps • Marketing Design Manager
Drew Fitzgerald • Marketing Content Associate
Heather Doornink • Vice President of Production
Drew Gill • Art Director
Hilary DiLoreto • Print Manager
Tricia Ramos • Traffic Manager
Melissa Gifford • Content Manager
Erika Schnatz • Senior Production Artist
Wesley Griffith • Production Artist
Rich Fowlks • Production Artist

imagecomics.com

GABE DINGER
production assistant

ERIKA SCHNATZ
production design

DEADLY CLASS VOLUME 12: A FOND FAREWELL, PART TWO. First printing. November 2022. Published by Image Comics, Inc. Office of publication: PO BOX 14458, Portland, OR 97293. Copyright © 2022 Rick Remender & Wes Craig. All rights reserved. Contains material originally published in single magazine form as DEADLY CLASS #53-56. DEADLY CLASS™ (including all prominent characters featured herein), its logo and all character likenesses are trademarks of Rick Remender & Wes Craig, unless otherwise noted. Image Comics® and its logos are registered trademarks of Image Comics, Inc. No part of this publication may be reproduced or transmitted, in any form or by any means (except for short excerpts for journalistic or review purposes), without the express written permission of Rick Remender, Wes Craig, or Image Comics, Inc. All names, characters, events, and locales in this publication are entirely fictional. Any resemblance to actual persons (living or dead), events, or places, without satirical intent, is coincidental. **PRINTED IN THE USA.** For international rights, contact: foreignlicensing@imagecomics.com. ISBN: 978-1-5343-2340-7

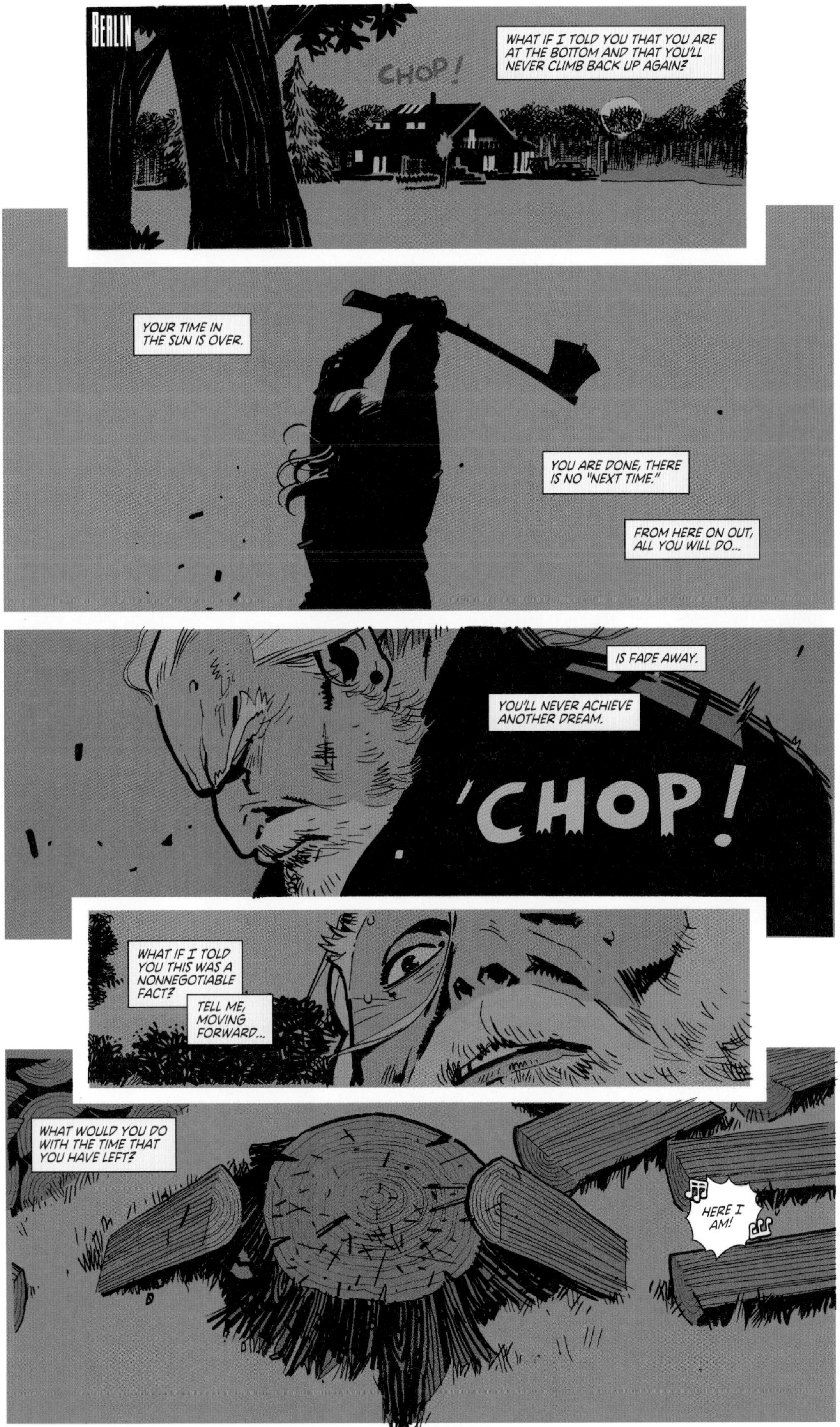
BERLIN
WHAT IF I TOLD YOU THAT YOU ARE AT THE BOTTOM AND THAT YOU'LL NEVER CLIMB BACK UP AGAIN?
CHOP!
YOUR TIME IN THE SUN IS OVER.
YOU ARE DONE, THERE IS NO "NEXT TIME."
FROM HERE ON OUT, ALL YOU WILL DO...
IS FADE AWAY.
YOU'LL NEVER ACHIEVE ANOTHER DREAM.
'CHOP!
WHAT IF I TOLD YOU THIS WAS A NONNEGOTIABLE FACT?
TELL ME, MOVING FORWARD...
WHAT WOULD YOU DO WITH THE TIME THAT YOU HAVE LEFT?
HERE I AM!

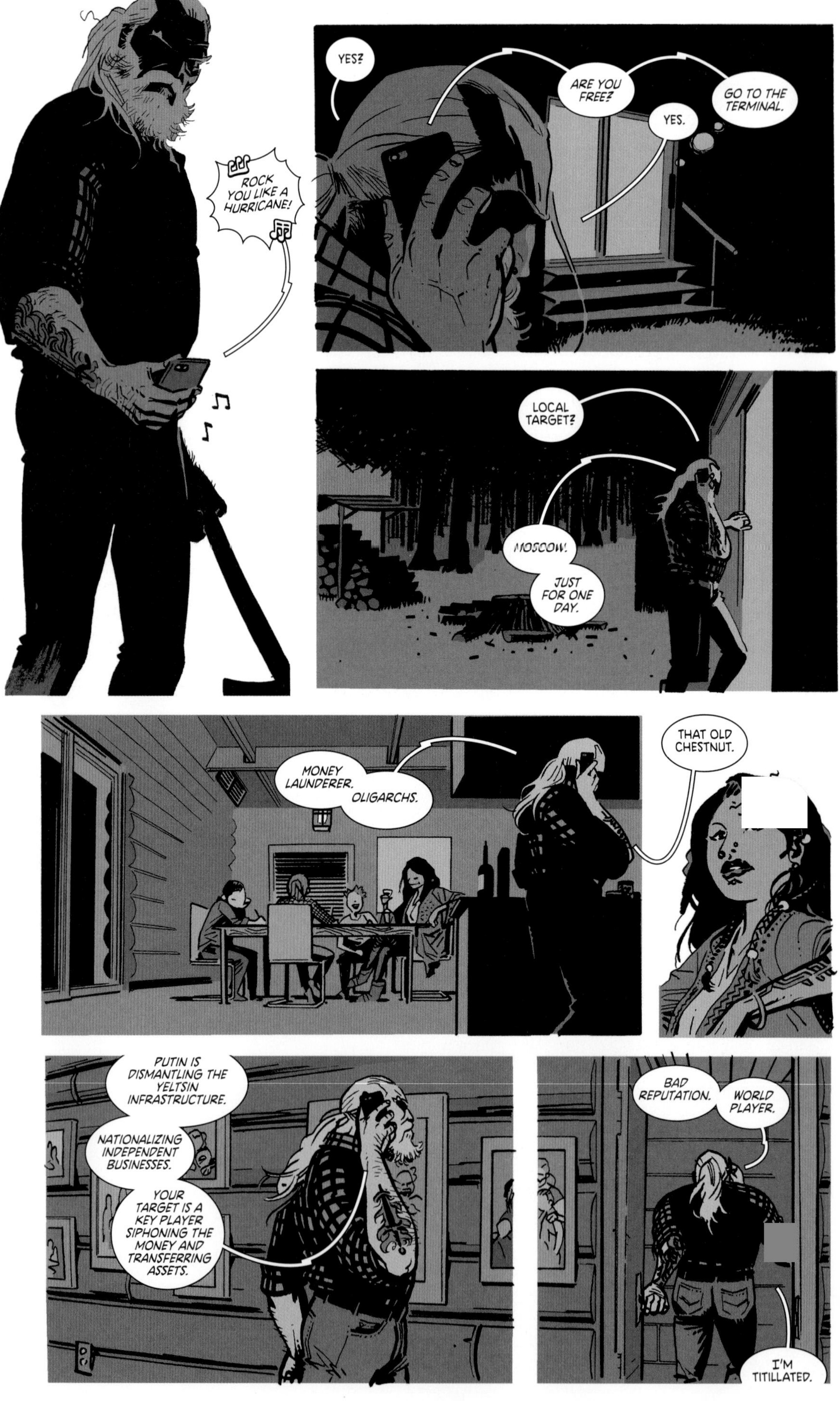
ROCK YOU LIKE A HURRICANE!
YES?
ARE YOU FREE?
YES.
GO TO THE TERMINAL.
LOCAL TARGET?
MOSCOW.
JUST FOR ONE DAY.
MONEY LAUNDERER.
OLIGARCHS.
THAT OLD CHESTNUT.
PUTIN IS DISMANTLING THE YELTSIN INFRASTRUCTURE.
NATIONALIZING INDEPENDENT BUSINESSES.
YOUR TARGET IS A KEY PLAYER SIPHONING THE MONEY AND TRANSFERRING ASSETS.
BAD REPUTATION.
WORLD PLAYER.
I'M TITILLATED.

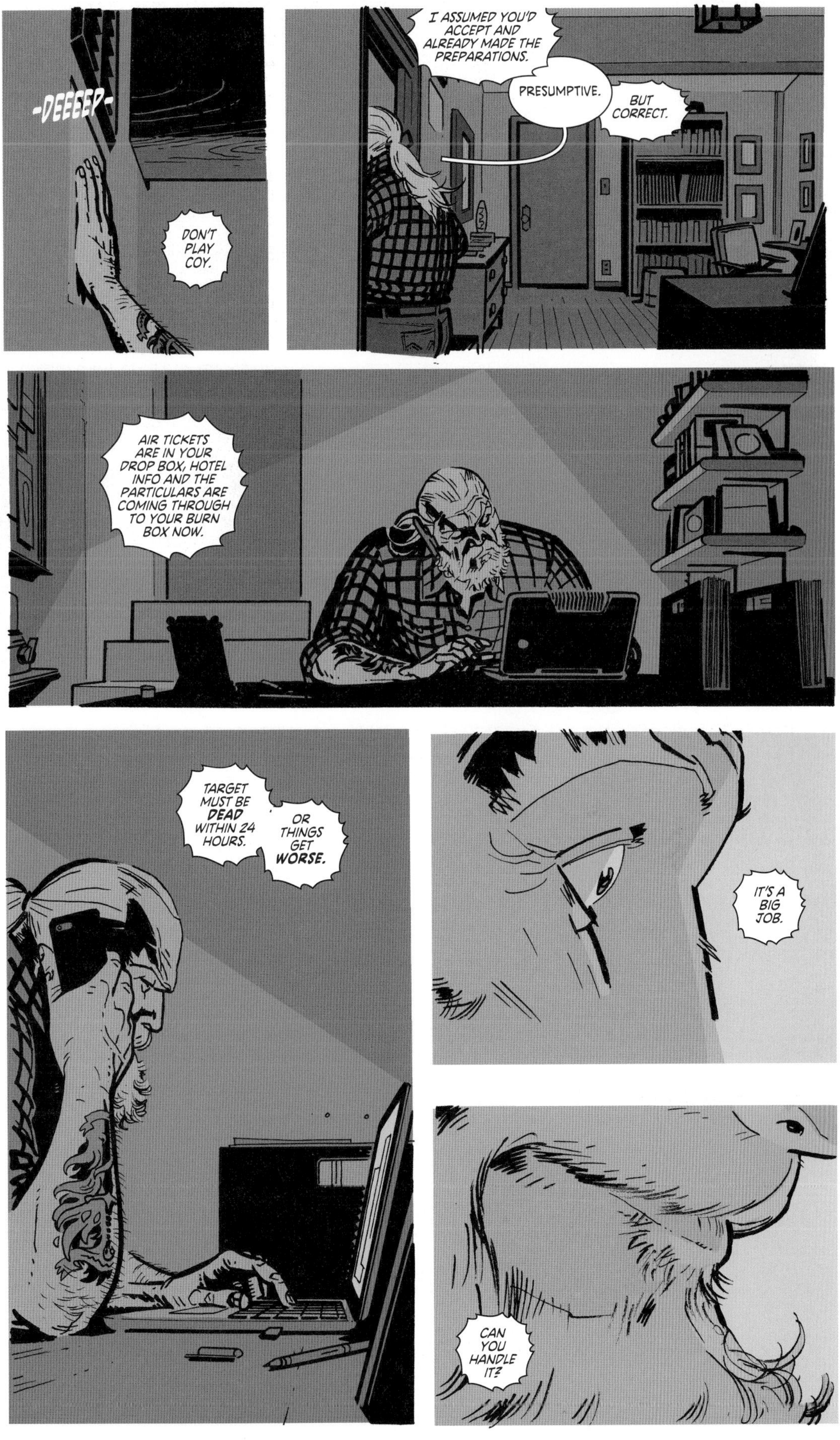
-DEEEEP-
DON'T PLAY COY.
I ASSUMED YOU'D ACCEPT AND ALREADY MADE THE PREPARATIONS.
PRESUMPTIVE.
BUT CORRECT.
AIR TICKETS ARE IN YOUR DROP BOX, HOTEL INFO AND THE PARTICULARS ARE COMING THROUGH TO YOUR BURN BOX NOW.
TARGET MUST BE **DEAD** WITHIN 24 HOURS.
OR THINGS GET **WORSE.**
IT'S A BIG JOB.
CAN YOU HANDLE IT?

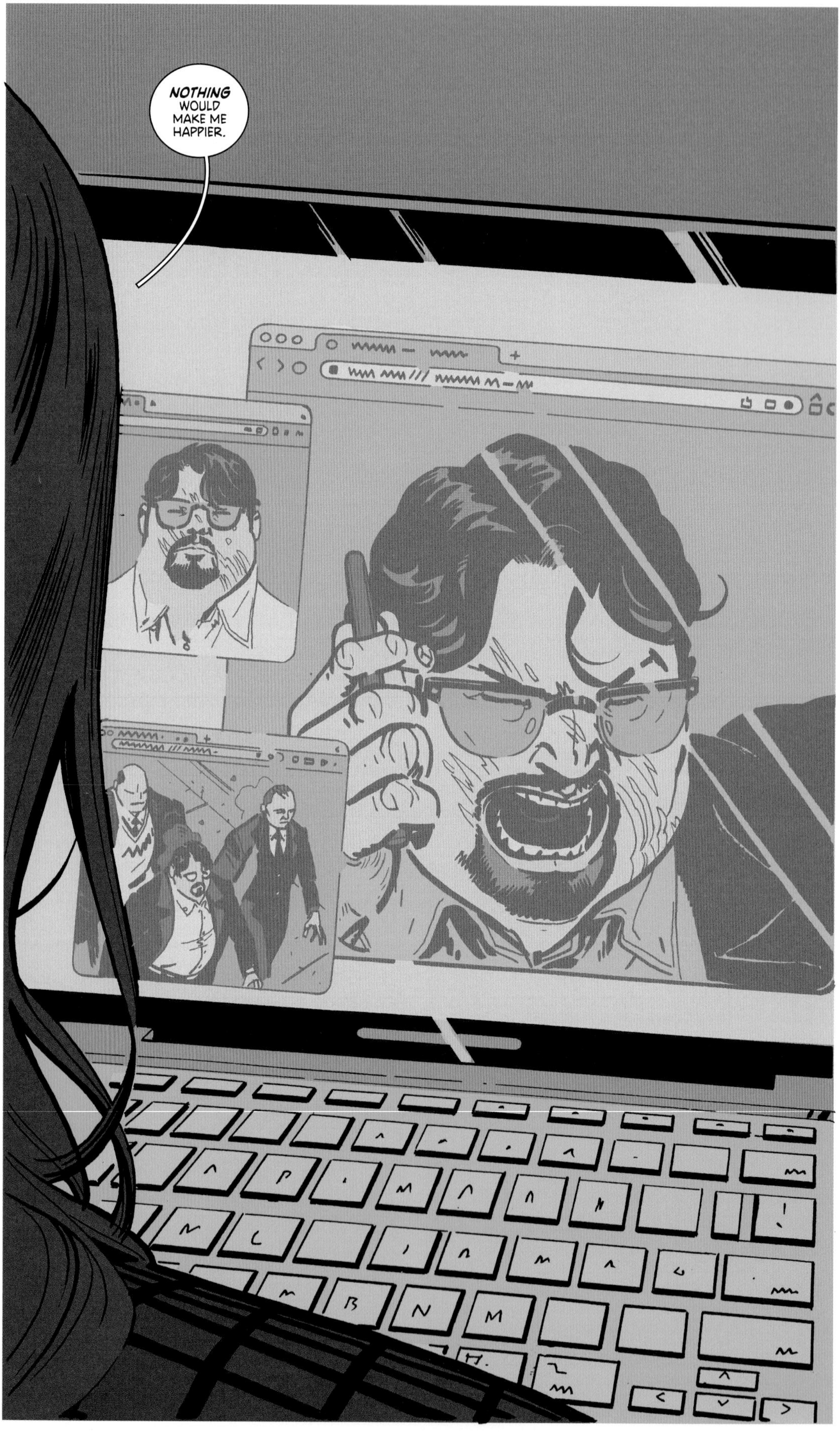
NOTHING WOULD MAKE ME HAPPIER.

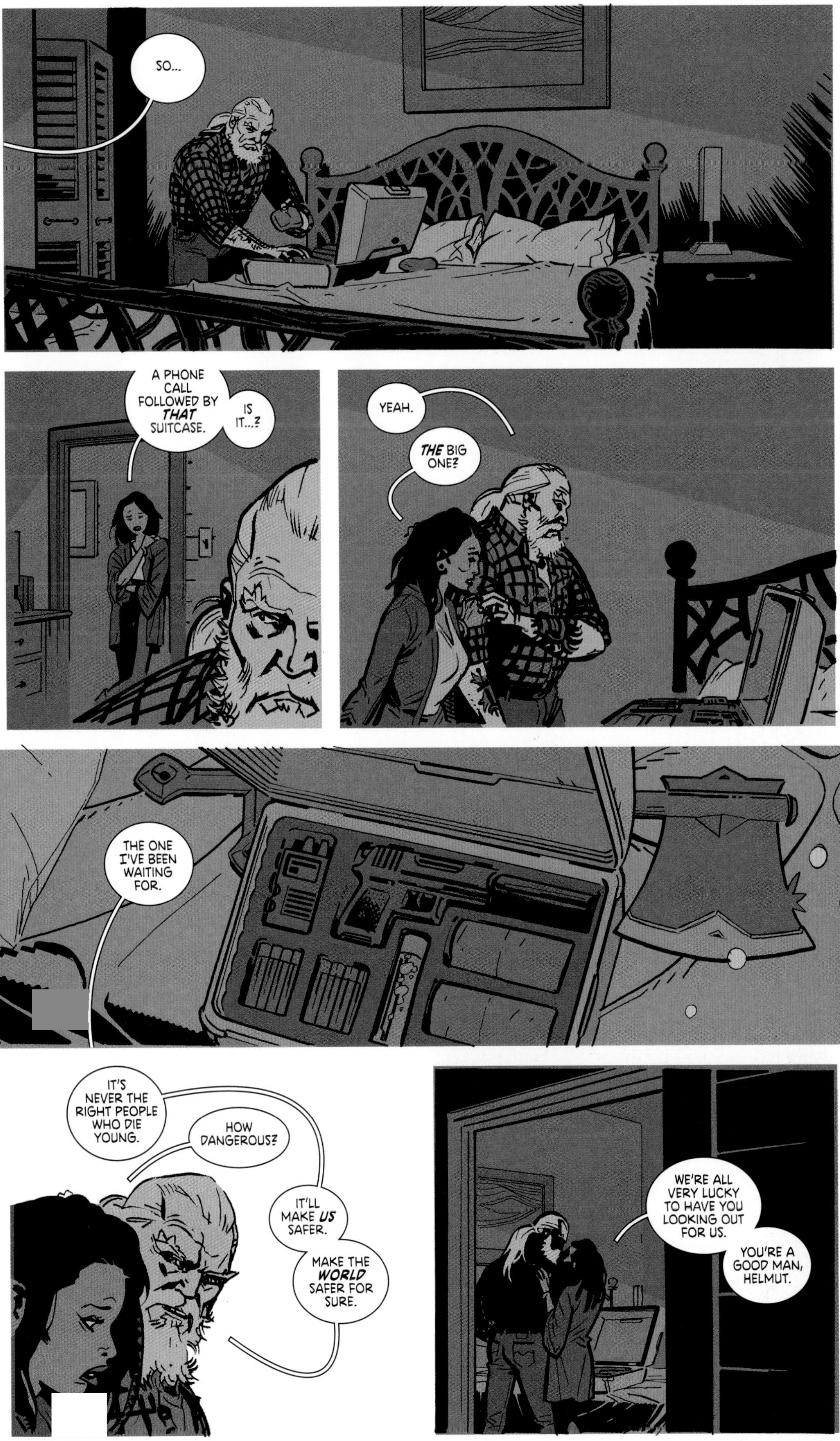
SO...
A PHONE CALL FOLLOWED BY THAT SUITCASE.
IS IT...?
YEAH.
THE BIG ONE?
THE ONE I'VE BEEN WAITING FOR.
IT'S NEVER THE RIGHT PEOPLE WHO DIE YOUNG.
HOW DANGEROUS?
IT'LL MAKE US SAFER.
MAKE THE WORLD SAFER FOR SURE.
WE'RE ALL VERY LUCKY TO HAVE YOU LOOKING OUT FOR US.
YOU'RE A GOOD MAN, HELMUT.

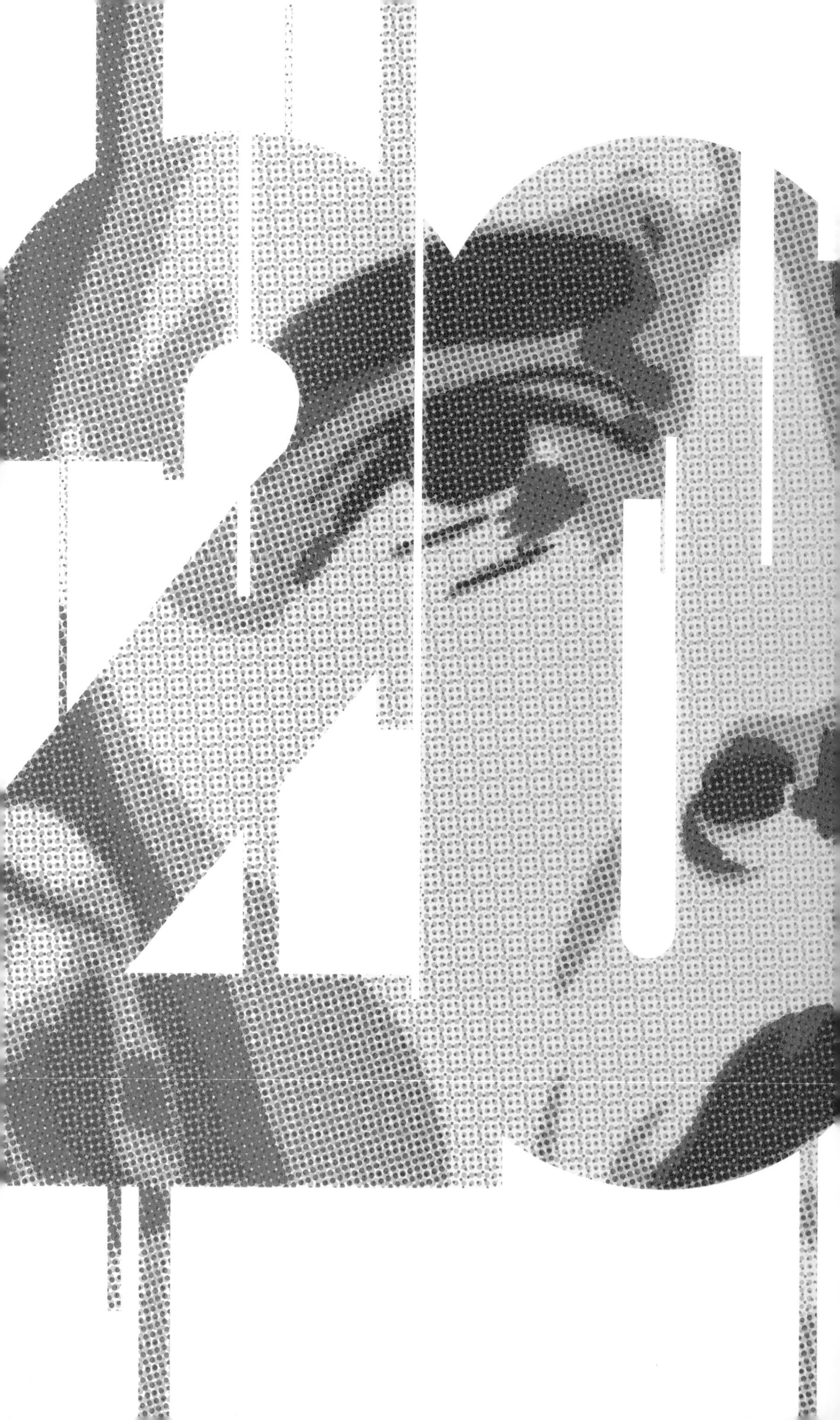

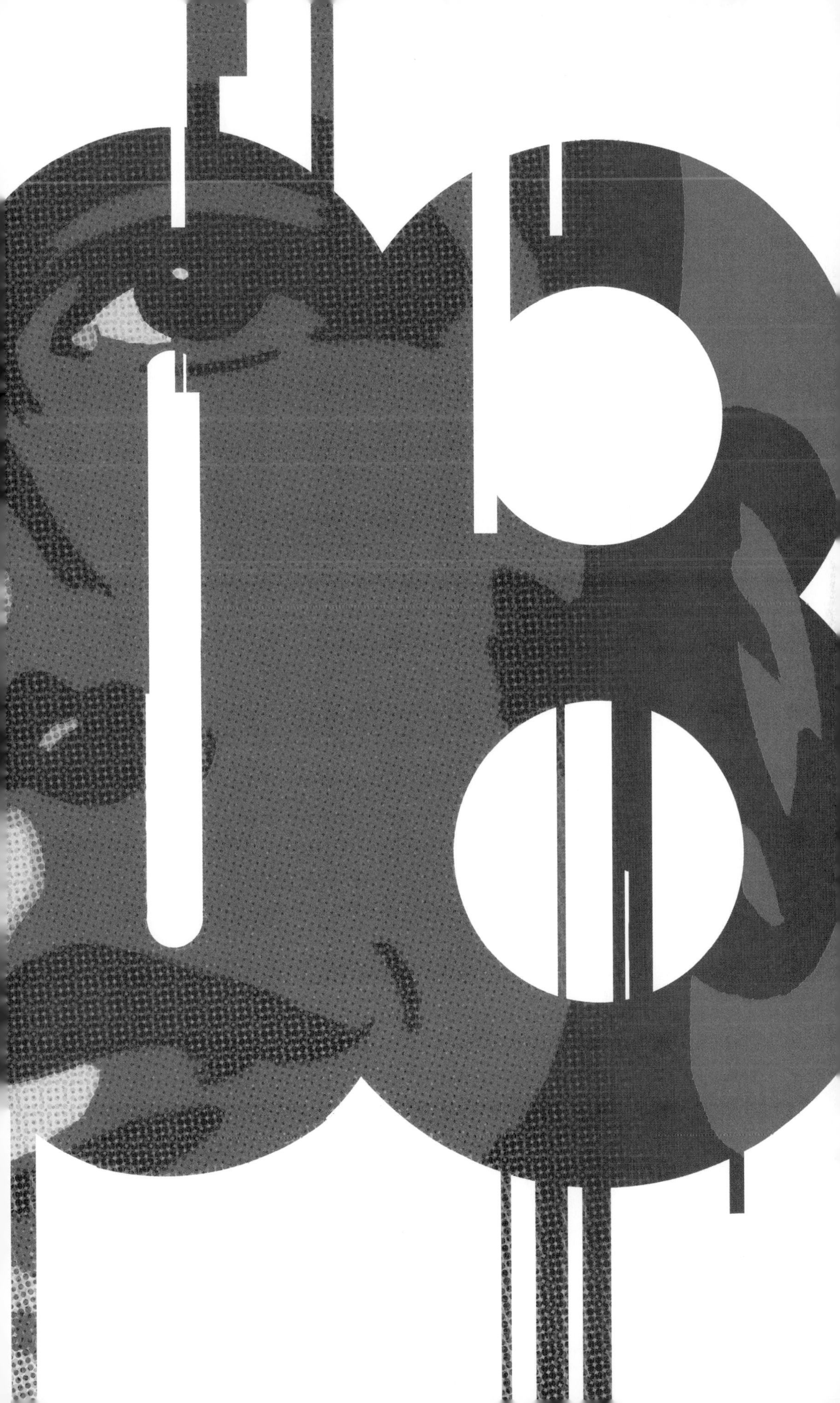

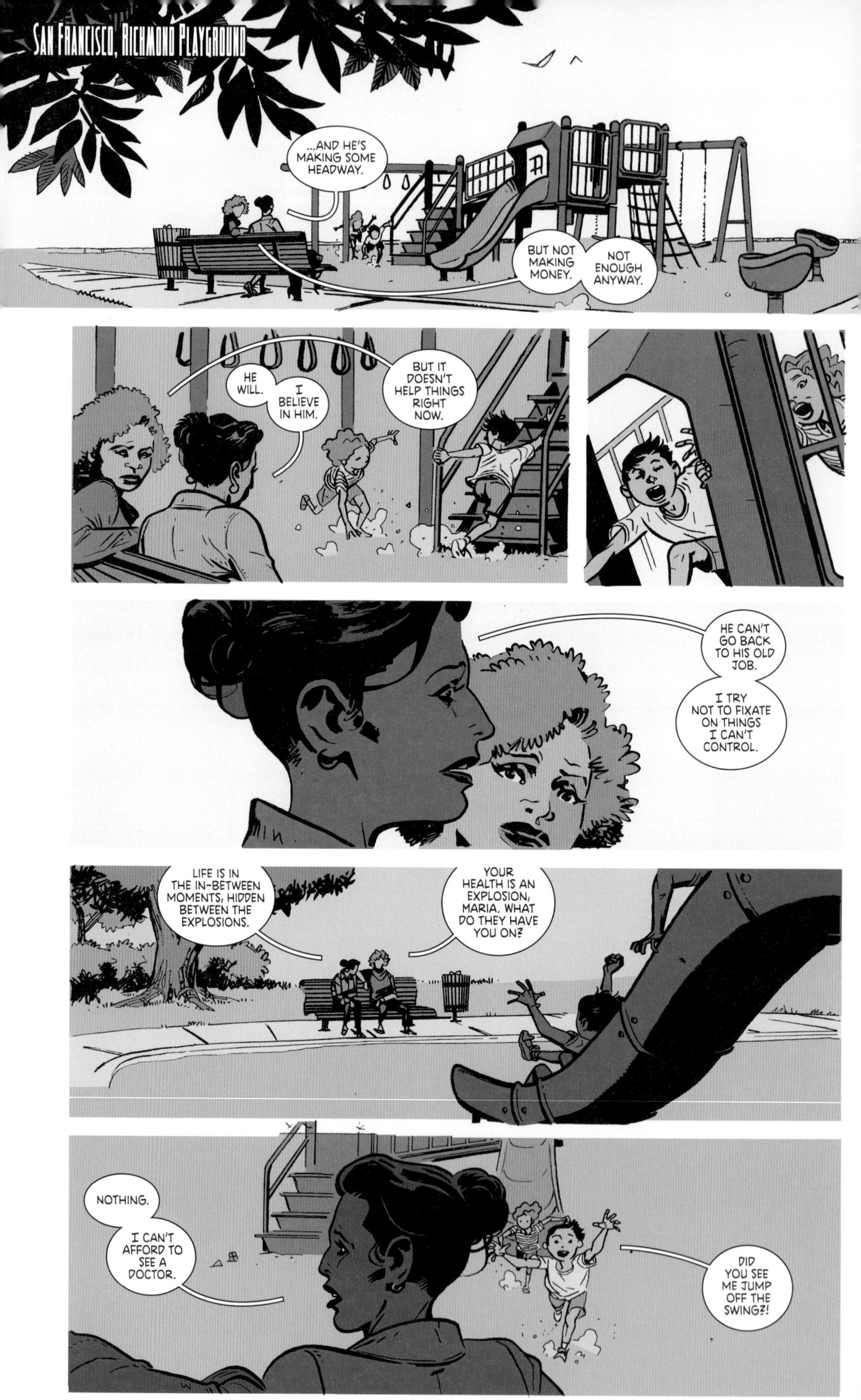
San Francisco, Richmond Playground
...AND HE'S MAKING SOME HEADWAY.
BUT NOT MAKING MONEY.
NOT ENOUGH ANYWAY.
HE WILL.
I BELIEVE IN HIM.
BUT IT DOESN'T HELP THINGS RIGHT NOW.
HE CAN'T GO BACK TO HIS OLD JOB.
I TRY NOT TO FIXATE ON THINGS I CAN'T CONTROL.
LIFE IS IN THE IN-BETWEEN MOMENTS, HIDDEN BETWEEN THE EXPLOSIONS.
YOUR HEALTH IS AN EXPLOSION, MARIA. WHAT DO THEY HAVE YOU ON?
NOTHING.
I CAN'T AFFORD TO SEE A DOCTOR.
DID YOU SEE ME JUMP OFF THE SWING?!

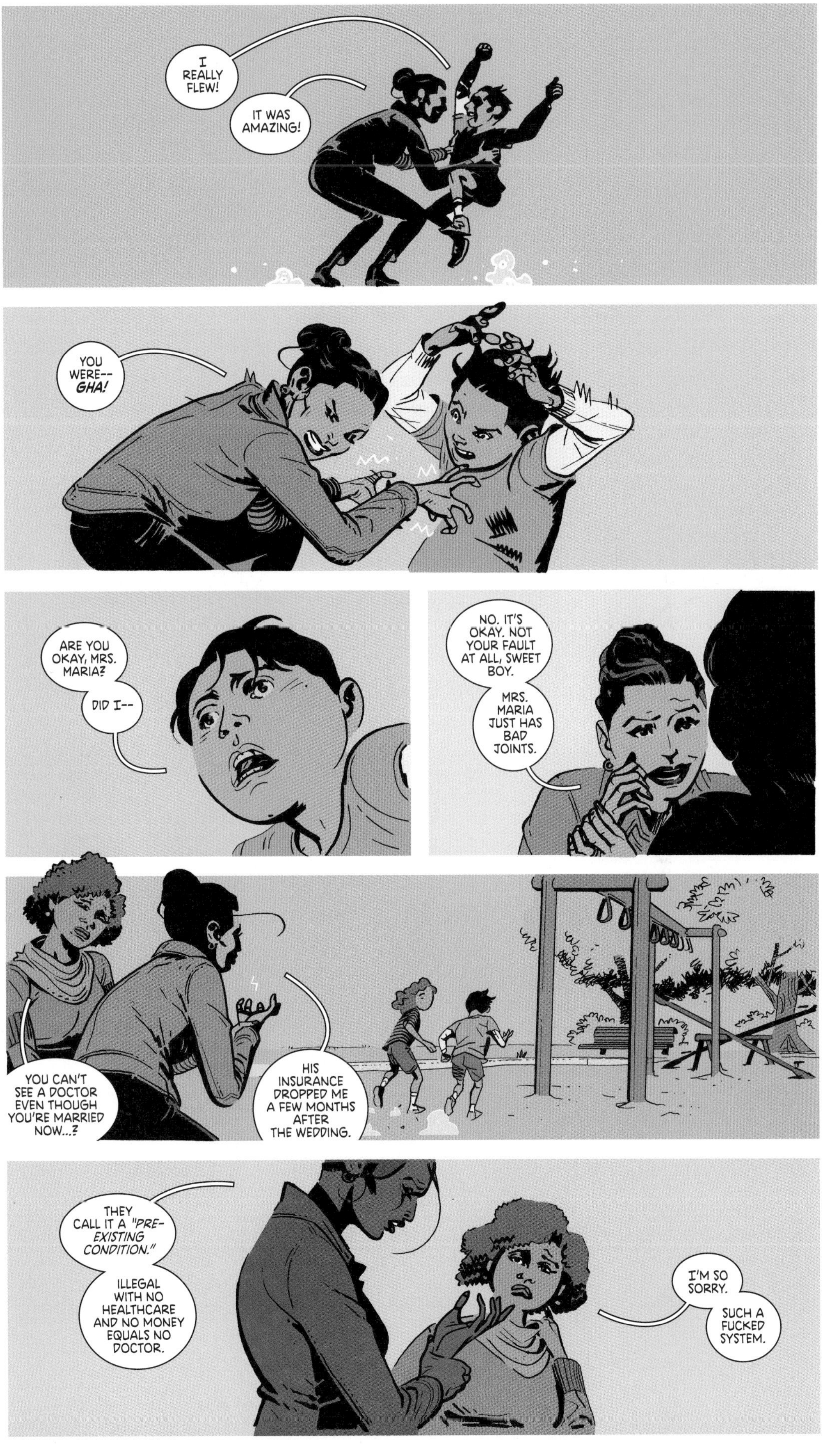
I REALLY FLEW!
IT WAS AMAZING!
YOU WERE-- *GHA!*
ARE YOU OKAY, MRS. MARIA?
DID I--
NO. IT'S OKAY. NOT YOUR FAULT AT ALL, SWEET BOY.
MRS. MARIA JUST HAS BAD JOINTS.
YOU CAN'T SEE A DOCTOR EVEN THOUGH YOU'RE MARRIED NOW...?
HIS INSURANCE DROPPED ME A FEW MONTHS AFTER THE WEDDING.
THEY CALL IT A *"PRE-EXISTING CONDITION."*
ILLEGAL WITH NO HEALTHCARE AND NO MONEY EQUALS NO DOCTOR.
I'M SO SORRY.
SUCH A FUCKED SYSTEM.

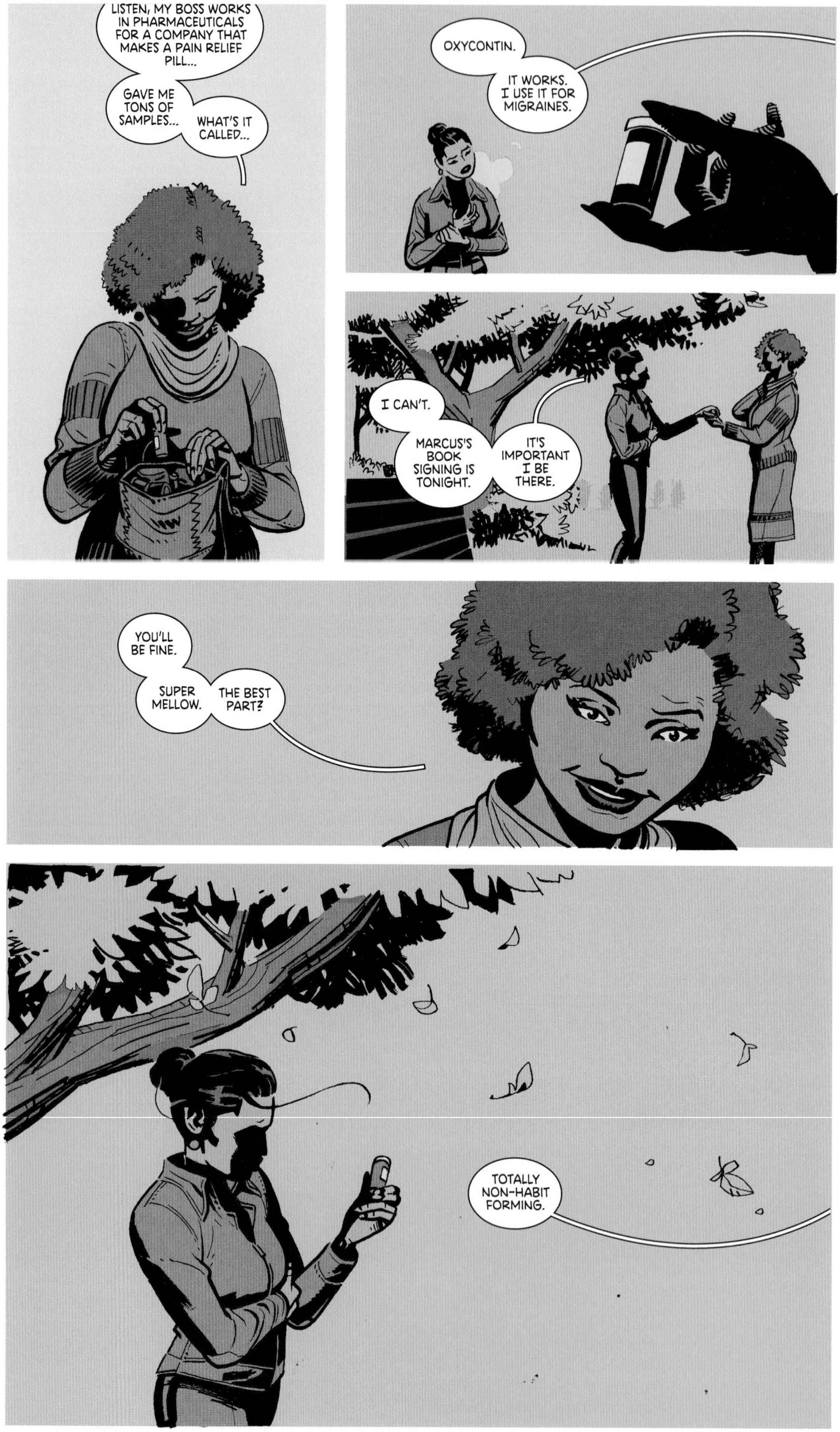

LISTEN, MY BOSS WORKS IN PHARMACEUTICALS FOR A COMPANY THAT MAKES A PAIN RELIEF PILL...
GAVE ME TONS OF SAMPLES...
WHAT'S IT CALLED...
OXYCONTIN.
IT WORKS. I USE IT FOR MIGRAINES.
I CAN'T.
MARCUS'S BOOK SIGNING IS TONIGHT.
IT'S IMPORTANT I BE THERE.
YOU'LL BE FINE.
SUPER MELLOW.
THE BEST PART?
TOTALLY NON-HABIT FORMING.

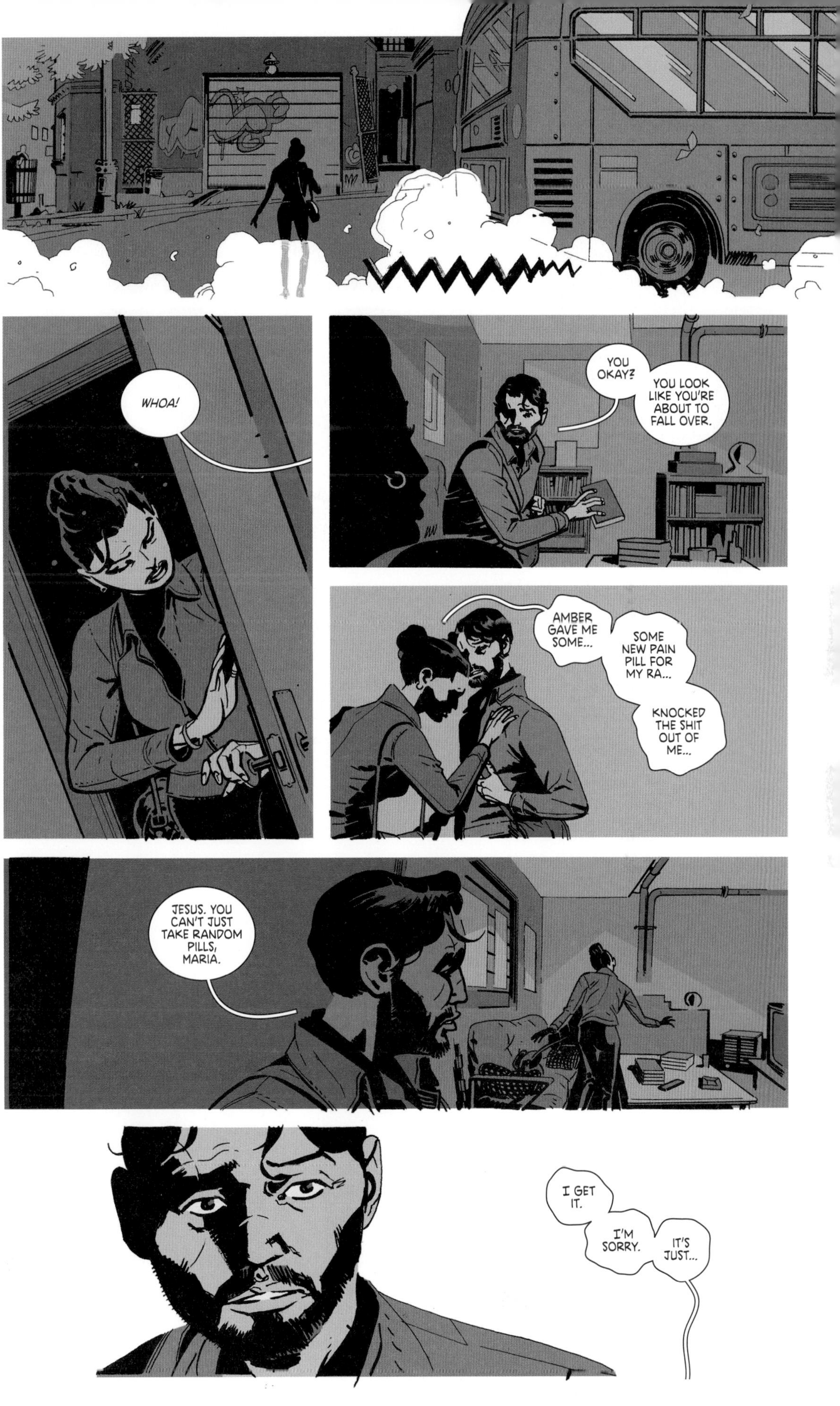
VVVVVVVVMMMM
WHOA!
YOU OKAY?
YOU LOOK LIKE YOU'RE ABOUT TO FALL OVER.
AMBER GAVE ME SOME...
SOME NEW PAIN PILL FOR MY RA...
KNOCKED THE SHIT OUT OF ME...
JESUS. YOU CAN'T JUST TAKE RANDOM PILLS, MARIA.
I GET IT.
I'M SORRY.
IT'S JUST...

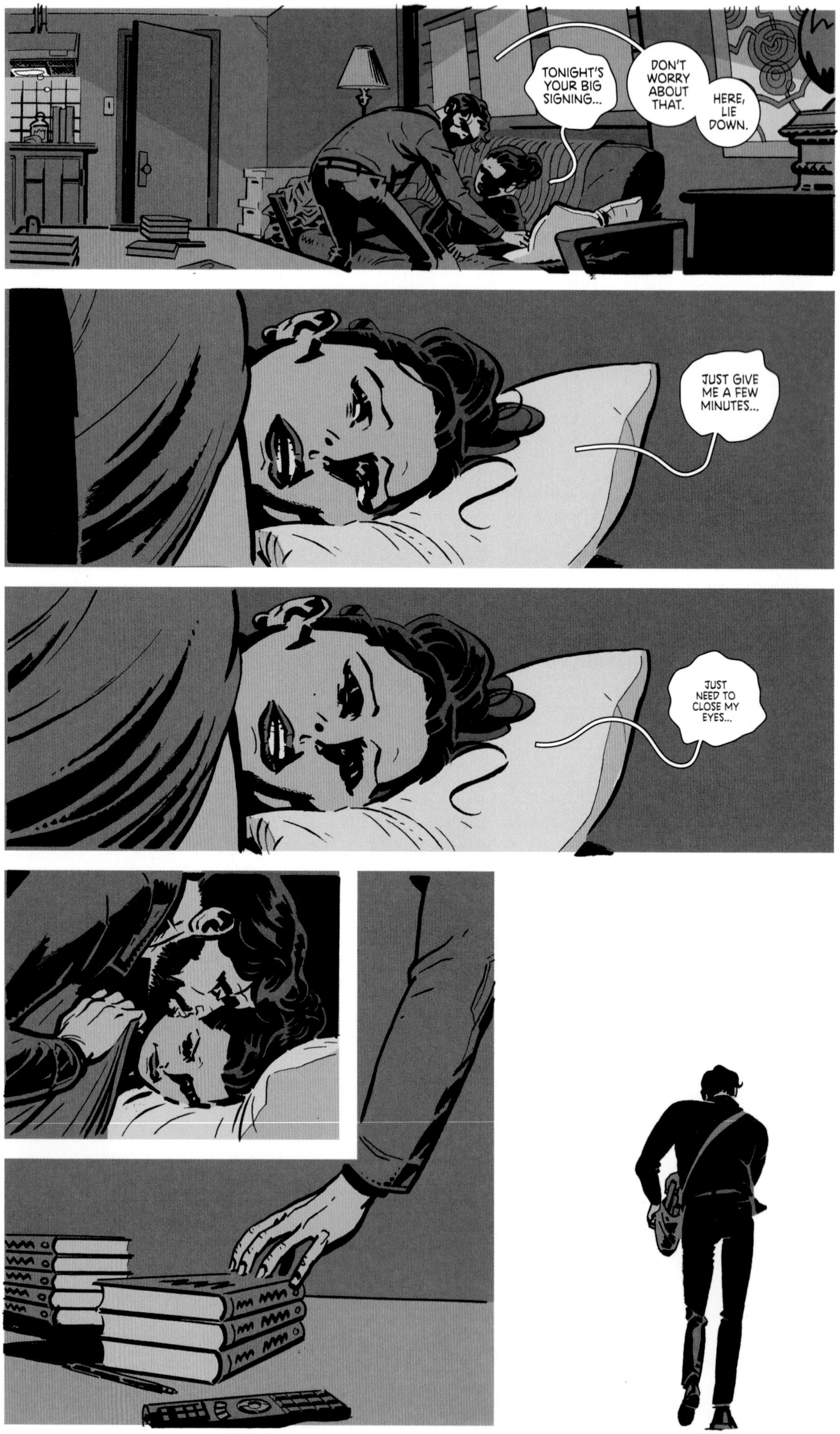
TONIGHT'S YOUR BIG SIGNING...
DON'T WORRY ABOUT THAT.
HERE, LIE DOWN.
JUST GIVE ME A FEW MINUTES...
JUST NEED TO CLOSE MY EYES...

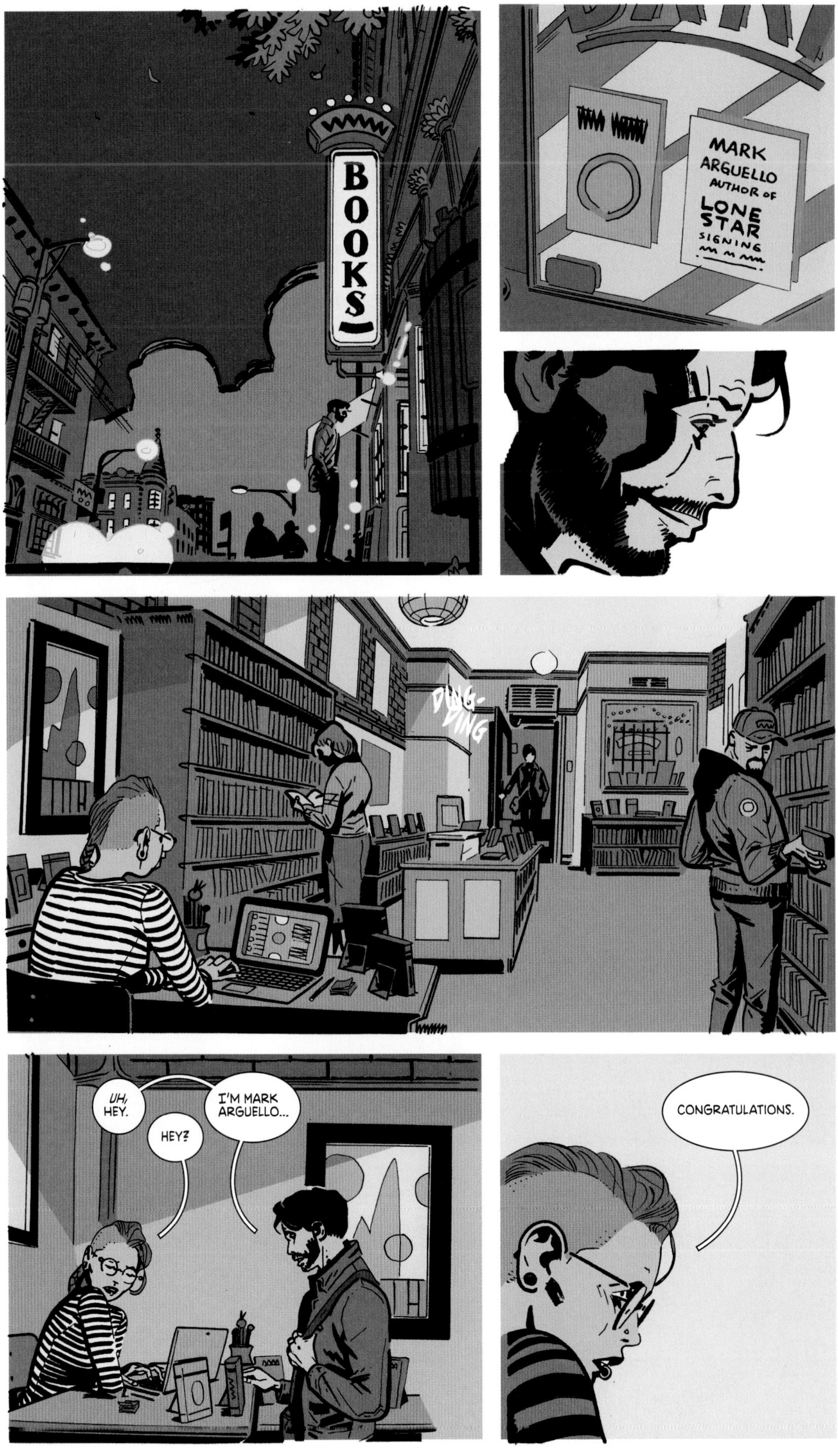
BOOKS
MARK ARGUELLO AUTHOR OF LONE STAR SIGNING
DING-DING
UH, HEY.
HEY?
I'M MARK ARGUELLO...
CONGRATULATIONS.

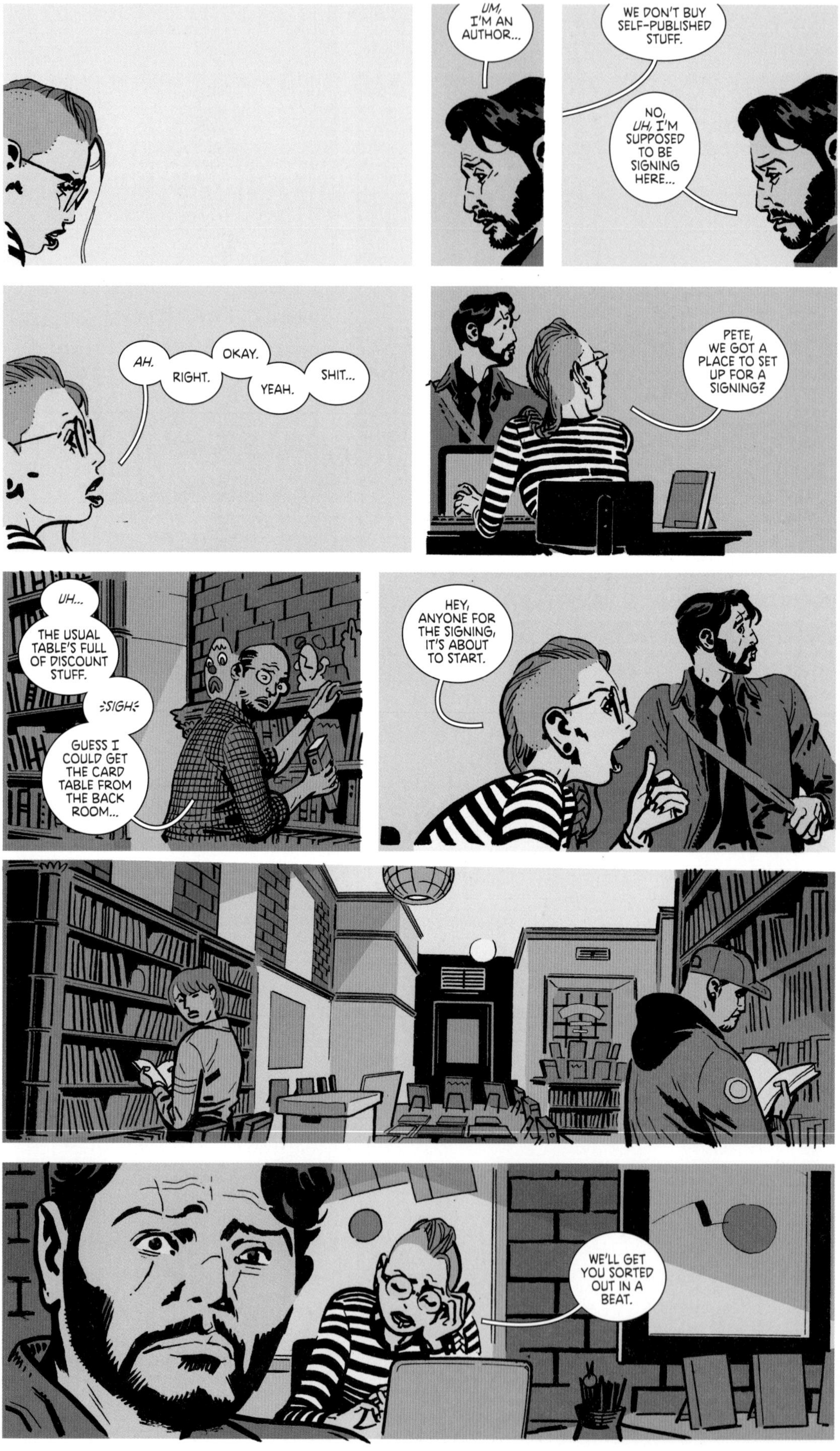
UM, I'M AN AUTHOR...
WE DON'T BUY SELF-PUBLISHED STUFF.
NO, UH, I'M SUPPOSED TO BE SIGNING HERE...
AH.
RIGHT.
OKAY.
YEAH.
SHIT...
PETE, WE GOT A PLACE TO SET UP FOR A SIGNING?
UH...
THE USUAL TABLE'S FULL OF DISCOUNT STUFF.
SIGH
GUESS I COULD GET THE CARD TABLE FROM THE BACK ROOM...
HEY, ANYONE FOR THE SIGNING, IT'S ABOUT TO START.
WE'LL GET YOU SORTED OUT IN A BEAT.

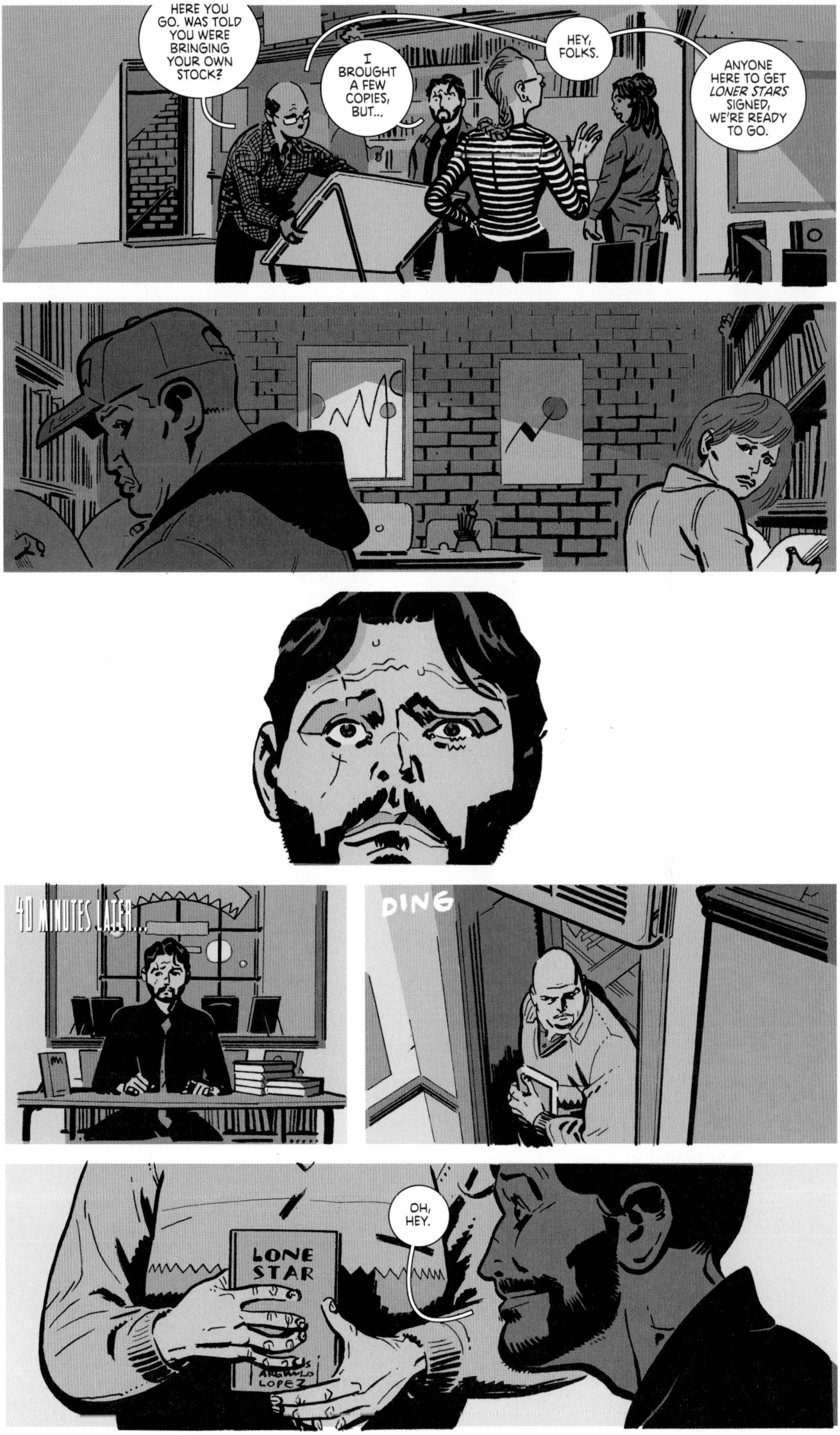
HERE YOU GO. WAS TOLD YOU WERE BRINGING YOUR OWN STOCK?
I BROUGHT A FEW COPIES, BUT...
HEY, FOLKS.
ANYONE HERE TO GET *LONER STARS* SIGNED, WE'RE READY TO GO.
40 MINUTES LATER...
DING
OH, HEY.
LONE STAR

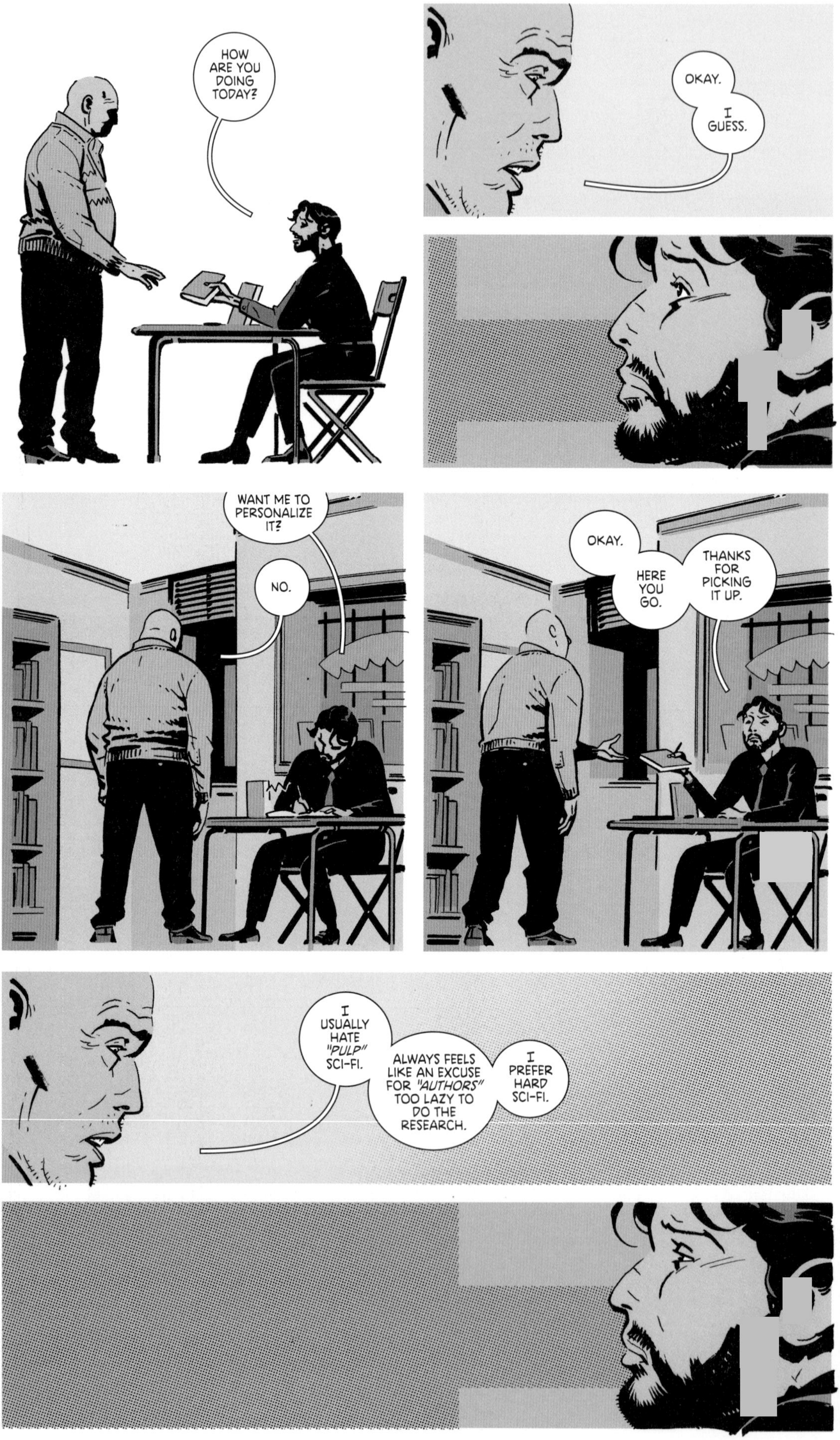
HOW ARE YOU DOING TODAY?
OKAY.
I GUESS.
WANT ME TO PERSONALIZE IT?
NO.
OKAY.
HERE YOU GO.
THANKS FOR PICKING IT UP.
I USUALLY HATE "PULP" SCI-FI.
ALWAYS FEELS LIKE AN EXCUSE FOR "AUTHORS" TOO LAZY TO DO THE RESEARCH.
I PREFER HARD SCI-FI.

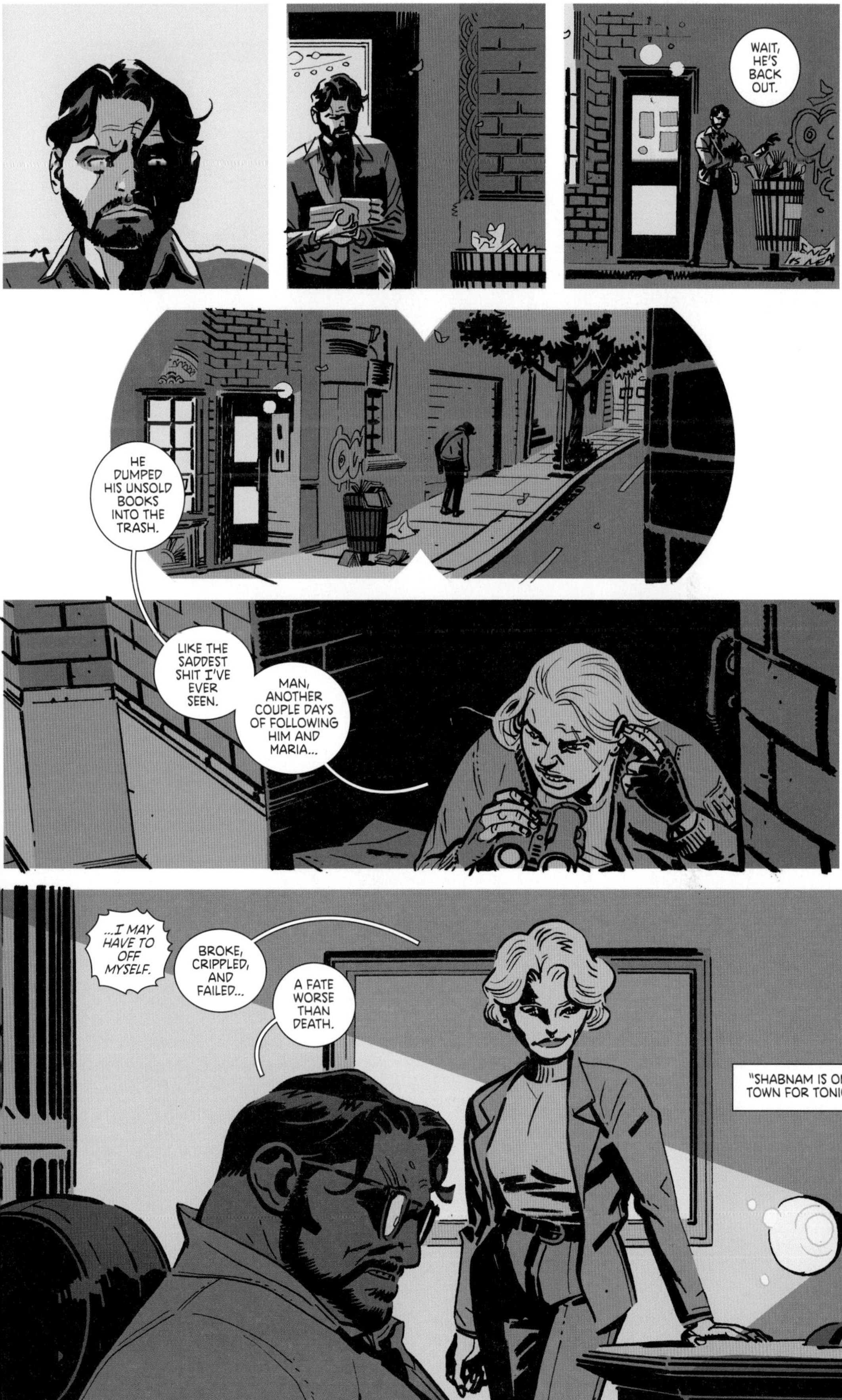
WAIT, HE'S BACK OUT.
HE DUMPED HIS UNSOLD BOOKS INTO THE TRASH.
LIKE THE SADDEST SHIT I'VE EVER SEEN.
MAN, ANOTHER COUPLE DAYS OF FOLLOWING HIM AND MARIA...
...I MAY HAVE TO OFF MYSELF.
BROKE, CRIPPLED, AND FAILED...
A FATE WORSE THAN DEATH.
"SHABNAM IS ONLY IN TOWN FOR TONIGHT..."

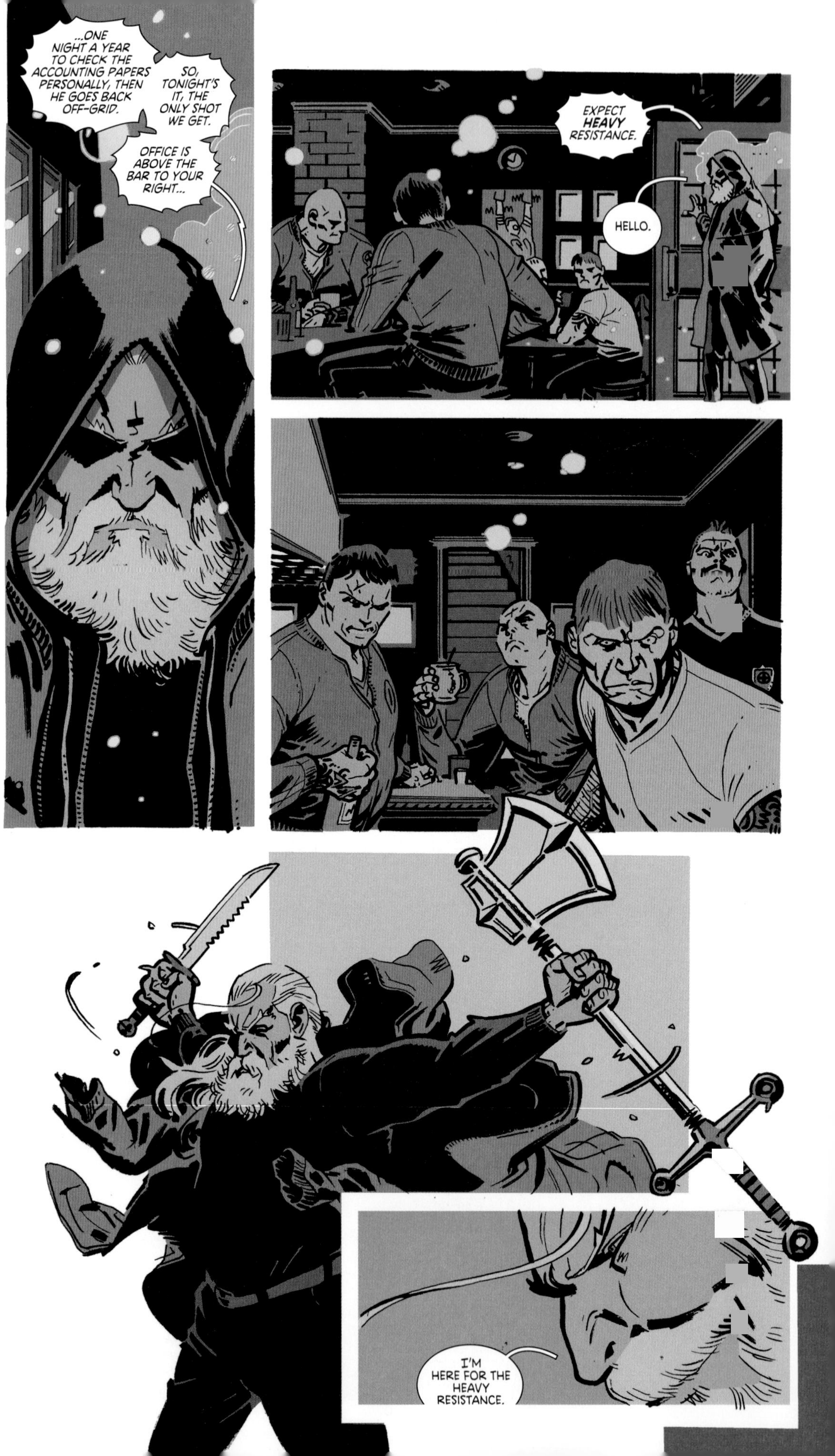

...ONE NIGHT A YEAR TO CHECK THE ACCOUNTING PAPERS PERSONALLY, THEN HE GOES BACK OFF-GRID.
SO, TONIGHT'S IT, THE ONLY SHOT WE GET.
OFFICE IS ABOVE THE BAR TO YOUR RIGHT...
EXPECT **HEAVY** RESISTANCE.
HELLO.
I'M HERE FOR THE HEAVY RESISTANCE.

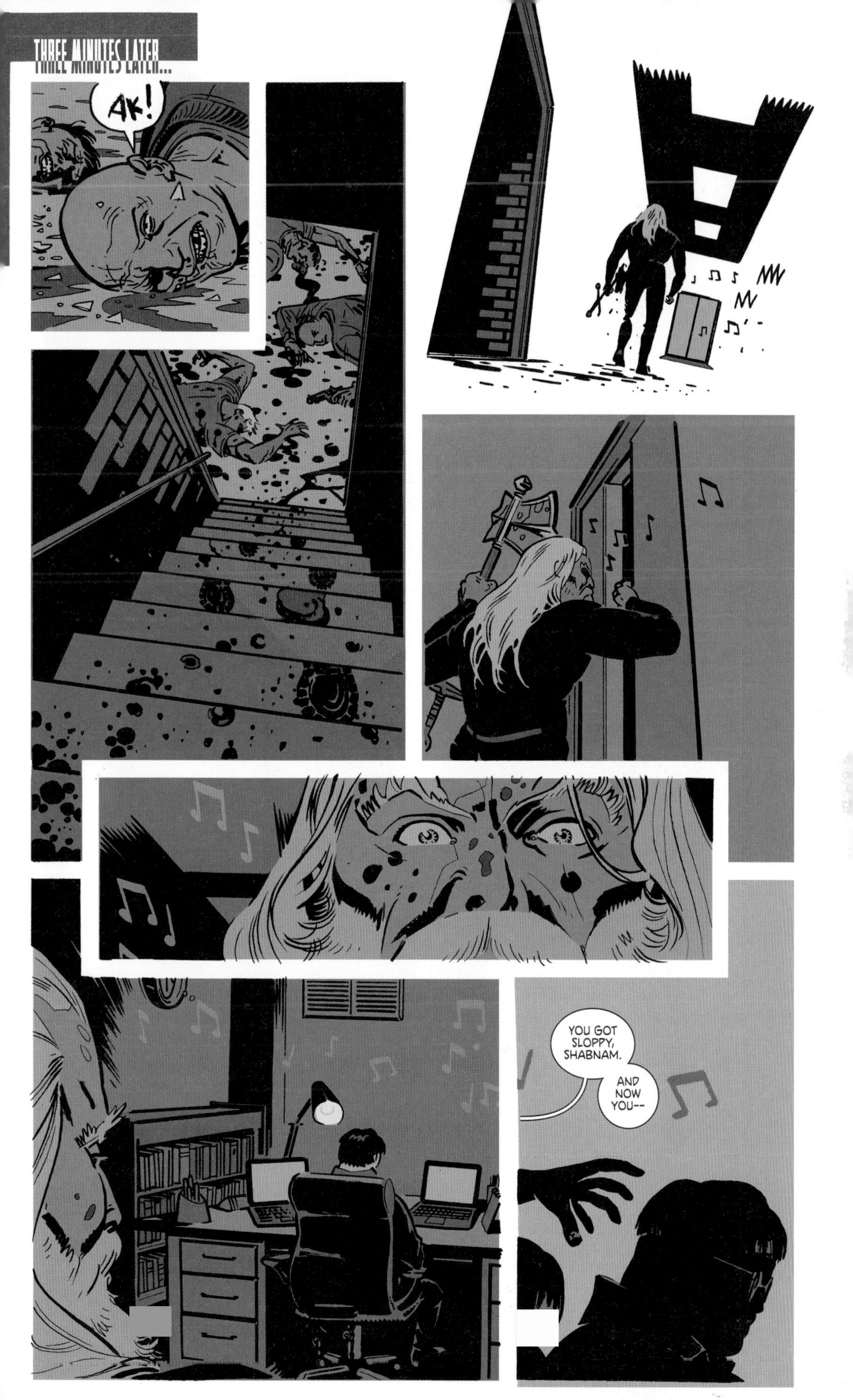

THREE MINUTES LATER...
AK!
YOU GOT SLOPPY, SHABNAM.
AND NOW YOU--

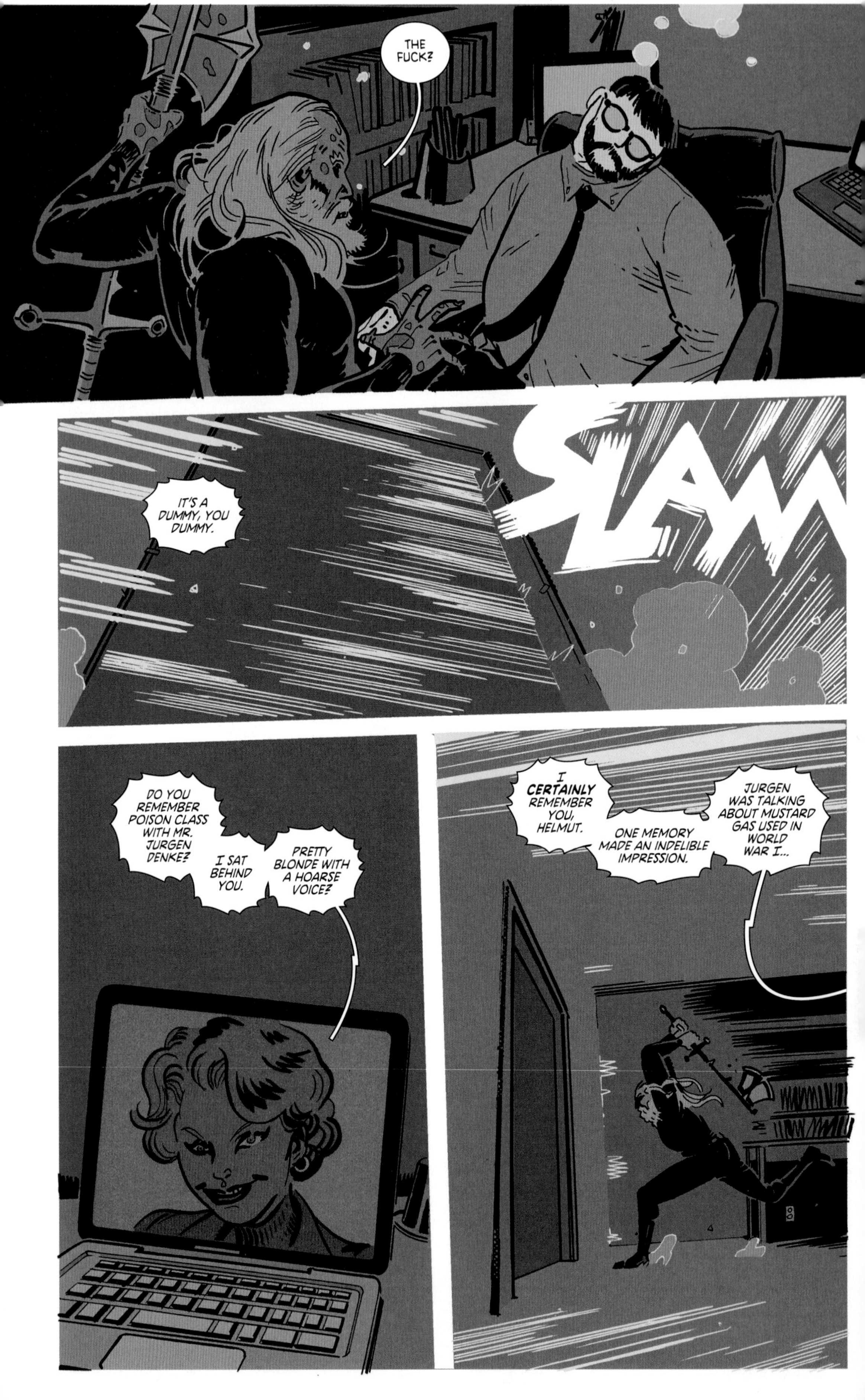
THE FUCK?
IT'S A DUMMY, YOU DUMMY.
SLAM
DO YOU REMEMBER POISON CLASS WITH MR. JURGEN DENKE?
I SAT BEHIND YOU.
PRETTY BLONDE WITH A HOARSE VOICE?
I CERTAINLY REMEMBER YOU, HELMUT.
ONE MEMORY MADE AN INDELIBLE IMPRESSION.
JURGEN WAS TALKING ABOUT MUSTARD GAS USED IN WORLD WAR I...

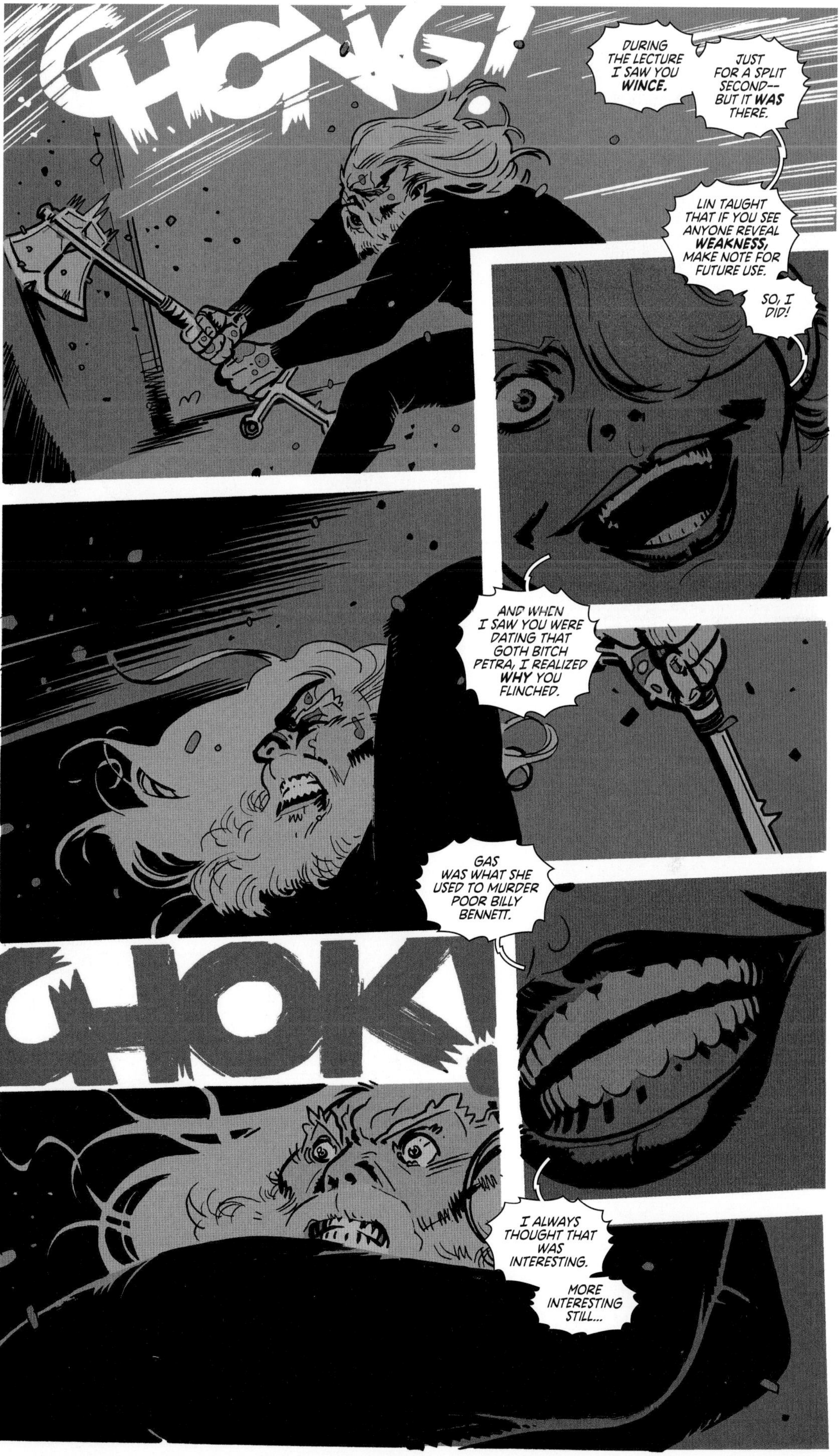
CHONG!
DURING THE LECTURE I SAW YOU WINCE.
JUST FOR A SPLIT SECOND-- BUT IT WAS THERE.
LIN TAUGHT THAT IF YOU SEE ANYONE REVEAL WEAKNESS, MAKE NOTE FOR FUTURE USE.
SO, I DID!
AND WHEN I SAW YOU WERE DATING THAT GOTH BITCH PETRA, I REALIZED WHY YOU FLINCHED.
GAS WAS WHAT SHE USED TO MURDER POOR BILLY BENNETT.
CHOK!
I ALWAYS THOUGHT THAT WAS INTERESTING.
MORE INTERESTING STILL...

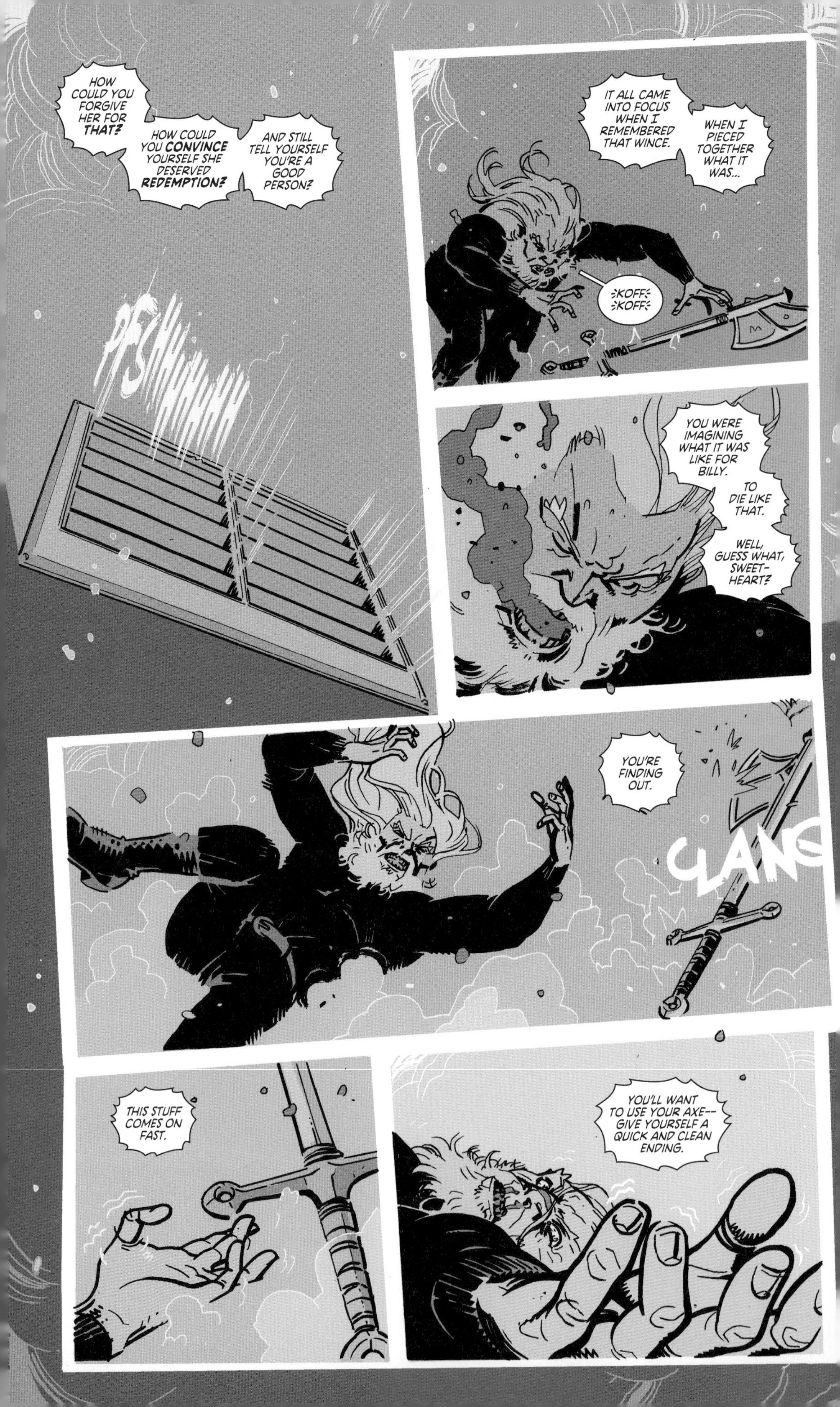
HOW COULD YOU FORGIVE HER FOR THAT?
HOW COULD YOU CONVINCE YOURSELF SHE DESERVED REDEMPTION?
AND STILL TELL YOURSELF YOU'RE A GOOD PERSON?
PFSHHHHHH
IT ALL CAME INTO FOCUS WHEN I REMEMBERED THAT WINCE.
WHEN I PIECED TOGETHER WHAT IT WAS...
KOFF KOFF
YOU WERE IMAGINING WHAT IT WAS LIKE FOR BILLY.
TO DIE LIKE THAT.
WELL, GUESS WHAT, SWEET-HEART?
YOU'RE FINDING OUT.
CLANG
THIS STUFF COMES ON FAST.
YOU'LL WANT TO USE YOUR AXE-- GIVE YOURSELF A QUICK AND CLEAN ENDING.

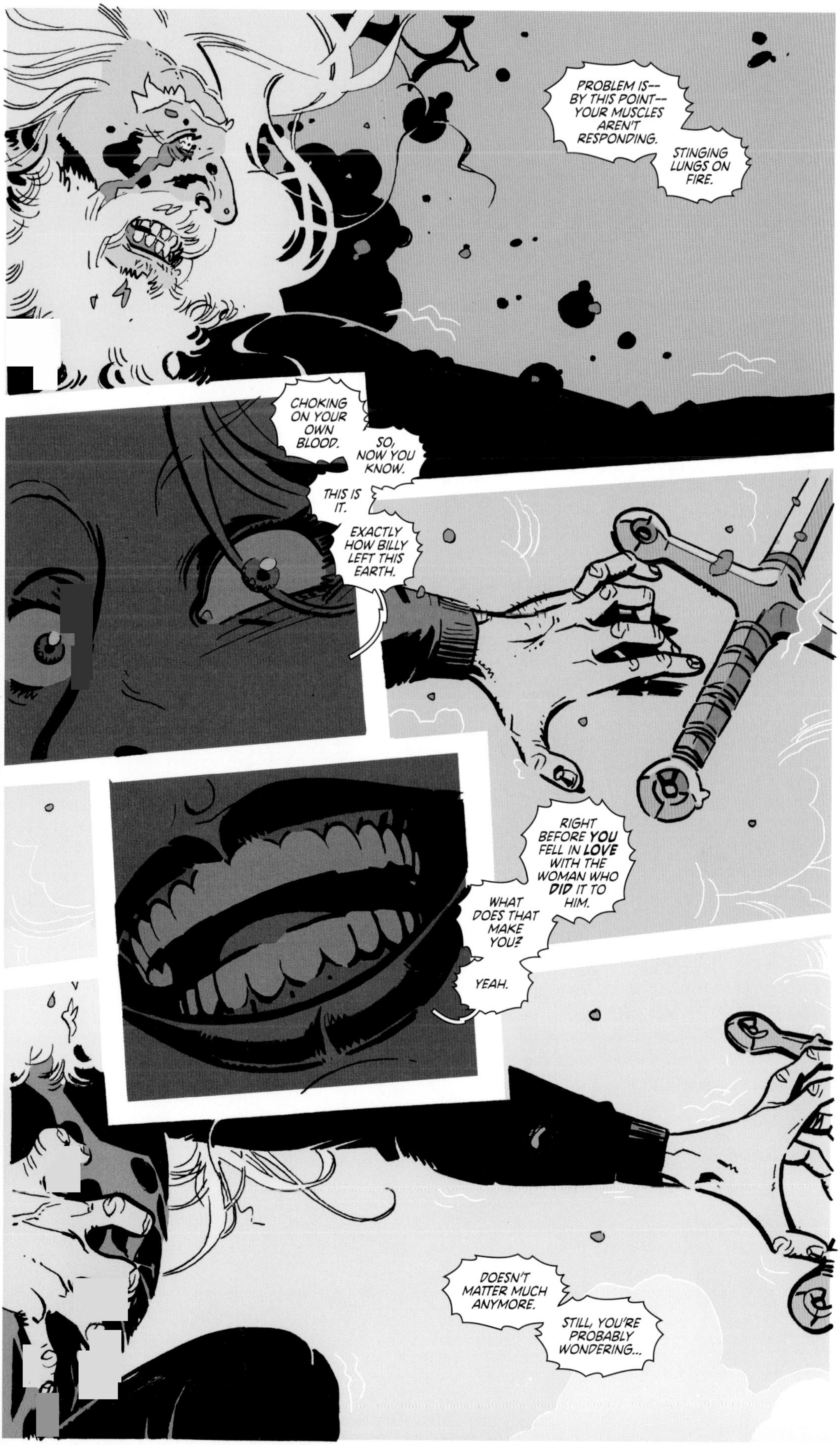
PROBLEM IS-- BY THIS POINT-- YOUR MUSCLES AREN'T RESPONDING.
STINGING LUNGS ON FIRE.
CHOKING ON YOUR OWN BLOOD.
SO, NOW YOU KNOW.
THIS IS IT.
EXACTLY HOW BILLY LEFT THIS EARTH.
RIGHT BEFORE YOU FELL IN LOVE WITH THE WOMAN WHO DID IT TO HIM.
WHAT DOES THAT MAKE YOU?
YEAH.
DOESN'T MATTER MUCH ANYMORE.
STILL, YOU'RE PROBABLY WONDERING...

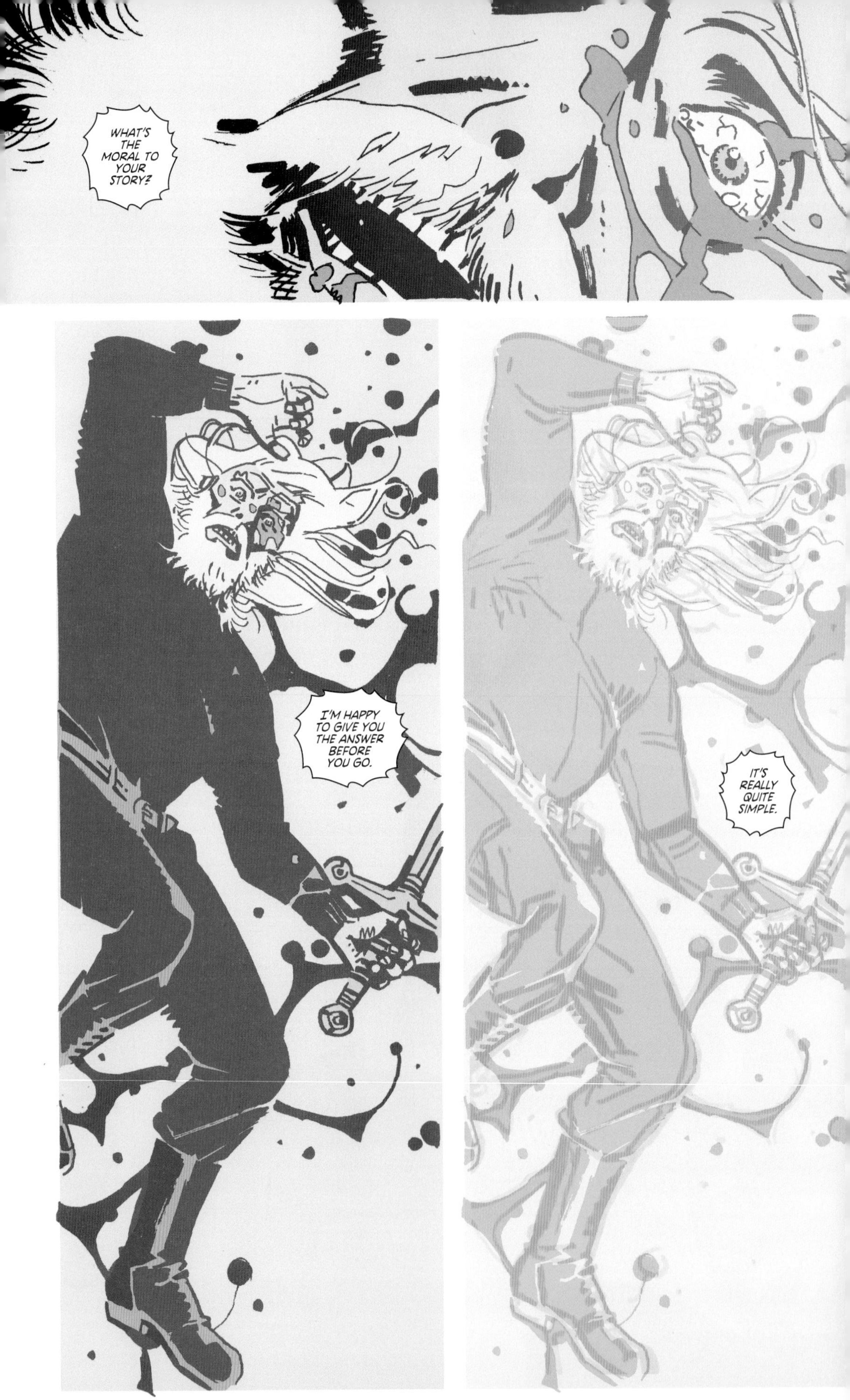
WHAT'S THE MORAL TO YOUR STORY?
I'M HAPPY TO GIVE YOU THE ANSWER BEFORE YOU GO.
IT'S REALLY QUITE SIMPLE.

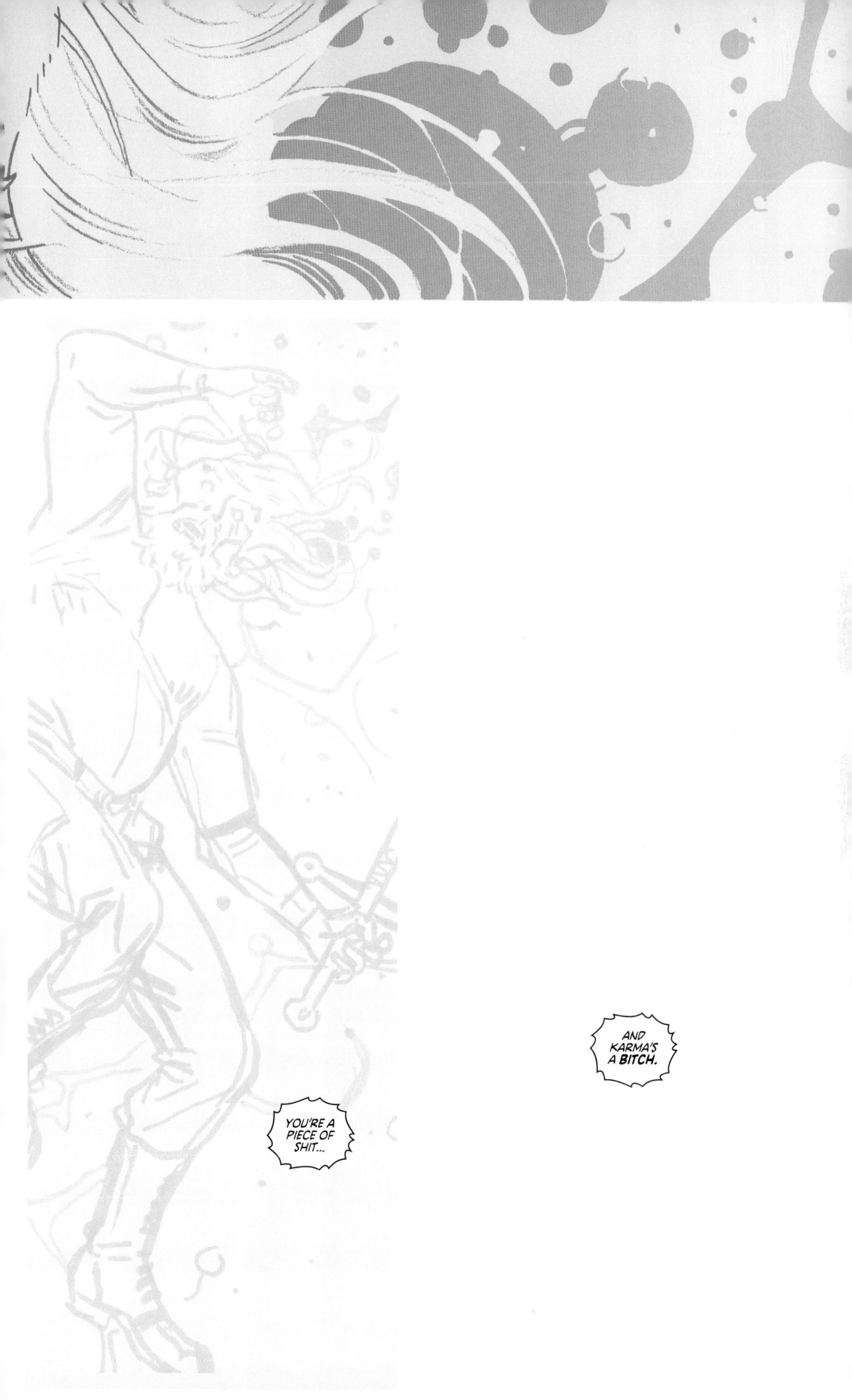
YOU'RE A PIECE OF SHIT...
AND KARMA'S A BITCH.

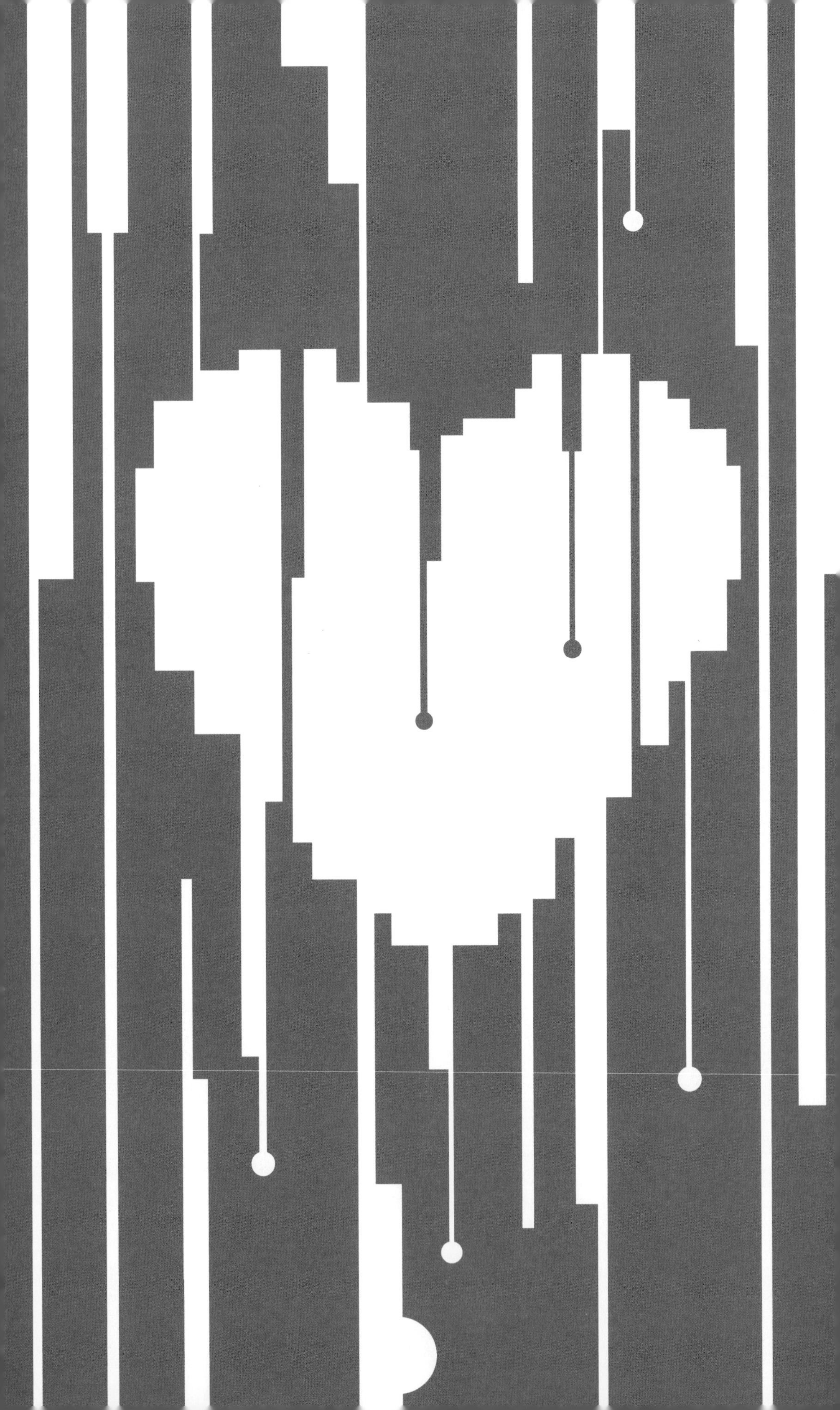

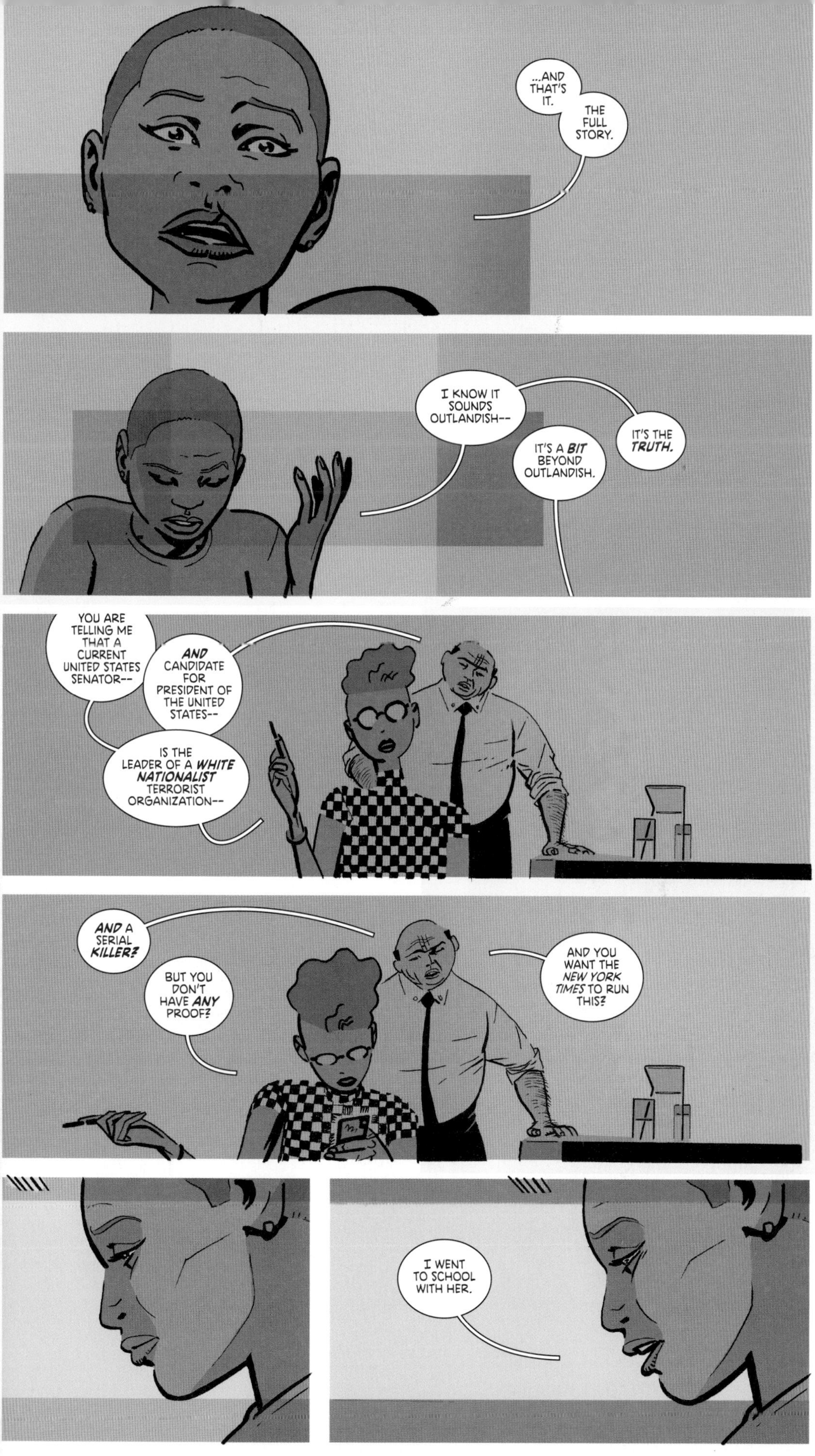

...AND THAT'S IT.
THE FULL STORY.
I KNOW IT SOUNDS OUTLANDISH--
IT'S THE TRUTH.
IT'S A BIT BEYOND OUTLANDISH.
YOU ARE TELLING ME THAT A CURRENT UNITED STATES SENATOR--
AND CANDIDATE FOR PRESIDENT OF THE UNITED STATES--
IS THE LEADER OF A WHITE NATIONALIST TERRORIST ORGANIZATION--
AND A SERIAL KILLER?
BUT YOU DON'T HAVE ANY PROOF?
AND YOU WANT THE NEW YORK TIMES TO RUN THIS?
I WENT TO SCHOOL WITH HER.

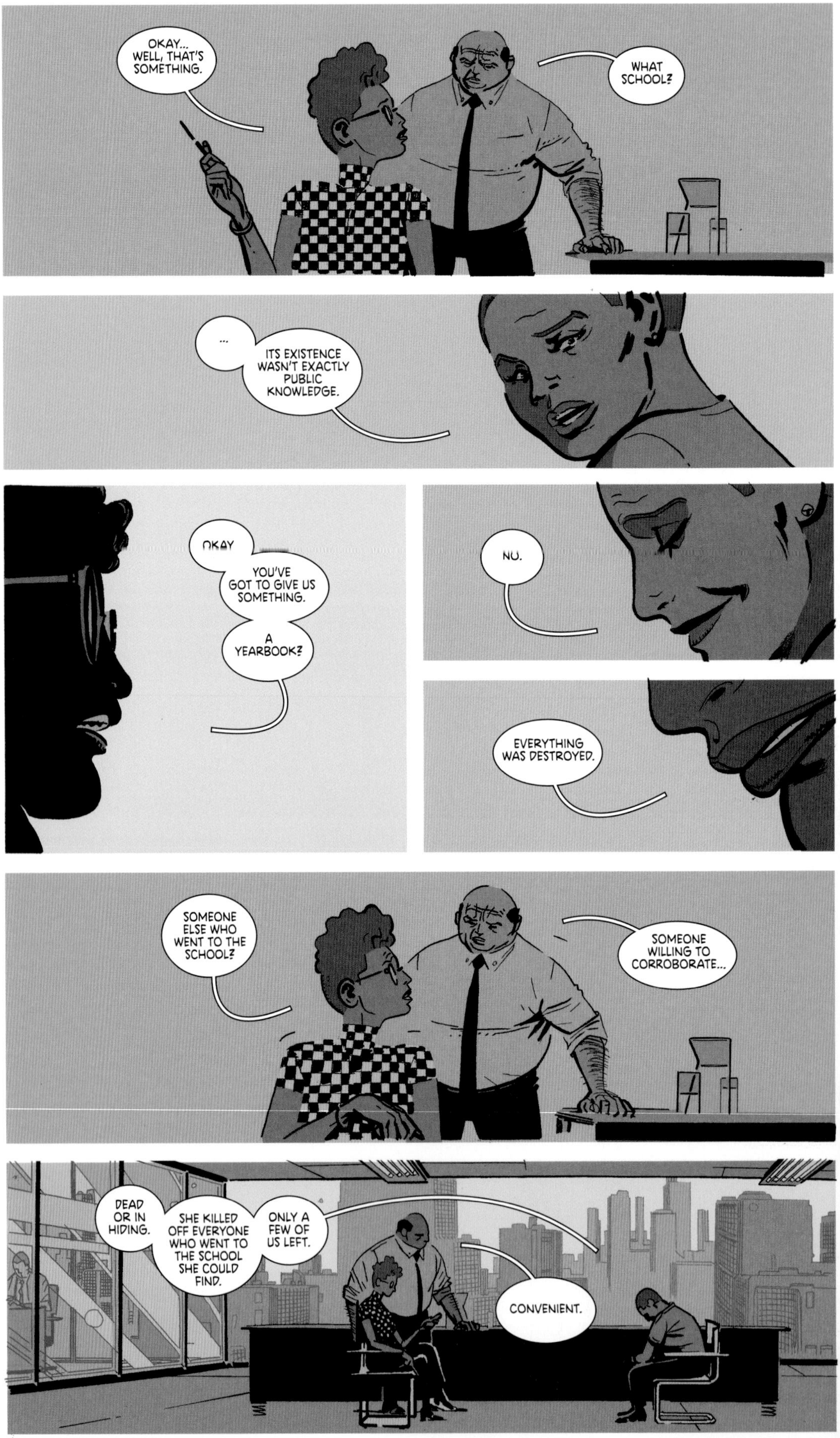
OKAY... WELL, THAT'S SOMETHING.
WHAT SCHOOL?
...
ITS EXISTENCE WASN'T EXACTLY PUBLIC KNOWLEDGE.
OKAY
YOU'VE GOT TO GIVE US SOMETHING.
A YEARBOOK?
NO.
EVERYTHING WAS DESTROYED.
SOMEONE ELSE WHO WENT TO THE SCHOOL?
SOMEONE WILLING TO CORROBORATE...
DEAD OR IN HIDING.
SHE KILLED OFF EVERYONE WHO WENT TO THE SCHOOL SHE COULD FIND.
ONLY A FEW OF US LEFT.
CONVENIENT.

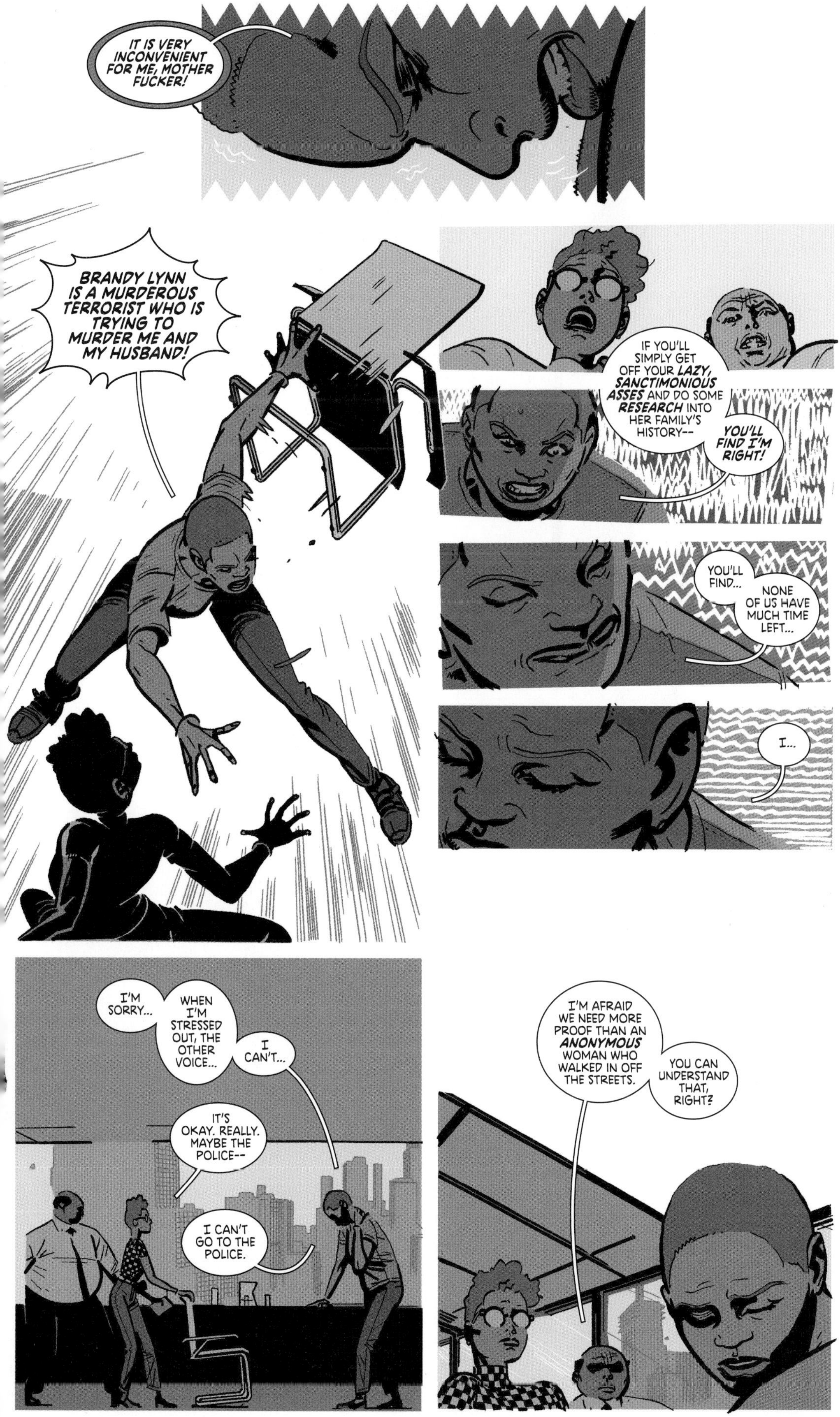
IT IS VERY INCONVENIENT FOR ME, MOTHER FUCKER!
BRANDY LYNN IS A MURDEROUS TERRORIST WHO IS TRYING TO MURDER ME AND MY HUSBAND!
IF YOU'LL SIMPLY GET OFF YOUR LAZY, SANCTIMONIOUS ASSES AND DO SOME RESEARCH INTO HER FAMILY'S HISTORY--
YOU'LL FIND I'M RIGHT!
YOU'LL FIND...
NONE OF US HAVE MUCH TIME LEFT...
I...
I'M SORRY...
WHEN I'M STRESSED OUT, THE OTHER VOICE...
I CAN'T...
IT'S OKAY. REALLY. MAYBE THE POLICE--
I CAN'T GO TO THE POLICE.
I'M AFRAID WE NEED MORE PROOF THAN AN ANONYMOUS WOMAN WHO WALKED IN OFF THE STREETS.
YOU CAN UNDERSTAND THAT, RIGHT?

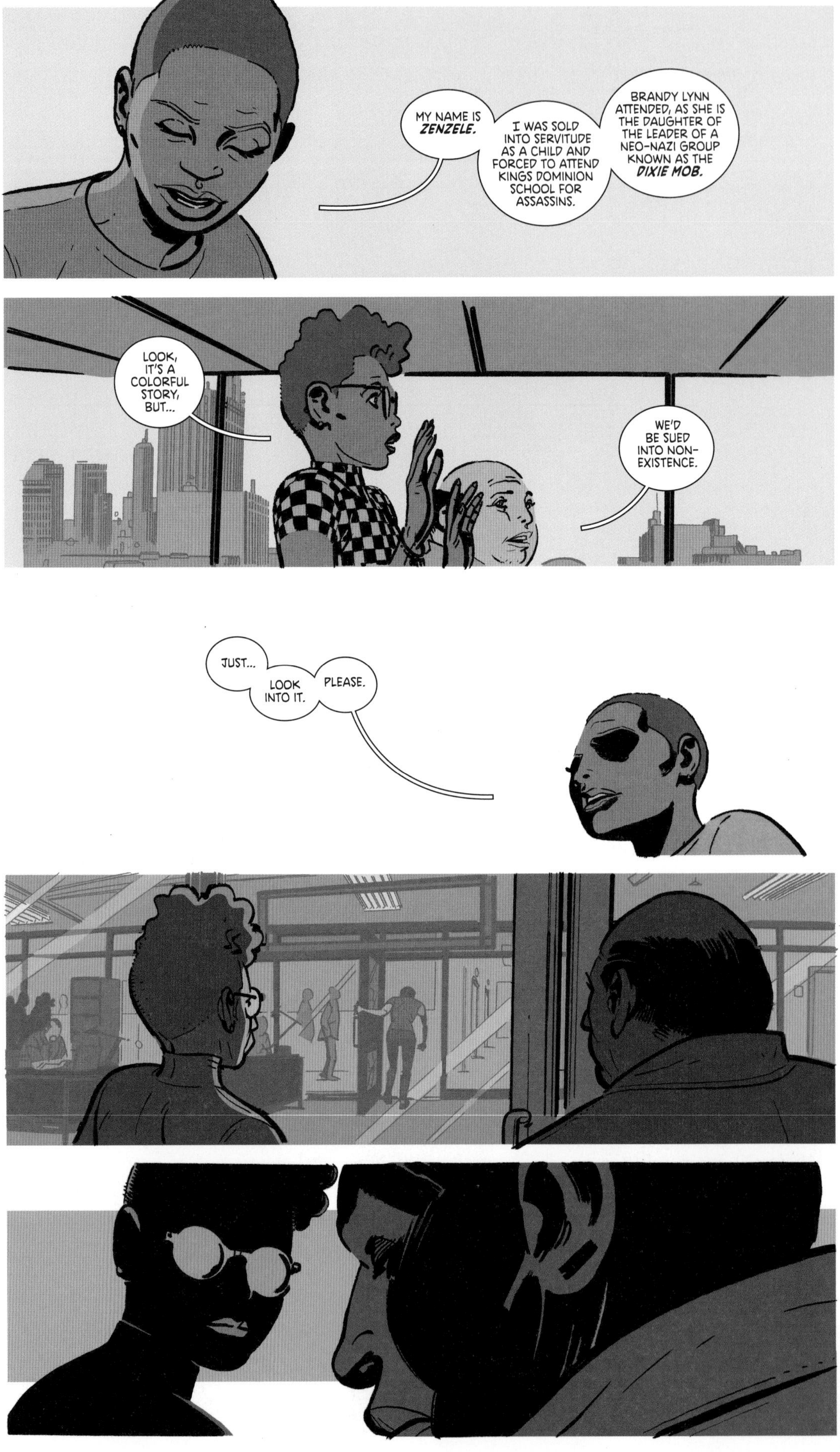
MY NAME IS *ZENZELE.*
I WAS SOLD INTO SERVITUDE AS A CHILD AND FORCED TO ATTEND KINGS DOMINION SCHOOL FOR ASSASSINS.
BRANDY LYNN ATTENDED, AS SHE IS THE DAUGHTER OF THE LEADER OF A NEO-NAZI GROUP KNOWN AS THE *DIXIE MOB.*
LOOK, IT'S A COLORFUL STORY, BUT...
WE'D BE SUED INTO NON-EXISTENCE.
JUST...
LOOK INTO IT.
PLEASE.

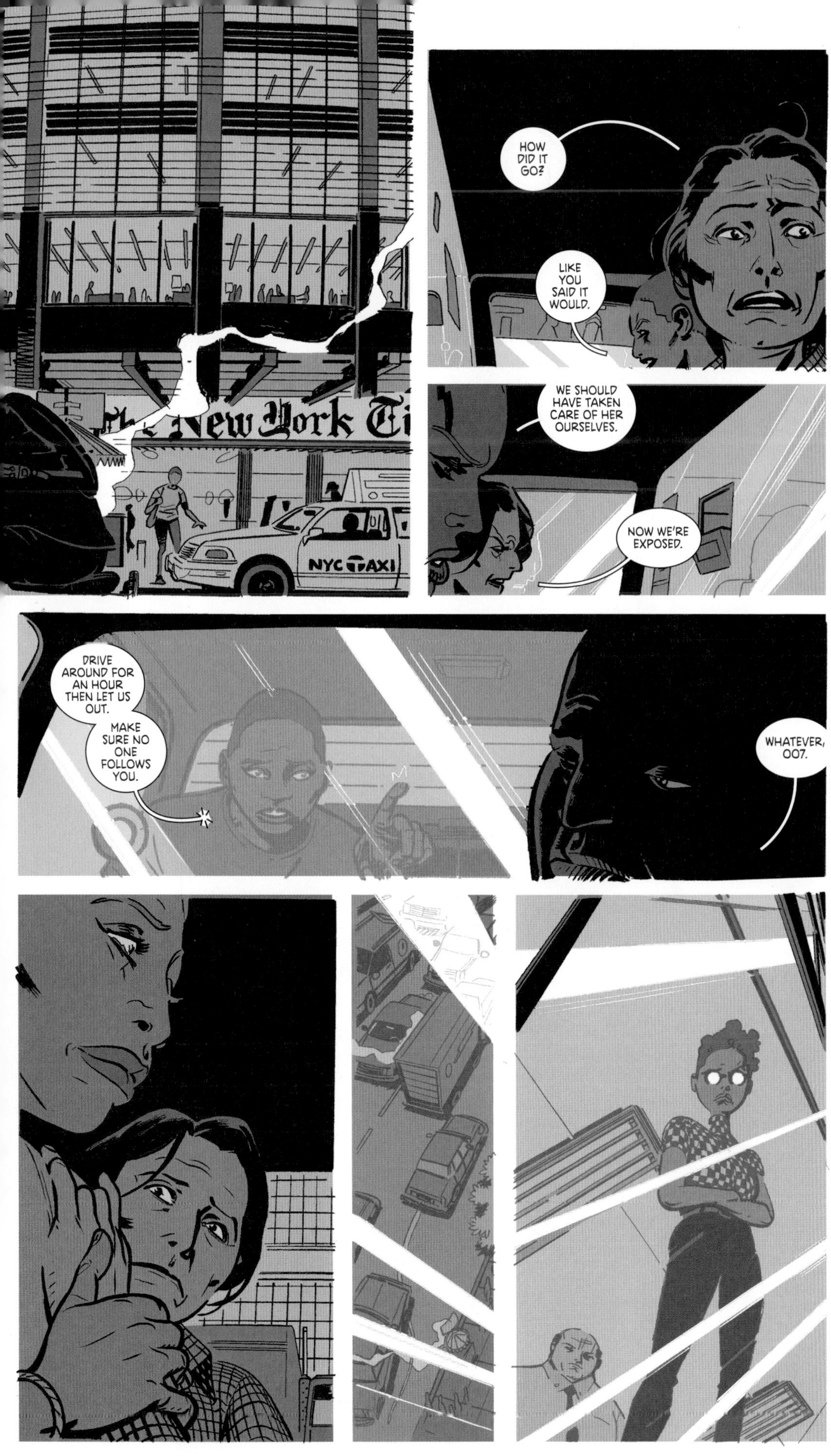
The New York Times
NYC TAXI
HOW DID IT GO?
LIKE YOU SAID IT WOULD.
WE SHOULD HAVE TAKEN CARE OF HER OURSELVES.
NOW WE'RE EXPOSED.
DRIVE AROUND FOR AN HOUR THEN LET US OUT.
MAKE SURE NO ONE FOLLOWS YOU.
WHATEVER, 007.

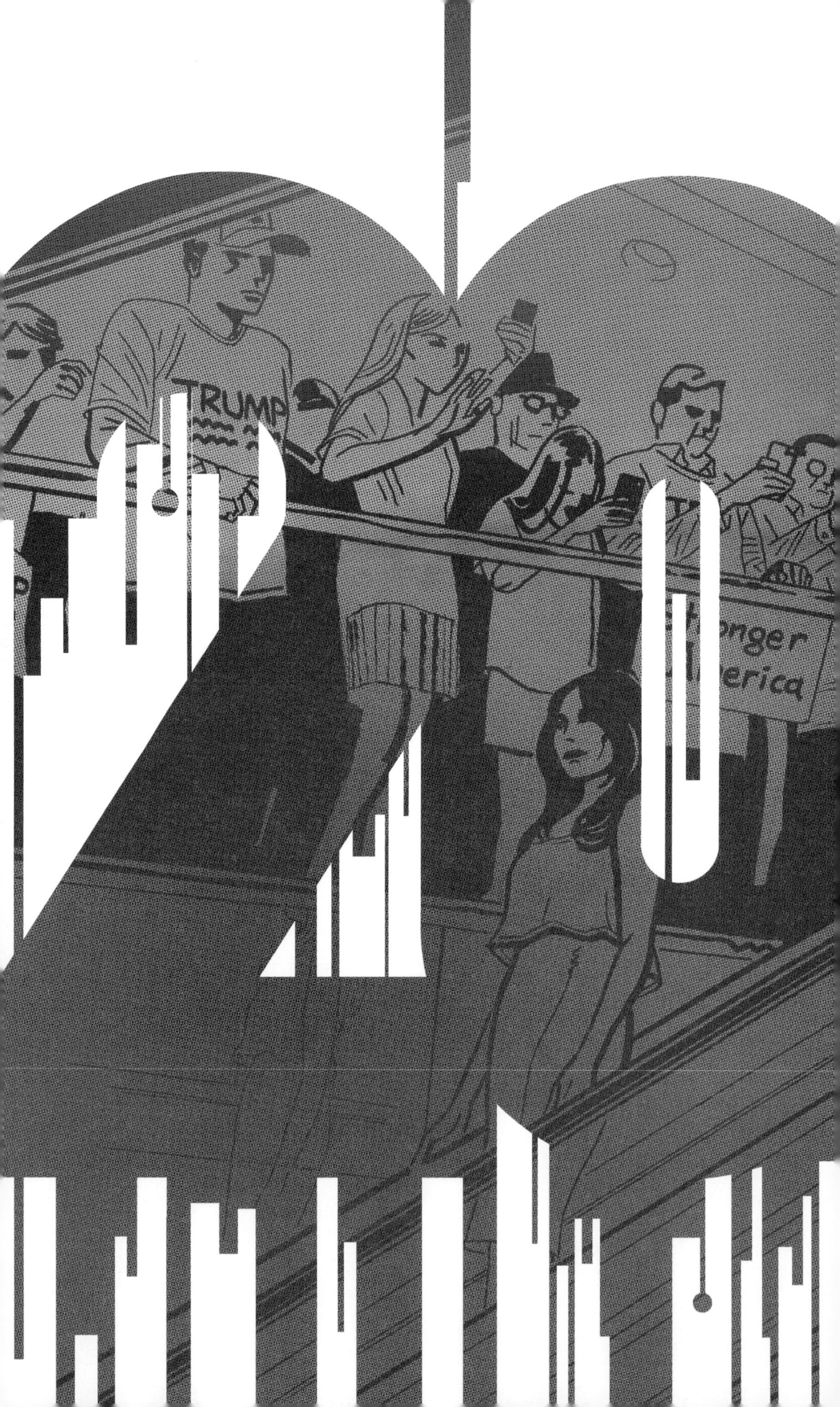
TRUMP

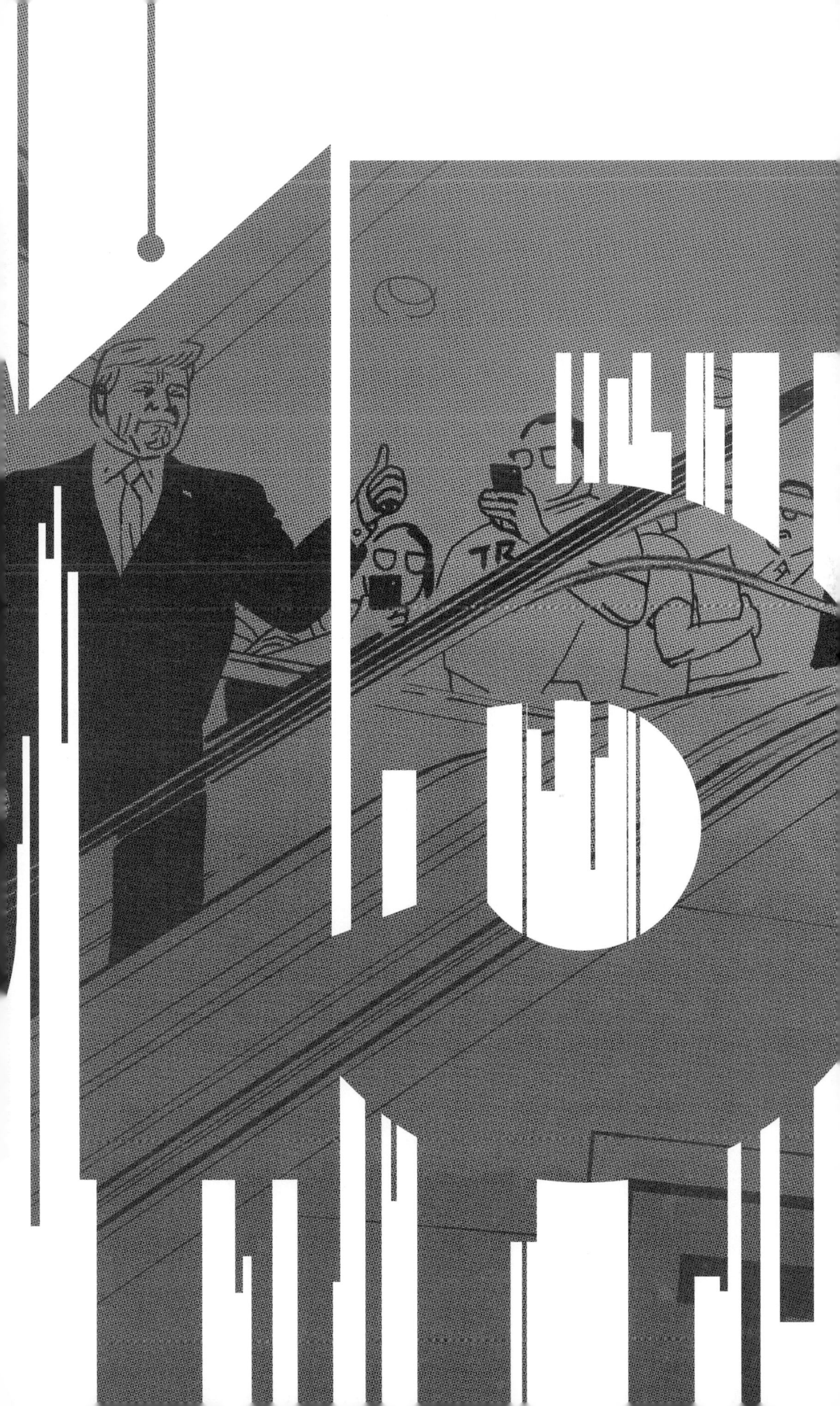

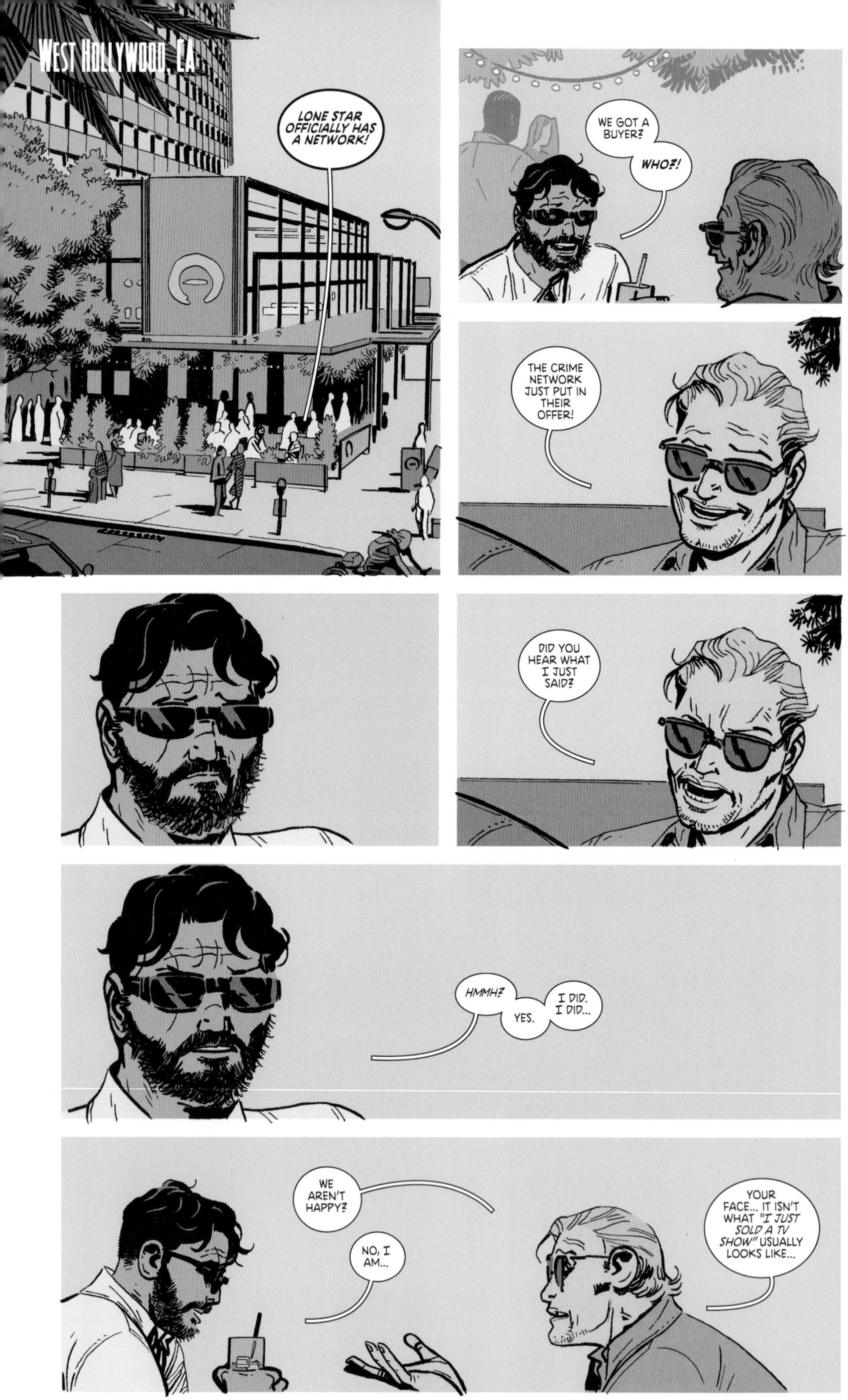
West Hollywood, CA
LONE STAR OFFICIALLY HAS A NETWORK!
WE GOT A BUYER?
WHO?!
THE CRIME NETWORK JUST PUT IN THEIR OFFER!
DID YOU HEAR WHAT I JUST SAID?
HMMH?
YES.
I DID. I DID...
WE AREN'T HAPPY?
NO, I AM...
YOUR FACE... IT ISN'T WHAT "I JUST SOLD A TV SHOW" USUALLY LOOKS LIKE...

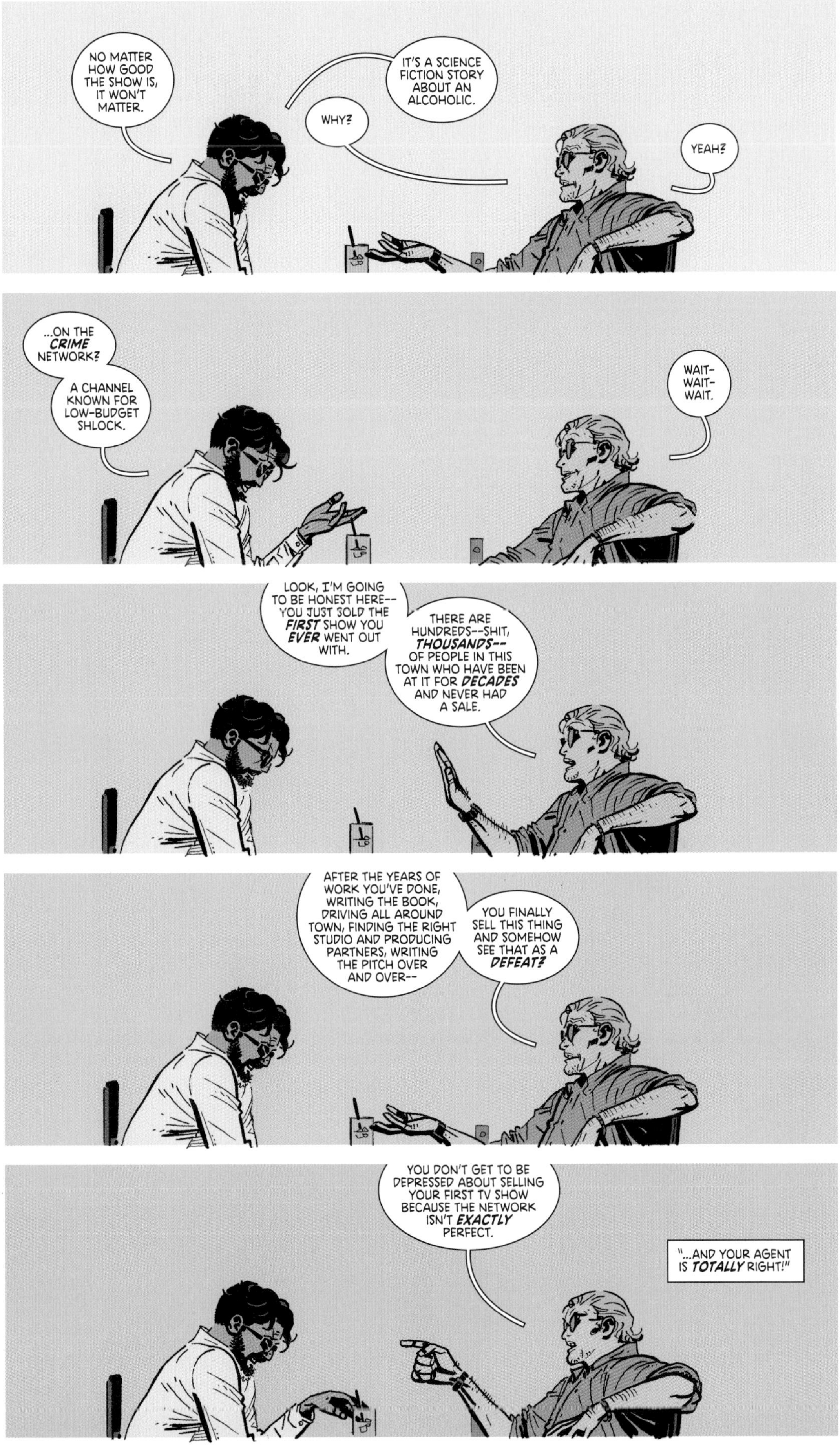

NO MATTER HOW GOOD THE SHOW IS, IT WON'T MATTER.
WHY?
IT'S A SCIENCE FICTION STORY ABOUT AN ALCOHOLIC.
YEAH?
...ON THE CRIME NETWORK?
A CHANNEL KNOWN FOR LOW-BUDGET SHLOCK.
WAIT-WAIT-WAIT.
LOOK, I'M GOING TO BE HONEST HERE--YOU JUST SOLD THE FIRST SHOW YOU EVER WENT OUT WITH.
THERE ARE HUNDREDS--SHIT, THOUSANDS--OF PEOPLE IN THIS TOWN WHO HAVE BEEN AT IT FOR DECADES AND NEVER HAD A SALE.
AFTER THE YEARS OF WORK YOU'VE DONE, WRITING THE BOOK, DRIVING ALL AROUND TOWN, FINDING THE RIGHT STUDIO AND PRODUCING PARTNERS, WRITING THE PITCH OVER AND OVER--
YOU FINALLY SELL THIS THING AND SOMEHOW SEE THAT AS A DEFEAT?
YOU DON'T GET TO BE DEPRESSED ABOUT SELLING YOUR FIRST TV SHOW BECAUSE THE NETWORK ISN'T EXACTLY PERFECT.
"...AND YOUR AGENT IS TOTALLY RIGHT!"

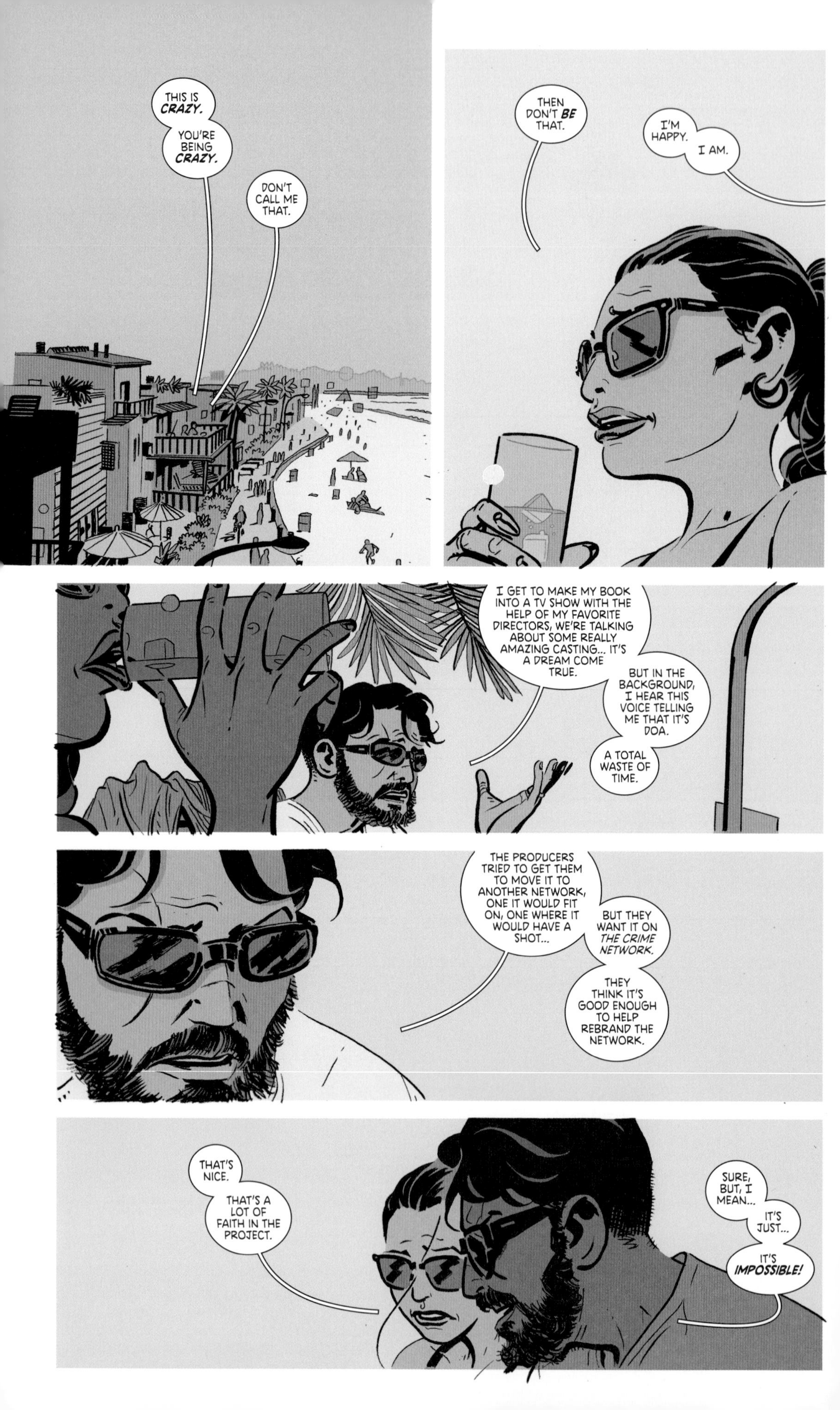
THIS IS CRAZY.
YOU'RE BEING CRAZY.
DON'T CALL ME THAT.
THEN DON'T BE THAT.
I'M HAPPY.
I AM.
I GET TO MAKE MY BOOK INTO A TV SHOW WITH THE HELP OF MY FAVORITE DIRECTORS, WE'RE TALKING ABOUT SOME REALLY AMAZING CASTING... IT'S A DREAM COME TRUE.
BUT IN THE BACKGROUND, I HEAR THIS VOICE TELLING ME THAT IT'S DOA.
A TOTAL WASTE OF TIME.
THE PRODUCERS TRIED TO GET THEM TO MOVE IT TO ANOTHER NETWORK, ONE IT WOULD FIT ON, ONE WHERE IT WOULD HAVE A SHOT...
BUT THEY WANT IT ON THE CRIME NETWORK.
THEY THINK IT'S GOOD ENOUGH TO HELP REBRAND THE NETWORK.
THAT'S NICE.
THAT'S A LOT OF FAITH IN THE PROJECT.
SURE, BUT, I MEAN...
IT'S JUST...
IT'S IMPOSSIBLE!

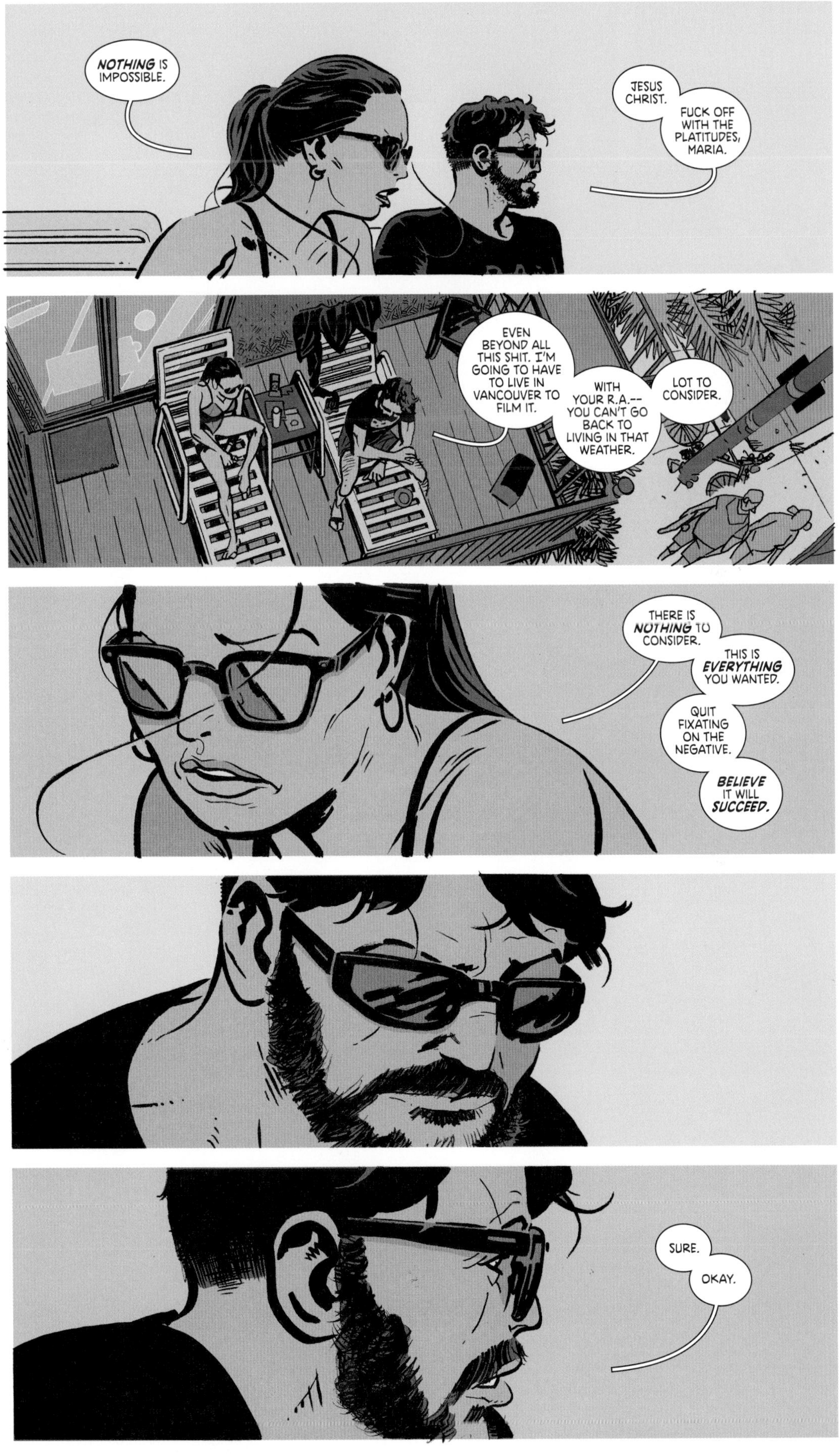
NOTHING IS IMPOSSIBLE.
JESUS CHRIST.
FUCK OFF WITH THE PLATITUDES, MARIA.
EVEN BEYOND ALL THIS SHIT. I'M GOING TO HAVE TO LIVE IN VANCOUVER TO FILM IT.
WITH YOUR R.A.-- YOU CAN'T GO BACK TO LIVING IN THAT WEATHER.
LOT TO CONSIDER.
THERE IS NOTHING TO CONSIDER.
THIS IS EVERYTHING YOU WANTED.
QUIT FIXATING ON THE NEGATIVE.
BELIEVE IT WILL SUCCEED.
SURE.
OKAY.

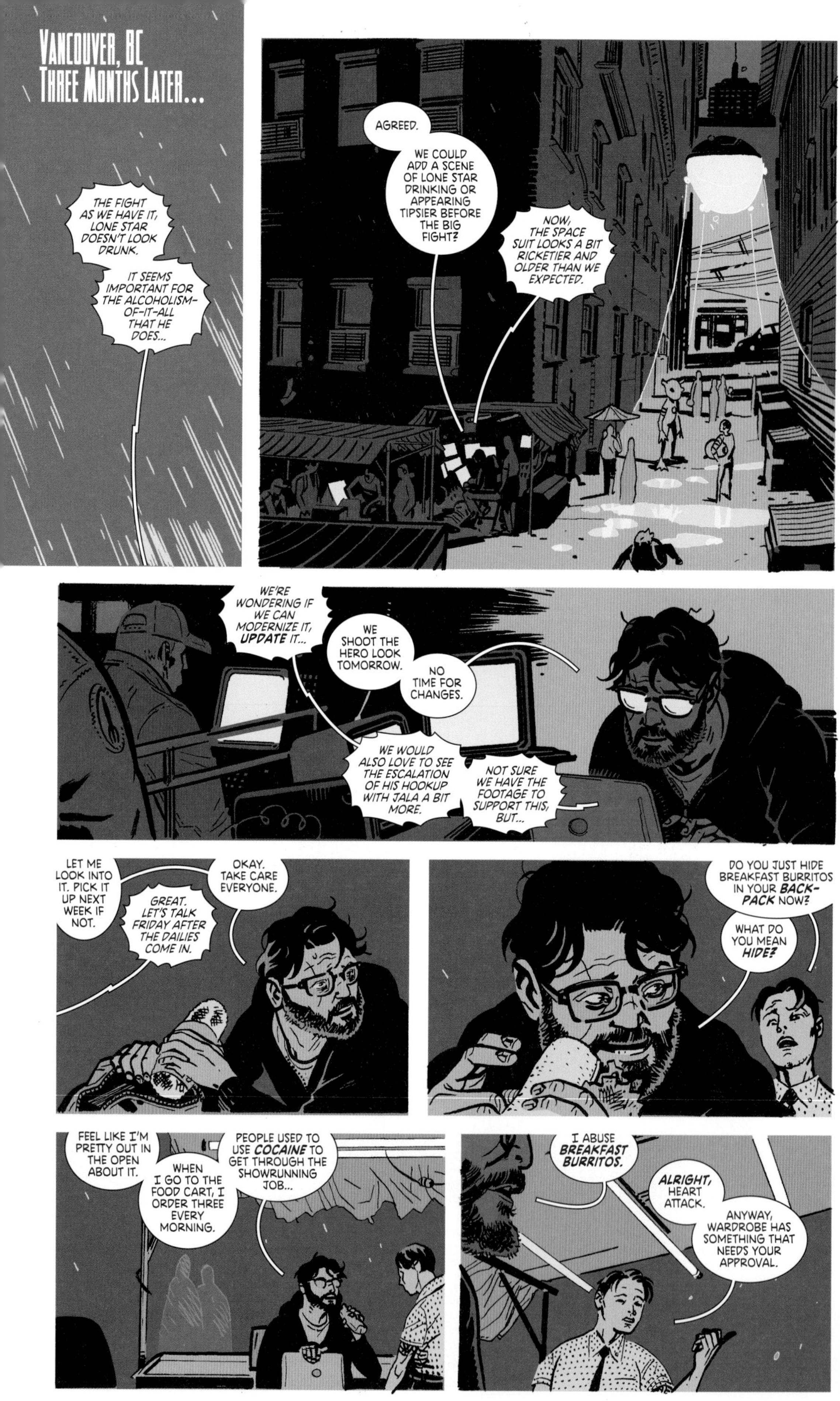
VANCOUVER, BC
THREE MONTHS LATER...
THE FIGHT AS WE HAVE IT, LONE STAR DOESN'T LOOK DRUNK.
IT SEEMS IMPORTANT FOR THE ALCOHOLISM-OF-IT-ALL THAT HE DOES...
AGREED.
WE COULD ADD A SCENE OF LONE STAR DRINKING OR APPEARING TIPSIER BEFORE THE BIG FIGHT?
NOW, THE SPACE SUIT LOOKS A BIT RICKETIER AND OLDER THAN WE EXPECTED.
WE'RE WONDERING IF WE CAN MODERNIZE IT, UPDATE IT...
WE SHOOT THE HERO LOOK TOMORROW.
NO TIME FOR CHANGES.
WE WOULD ALSO LOVE TO SEE THE ESCALATION OF HIS HOOKUP WITH JALA A BIT MORE.
NOT SURE WE HAVE THE FOOTAGE TO SUPPORT THIS, BUT...
LET ME LOOK INTO IT. PICK IT UP NEXT WEEK IF NOT.
GREAT. LET'S TALK FRIDAY AFTER THE DAILIES COME IN.
OKAY. TAKE CARE EVERYONE.
DO YOU JUST HIDE BREAKFAST BURRITOS IN YOUR BACK-PACK NOW?
WHAT DO YOU MEAN HIDE?
FEEL LIKE I'M PRETTY OUT IN THE OPEN ABOUT IT.
WHEN I GO TO THE FOOD CART, I ORDER THREE EVERY MORNING.
PEOPLE USED TO USE COCAINE TO GET THROUGH THE SHOWRUNNING JOB...
I ABUSE BREAKFAST BURRITOS.
ALRIGHT, HEART ATTACK.
ANYWAY, WARDROBE HAS SOMETHING THAT NEEDS YOUR APPROVAL.

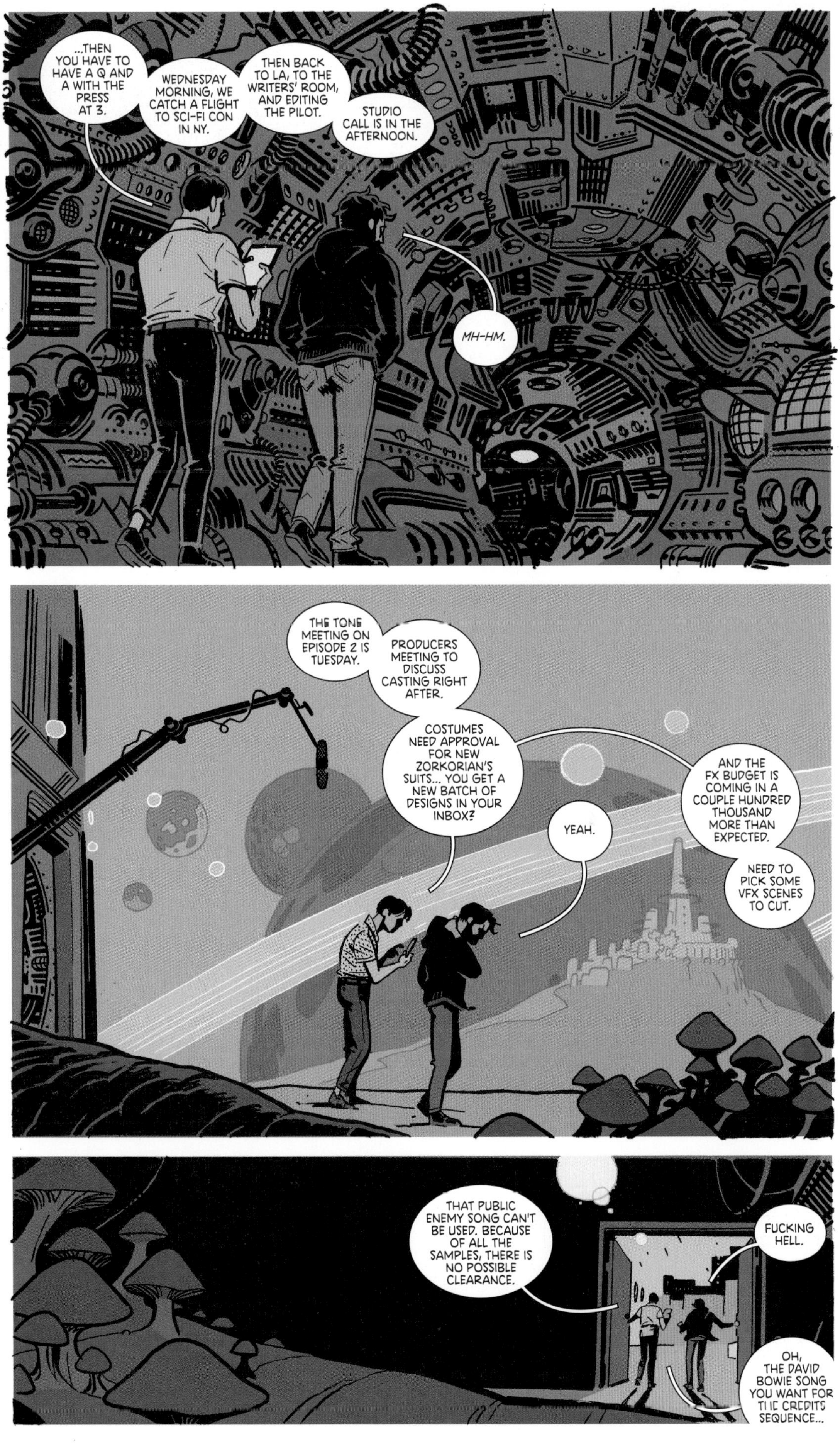
...THEN YOU HAVE TO HAVE A Q AND A WITH THE PRESS AT 3.
WEDNESDAY MORNING, WE CATCH A FLIGHT TO SCI-FI CON IN NY.
THEN BACK TO LA, TO THE WRITERS' ROOM, AND EDITING THE PILOT.
STUDIO CALL IS IN THE AFTERNOON.
MH-HM.
THE TONE MEETING ON EPISODE 2 IS TUESDAY.
PRODUCERS MEETING TO DISCUSS CASTING RIGHT AFTER.
COSTUMES NEED APPROVAL FOR NEW ZORKORIAN'S SUITS... YOU GET A NEW BATCH OF DESIGNS IN YOUR INBOX?
YEAH.
AND THE FX BUDGET IS COMING IN A COUPLE HUNDRED THOUSAND MORE THAN EXPECTED.
NEED TO PICK SOME VFX SCENES TO CUT.
THAT PUBLIC ENEMY SONG CAN'T BE USED. BECAUSE OF ALL THE SAMPLES, THERE IS NO POSSIBLE CLEARANCE.
FUCKING HELL.
OH, THE DAVID BOWIE SONG YOU WANT FOR THE CREDITS SEQUENCE...

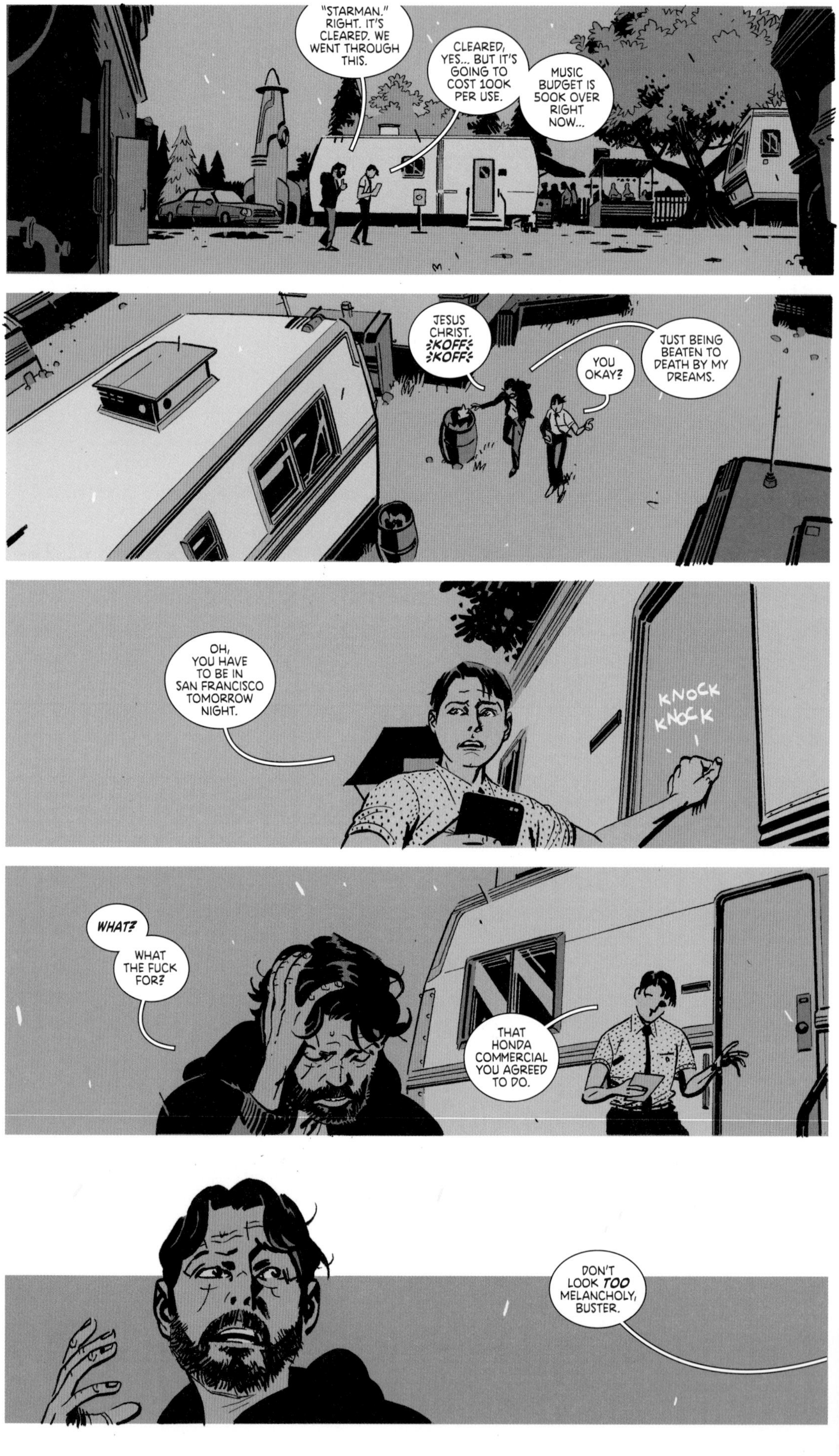

"STARMAN." RIGHT. IT'S CLEARED. WE WENT THROUGH THIS.
CLEARED, YES... BUT IT'S GOING TO COST 100K PER USE.
MUSIC BUDGET IS 500K OVER RIGHT NOW...
JESUS CHRIST. KOFF KOFF
YOU OKAY?
JUST BEING BEATEN TO DEATH BY MY DREAMS.
OH, YOU HAVE TO BE IN SAN FRANCISCO TOMORROW NIGHT.
KNOCK KNOCK
WHAT?
WHAT THE FUCK FOR?
THAT HONDA COMMERCIAL YOU AGREED TO DO.
DON'T LOOK TOO MELANCHOLY, BUSTER.

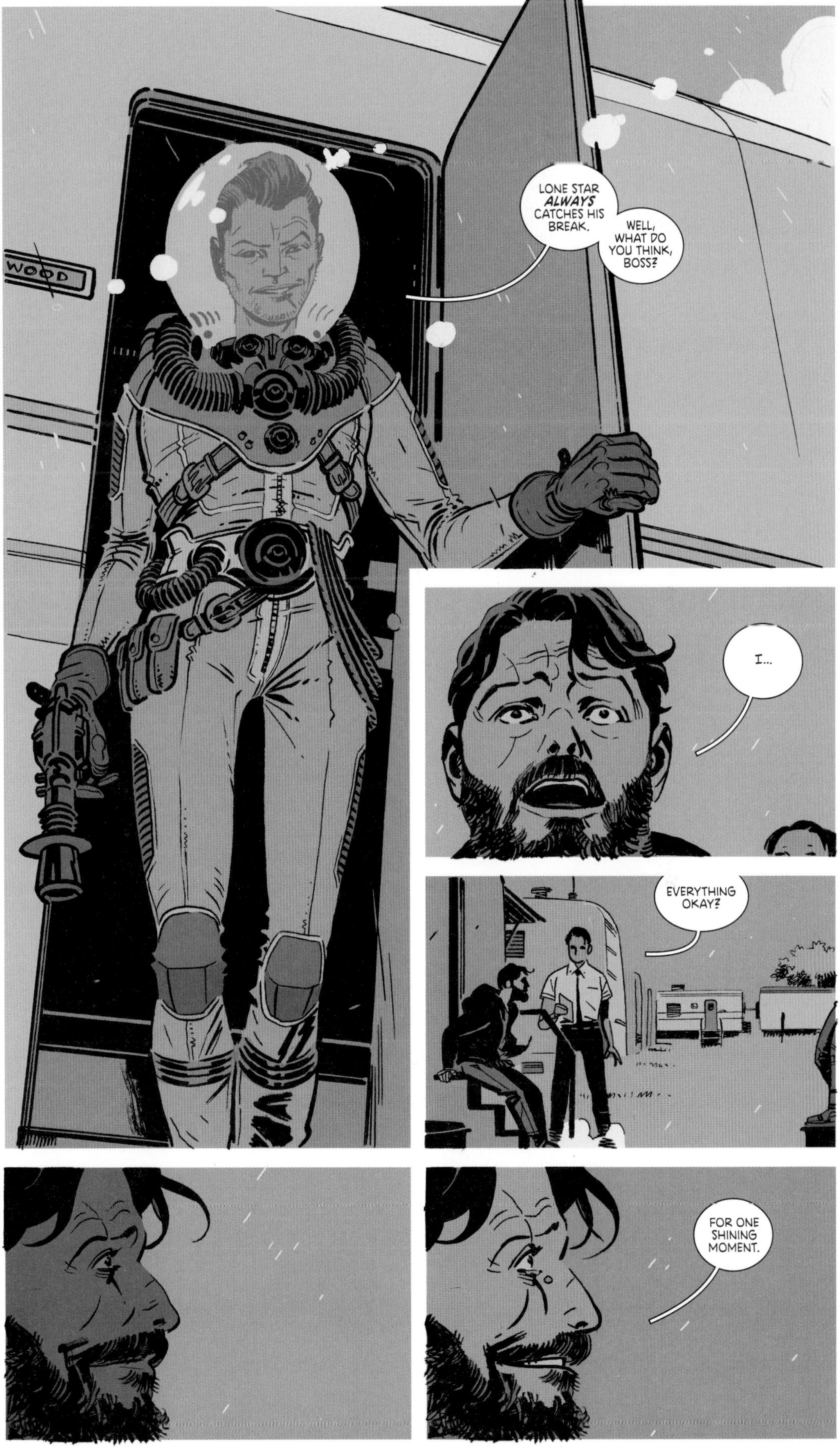

WOOD
LONE STAR ALWAYS CATCHES HIS BREAK.
WELL, WHAT DO YOU THINK, BOSS?
I...
EVERYTHING OKAY?
FOR ONE SHINING MOMENT.

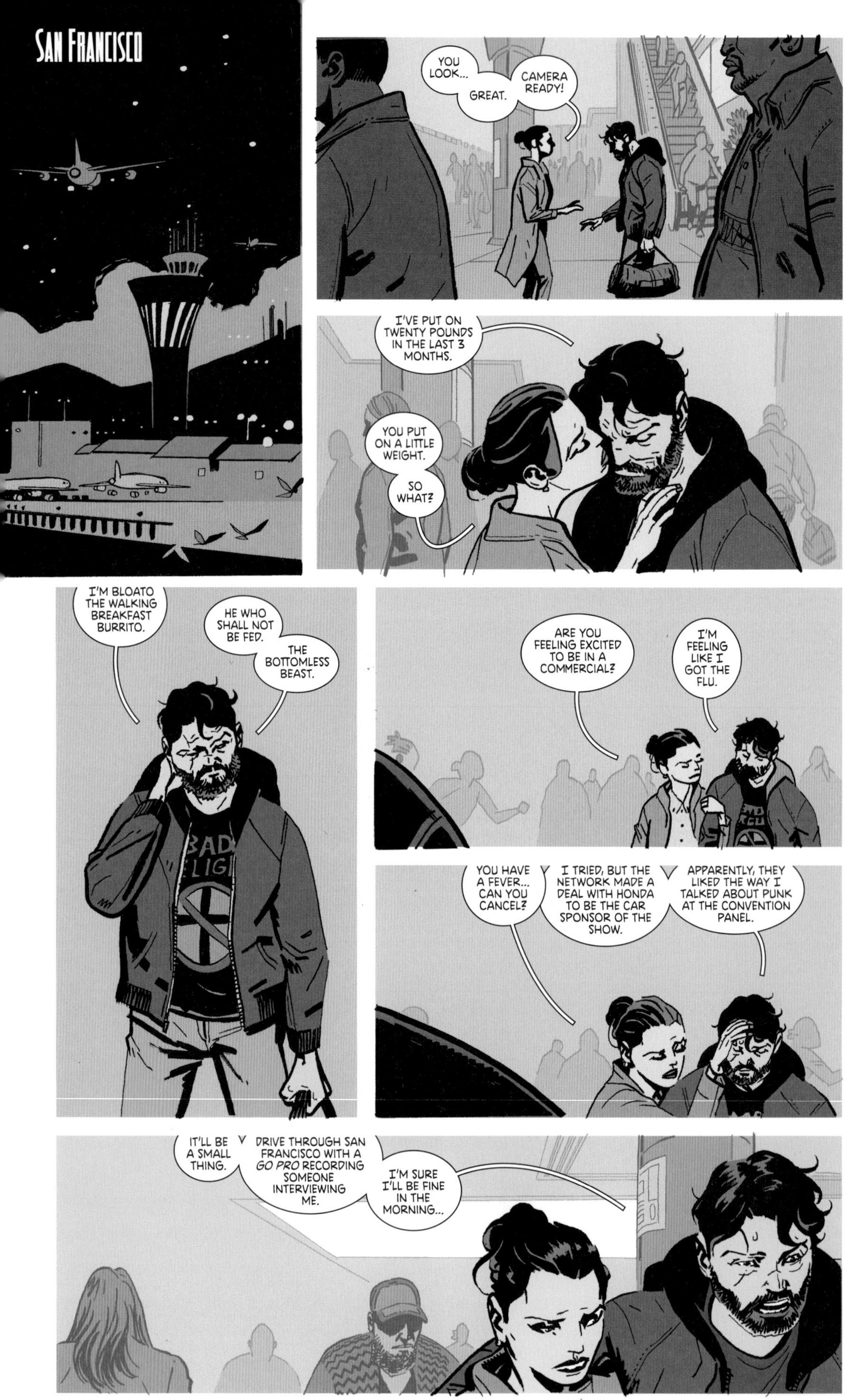
SAN FRANCISCO
YOU LOOK...
GREAT.
CAMERA READY!
I'VE PUT ON TWENTY POUNDS IN THE LAST 3 MONTHS.
YOU PUT ON A LITTLE WEIGHT.
SO WHAT?
I'M BLOATO THE WALKING BREAKFAST BURRITO.
HE WHO SHALL NOT BE FED.
THE BOTTOMLESS BEAST.
ARE YOU FEELING EXCITED TO BE IN A COMMERCIAL?
I'M FEELING LIKE I GOT THE FLU.
YOU HAVE A FEVER... CAN YOU CANCEL?
I TRIED, BUT THE NETWORK MADE A DEAL WITH HONDA TO BE THE CAR SPONSOR OF THE SHOW.
APPARENTLY, THEY LIKED THE WAY I TALKED ABOUT PUNK AT THE CONVENTION PANEL.
IT'LL BE A SMALL THING.
DRIVE THROUGH SAN FRANCISCO WITH A *GO PRO* RECORDING SOMEONE INTERVIEWING ME.
I'M SURE I'LL BE FINE IN THE MORNING...

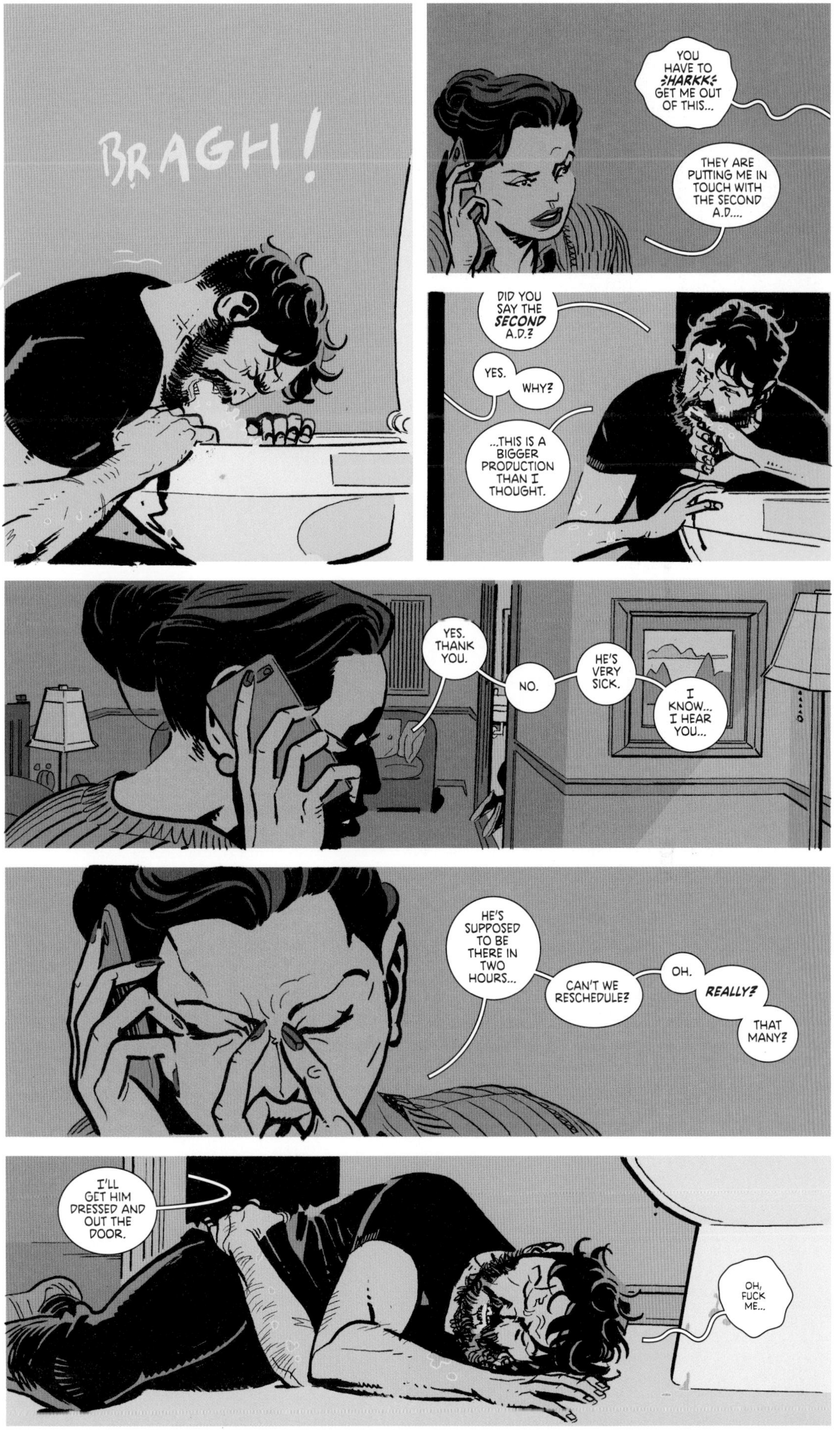
BRAGH!
YOU HAVE TO -HARKK- GET ME OUT OF THIS...
THEY ARE PUTTING ME IN TOUCH WITH THE SECOND A.D....
DID YOU SAY THE SECOND A.D.?
YES.
WHY?
...THIS IS A BIGGER PRODUCTION THAN I THOUGHT.
YES. THANK YOU.
NO.
HE'S VERY SICK.
I KNOW... I HEAR YOU...
HE'S SUPPOSED TO BE THERE IN TWO HOURS...
CAN'T WE RESCHEDULE?
OH.
REALLY?
THAT MANY?
I'LL GET HIM DRESSED AND OUT THE DOOR.
OH, FUCK ME...

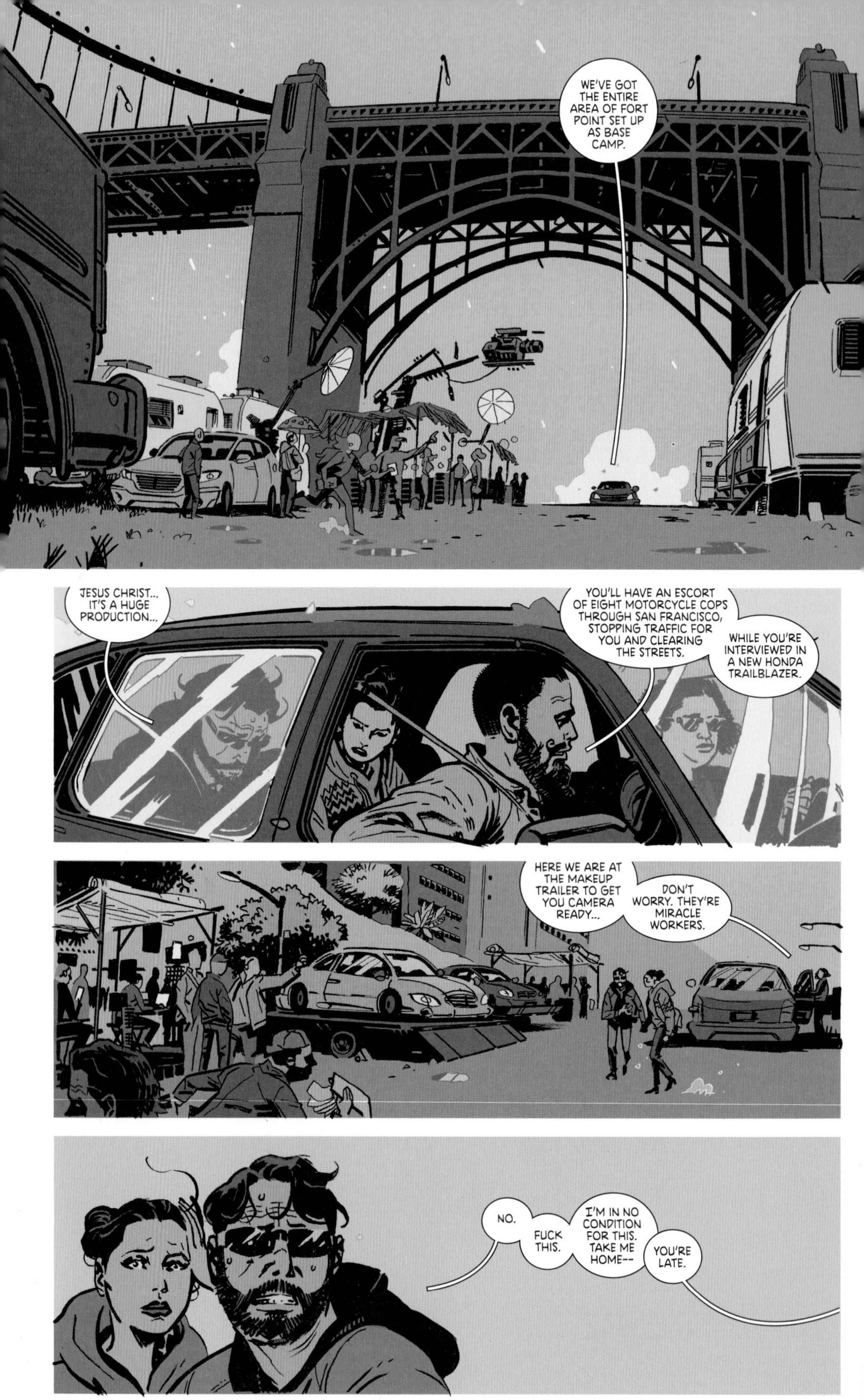
WE'VE GOT THE ENTIRE AREA OF FORT POINT SET UP AS BASE CAMP.
JESUS CHRIST... IT'S A HUGE PRODUCTION...
YOU'LL HAVE AN ESCORT OF EIGHT MOTORCYCLE COPS THROUGH SAN FRANCISCO, STOPPING TRAFFIC FOR YOU AND CLEARING THE STREETS.
WHILE YOU'RE INTERVIEWED IN A NEW HONDA TRAILBLAZER.
HERE WE ARE AT THE MAKEUP TRAILER TO GET YOU CAMERA READY...
DON'T WORRY. THEY'RE MIRACLE WORKERS.
NO.
FUCK THIS.
I'M IN NO CONDITION FOR THIS. TAKE ME HOME--
YOU'RE LATE.

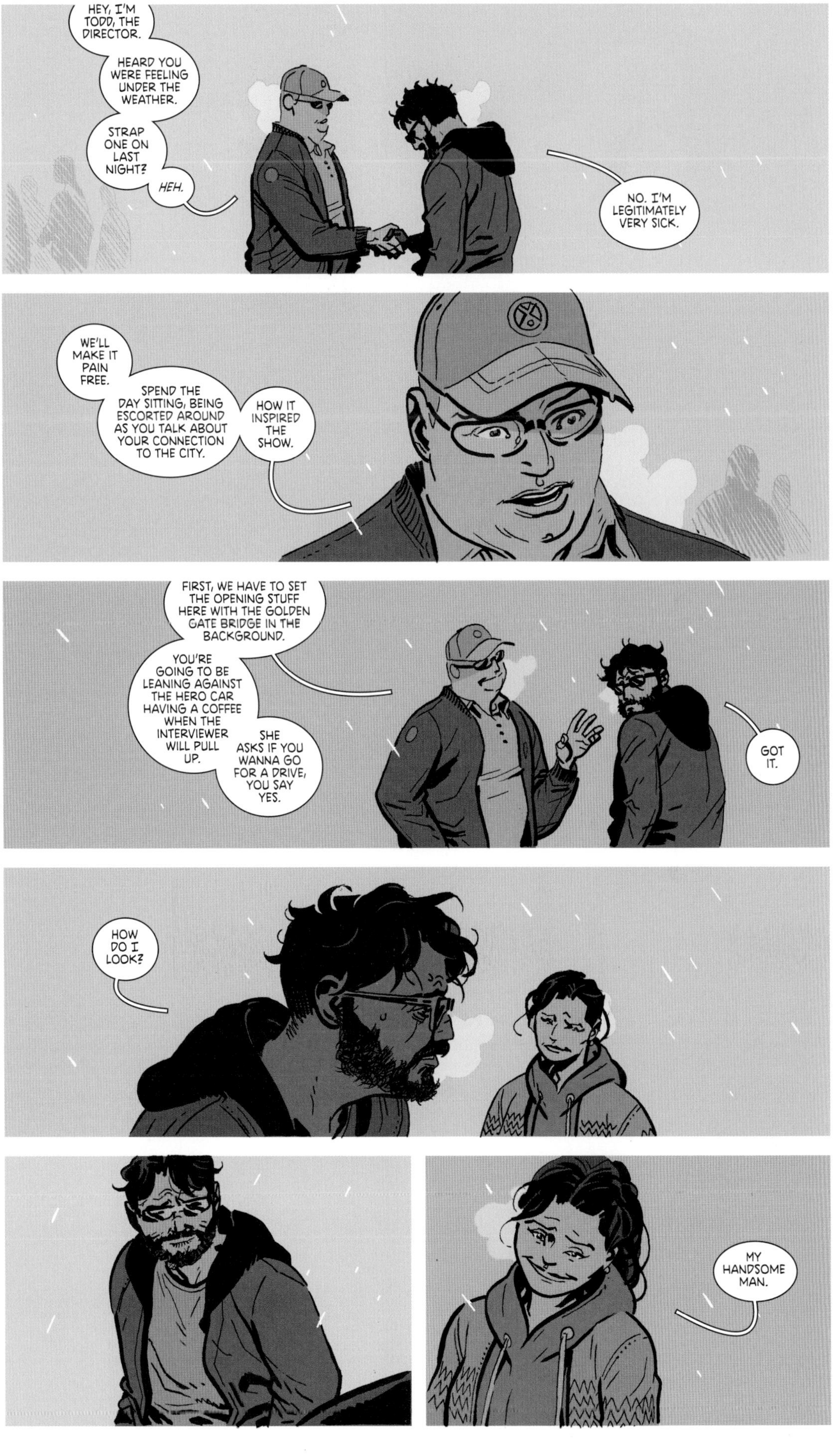

HEY, I'M TODD, THE DIRECTOR.
HEARD YOU WERE FEELING UNDER THE WEATHER.
STRAP ONE ON LAST NIGHT?
HEH.
NO. I'M LEGITIMATELY VERY SICK.
WE'LL MAKE IT PAIN FREE.
SPEND THE DAY SITTING, BEING ESCORTED AROUND AS YOU TALK ABOUT YOUR CONNECTION TO THE CITY.
HOW IT INSPIRED THE SHOW.
FIRST, WE HAVE TO SET THE OPENING STUFF HERE WITH THE GOLDEN GATE BRIDGE IN THE BACKGROUND.
YOU'RE GOING TO BE LEANING AGAINST THE HERO CAR HAVING A COFFEE WHEN THE INTERVIEWER WILL PULL UP.
SHE ASKS IF YOU WANNA GO FOR A DRIVE, YOU SAY YES.
GOT IT.
HOW DO I LOOK?
MY HANDSOME MAN.

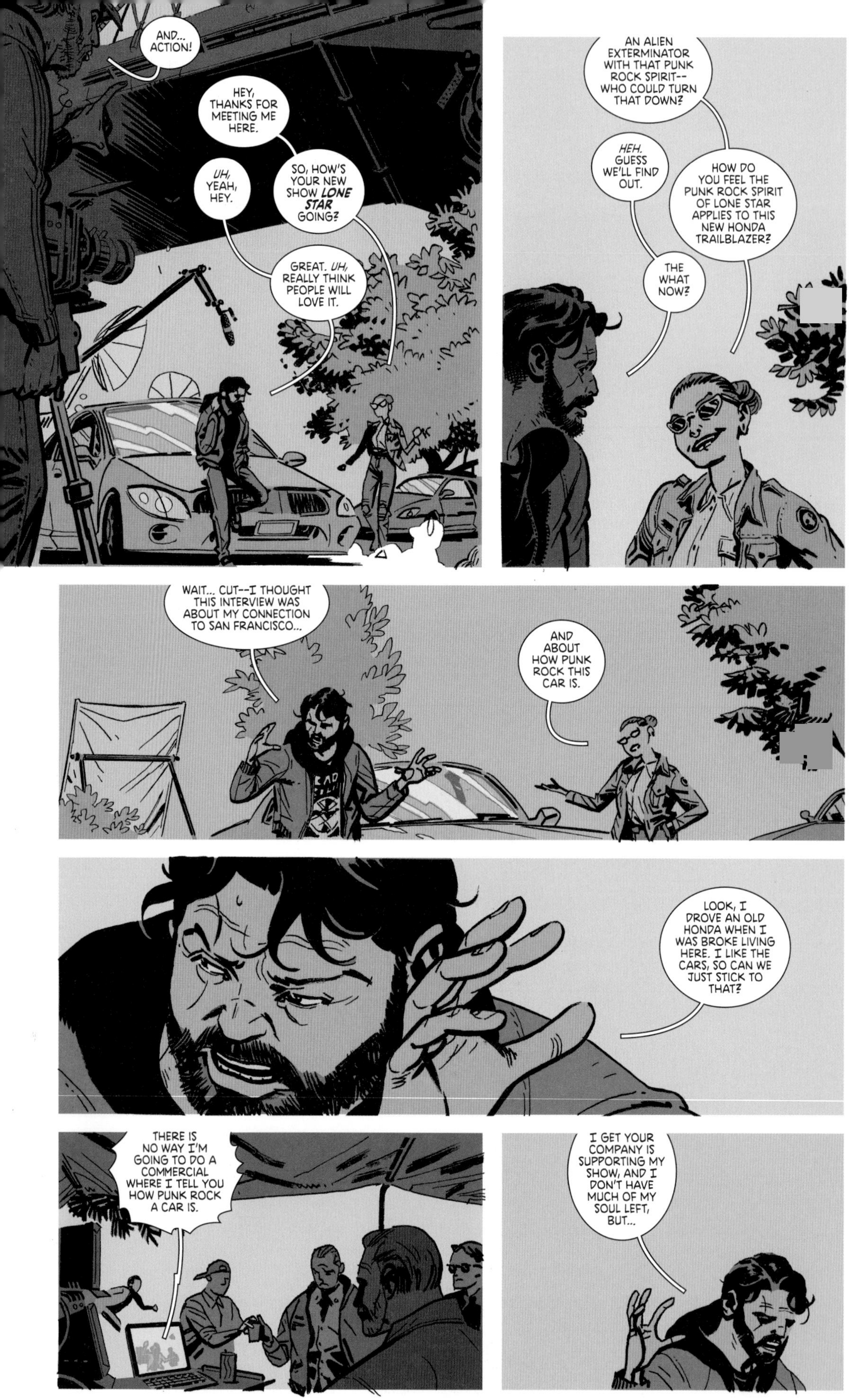
AND... ACTION!
HEY, THANKS FOR MEETING ME HERE.
UH, YEAH, HEY.
SO, HOW'S YOUR NEW SHOW LONE STAR GOING?
GREAT. UH, REALLY THINK PEOPLE WILL LOVE IT.
AN ALIEN EXTERMINATOR WITH THAT PUNK ROCK SPIRIT-- WHO COULD TURN THAT DOWN?
HEH. GUESS WE'LL FIND OUT.
HOW DO YOU FEEL THE PUNK ROCK SPIRIT OF LONE STAR APPLIES TO THIS NEW HONDA TRAILBLAZER?
THE WHAT NOW?
WAIT... CUT--I THOUGHT THIS INTERVIEW WAS ABOUT MY CONNECTION TO SAN FRANCISCO...
AND ABOUT HOW PUNK ROCK THIS CAR IS.
LOOK, I DROVE AN OLD HONDA WHEN I WAS BROKE LIVING HERE. I LIKE THE CARS, SO CAN WE JUST STICK TO THAT?
THERE IS NO WAY I'M GOING TO DO A COMMERCIAL WHERE I TELL YOU HOW PUNK ROCK A CAR IS.
I GET YOUR COMPANY IS SUPPORTING MY SHOW, AND I DON'T HAVE MUCH OF MY SOUL LEFT, BUT...

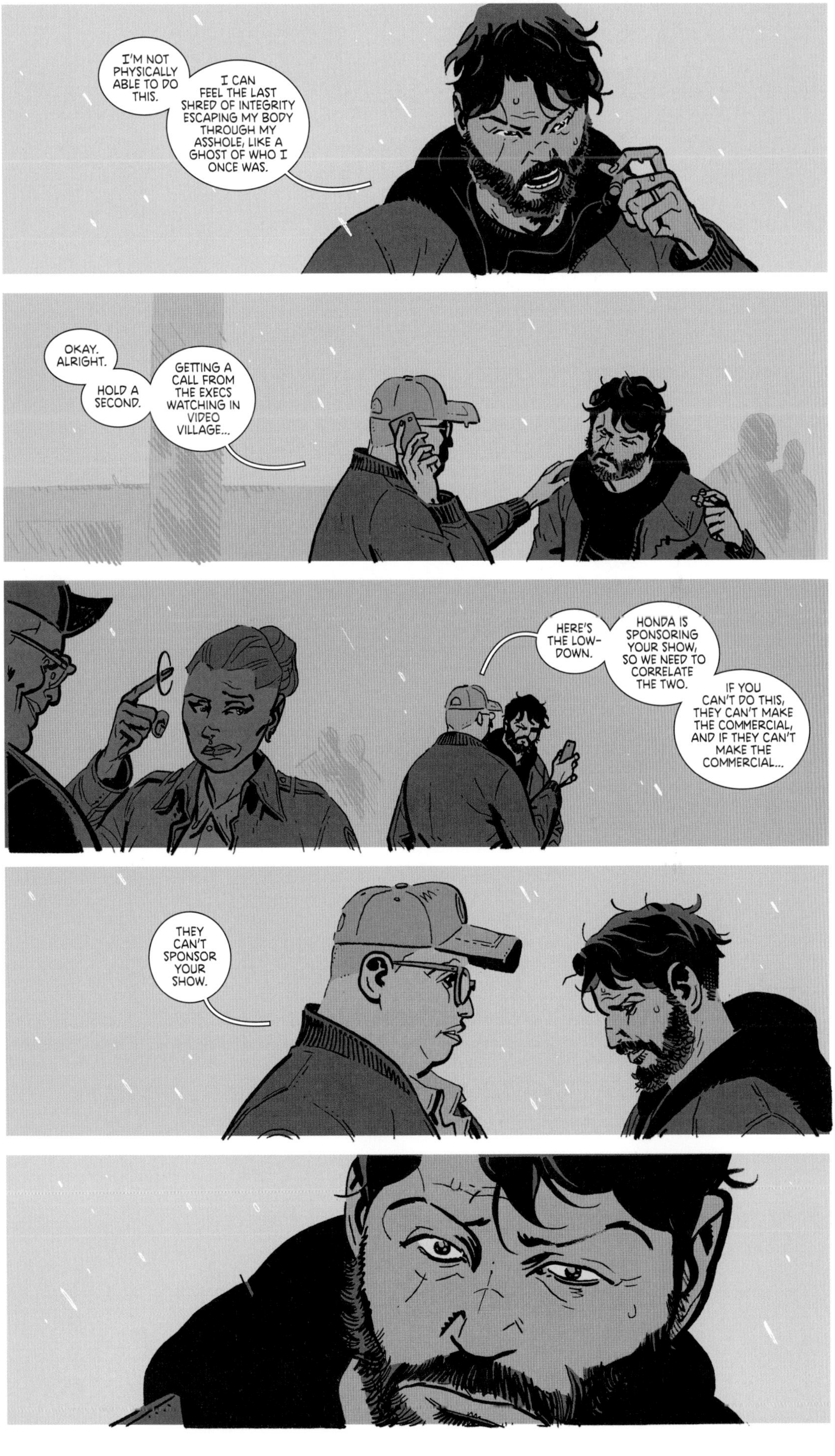
I'M NOT PHYSICALLY ABLE TO DO THIS.
I CAN FEEL THE LAST SHRED OF INTEGRITY ESCAPING MY BODY THROUGH MY ASSHOLE, LIKE A GHOST OF WHO I ONCE WAS.
OKAY. ALRIGHT.
HOLD A SECOND.
GETTING A CALL FROM THE EXECS WATCHING IN VIDEO VILLAGE...
HERE'S THE LOW-DOWN.
HONDA IS SPONSORING YOUR SHOW, SO WE NEED TO CORRELATE THE TWO.
IF YOU CAN'T DO THIS, THEY CAN'T MAKE THE COMMERCIAL, AND IF THEY CAN'T MAKE THE COMMERCIAL...
THEY CAN'T SPONSOR YOUR SHOW.

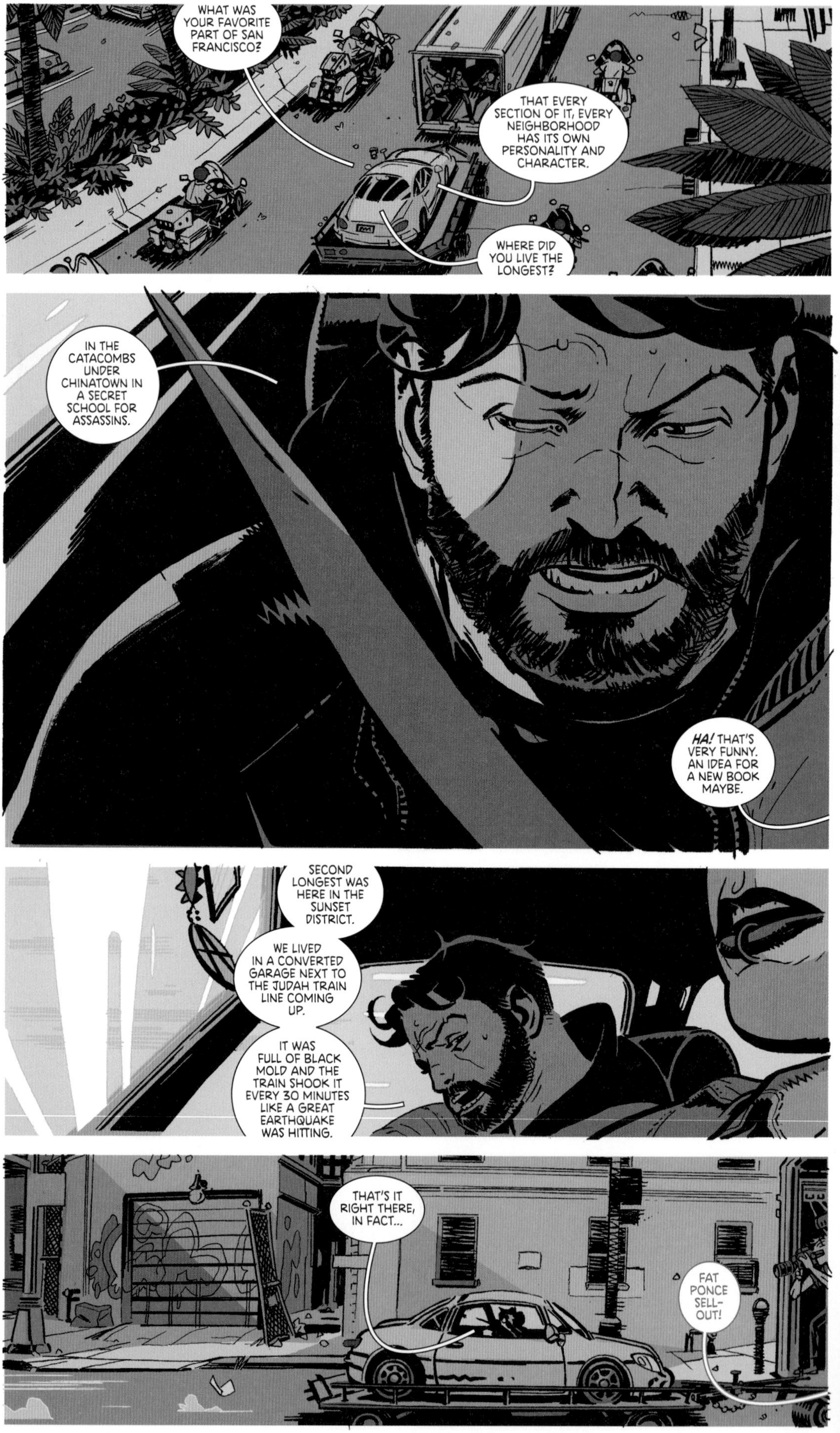

WHAT WAS YOUR FAVORITE PART OF SAN FRANCISCO?
THAT EVERY SECTION OF IT, EVERY NEIGHBORHOOD HAS ITS OWN PERSONALITY AND CHARACTER.
WHERE DID YOU LIVE THE LONGEST?
IN THE CATACOMBS UNDER CHINATOWN IN A SECRET SCHOOL FOR ASSASSINS.
HA! THAT'S VERY FUNNY. AN IDEA FOR A NEW BOOK MAYBE.
SECOND LONGEST WAS HERE IN THE SUNSET DISTRICT.
WE LIVED IN A CONVERTED GARAGE NEXT TO THE JUDAH TRAIN LINE COMING UP.
IT WAS FULL OF BLACK MOLD AND THE TRAIN SHOOK IT EVERY 30 MINUTES LIKE A GREAT EARTHQUAKE WAS HITTING.
THAT'S IT RIGHT THERE, IN FACT...
FAT PONCE SELL-OUT!

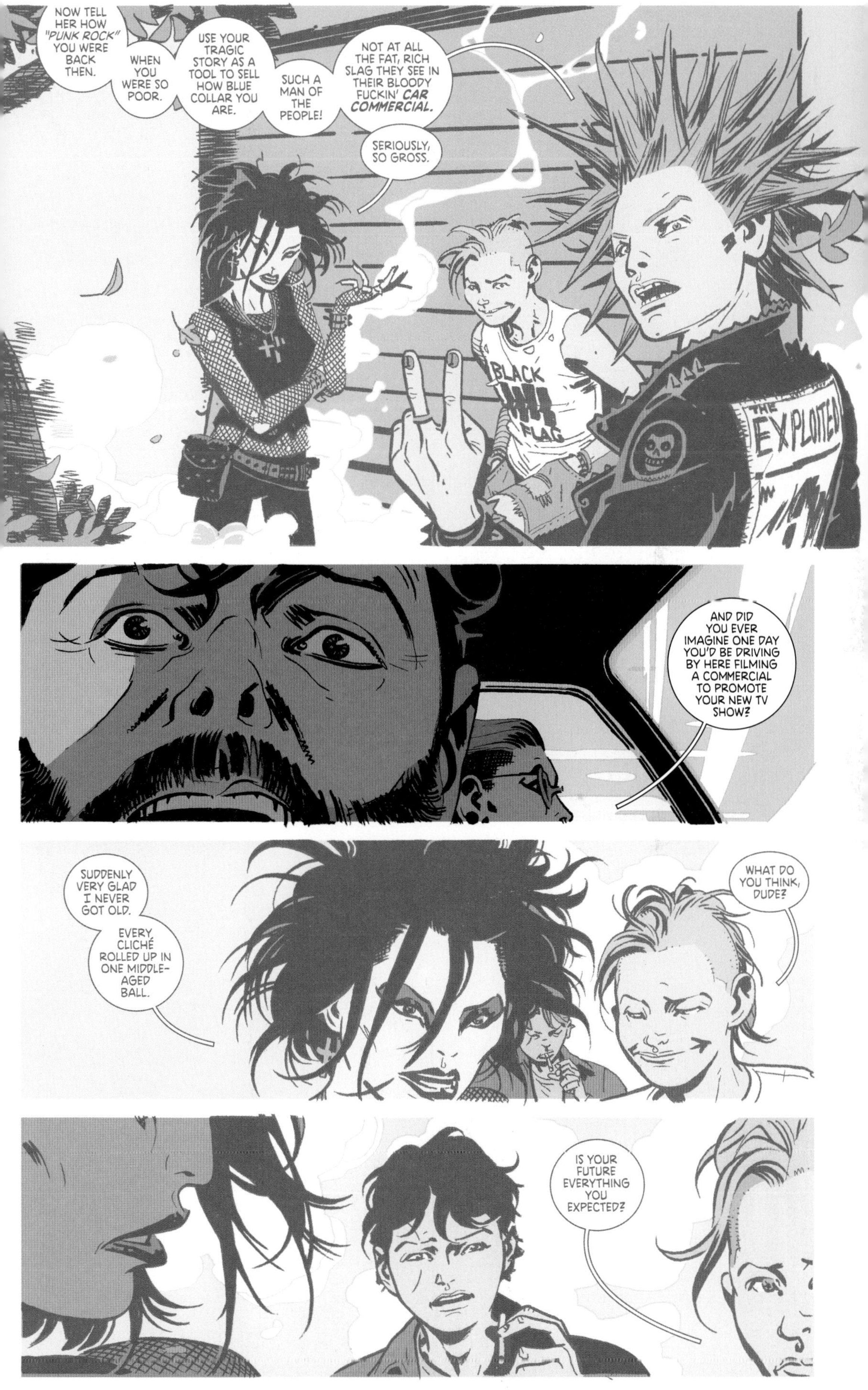
NOW TELL HER HOW "PUNK ROCK" YOU WERE BACK THEN.
WHEN YOU WERE SO POOR.
USE YOUR TRAGIC STORY AS A TOOL TO SELL HOW BLUE COLLAR YOU ARE.
SUCH A MAN OF THE PEOPLE!
NOT AT ALL THE FAT, RICH SLAG THEY SEE IN THEIR BLOODY FUCKIN' CAR COMMERCIAL.
SERIOUSLY, SO GROSS.
BLACK FLAG
THE EXPLOITED
AND DID YOU EVER IMAGINE ONE DAY YOU'D BE DRIVING BY HERE FILMING A COMMERCIAL TO PROMOTE YOUR NEW TV SHOW?
SUDDENLY VERY GLAD I NEVER GOT OLD.
EVERY CLICHÉ ROLLED UP IN ONE MIDDLE-AGED BALL.
WHAT DO YOU THINK, DUDE?
IS YOUR FUTURE EVERYTHING YOU EXPECTED?

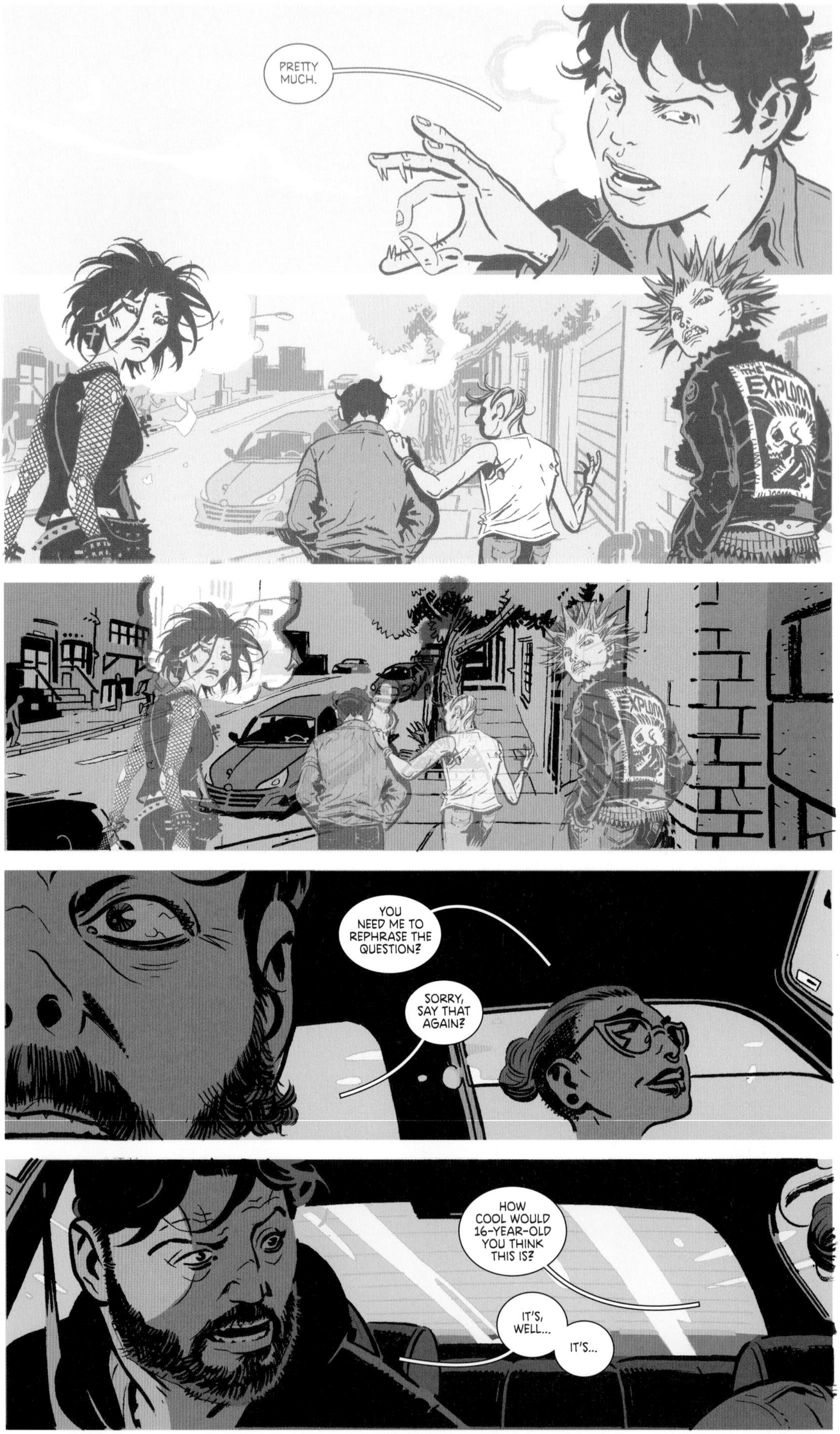

PRETTY MUCH.
THE EXPLOITED
THE EXPLOITED
YOU NEED ME TO REPHRASE THE QUESTION?
SORRY, SAY THAT AGAIN?
HOW COOL WOULD 16-YEAR-OLD YOU THINK THIS IS?
IT'S, WELL...
IT'S...

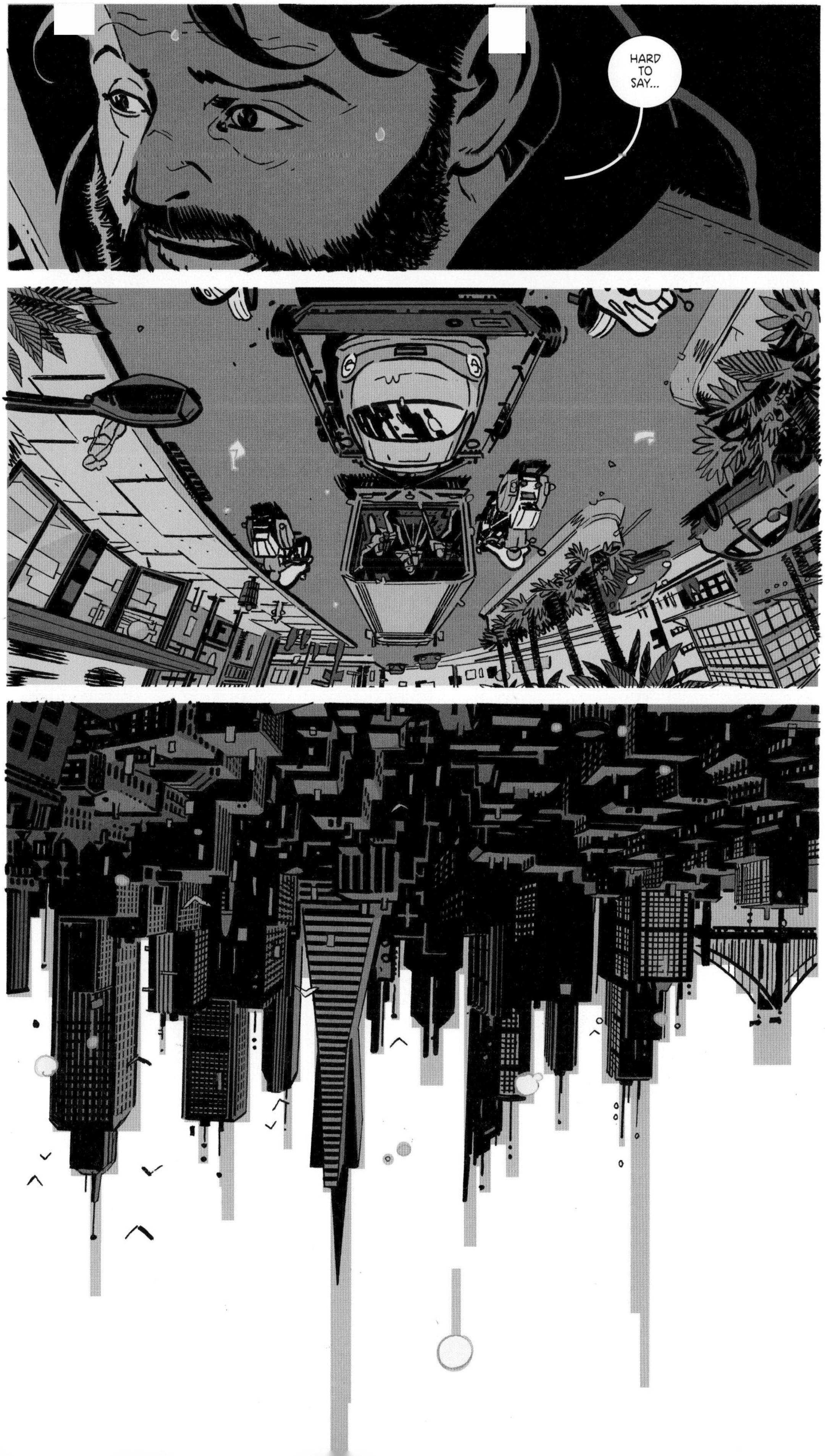
HARD TO SAY...

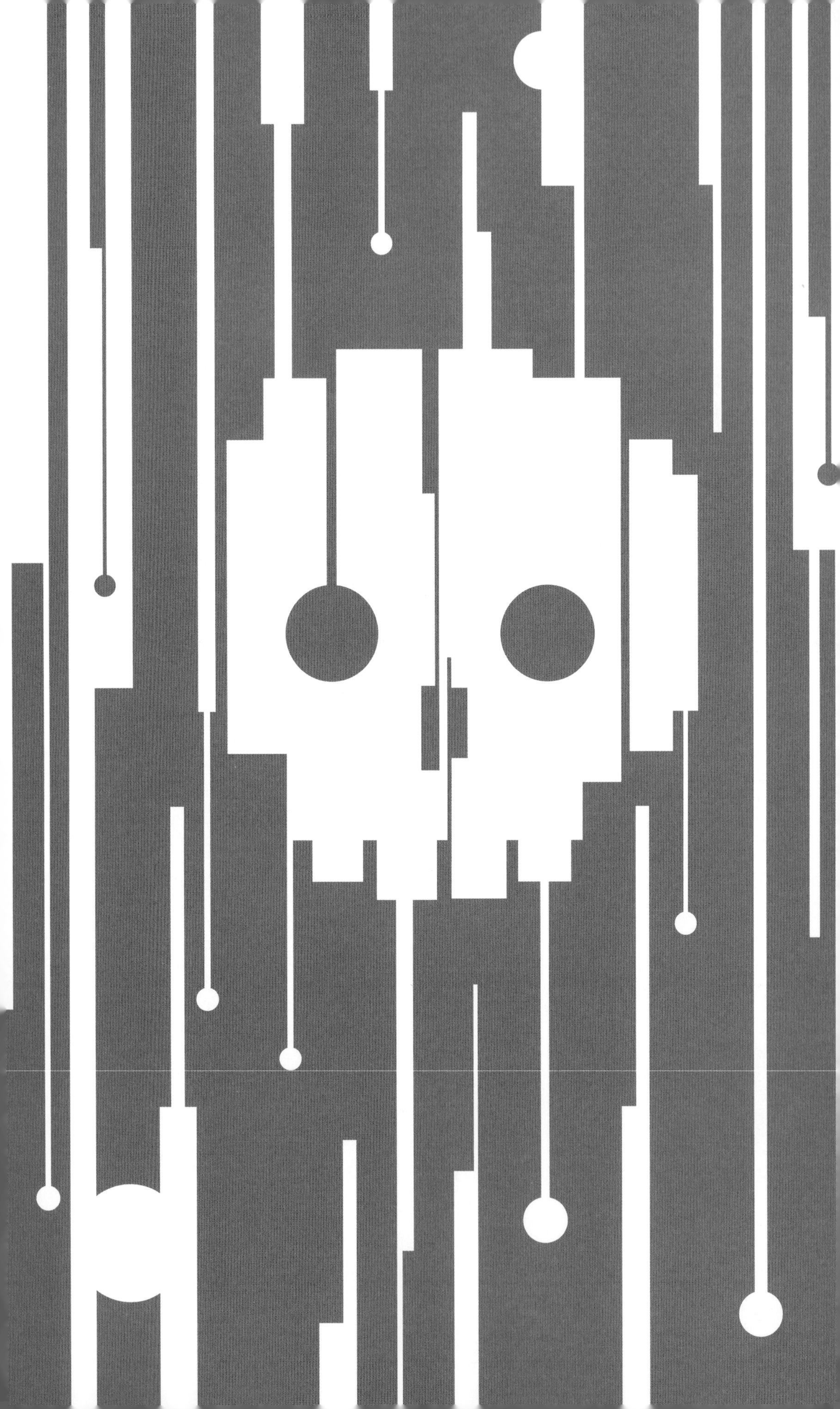

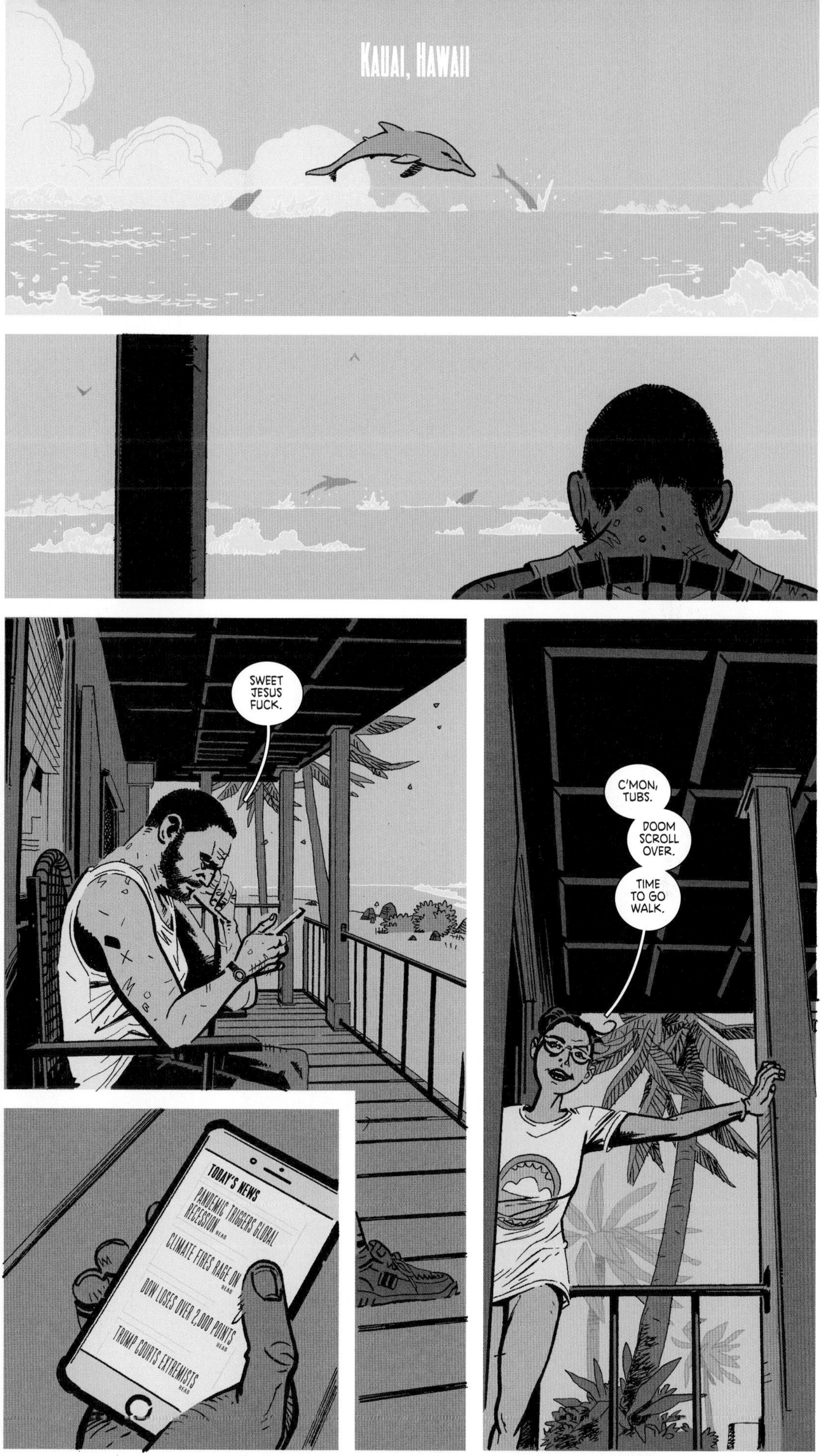
Kauai, Hawaii
SWEET JESUS FUCK.
C'MON, TUBS.
DOOM SCROLL OVER.
TIME TO GO WALK.
TODAY'S NEWS
PANDEMIC TRIGGERS GLOBAL RECESSION
CLIMATE FIRES RAGE ON
DOW LOSES OVER 2,000 POINTS
TRUMP COURTS EXTREMISTS

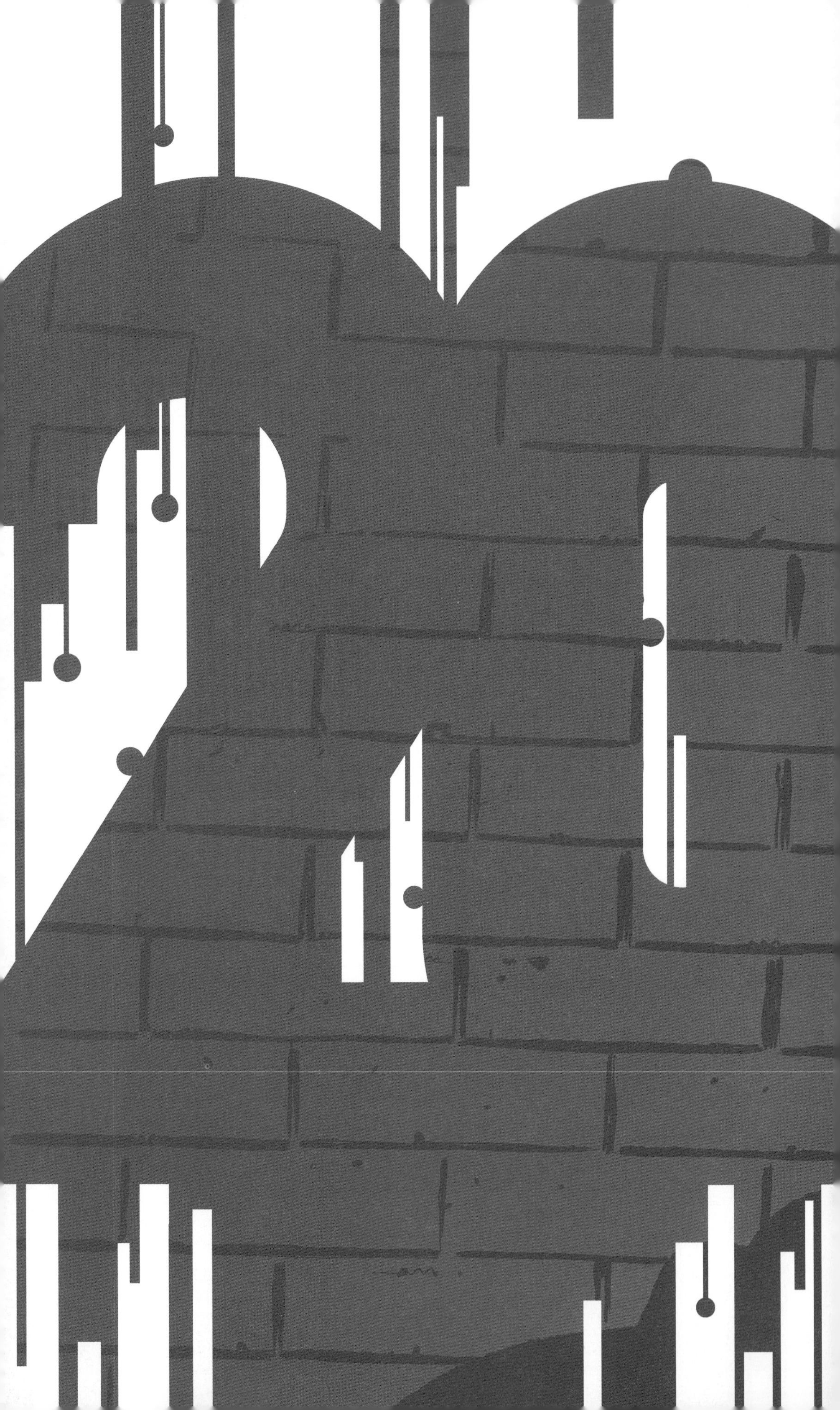

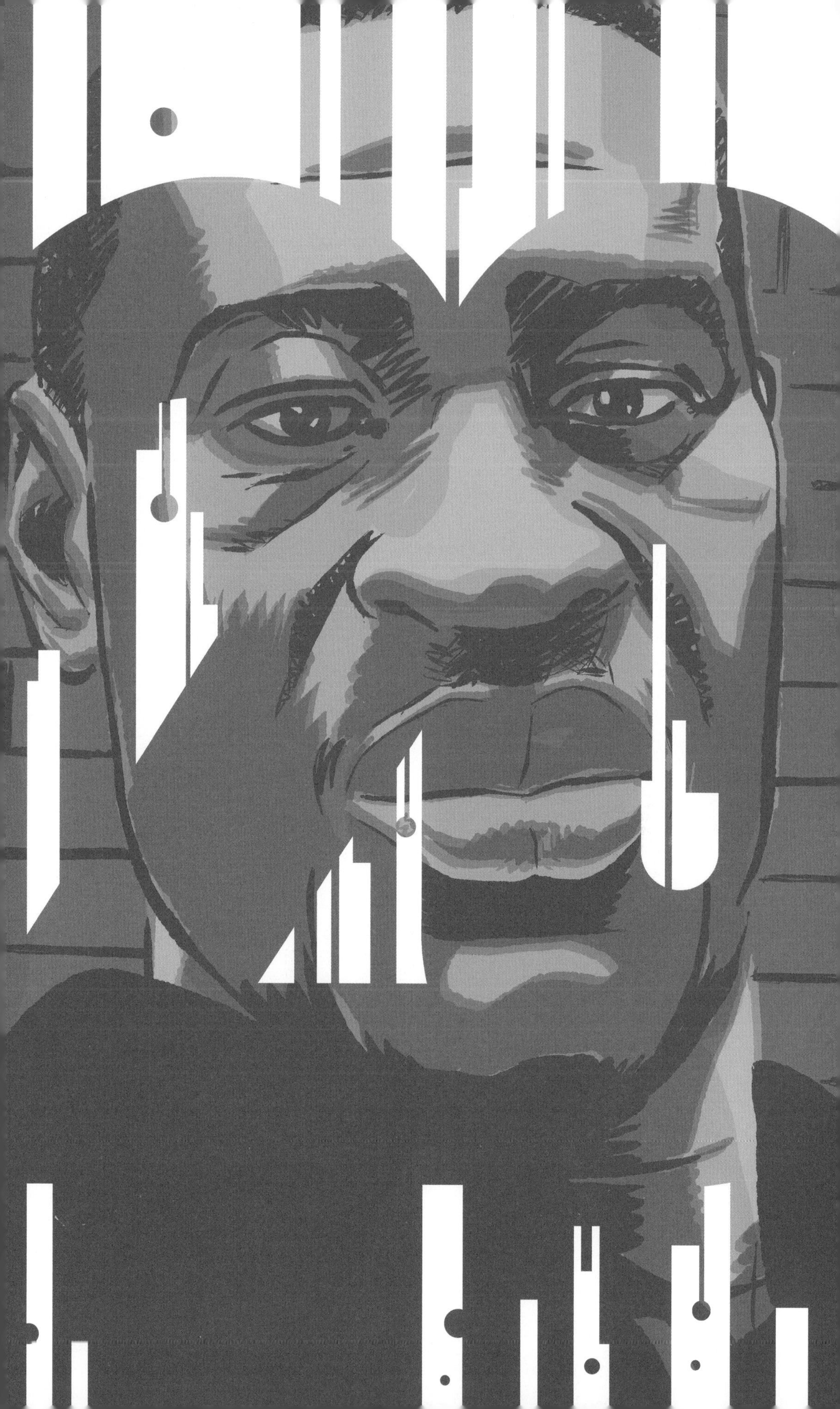

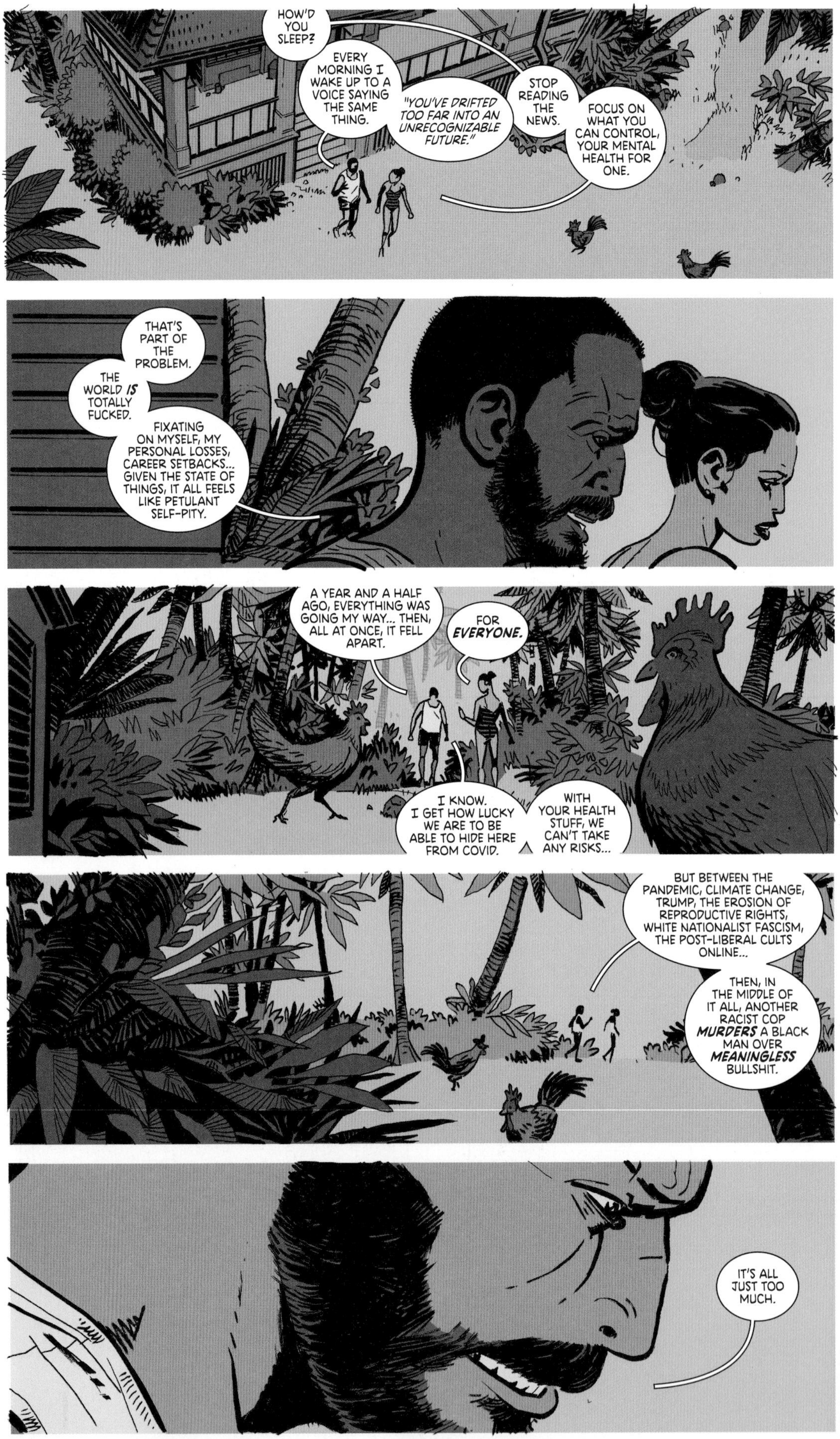
HOW'D YOU SLEEP?
EVERY MORNING I WAKE UP TO A VOICE SAYING THE SAME THING.
"YOU'VE DRIFTED TOO FAR INTO AN UNRECOGNIZABLE FUTURE."
STOP READING THE NEWS.
FOCUS ON WHAT YOU CAN CONTROL, YOUR MENTAL HEALTH FOR ONE.
THAT'S PART OF THE PROBLEM.
THE WORLD *IS* TOTALLY FUCKED.
FIXATING ON MYSELF, MY PERSONAL LOSSES, CAREER SETBACKS... GIVEN THE STATE OF THINGS, IT ALL FEELS LIKE PETULANT SELF-PITY.
A YEAR AND A HALF AGO, EVERYTHING WAS GOING MY WAY... THEN, ALL AT ONCE, IT FELL APART.
FOR ***EVERYONE.***
I KNOW. I GET HOW LUCKY WE ARE TO BE ABLE TO HIDE HERE FROM COVID.
WITH YOUR HEALTH STUFF, WE CAN'T TAKE ANY RISKS...
BUT BETWEEN THE PANDEMIC, CLIMATE CHANGE, TRUMP, THE EROSION OF REPRODUCTIVE RIGHTS, WHITE NATIONALIST FASCISM, THE POST-LIBERAL CULTS ONLINE...
THEN, IN THE MIDDLE OF IT ALL, ANOTHER RACIST COP ***MURDERS*** A BLACK MAN OVER ***MEANINGLESS*** BULLSHIT.
IT'S ALL JUST TOO MUCH.

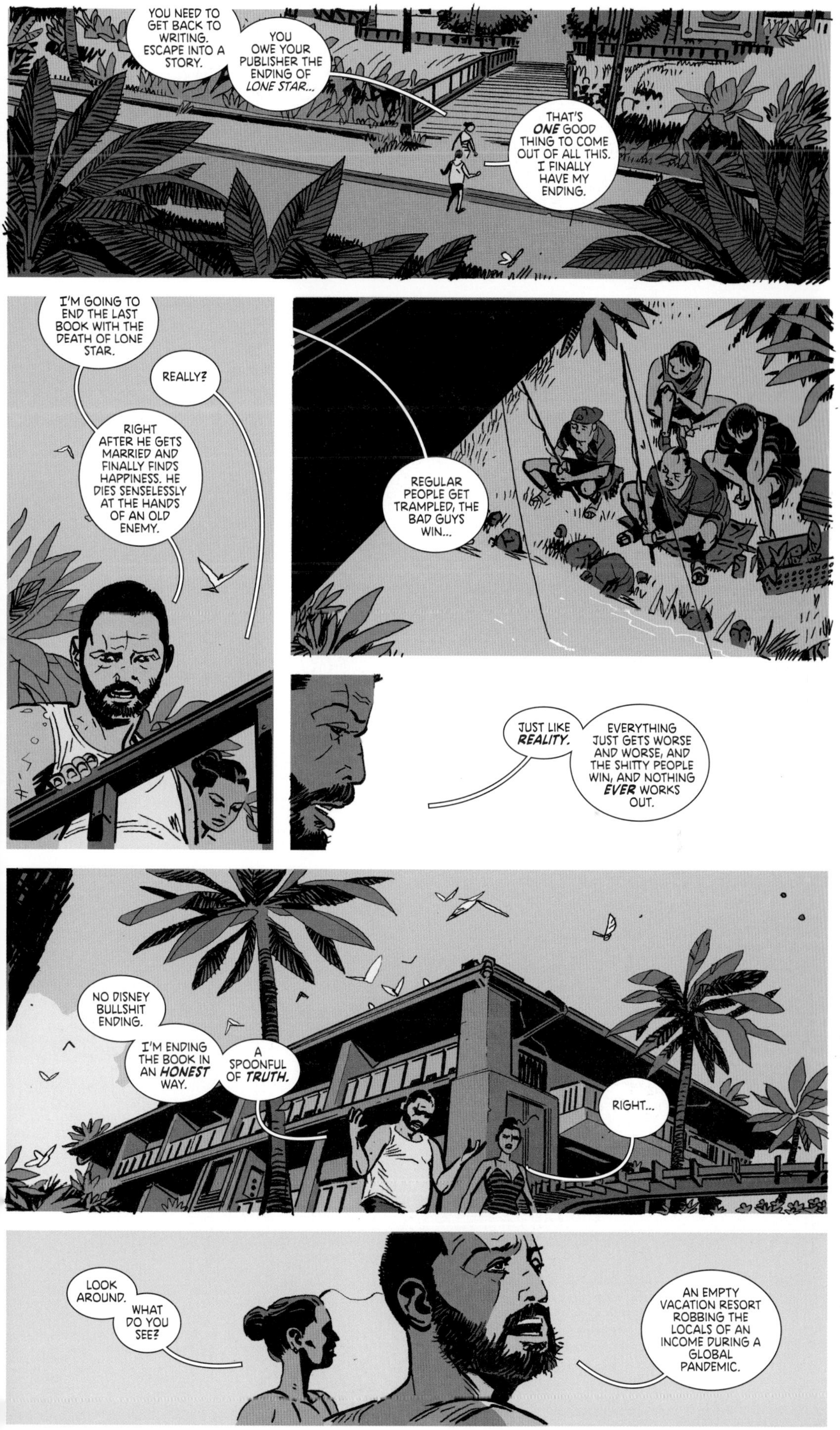
YOU NEED TO GET BACK TO WRITING. ESCAPE INTO A STORY.
YOU OWE YOUR PUBLISHER THE ENDING OF LONE STAR...
THAT'S ONE GOOD THING TO COME OUT OF ALL THIS. I FINALLY HAVE MY ENDING.
I'M GOING TO END THE LAST BOOK WITH THE DEATH OF LONE STAR.
REALLY?
RIGHT AFTER HE GETS MARRIED AND FINALLY FINDS HAPPINESS. HE DIES SENSELESSLY AT THE HANDS OF AN OLD ENEMY.
REGULAR PEOPLE GET TRAMPLED, THE BAD GUYS WIN...
JUST LIKE REALITY.
EVERYTHING JUST GETS WORSE AND WORSE, AND THE SHITTY PEOPLE WIN, AND NOTHING EVER WORKS OUT.
NO DISNEY BULLSHIT ENDING.
I'M ENDING THE BOOK IN AN HONEST WAY.
A SPOONFUL OF TRUTH.
RIGHT...
LOOK AROUND.
WHAT DO YOU SEE?
AN EMPTY VACATION RESORT ROBBING THE LOCALS OF AN INCOME DURING A GLOBAL PANDEMIC.

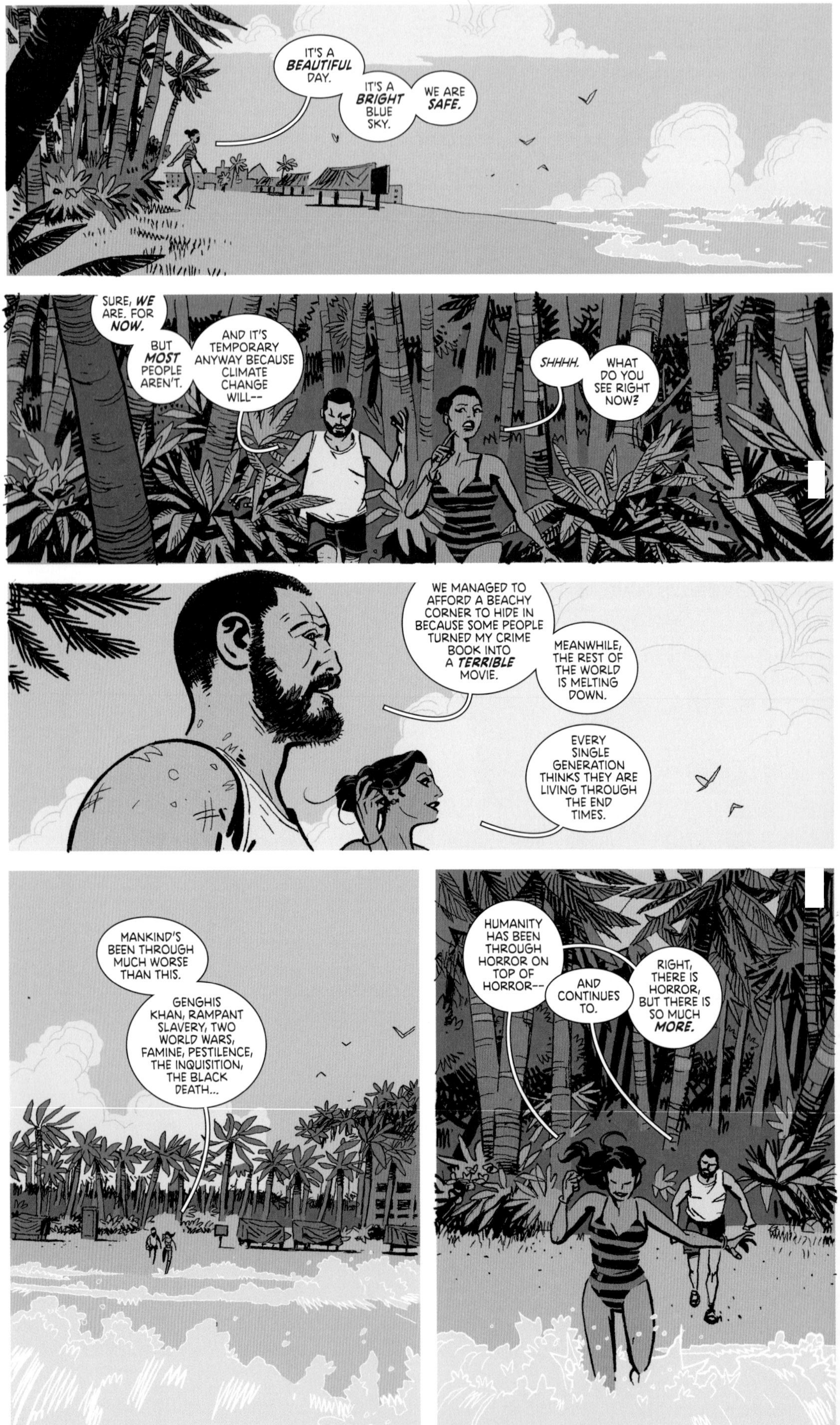
IT'S A BEAUTIFUL DAY.
IT'S A BRIGHT BLUE SKY.
WE ARE SAFE.
SURE, WE ARE. FOR NOW.
BUT MOST PEOPLE AREN'T.
AND IT'S TEMPORARY ANYWAY BECAUSE CLIMATE CHANGE WILL--
SHHHH.
WHAT DO YOU SEE RIGHT NOW?
WE MANAGED TO AFFORD A BEACHY CORNER TO HIDE IN BECAUSE SOME PEOPLE TURNED MY CRIME BOOK INTO A TERRIBLE MOVIE.
MEANWHILE, THE REST OF THE WORLD IS MELTING DOWN.
EVERY SINGLE GENERATION THINKS THEY ARE LIVING THROUGH THE END TIMES.
MANKIND'S BEEN THROUGH MUCH WORSE THAN THIS.
GENGHIS KHAN, RAMPANT SLAVERY, TWO WORLD WARS, FAMINE, PESTILENCE, THE INQUISITION, THE BLACK DEATH...
HUMANITY HAS BEEN THROUGH HORROR ON TOP OF HORROR--
AND CONTINUES TO.
RIGHT, THERE IS HORROR, BUT THERE IS SO MUCH MORE.

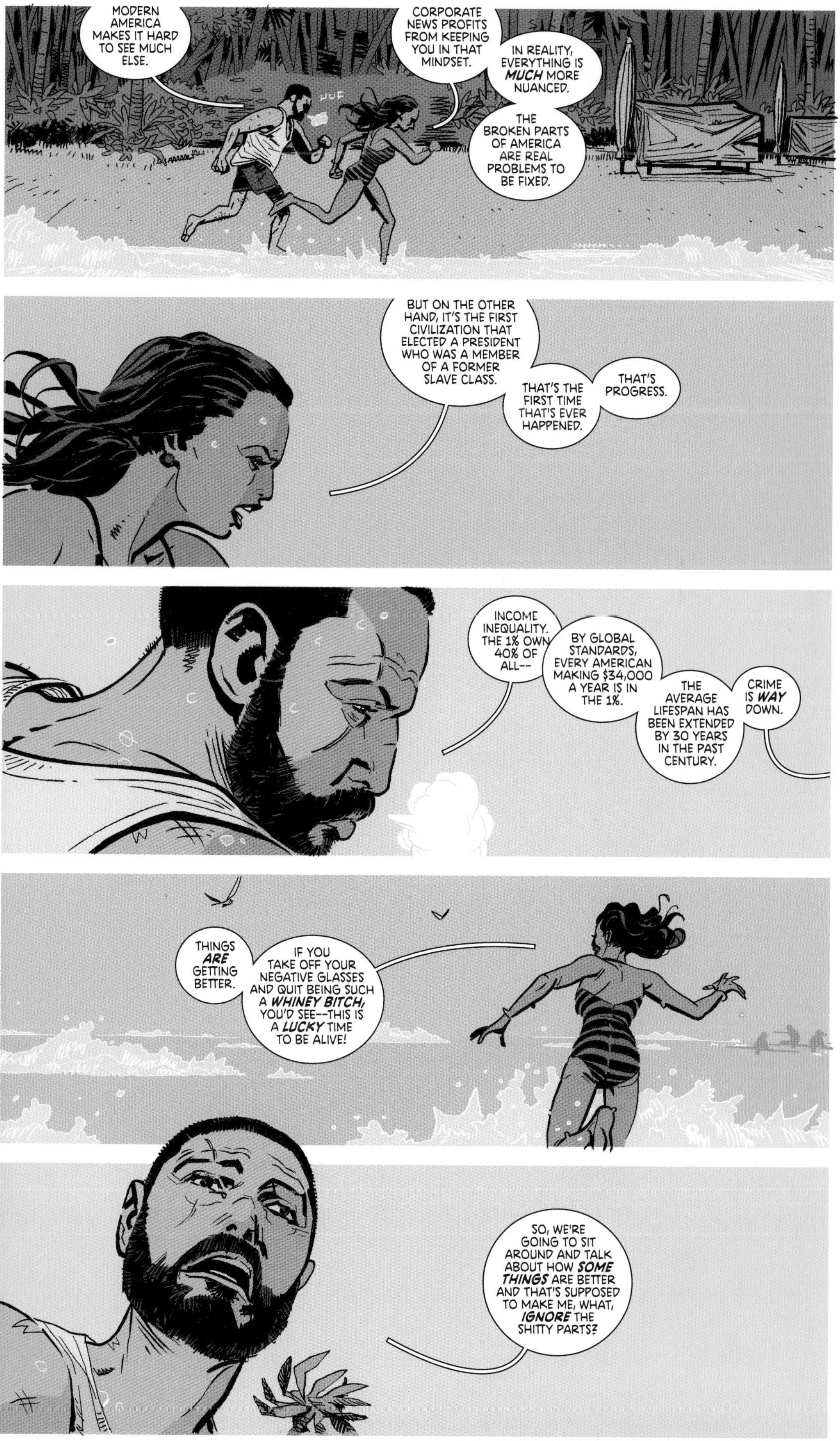
MODERN AMERICA MAKES IT HARD TO SEE MUCH ELSE.
HUF
CORPORATE NEWS PROFITS FROM KEEPING YOU IN THAT MINDSET.
IN REALITY, EVERYTHING IS MUCH MORE NUANCED.
THE BROKEN PARTS OF AMERICA ARE REAL PROBLEMS TO BE FIXED.
BUT ON THE OTHER HAND, IT'S THE FIRST CIVILIZATION THAT ELECTED A PRESIDENT WHO WAS A MEMBER OF A FORMER SLAVE CLASS.
THAT'S THE FIRST TIME THAT'S EVER HAPPENED.
THAT'S PROGRESS.
INCOME INEQUALITY. THE 1% OWN 40% OF ALL--
BY GLOBAL STANDARDS, EVERY AMERICAN MAKING $34,000 A YEAR IS IN THE 1%.
THE AVERAGE LIFESPAN HAS BEEN EXTENDED BY 30 YEARS IN THE PAST CENTURY.
CRIME IS WAY DOWN.
THINGS ARE GETTING BETTER.
IF YOU TAKE OFF YOUR NEGATIVE GLASSES AND QUIT BEING SUCH A WHINEY BITCH, YOU'D SEE--THIS IS A LUCKY TIME TO BE ALIVE!
SO, WE'RE GOING TO SIT AROUND AND TALK ABOUT HOW SOME THINGS ARE BETTER AND THAT'S SUPPOSED TO MAKE ME, WHAT, IGNORE THE SHITTY PARTS?

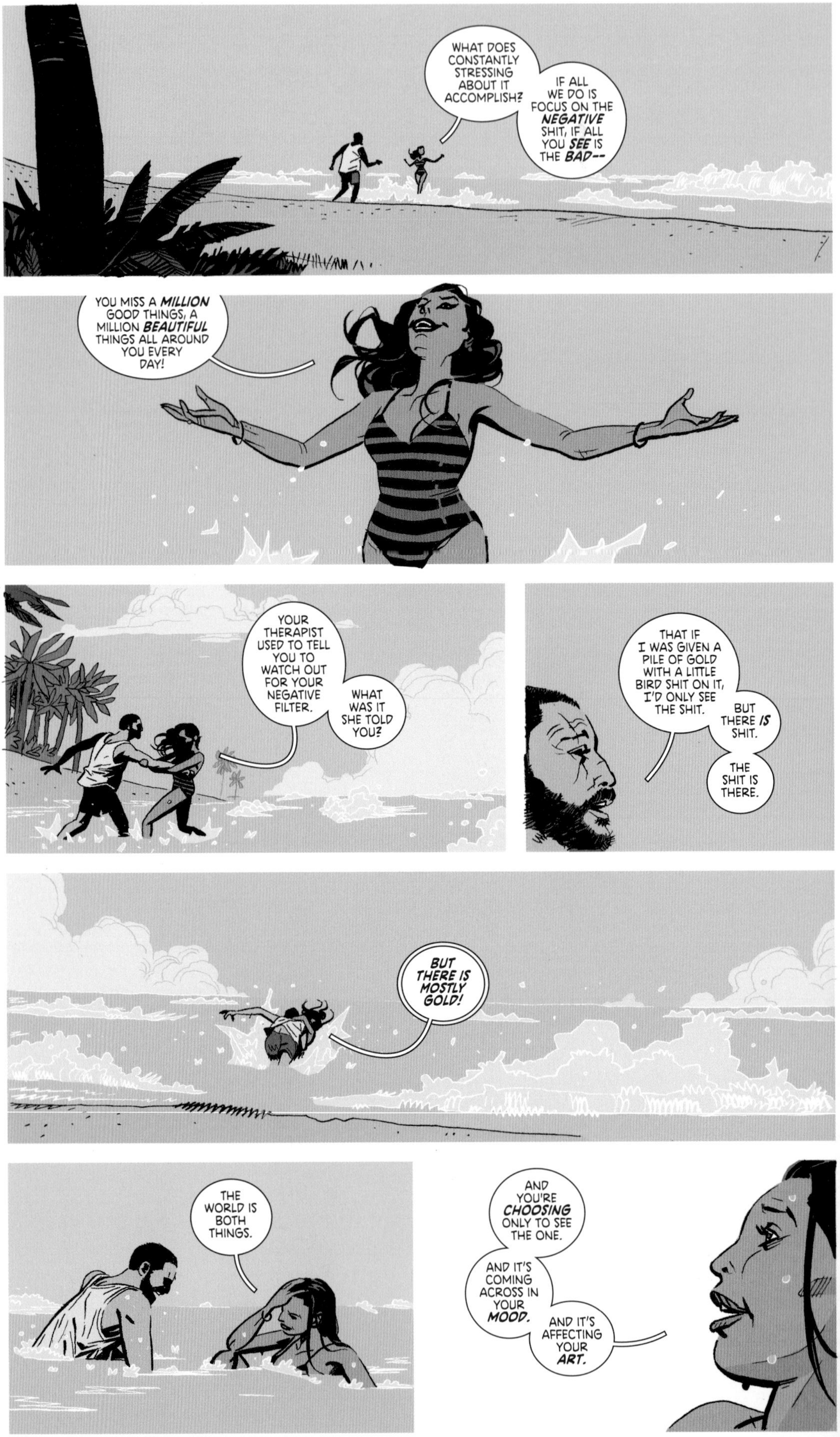
WHAT DOES CONSTANTLY STRESSING ABOUT IT ACCOMPLISH?
IF ALL WE DO IS FOCUS ON THE NEGATIVE SHIT, IF ALL YOU SEE IS THE BAD--
YOU MISS A MILLION GOOD THINGS, A MILLION BEAUTIFUL THINGS ALL AROUND YOU EVERY DAY!
YOUR THERAPIST USED TO TELL YOU TO WATCH OUT FOR YOUR NEGATIVE FILTER.
WHAT WAS IT SHE TOLD YOU?
THAT IF I WAS GIVEN A PILE OF GOLD WITH A LITTLE BIRD SHIT ON IT, I'D ONLY SEE THE SHIT.
BUT THERE IS SHIT.
THE SHIT IS THERE.
BUT THERE IS MOSTLY GOLD!
THE WORLD IS BOTH THINGS.
AND YOU'RE CHOOSING ONLY TO SEE THE ONE.
AND IT'S COMING ACROSS IN YOUR MOOD.
AND IT'S AFFECTING YOUR ART.

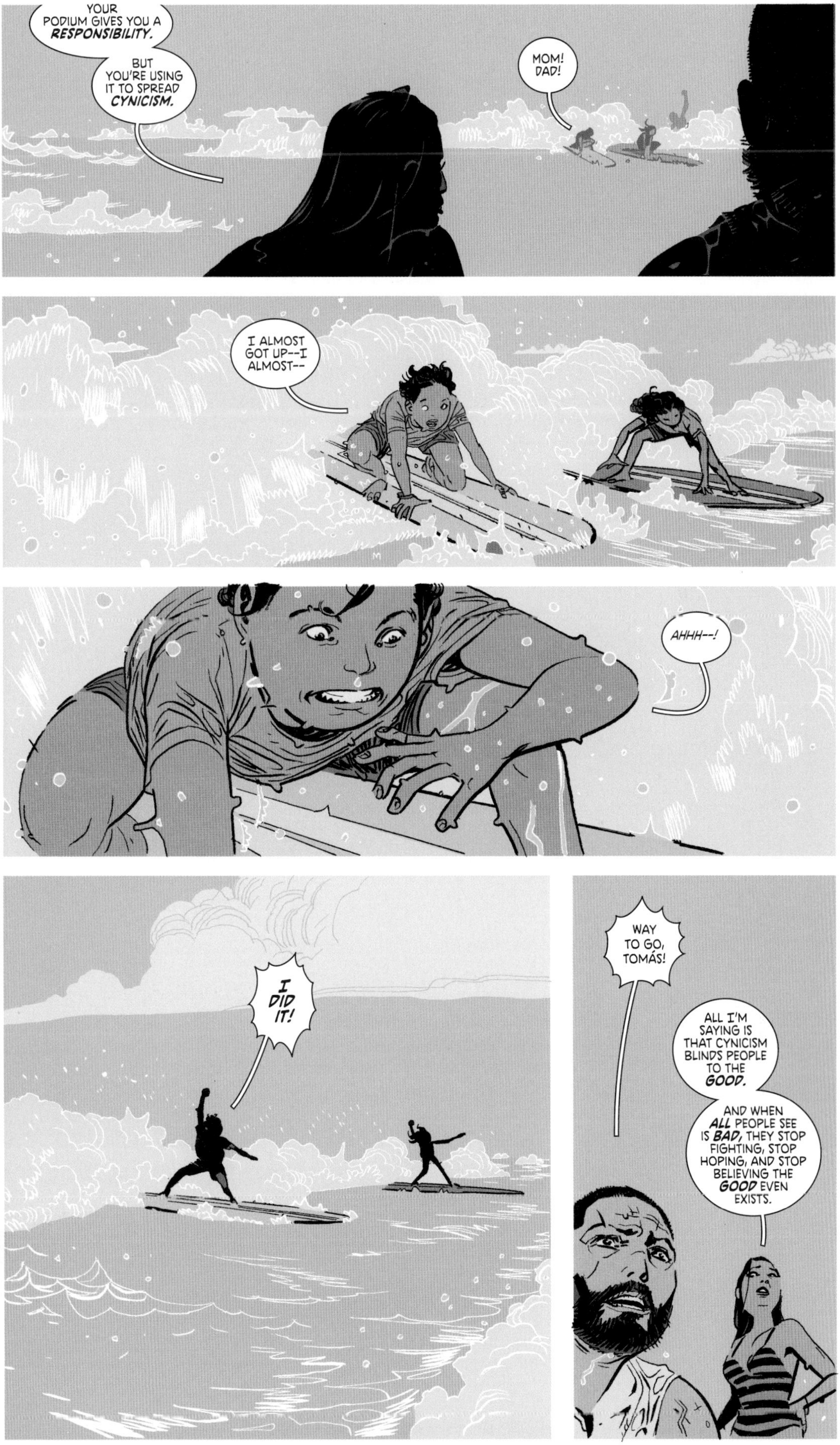
YOUR PODIUM GIVES YOU A *RESPONSIBILITY.*
BUT YOU'RE USING IT TO SPREAD *CYNICISM.*
MOM! DAD!
I ALMOST GOT UP--I ALMOST--
AHHH--!
I DID IT!
WAY TO GO, TOMÁS!
ALL I'M SAYING IS THAT CYNICISM BLINDS PEOPLE TO THE *GOOD.*
AND WHEN *ALL* PEOPLE SEE IS *BAD,* THEY STOP FIGHTING, STOP HOPING, AND STOP BELIEVING THE *GOOD* EVEN EXISTS.

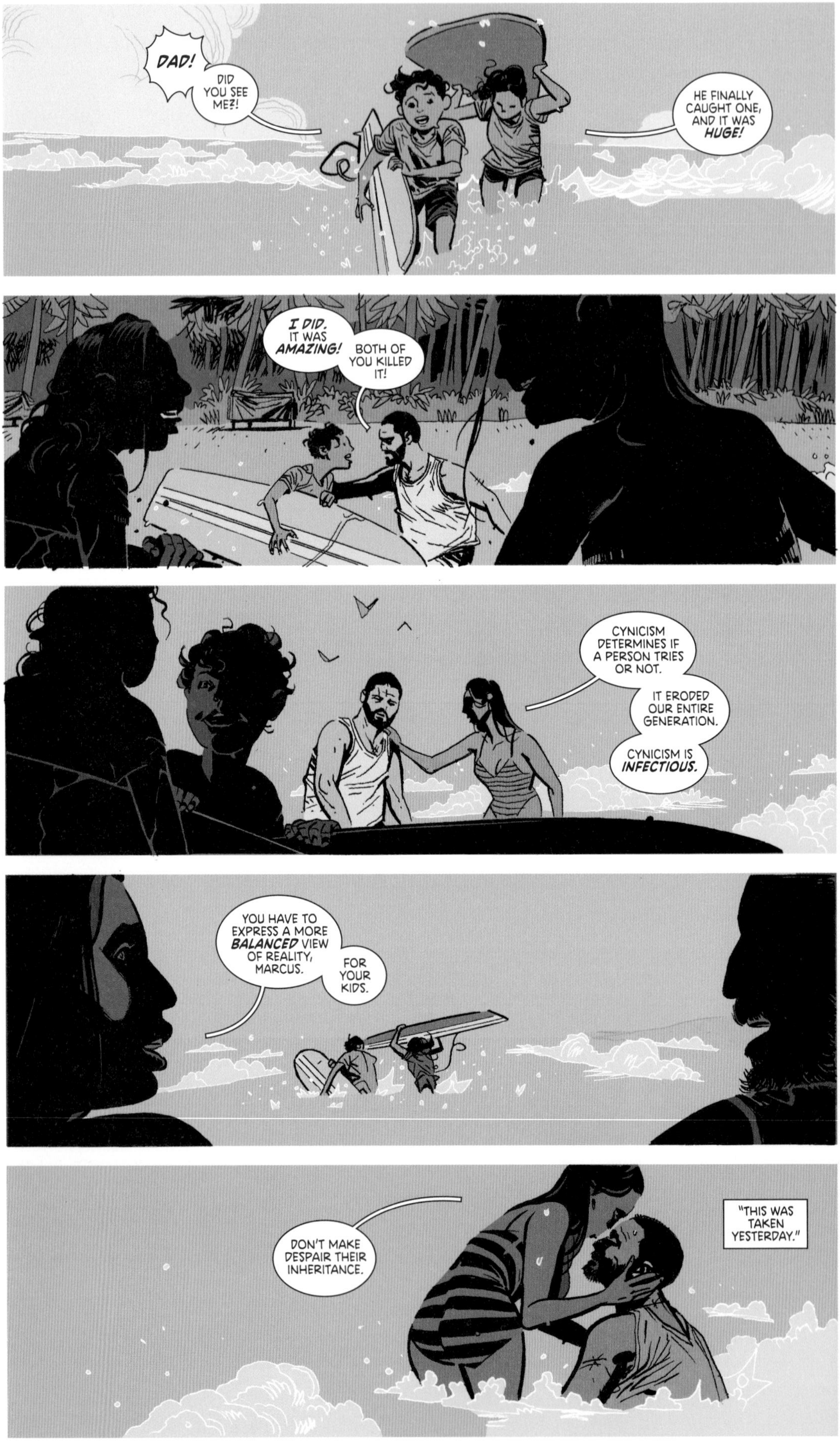
DAD!
DID YOU SEE ME?!
HE FINALLY CAUGHT ONE, AND IT WAS HUGE!
I DID. IT WAS AMAZING!
BOTH OF YOU KILLED IT!
CYNICISM DETERMINES IF A PERSON TRIES OR NOT.
IT ERODED OUR ENTIRE GENERATION.
CYNICISM IS INFECTIOUS.
YOU HAVE TO EXPRESS A MORE BALANCED VIEW OF REALITY, MARCUS.
FOR YOUR KIDS.
DON'T MAKE DESPAIR THEIR INHERITANCE.
"THIS WAS TAKEN YESTERDAY."

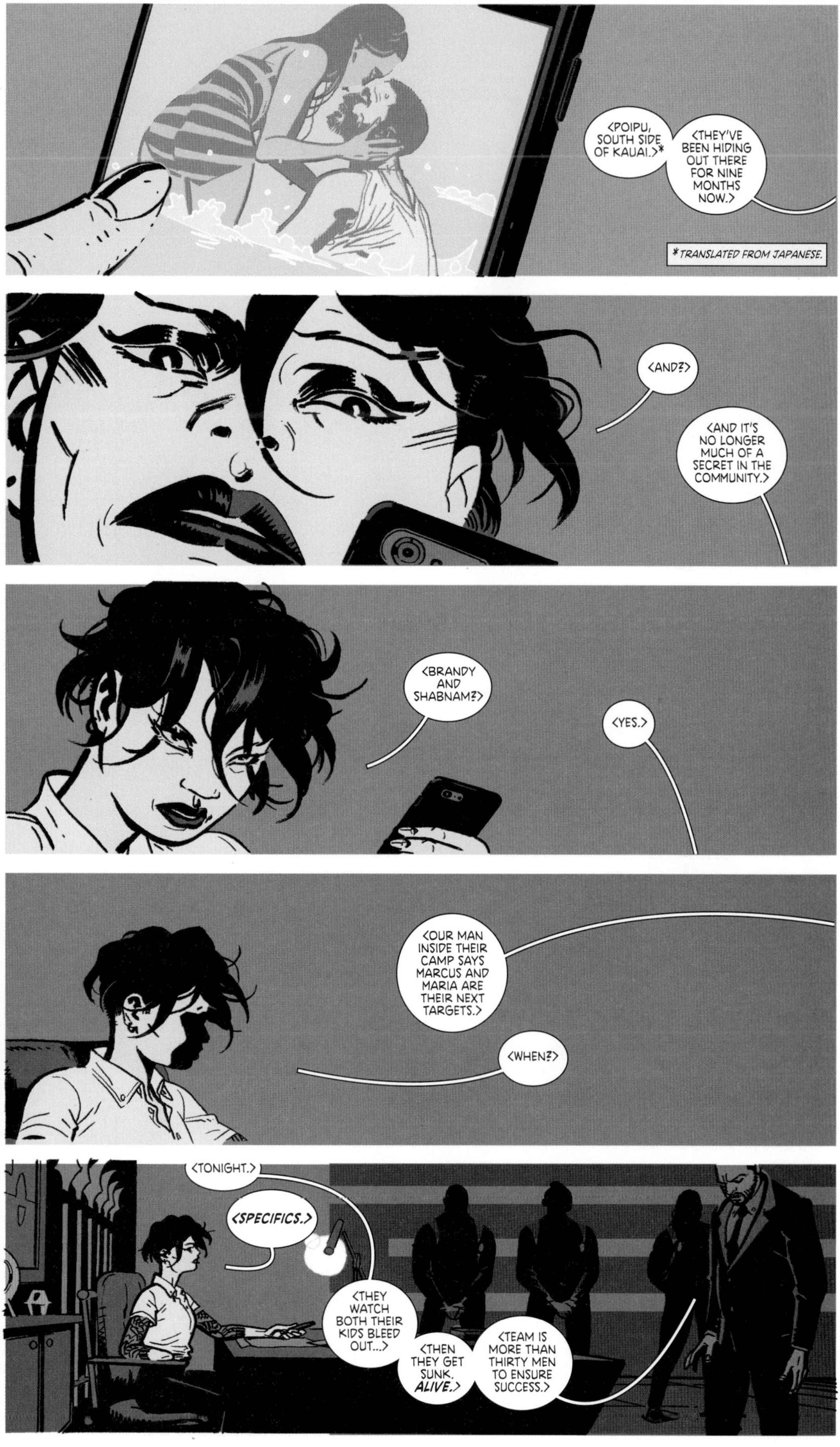
<POIPU, SOUTH SIDE OF KAUAI.>*
<THEY'VE BEEN HIDING OUT THERE FOR NINE MONTHS NOW.>
*TRANSLATED FROM JAPANESE.
<AND?>
<AND IT'S NO LONGER MUCH OF A SECRET IN THE COMMUNITY.>
<BRANDY AND SHABNAM?>
<YES.>
<OUR MAN INSIDE THEIR CAMP SAYS MARCUS AND MARIA ARE THEIR NEXT TARGETS.>
<WHEN?>
<TONIGHT.>
<SPECIFICS.>
<THEY WATCH BOTH THEIR KIDS BLEED OUT...>
<THEN THEY GET SUNK. ALIVE.>
<TEAM IS MORE THAN THIRTY MEN TO ENSURE SUCCESS.>

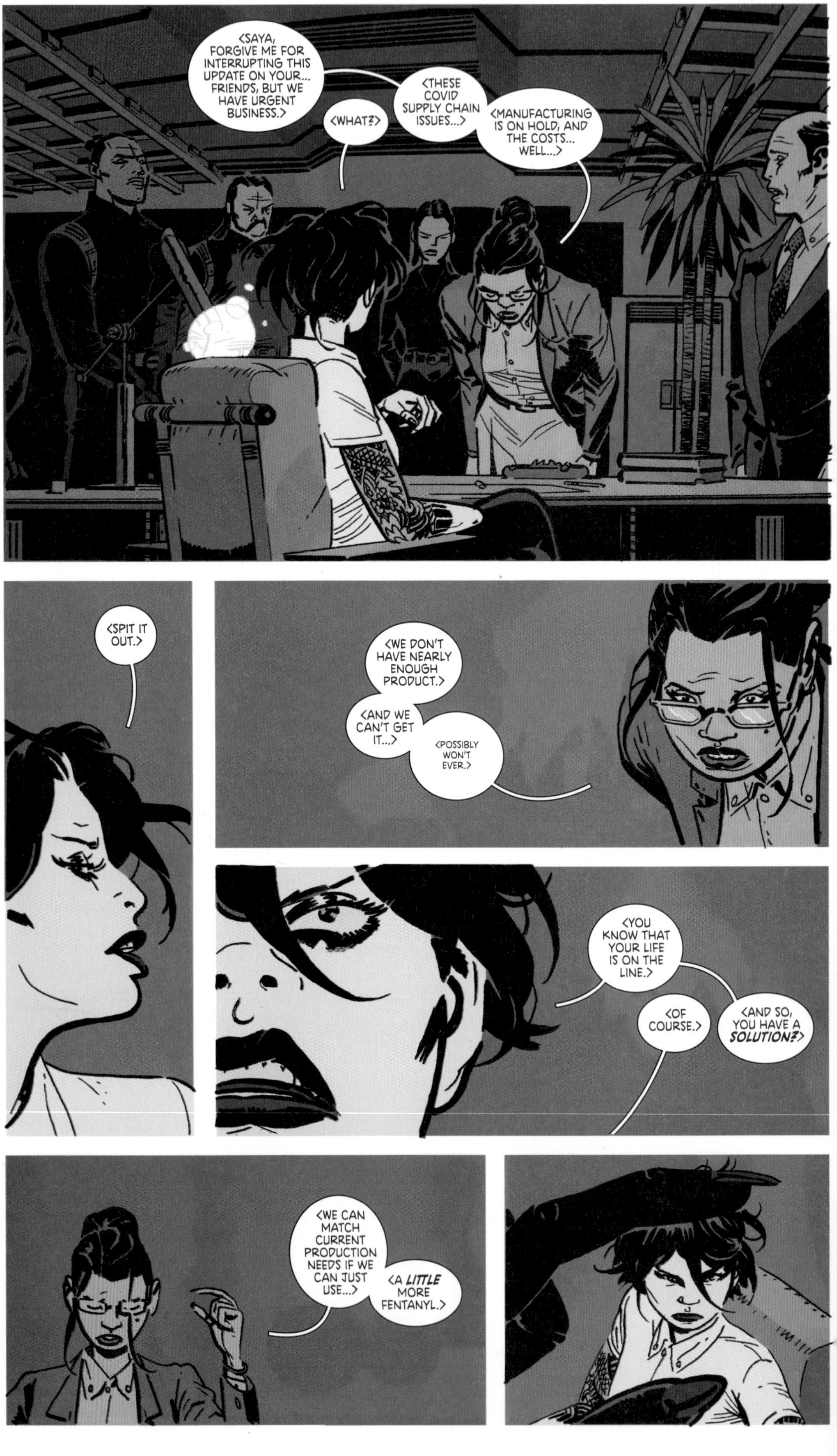
<SAYA, FORGIVE ME FOR INTERRUPTING THIS UPDATE ON YOUR... FRIENDS, BUT WE HAVE URGENT BUSINESS.>
<WHAT?!>
<THESE COVID SUPPLY CHAIN ISSUES...>
<MANUFACTURING IS ON HOLD, AND THE COSTS... WELL...>
<SPIT IT OUT.>
<WE DON'T HAVE NEARLY ENOUGH PRODUCT.>
<AND WE CAN'T GET IT...>
<POSSIBLY WON'T EVER.>
<YOU KNOW THAT YOUR LIFE IS ON THE LINE.>
<AND SO, YOU HAVE A ***SOLUTION?!***>
<OF COURSE.>
<WE CAN MATCH CURRENT PRODUCTION NEEDS IF WE CAN JUST USE...>
<A ***LITTLE*** MORE FENTANYL.>

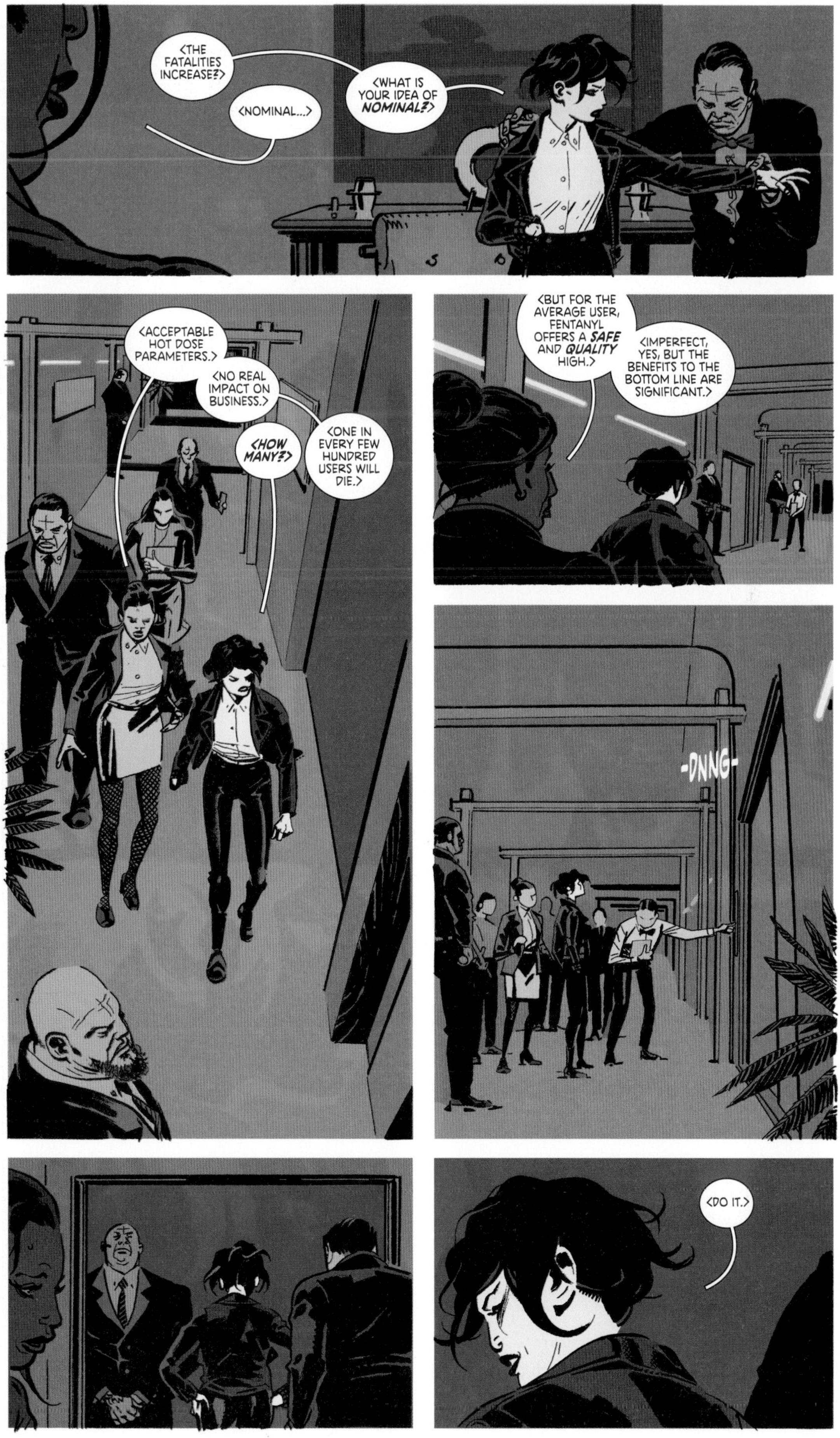
<THE FATALITIES INCREASE?>
<NOMINAL...>
<WHAT IS YOUR IDEA OF NOMINAL?>
<ACCEPTABLE HOT DOSE PARAMETERS.>
<NO REAL IMPACT ON BUSINESS.>
<HOW MANY?>
<ONE IN EVERY FEW HUNDRED USERS WILL DIE.>
<BUT FOR THE AVERAGE USER, FENTANYL OFFERS A SAFE AND QUALITY HIGH.>
<IMPERFECT, YES, BUT THE BENEFITS TO THE BOTTOM LINE ARE SIGNIFICANT.>
-DNNG-
<DO IT.>

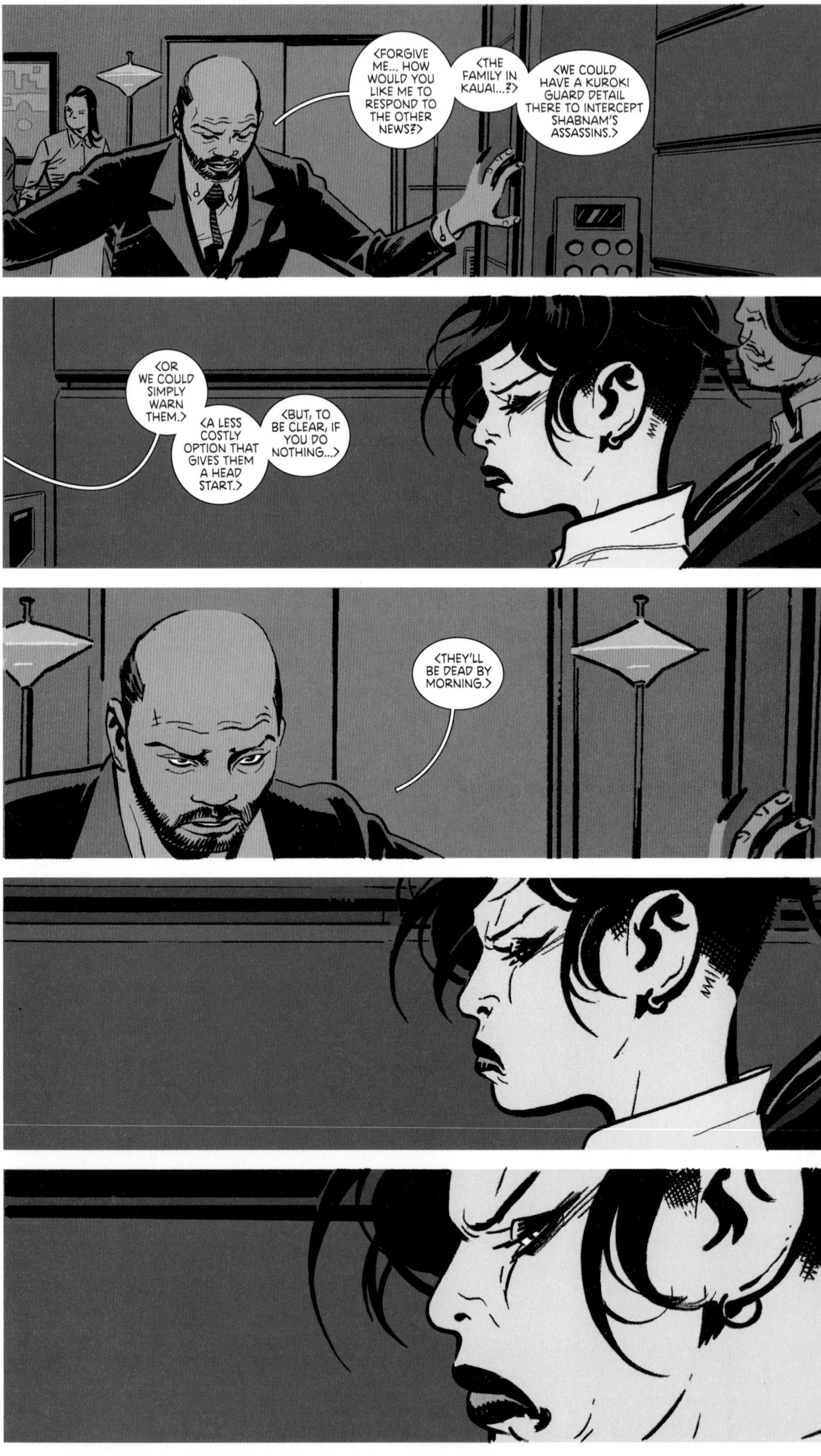
<FORGIVE ME... HOW WOULD YOU LIKE ME TO RESPOND TO THE OTHER NEWS?>
<THE FAMILY IN KAUAI...?>
<WE COULD HAVE A KUROKI GUARD DETAIL THERE TO INTERCEPT SHABNAM'S ASSASSINS.>
<OR WE COULD SIMPLY WARN THEM.>
<A LESS COSTLY OPTION THAT GIVES THEM A HEAD START.>
<BUT, TO BE CLEAR, IF YOU DO NOTHING...>
<THEY'LL BE DEAD BY MORNING.>

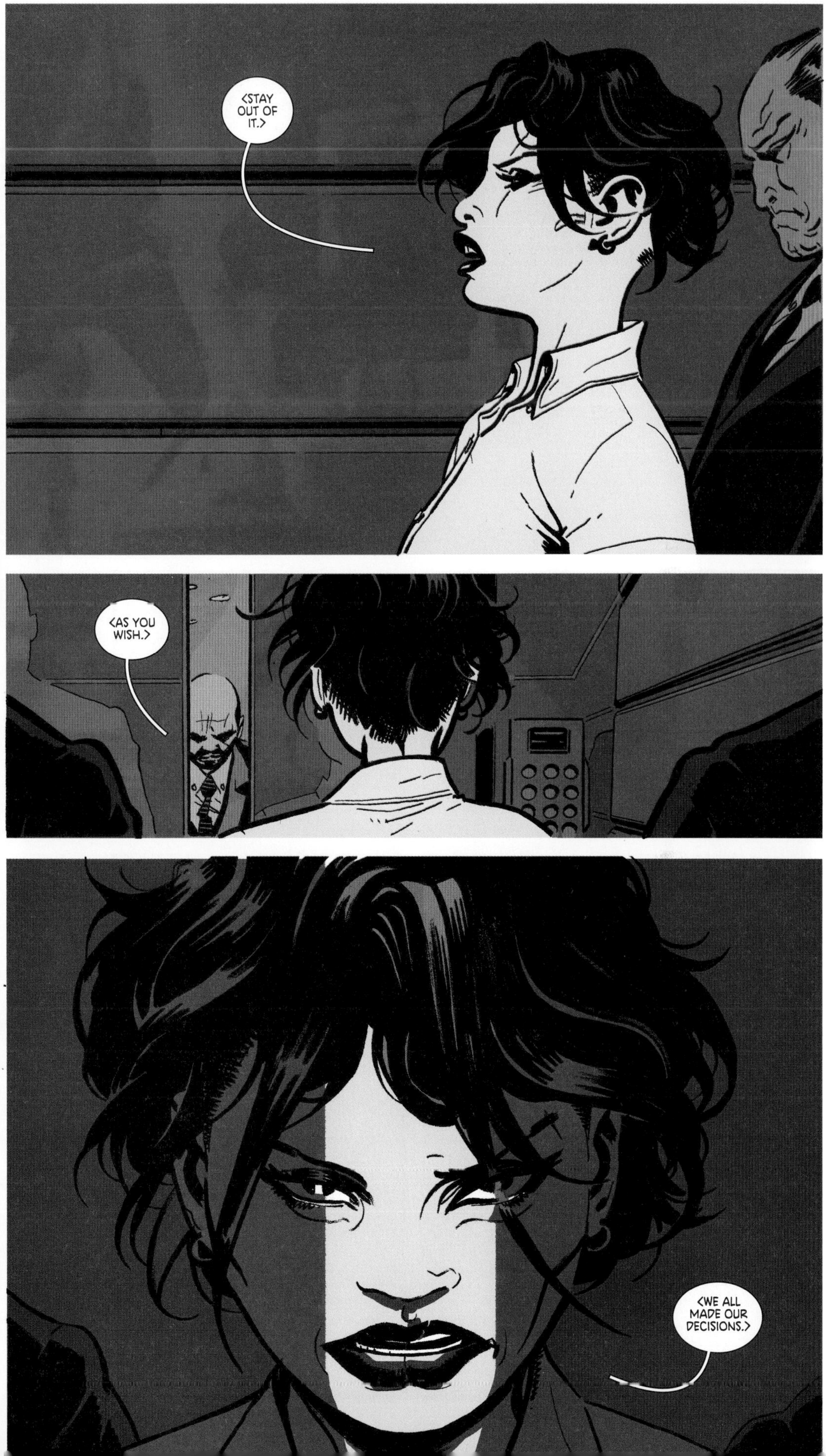
<STAY OUT OF IT.>
<AS YOU WISH.>
<WE ALL MADE OUR DECISIONS.>

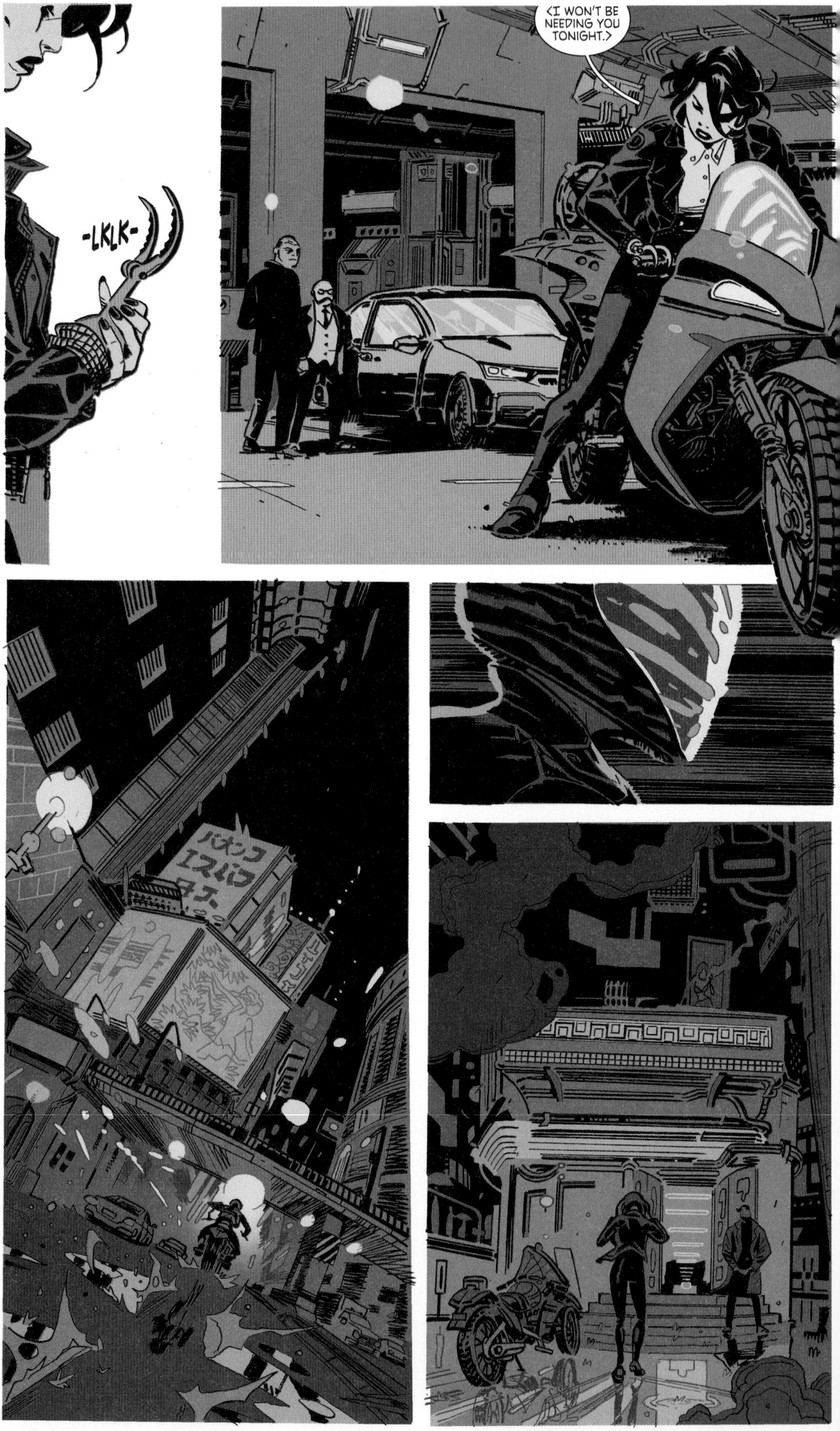
-LKLK-
<I WON'T BE NEEDING YOU TONIGHT.>

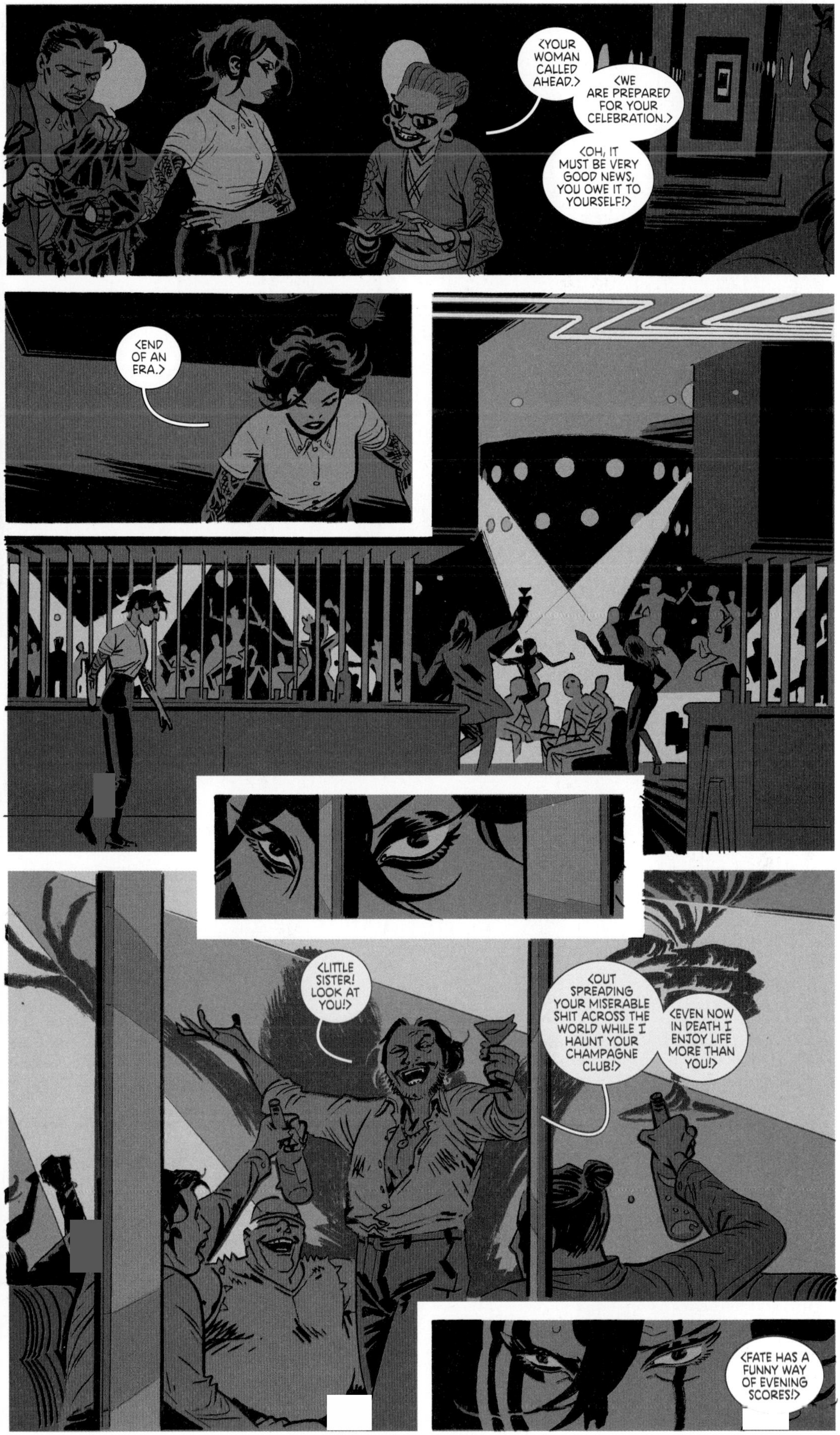
<YOUR WOMAN CALLED AHEAD.>
<WE ARE PREPARED FOR YOUR CELEBRATION.>
<OH, IT MUST BE VERY GOOD NEWS, YOU OWE IT TO YOURSELF!>
<END OF AN ERA.>
<LITTLE SISTER! LOOK AT YOU!>
<OUT SPREADING YOUR MISERABLE SHIT ACROSS THE WORLD WHILE I HAUNT YOUR CHAMPAGNE CLUB!>
<EVEN NOW IN DEATH I ENJOY LIFE MORE THAN YOU!>
<FATE HAS A FUNNY WAY OF EVENING SCORES!>

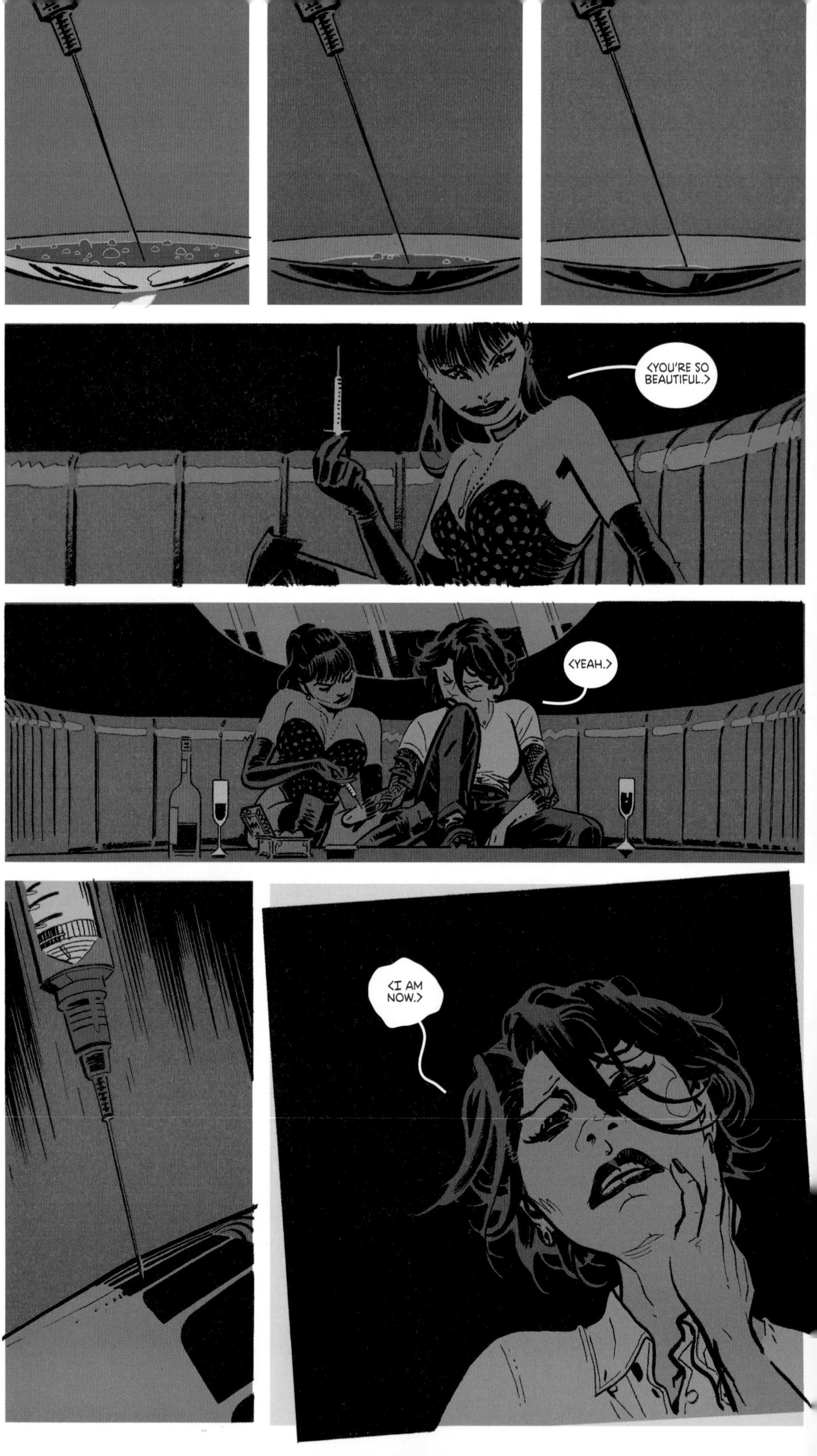
<YOU'RE SO BEAUTIFUL.>
<YEAH.>
<I AM NOW.>

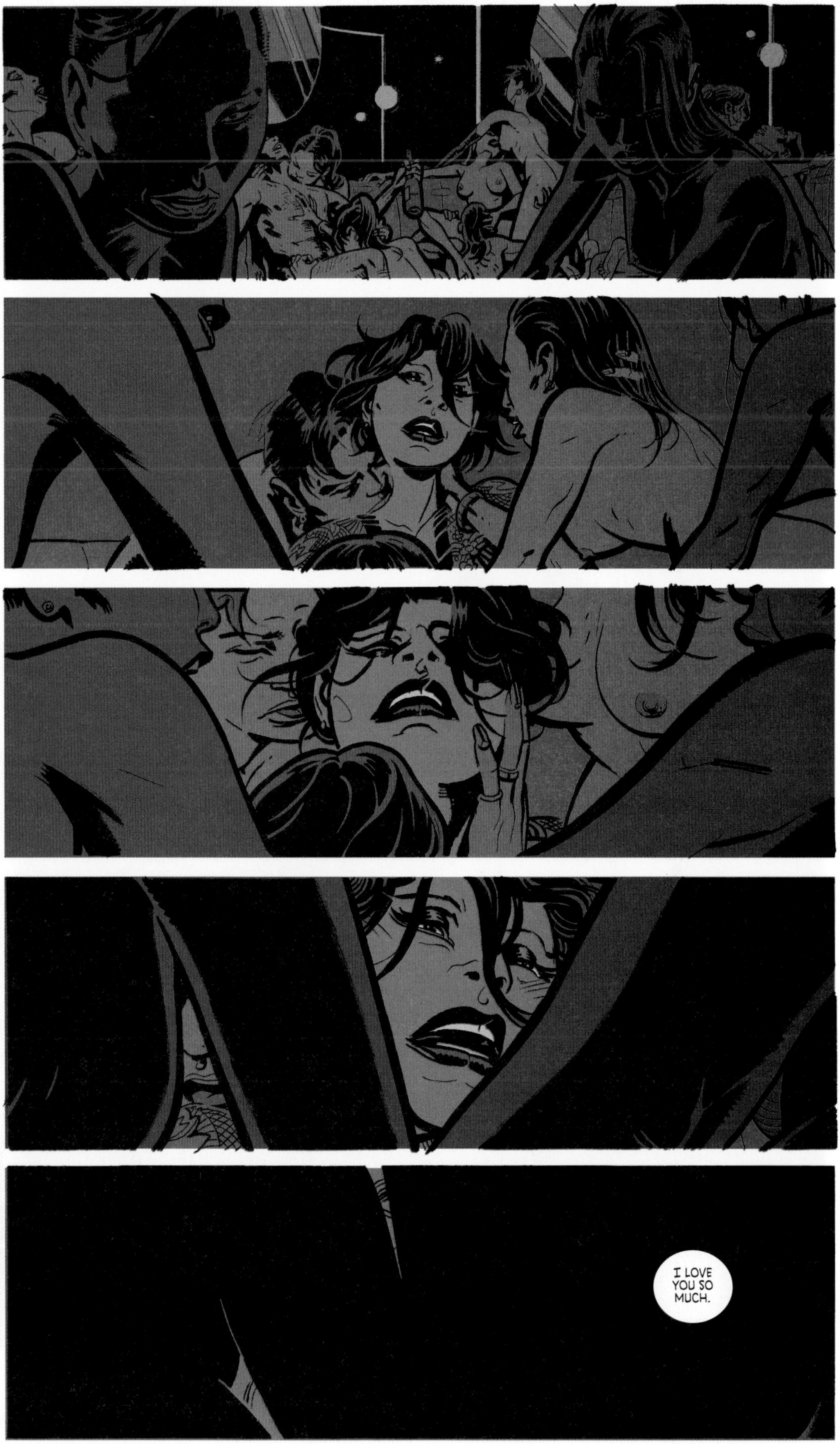
I LOVE YOU SO MUCH.

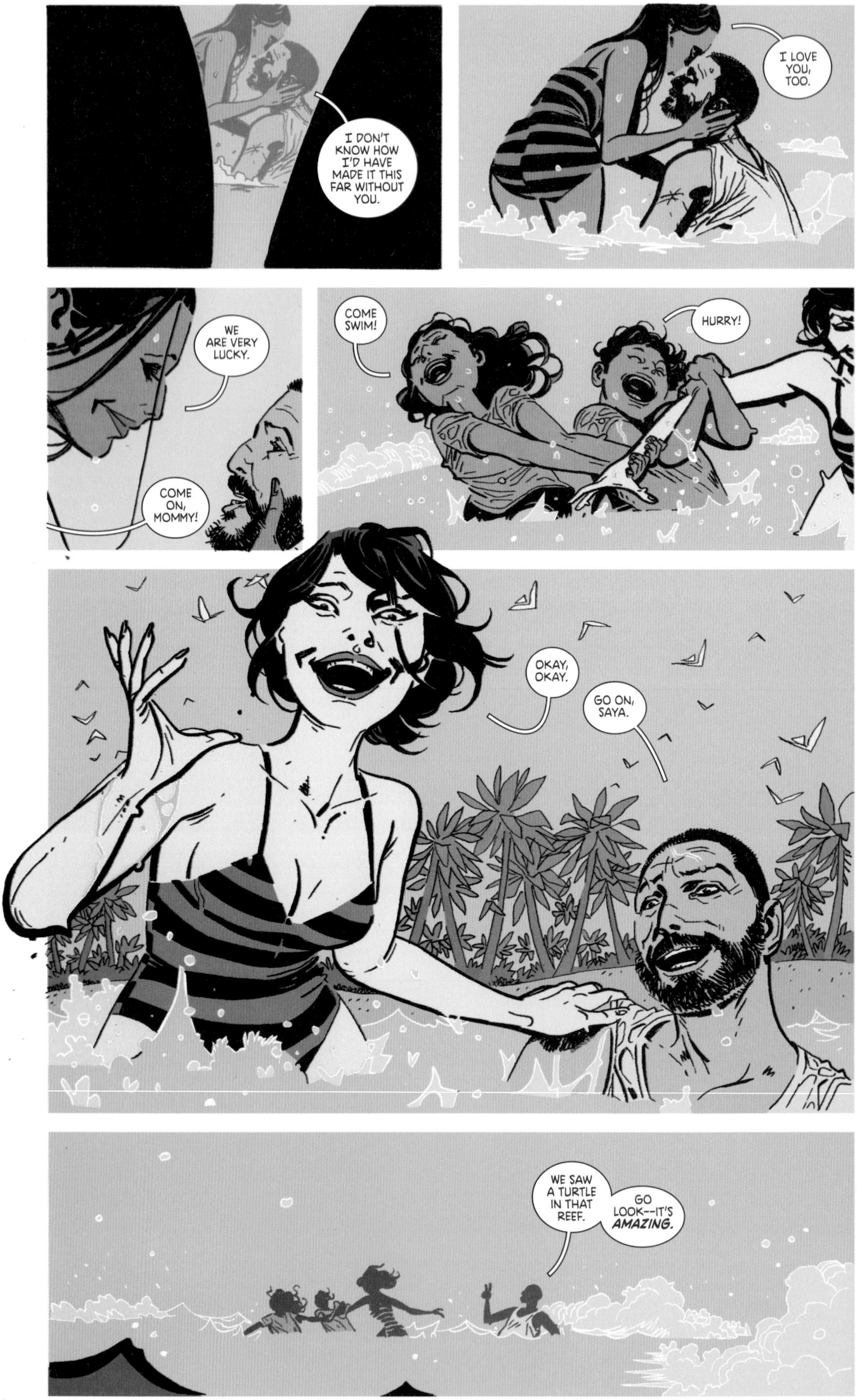

I DON'T KNOW HOW I'D HAVE MADE IT THIS FAR WITHOUT YOU.
I LOVE YOU, TOO.
WE ARE VERY LUCKY.
COME ON, MOMMY!
COME SWIM!
HURRY!
OKAY, OKAY.
GO ON, SAYA.
WE SAW A TURTLE IN THAT REEF.
GO LOOK--IT'S *AMAZING.*

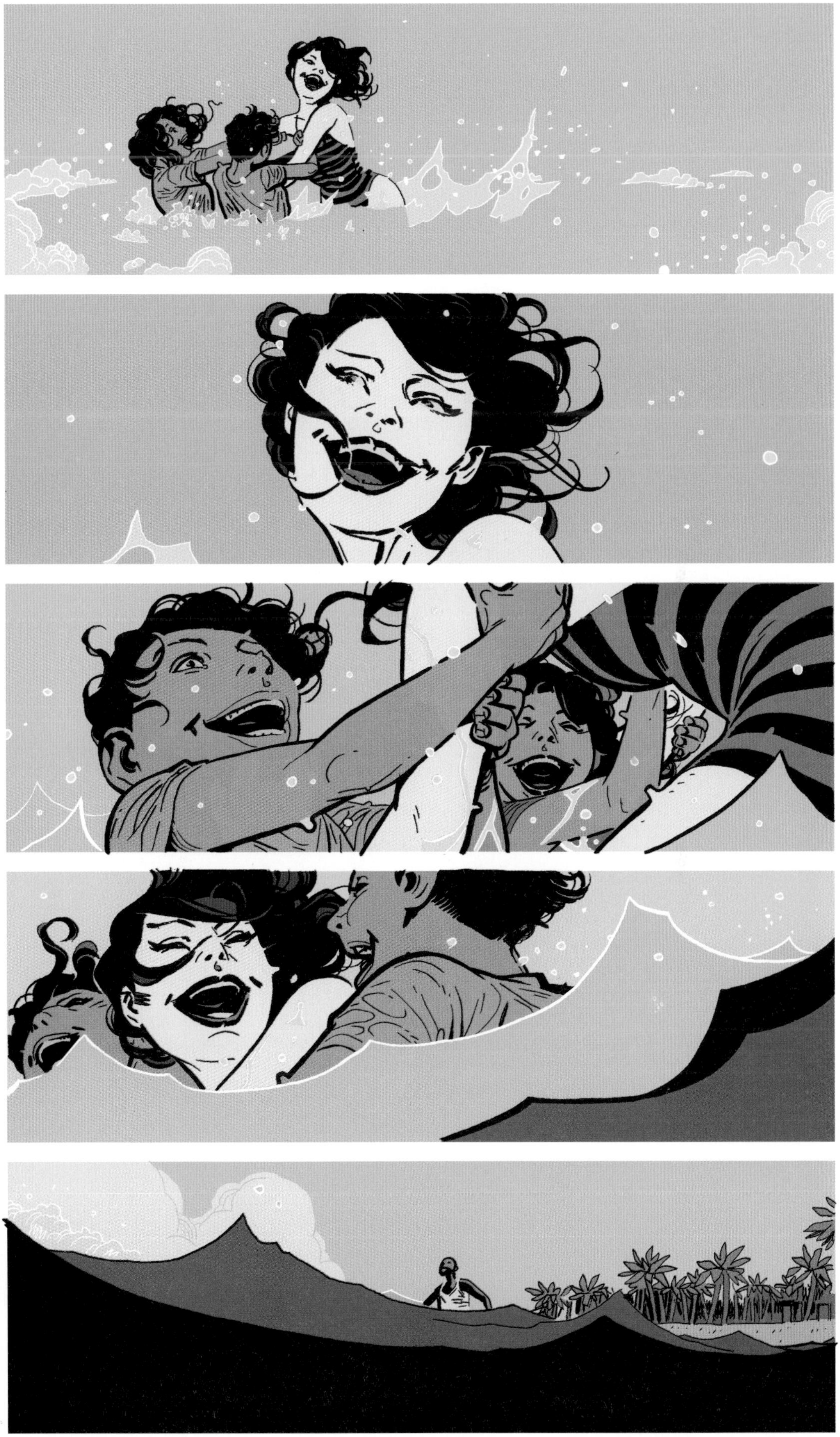

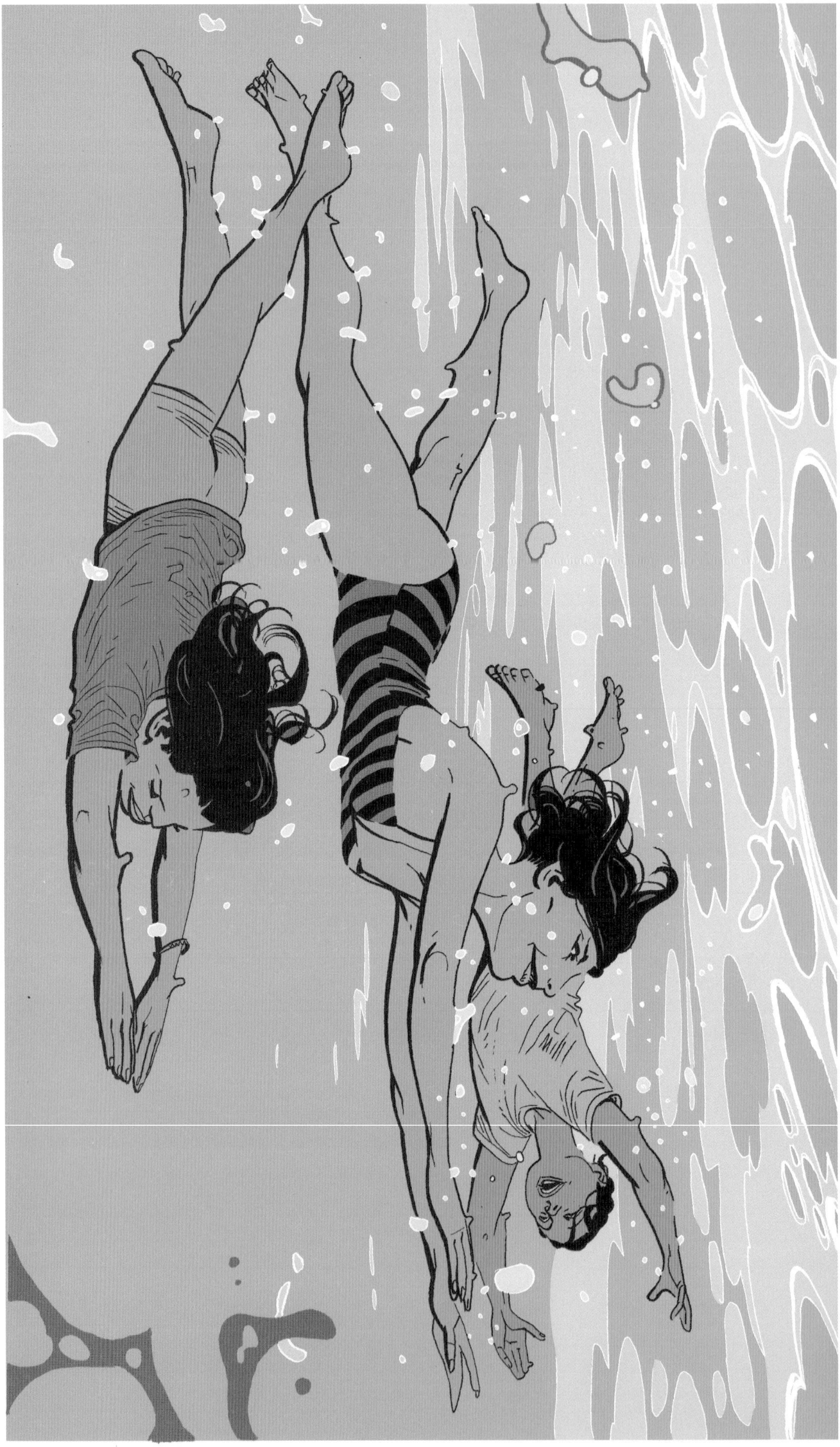

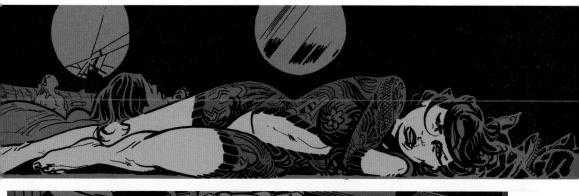

MURHH...?

<IF YOU DO NOTHING...>

<LADY?>

<PARDON ME.>

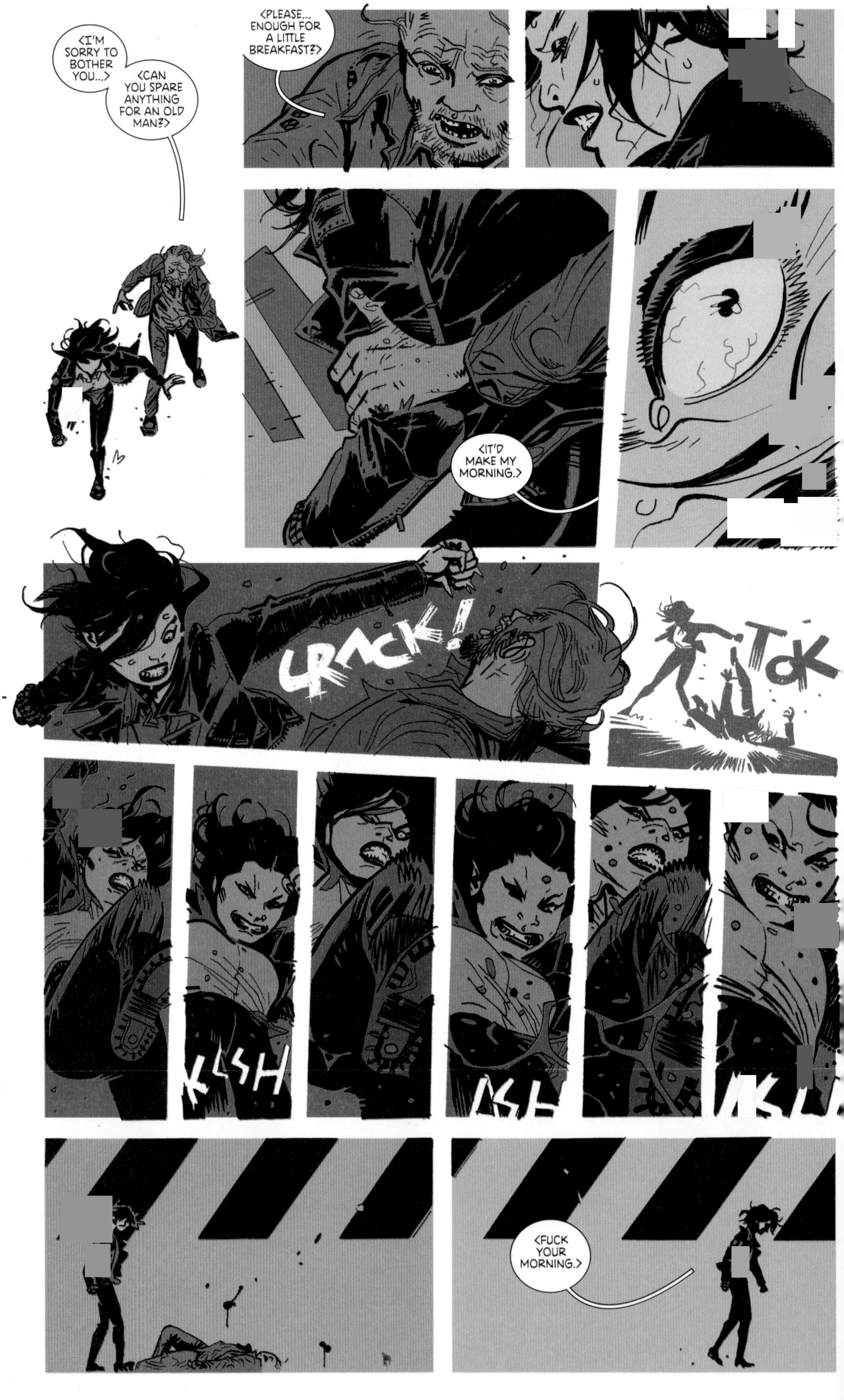

<I'M SORRY TO BOTHER YOU...>
<CAN YOU SPARE ANYTHING FOR AN OLD MAN?>
<PLEASE... ENOUGH FOR A LITTLE BREAKFAST?>
<IT'D MAKE MY MORNING.>
CRACK!
TOK
<FUCK YOUR MORNING.>

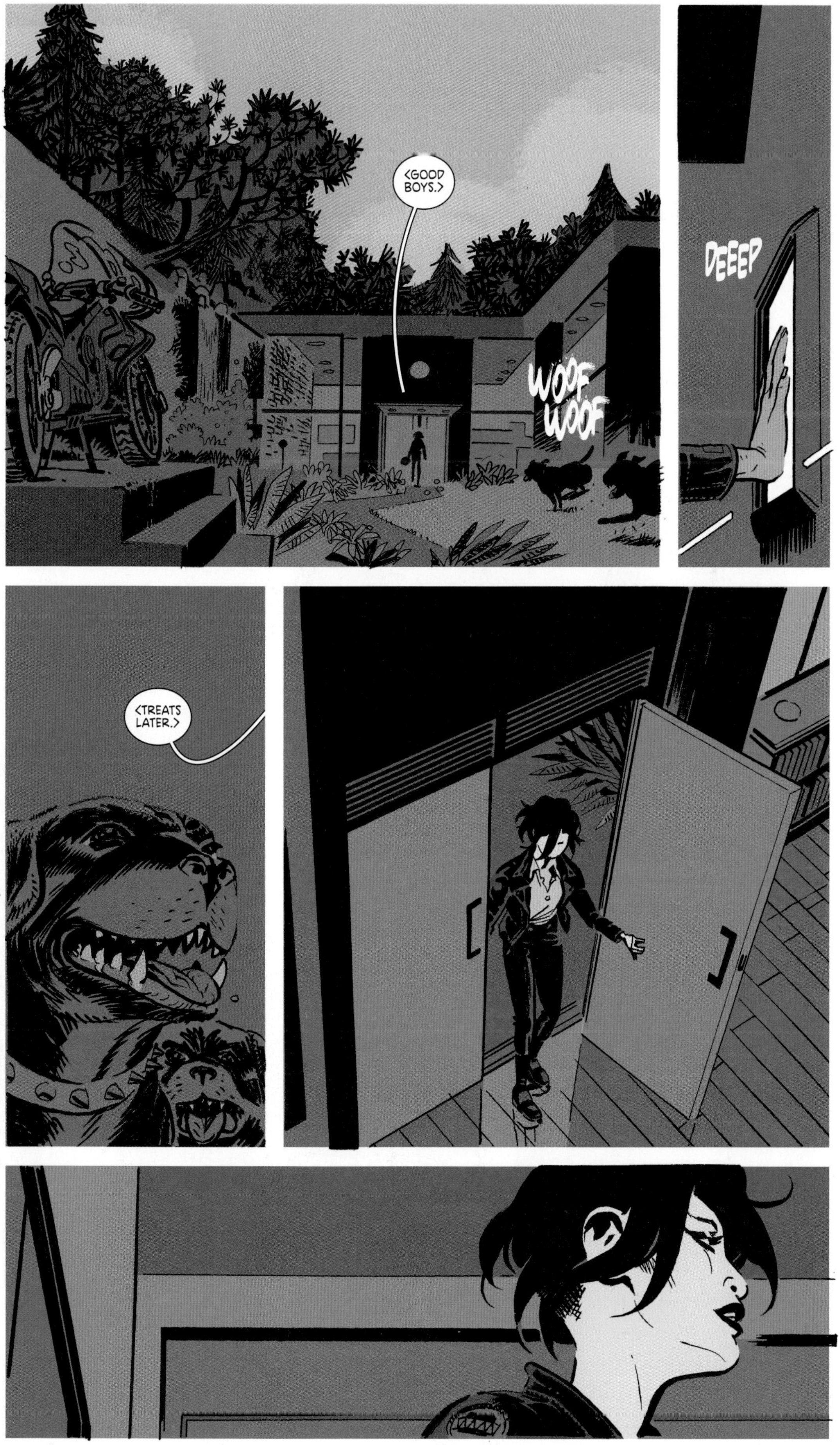
<GOOD BOYS.>
WOOF WOOF
DEEEP
<TREATS LATER.>

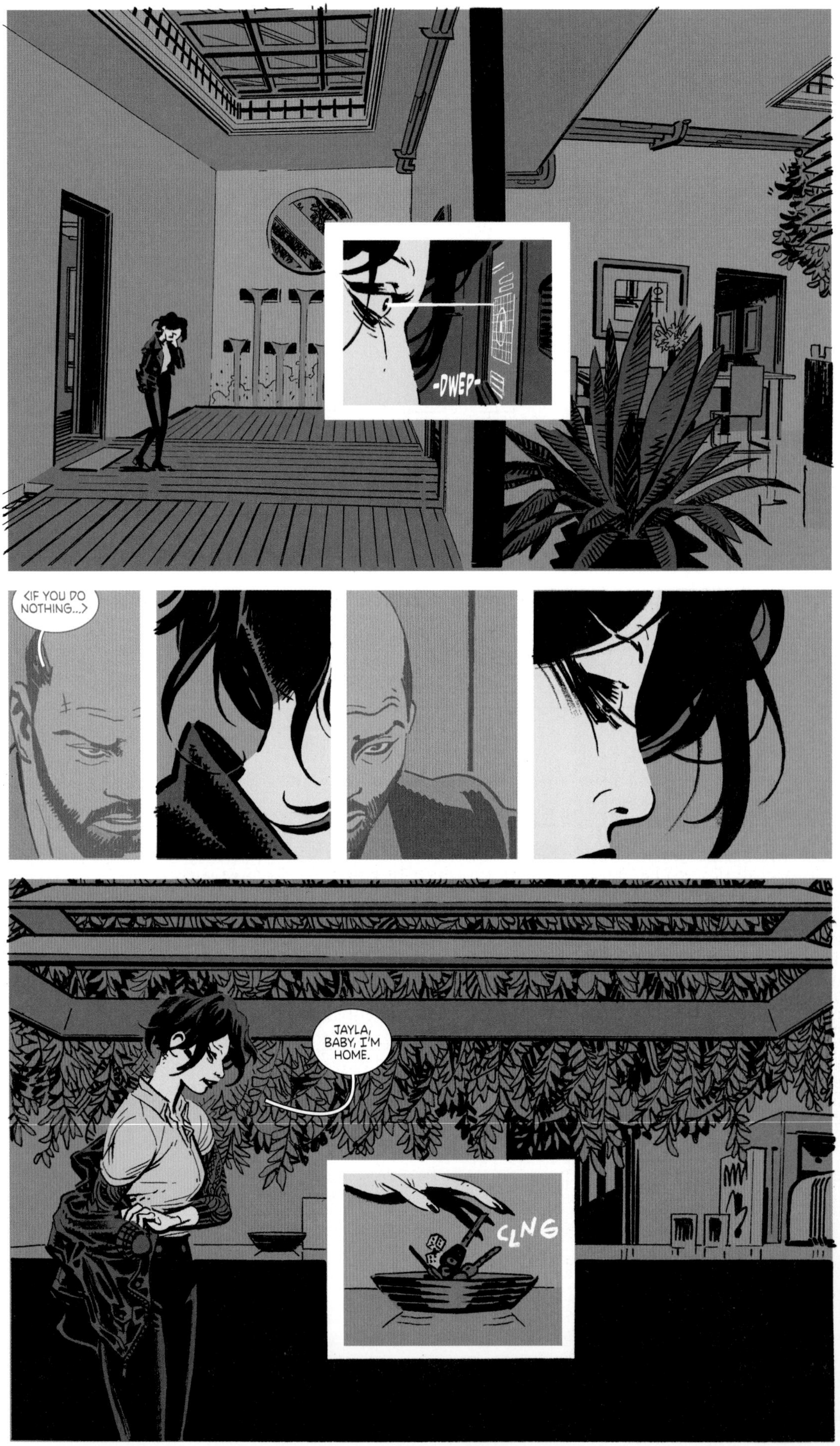
-DWEP-
<IF YOU DO NOTHING...>
JAYLA, BABY, I'M HOME.
CLNG

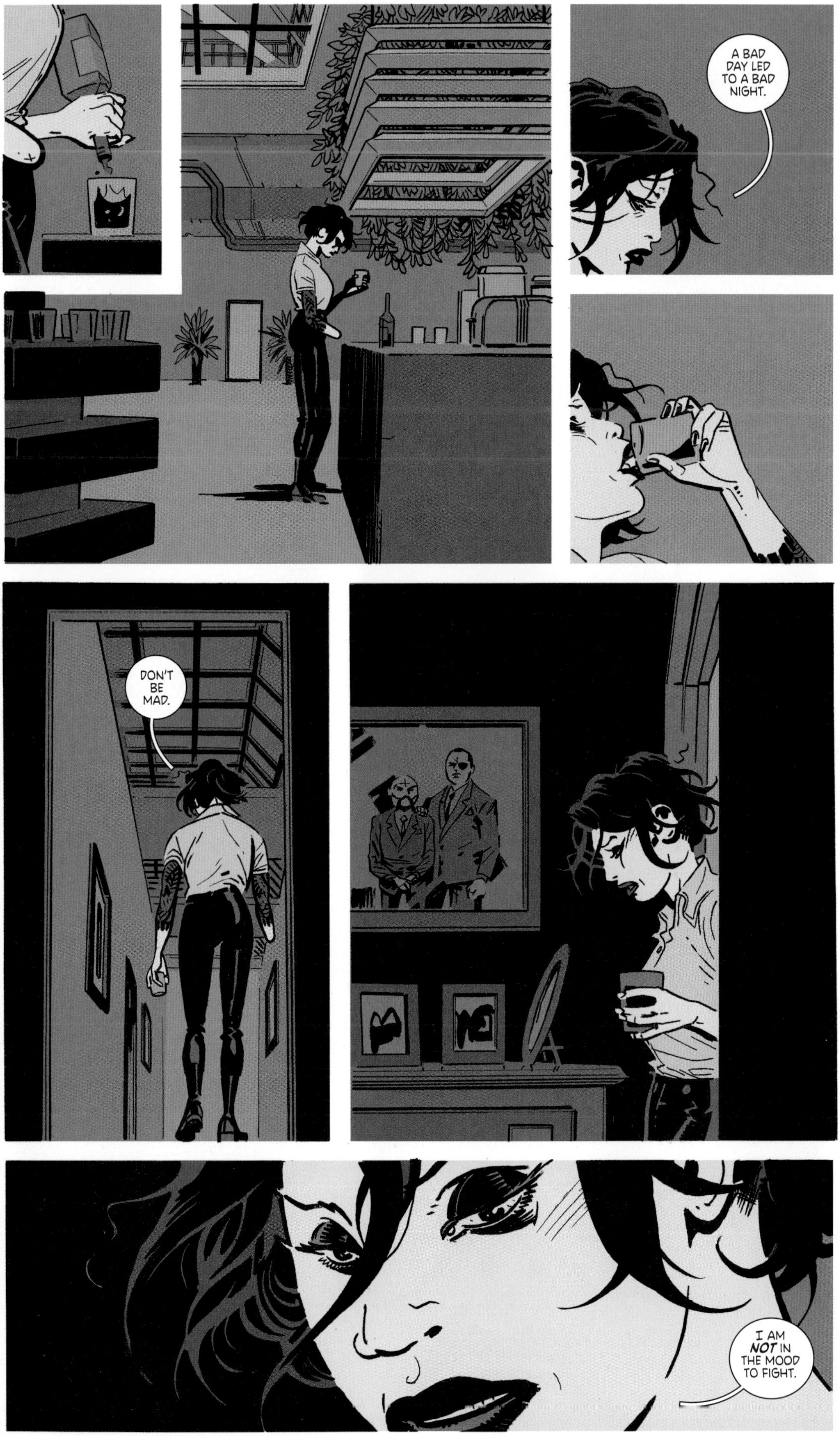
A BAD DAY LED TO A BAD NIGHT.
DON'T BE MAD.
I AM NOT IN THE MOOD TO FIGHT.

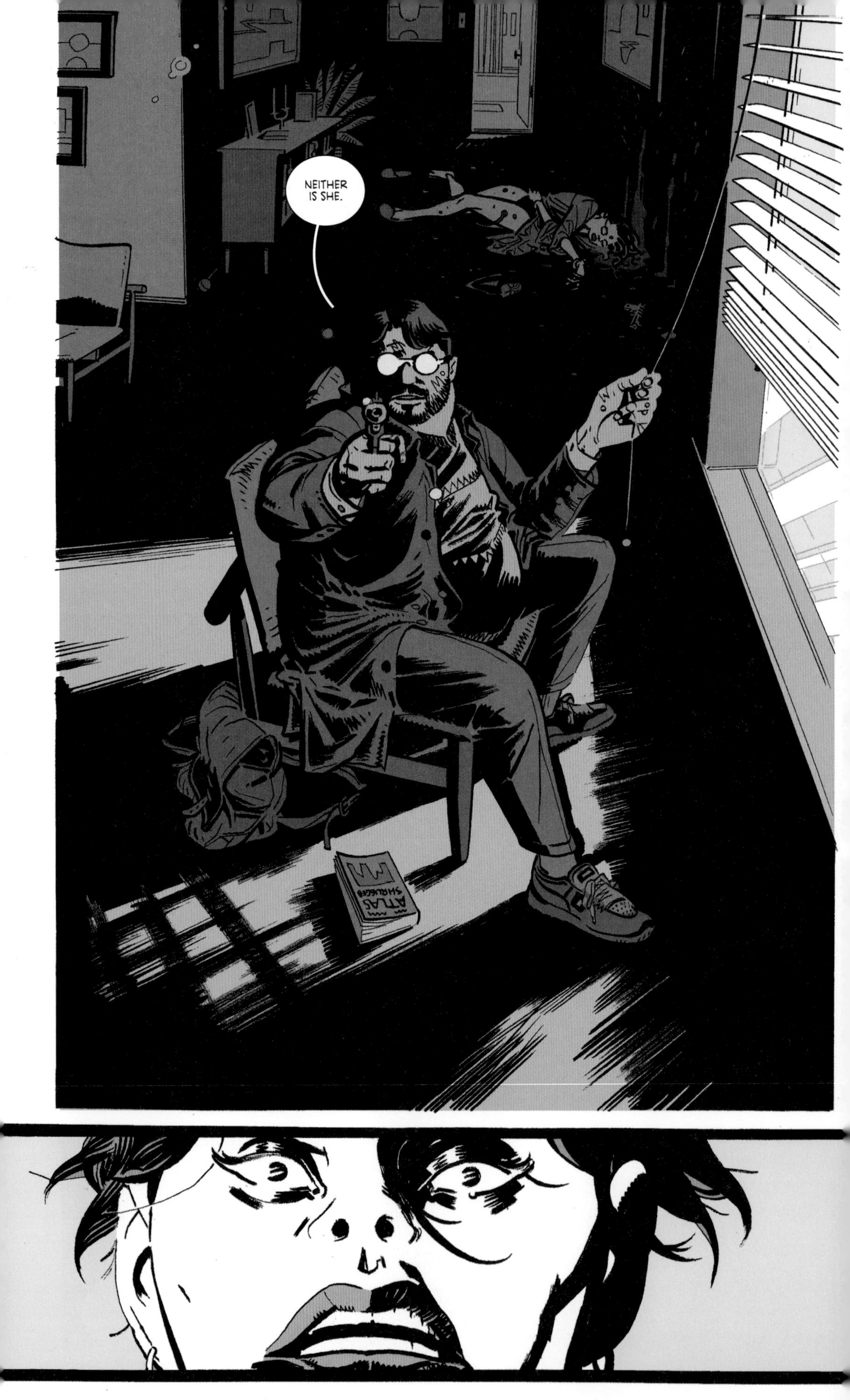
NEITHER IS SHE.
ATLAS SHRUGGED

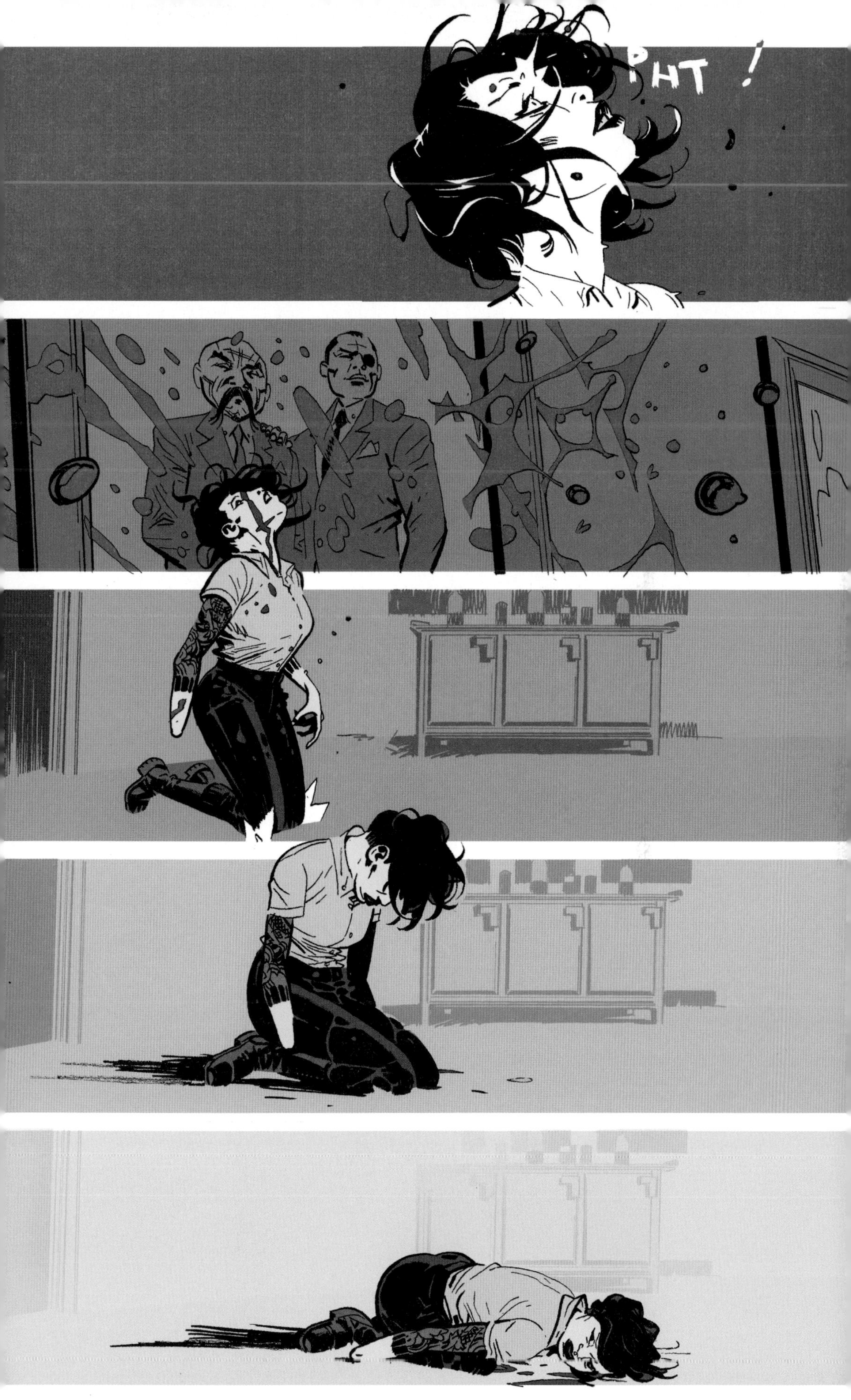
PHT !

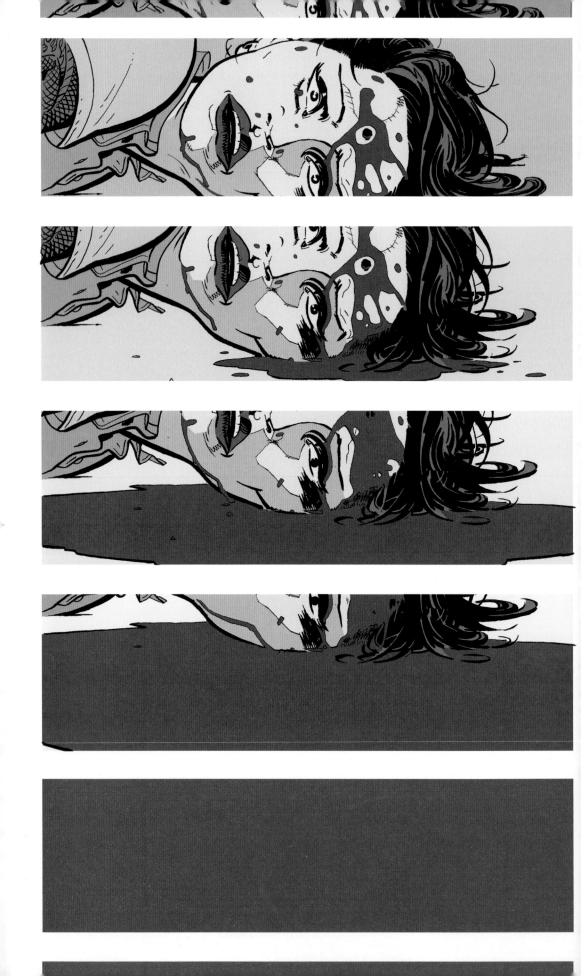

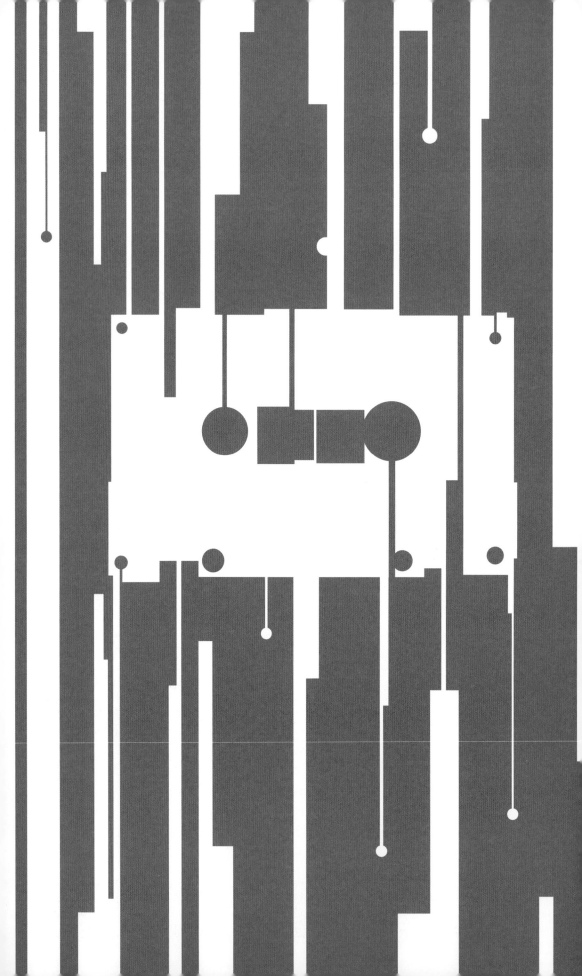

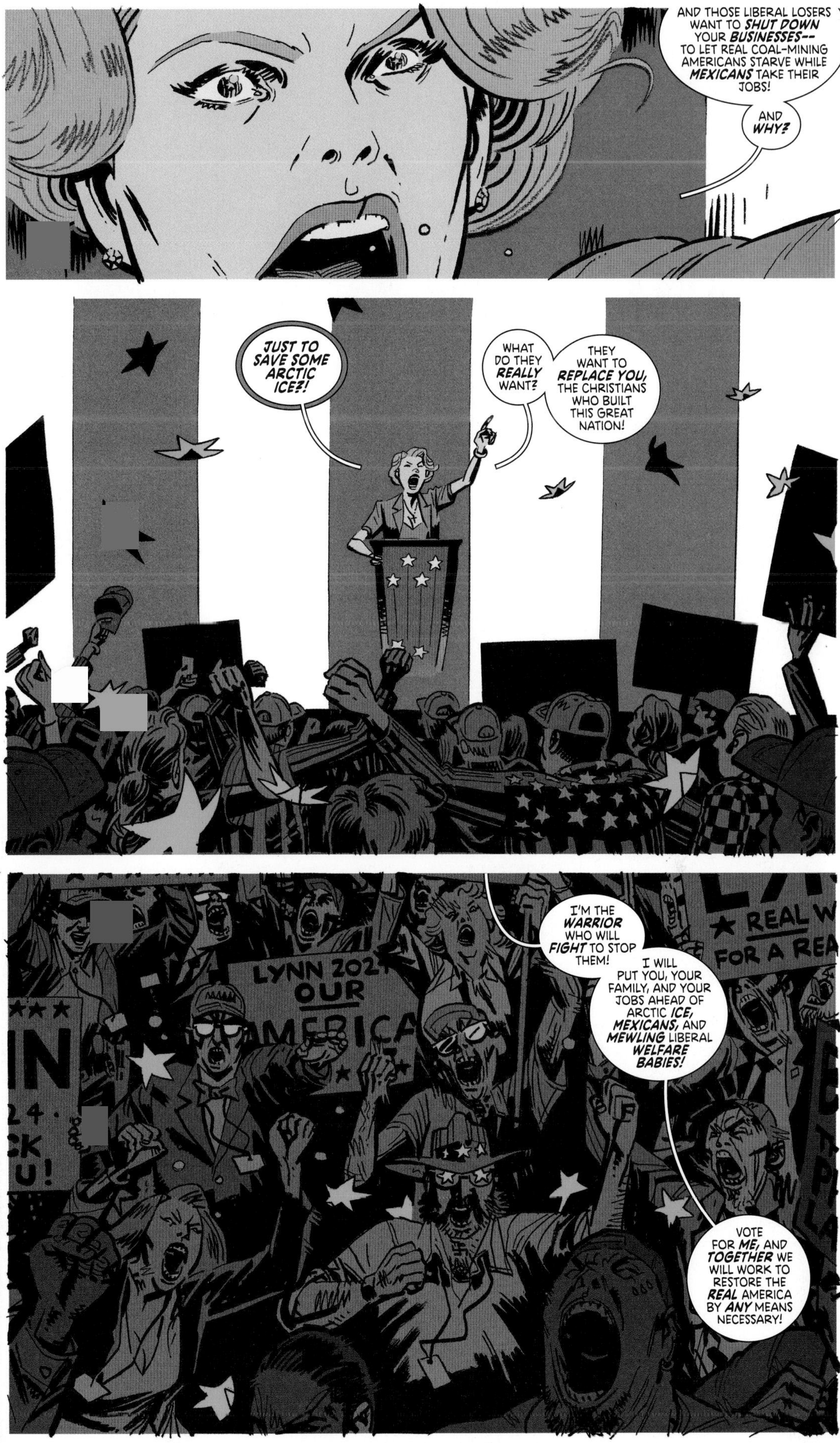
AND THOSE LIBERAL LOSERS WANT TO SHUT DOWN YOUR BUSINESSES-- TO LET REAL COAL-MINING AMERICANS STARVE WHILE MEXICANS TAKE THEIR JOBS!
AND WHY?
JUST TO SAVE SOME ARCTIC ICE?!
WHAT DO THEY REALLY WANT?
THEY WANT TO REPLACE YOU, THE CHRISTIANS WHO BUILT THIS GREAT NATION!
I'M THE WARRIOR WHO WILL FIGHT TO STOP THEM!
I WILL PUT YOU, YOUR FAMILY, AND YOUR JOBS AHEAD OF ARCTIC ICE, MEXICANS, AND MEWLING LIBERAL WELFARE BABIES!
VOTE FOR ME, AND TOGETHER WE WILL WORK TO RESTORE THE REAL AMERICA BY ANY MEANS NECESSARY!

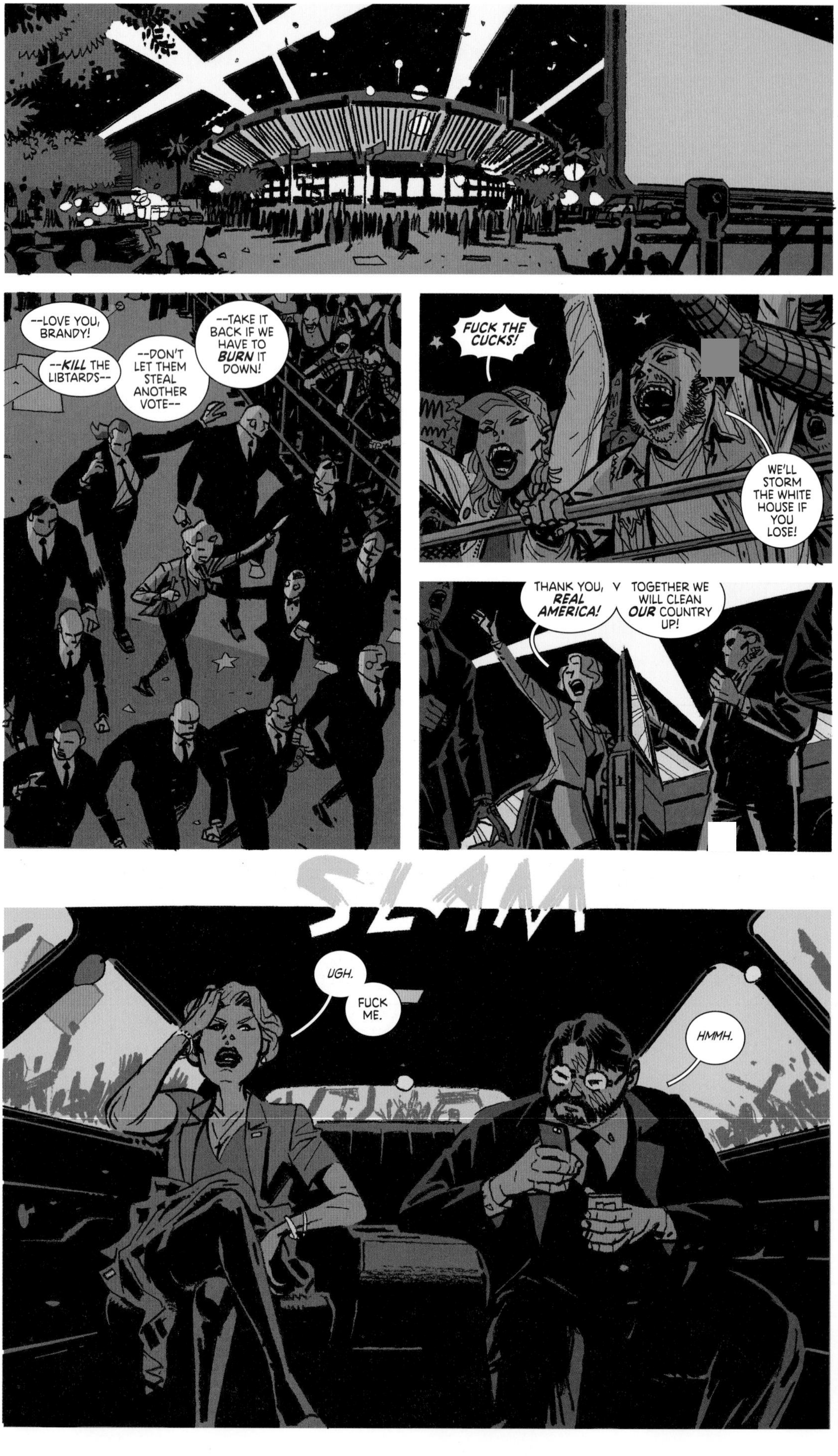
--LOVE YOU, BRANDY!
--KILL THE LIBTARDS--
--DON'T LET THEM STEAL ANOTHER VOTE--
--TAKE IT BACK IF WE HAVE TO BURN IT DOWN!
FUCK THE CUCKS!
WE'LL STORM THE WHITE HOUSE IF YOU LOSE!
THANK YOU, REAL AMERICA!
TOGETHER WE WILL CLEAN OUR COUNTRY UP!
SLAM
UGH.
FUCK ME.
HMMH.

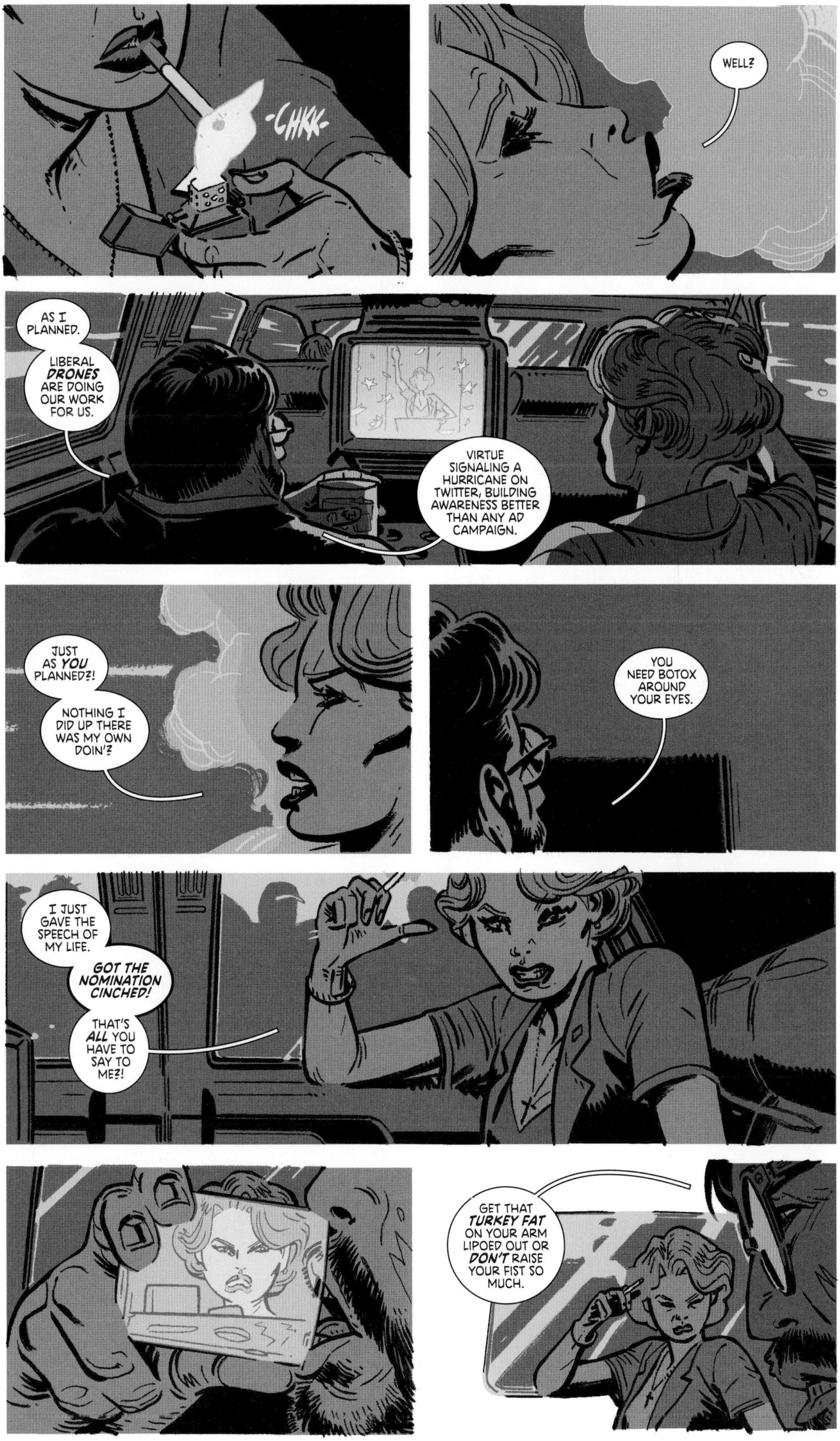

-CHKK-
WELL?
AS I PLANNED.
LIBERAL DRONES ARE DOING OUR WORK FOR US.
VIRTUE SIGNALING A HURRICANE ON TWITTER, BUILDING AWARENESS BETTER THAN ANY AD CAMPAIGN.
JUST AS YOU PLANNED?!
NOTHING I DID UP THERE WAS MY OWN DOIN'?
YOU NEED BOTOX AROUND YOUR EYES.
I JUST GAVE THE SPEECH OF MY LIFE.
GOT THE NOMINATION CINCHED!
THAT'S ALL YOU HAVE TO SAY TO ME?!
GET THAT TURKEY FAT ON YOUR ARM LIPOED OUT OR DON'T RAISE YOUR FIST SO MUCH.

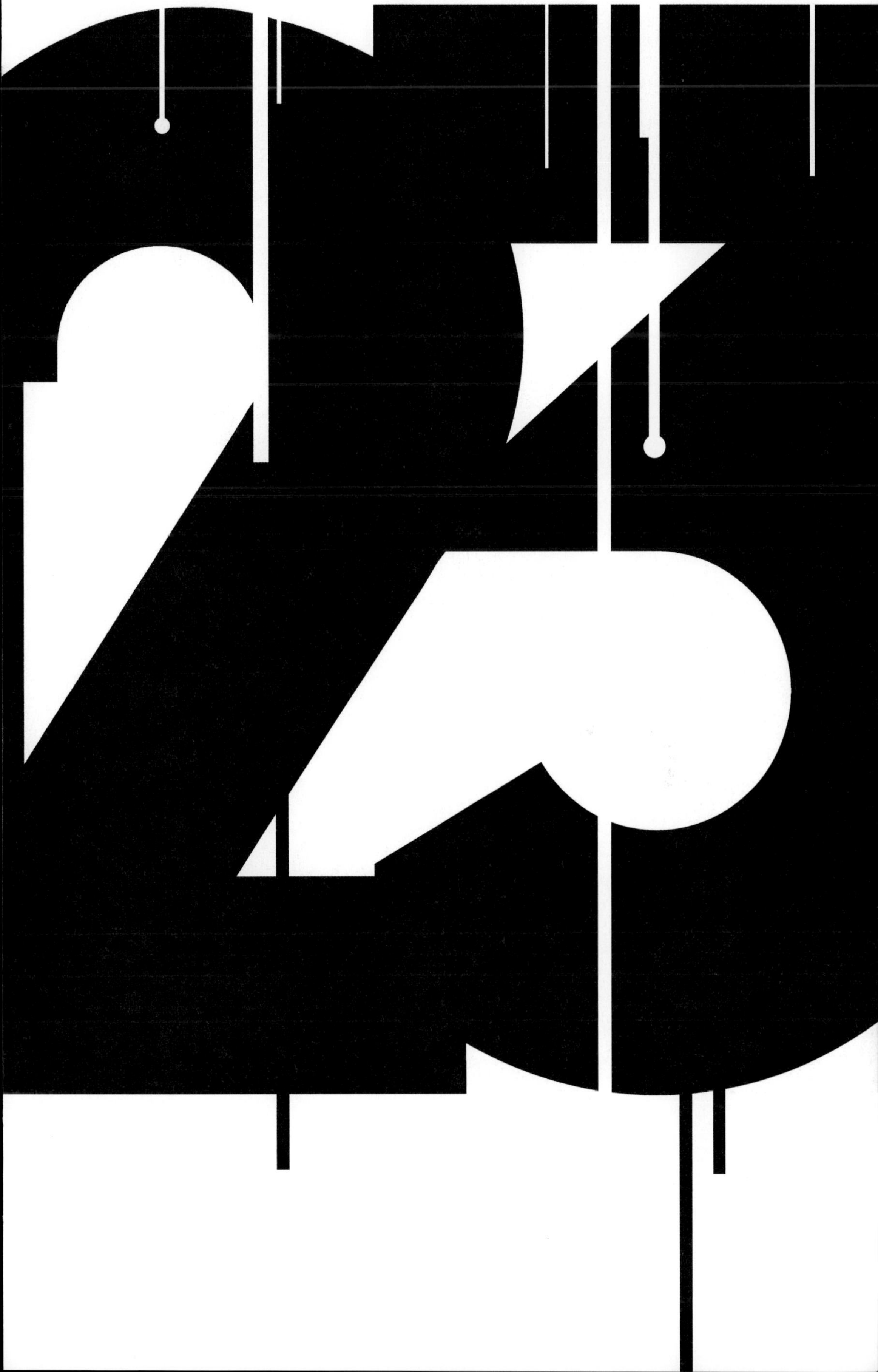
25

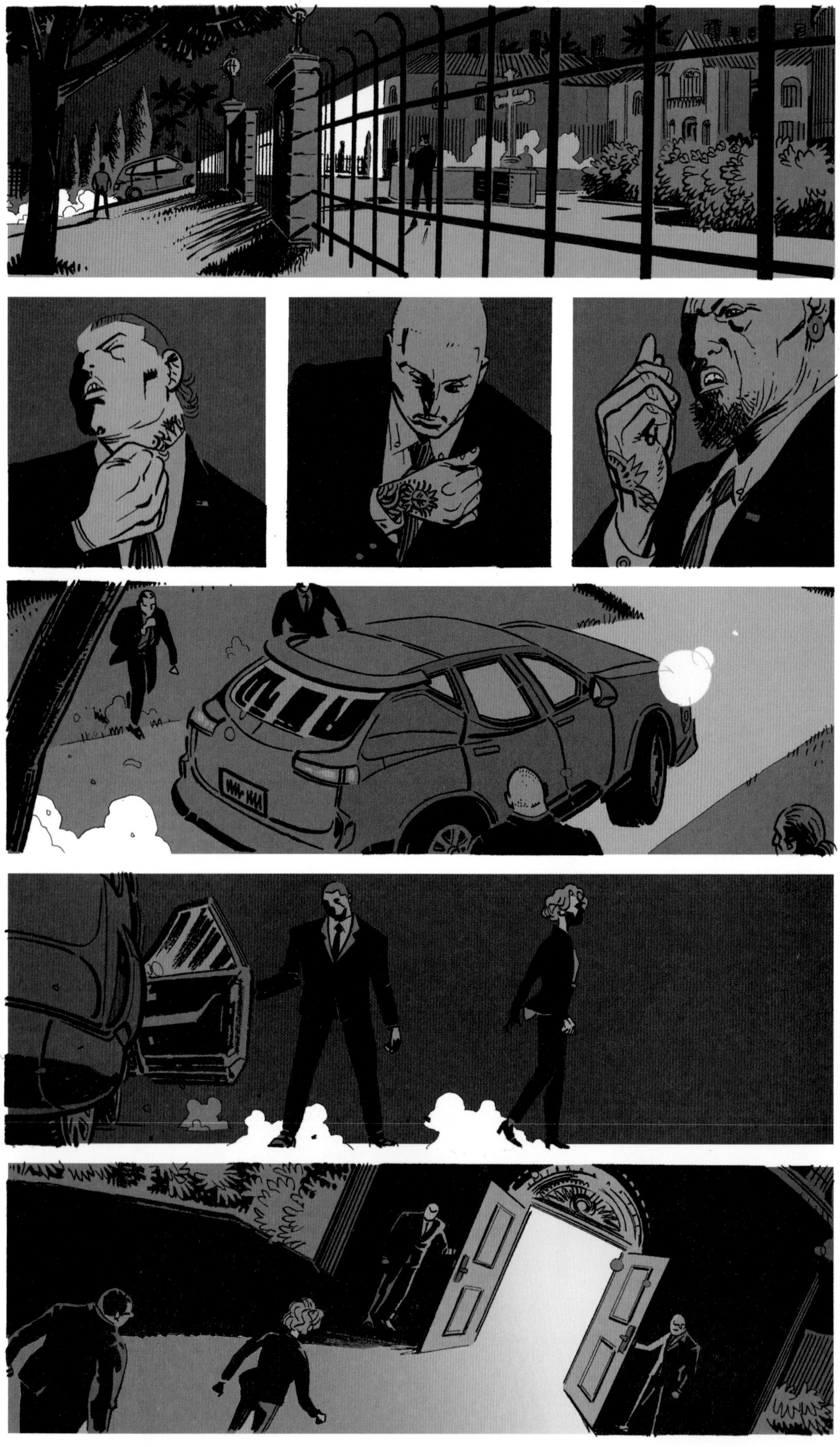

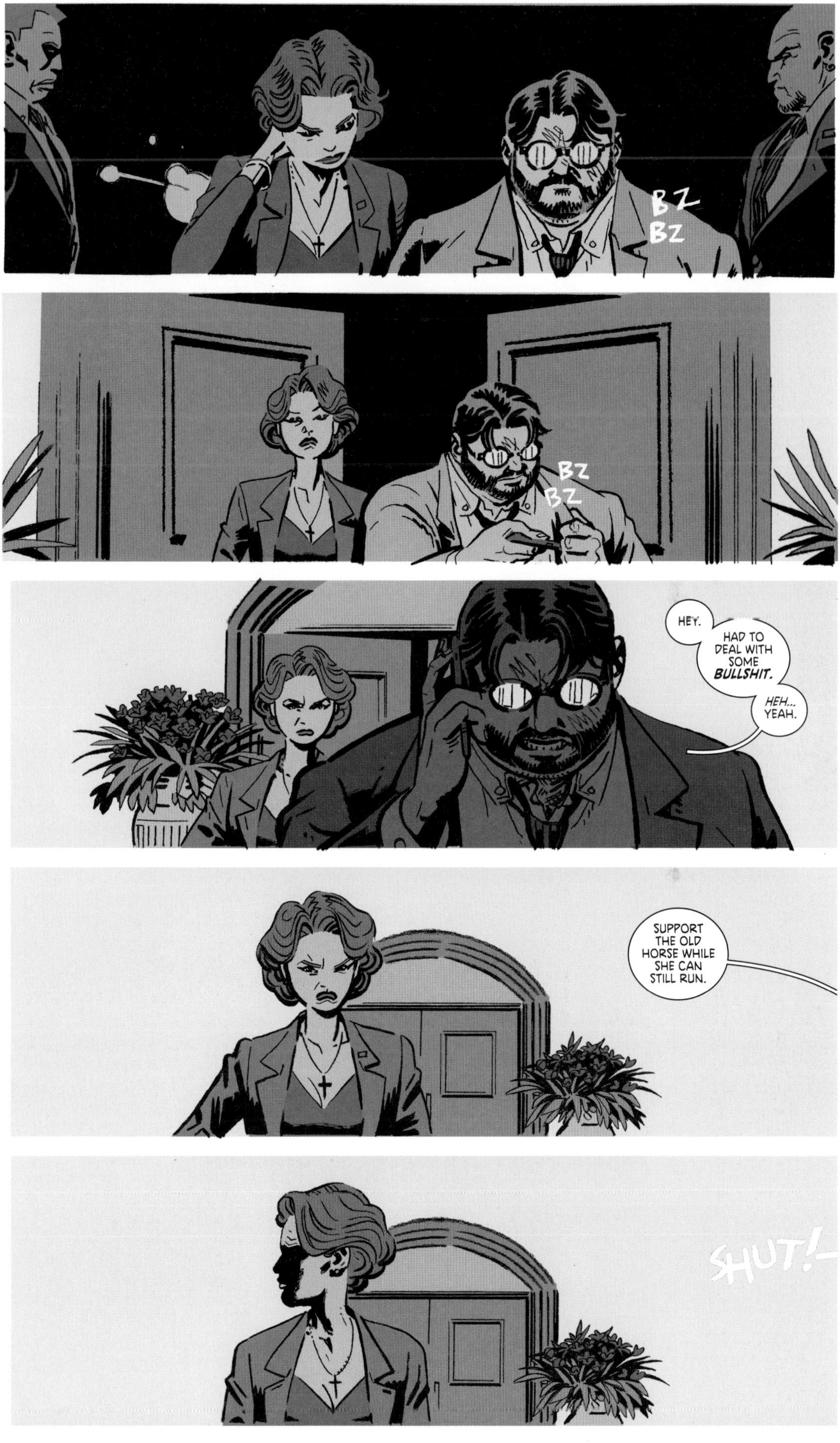
BZ
BZ
BZ
BZ
HEY.
HAD TO DEAL WITH SOME **BULLSHIT.**
HEH... YEAH.
SUPPORT THE OLD HORSE WHILE SHE CAN STILL RUN.
SHUT!

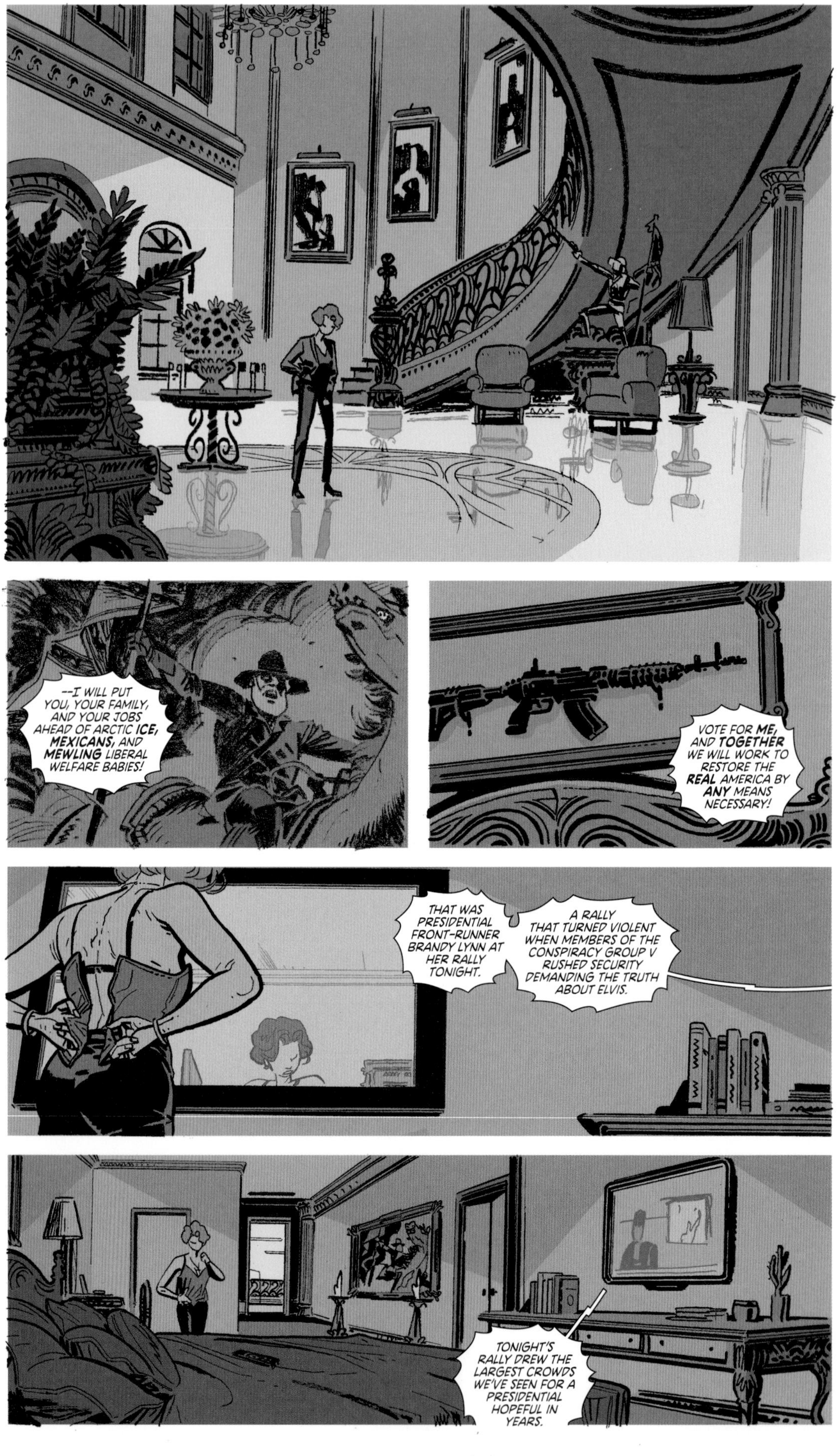
--I WILL PUT YOU, YOUR FAMILY, AND YOUR JOBS AHEAD OF ARCTIC ICE, MEXICANS, AND MEWLING LIBERAL WELFARE BABIES!
VOTE FOR ME, AND TOGETHER WE WILL WORK TO RESTORE THE REAL AMERICA BY ANY MEANS NECESSARY!
THAT WAS PRESIDENTIAL FRONT-RUNNER BRANDY LYNN AT HER RALLY TONIGHT.
A RALLY THAT TURNED VIOLENT WHEN MEMBERS OF THE CONSPIRACY GROUP V RUSHED SECURITY DEMANDING THE TRUTH ABOUT ELVIS.
TONIGHT'S RALLY DREW THE LARGEST CROWDS WE'VE SEEN FOR A PRESIDENTIAL HOPEFUL IN YEARS.

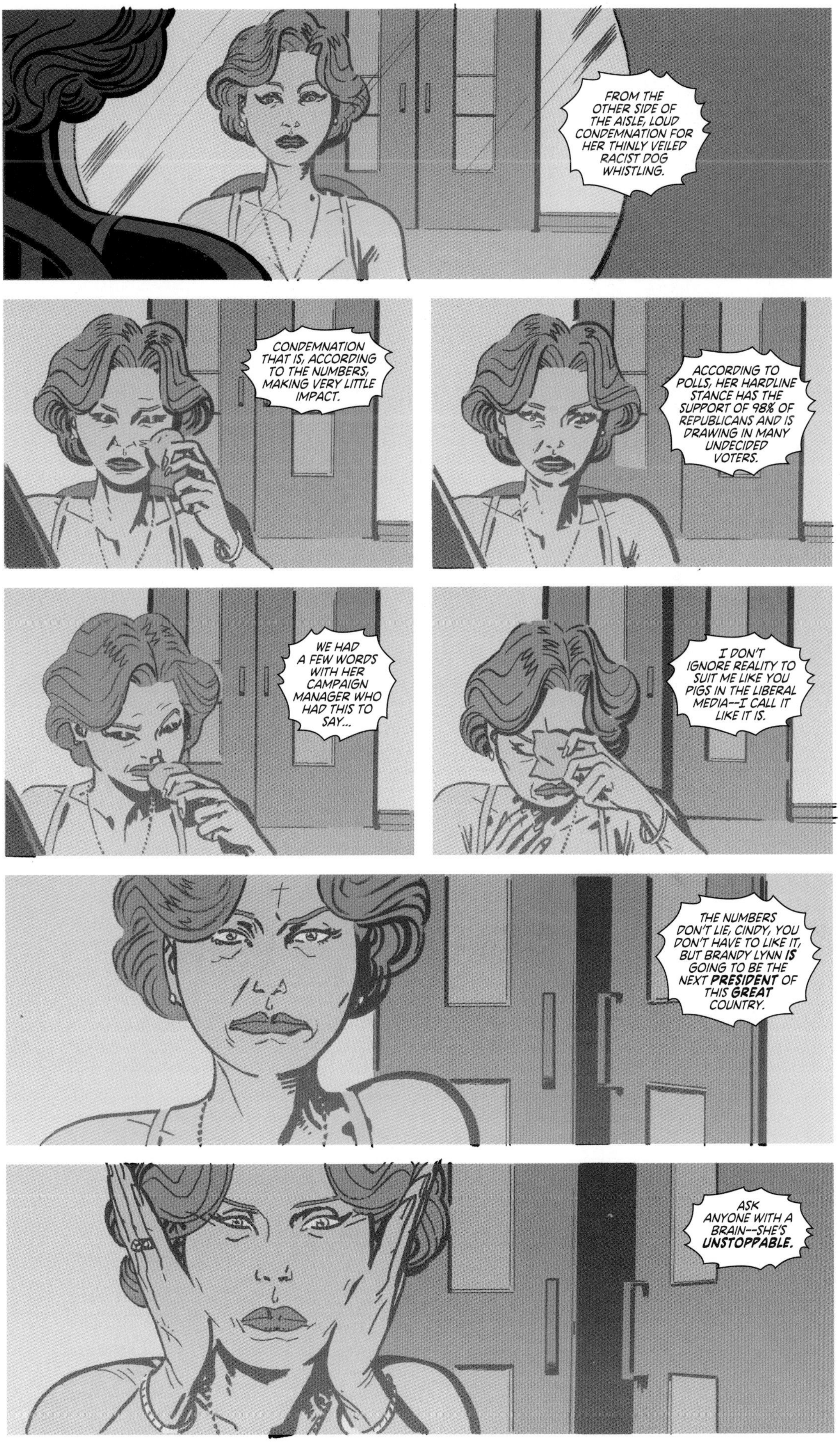
FROM THE OTHER SIDE OF THE AISLE, LOUD CONDEMNATION FOR HER THINLY VEILED RACIST DOG WHISTLING.
CONDEMNATION THAT IS, ACCORDING TO THE NUMBERS, MAKING VERY LITTLE IMPACT.
ACCORDING TO POLLS, HER HARDLINE STANCE HAS THE SUPPORT OF 98% OF REPUBLICANS AND IS DRAWING IN MANY UNDECIDED VOTERS.
WE HAD A FEW WORDS WITH HER CAMPAIGN MANAGER WHO HAD THIS TO SAY...
I DON'T IGNORE REALITY TO SUIT ME LIKE YOU PIGS IN THE LIBERAL MEDIA--I CALL IT LIKE IT IS.
THE NUMBERS DON'T LIE, CINDY, YOU DON'T HAVE TO LIKE IT, BUT BRANDY LYNN **IS** GOING TO BE THE NEXT **PRESIDENT** OF THIS **GREAT** COUNTRY.
ASK ANYONE WITH A BRAIN--SHE'S **UNSTOPPABLE.**

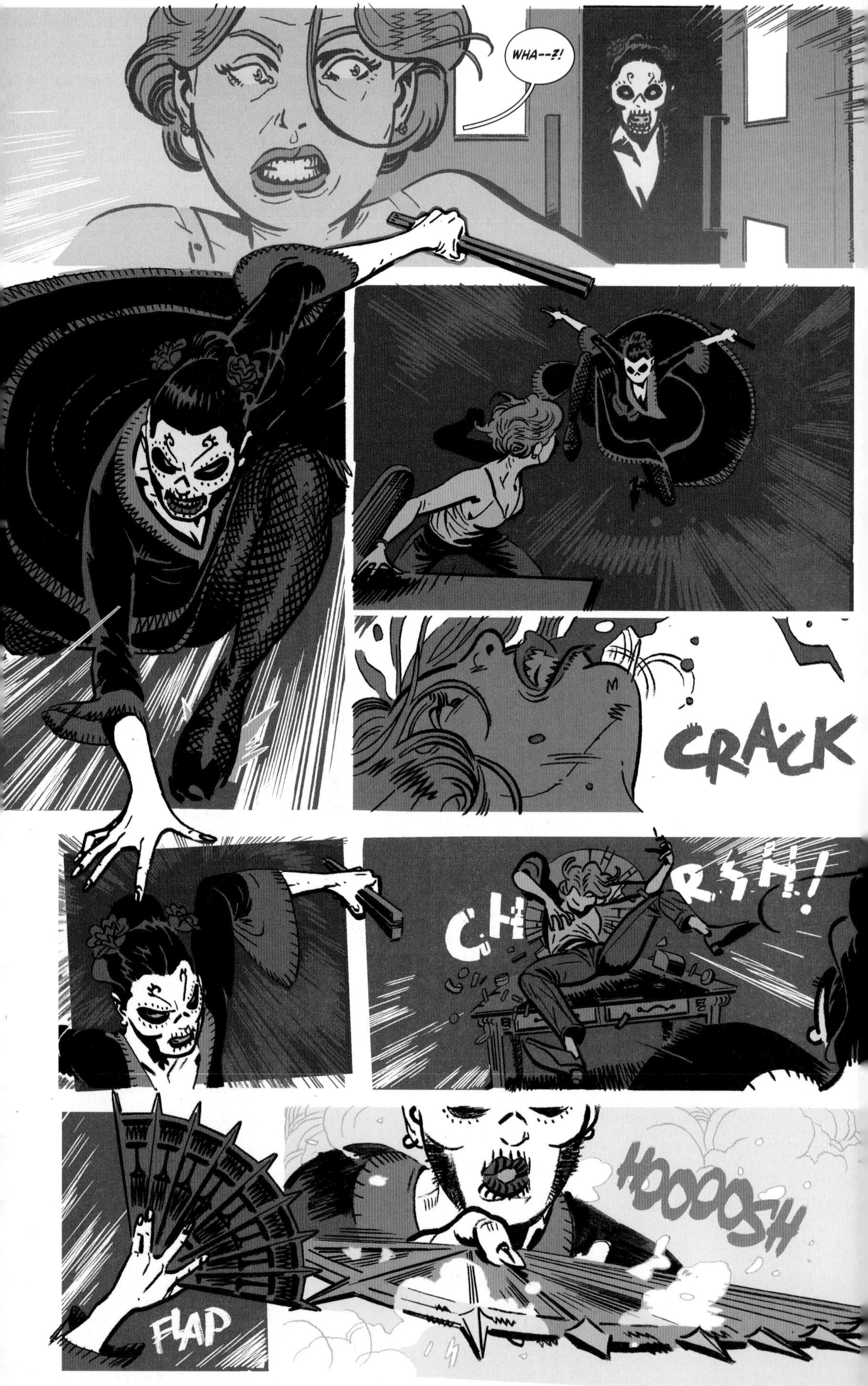
WHA--?!
CRACK
CH
RSH!
HOOOOSH
FLAP

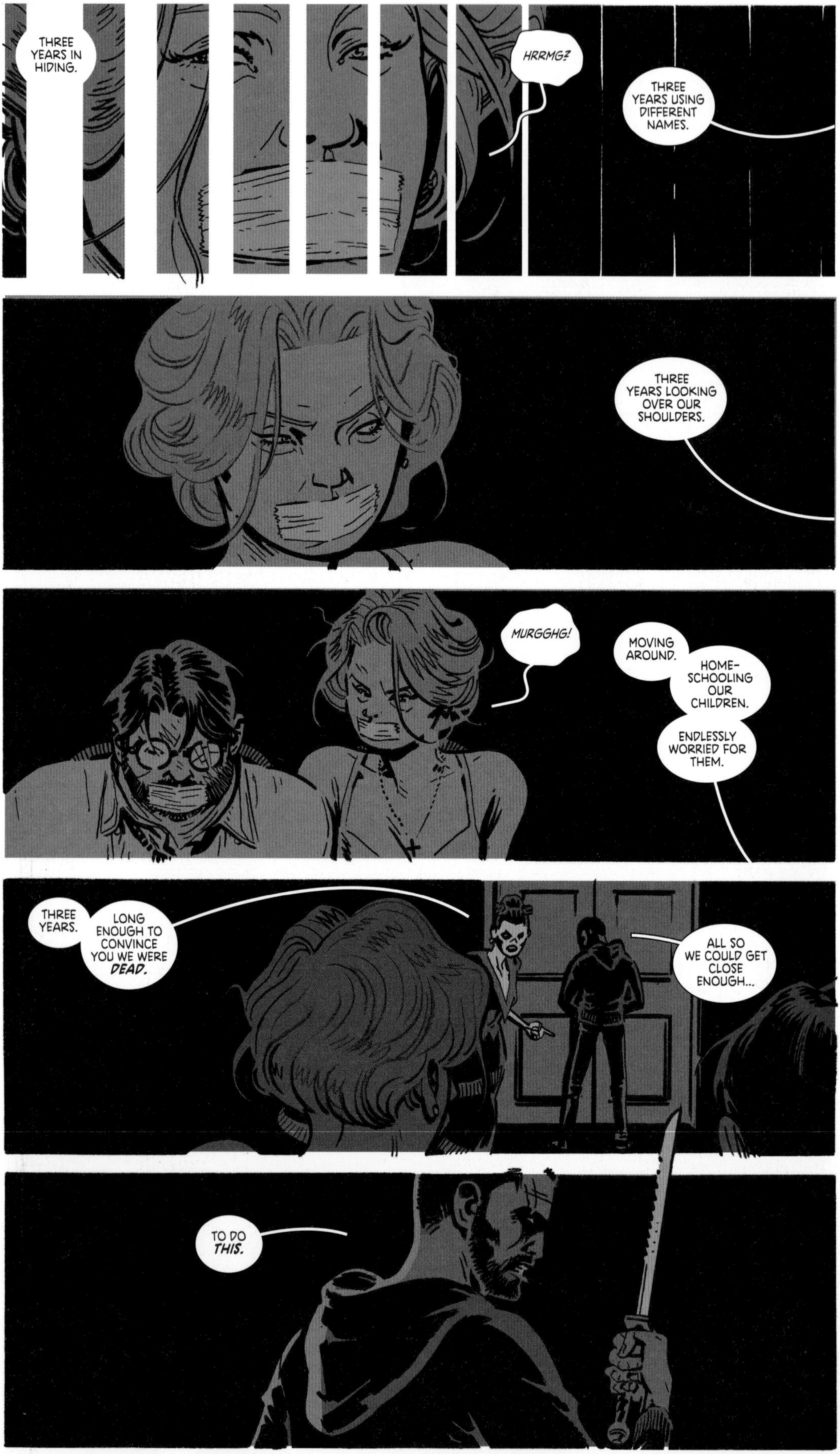
THREE YEARS IN HIDING.
HRRMG?
THREE YEARS USING DIFFERENT NAMES.
THREE YEARS LOOKING OVER OUR SHOULDERS.
MURGGHG!
MOVING AROUND.
HOME-SCHOOLING OUR CHILDREN.
ENDLESSLY WORRIED FOR THEM.
THREE YEARS.
LONG ENOUGH TO CONVINCE YOU WE WERE *DEAD.*
ALL SO WE COULD GET CLOSE ENOUGH...
TO DO *THIS.*

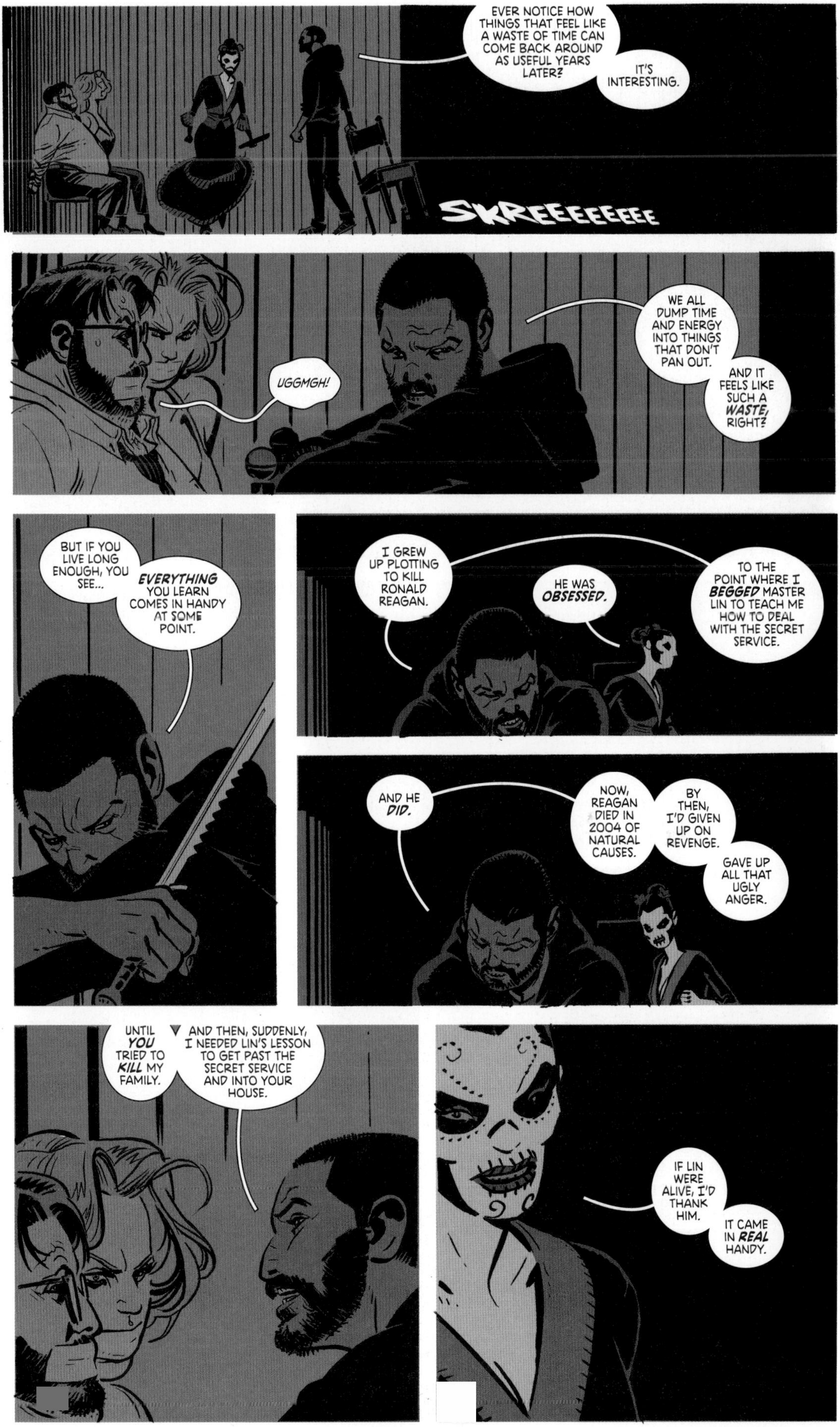

EVER NOTICE HOW THINGS THAT FEEL LIKE A WASTE OF TIME CAN COME BACK AROUND AS USEFUL YEARS LATER?
IT'S INTERESTING.
SKREEEEEEEE
WE ALL DUMP TIME AND ENERGY INTO THINGS THAT DON'T PAN OUT.
AND IT FEELS LIKE SUCH A WASTE, RIGHT?
UGGMGH!
BUT IF YOU LIVE LONG ENOUGH, YOU SEE...
EVERYTHING YOU LEARN COMES IN HANDY AT SOME POINT.
I GREW UP PLOTTING TO KILL RONALD REAGAN.
HE WAS OBSESSED.
TO THE POINT WHERE I BEGGED MASTER LIN TO TEACH ME HOW TO DEAL WITH THE SECRET SERVICE.
AND HE DID.
NOW, REAGAN DIED IN 2004 OF NATURAL CAUSES.
BY THEN, I'D GIVEN UP ON REVENGE.
GAVE UP ALL THAT UGLY ANGER.
UNTIL YOU TRIED TO KILL MY FAMILY.
AND THEN, SUDDENLY, I NEEDED LIN'S LESSON TO GET PAST THE SECRET SERVICE AND INTO YOUR HOUSE.
IF LIN WERE ALIVE, I'D THANK HIM.
IT CAME IN REAL HANDY.

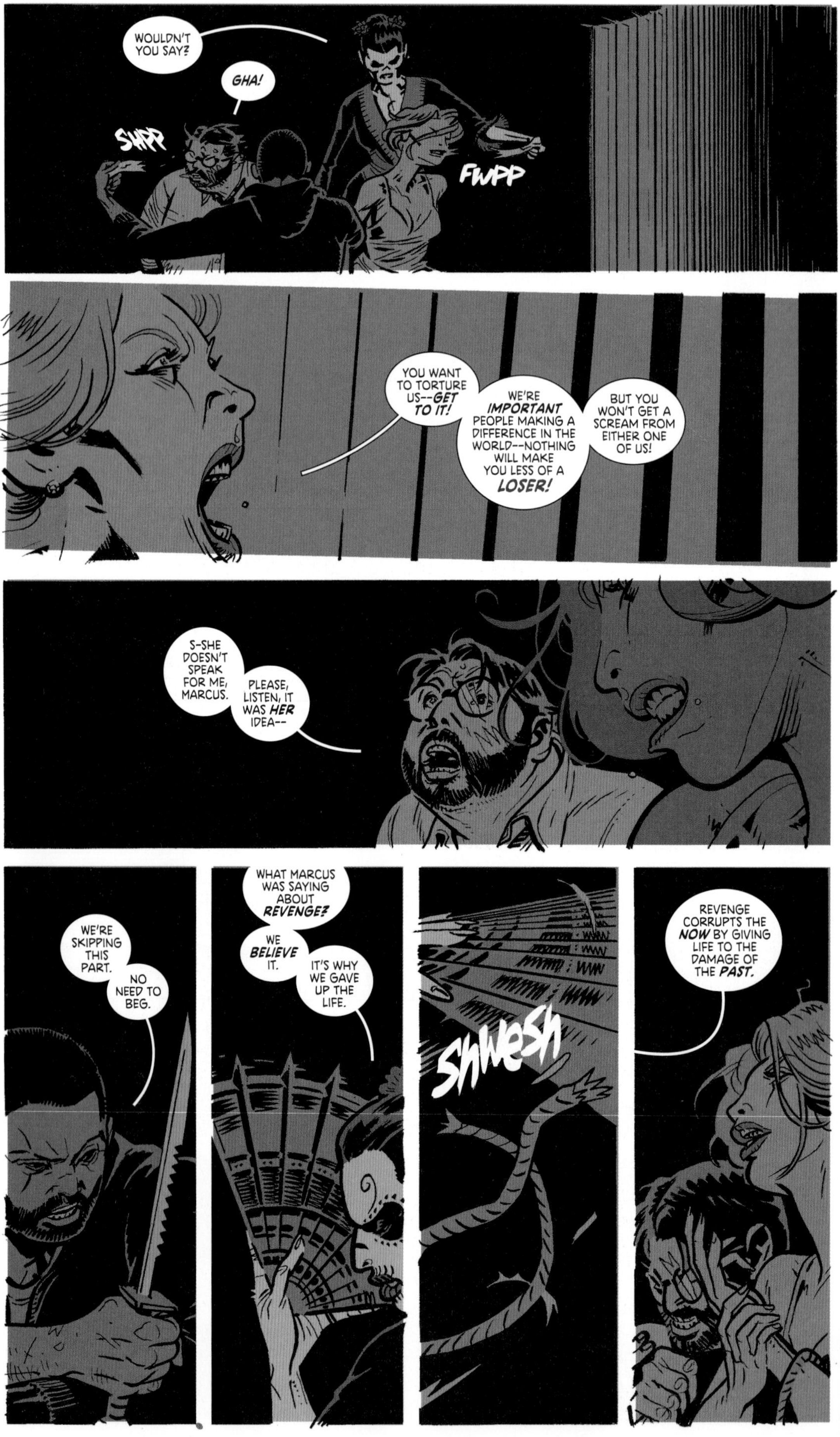
WOULDN'T YOU SAY?
GHA!
SHPP
FWPP
YOU WANT TO TORTURE US--GET TO IT!
WE'RE IMPORTANT PEOPLE MAKING A DIFFERENCE IN THE WORLD--NOTHING WILL MAKE YOU LESS OF A LOSER!
BUT YOU WON'T GET A SCREAM FROM EITHER ONE OF US!
S-SHE DOESN'T SPEAK FOR ME, MARCUS.
PLEASE, LISTEN, IT WAS HER IDEA--
WE'RE SKIPPING THIS PART.
NO NEED TO BEG.
WHAT MARCUS WAS SAYING ABOUT REVENGE?
WE BELIEVE IT.
IT'S WHY WE GAVE UP THE LIFE.
SHWESH
REVENGE CORRUPTS THE NOW BY GIVING LIFE TO THE DAMAGE OF THE PAST.

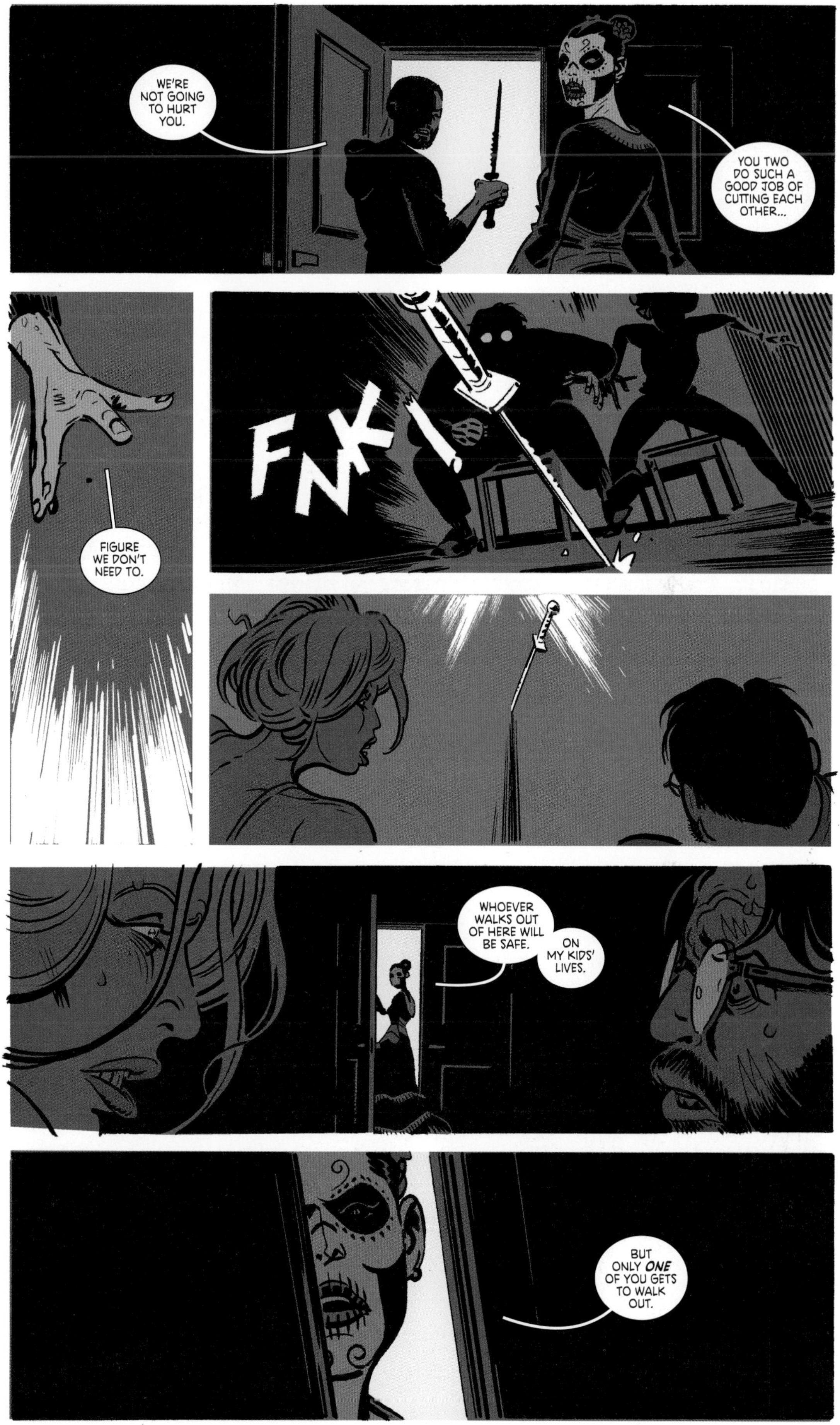
WE'RE NOT GOING TO HURT YOU.
YOU TWO DO SUCH A GOOD JOB OF CUTTING EACH OTHER...
FIGURE WE DON'T NEED TO.
FNK!
WHOEVER WALKS OUT OF HERE WILL BE SAFE.
ON MY KIDS' LIVES.
BUT ONLY *ONE* OF YOU GETS TO WALK OUT.

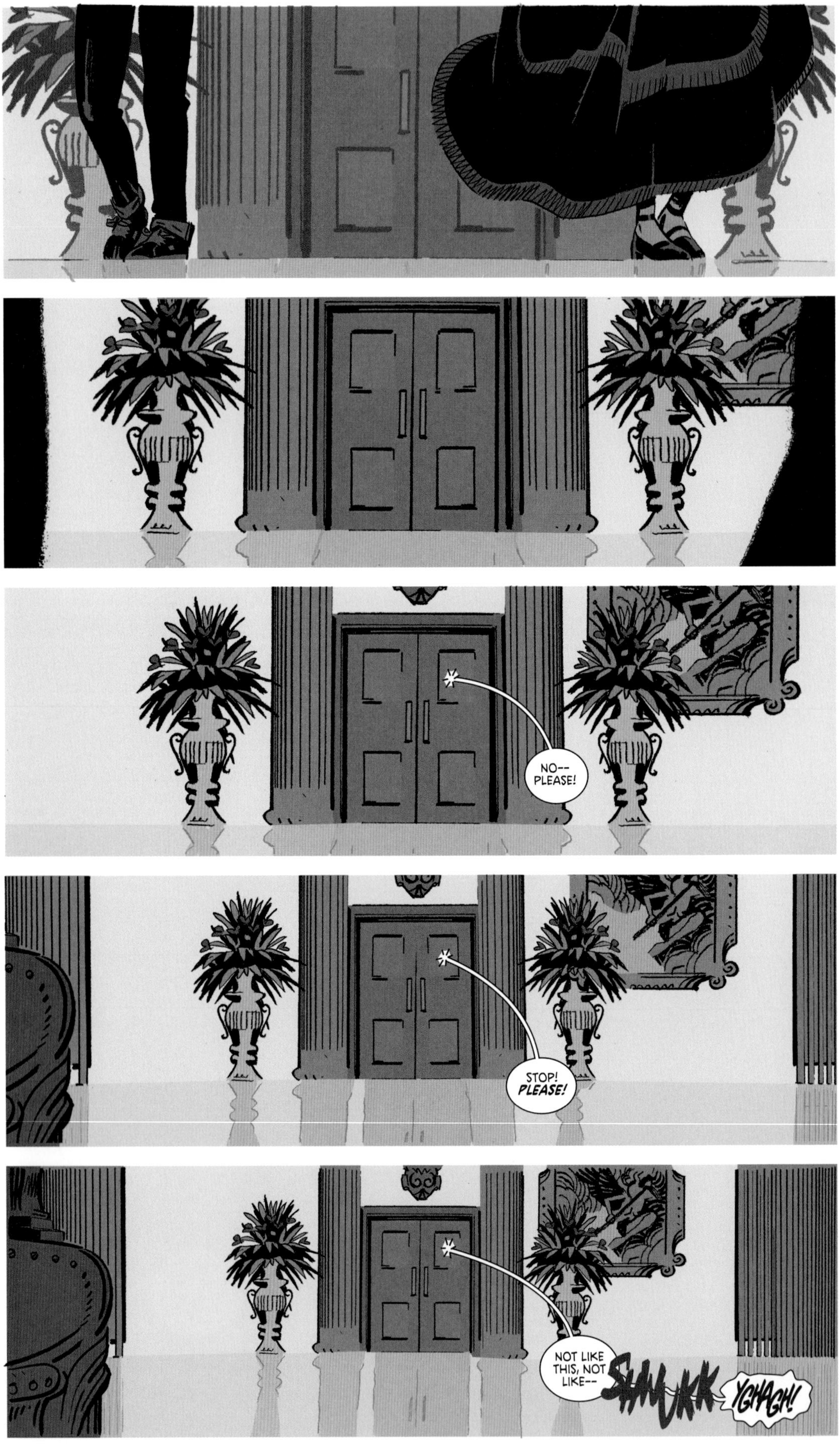

NO-- PLEASE!
STOP! PLEASE!
NOT LIKE THIS, NOT LIKE--
SHUKK
YGHAGH!

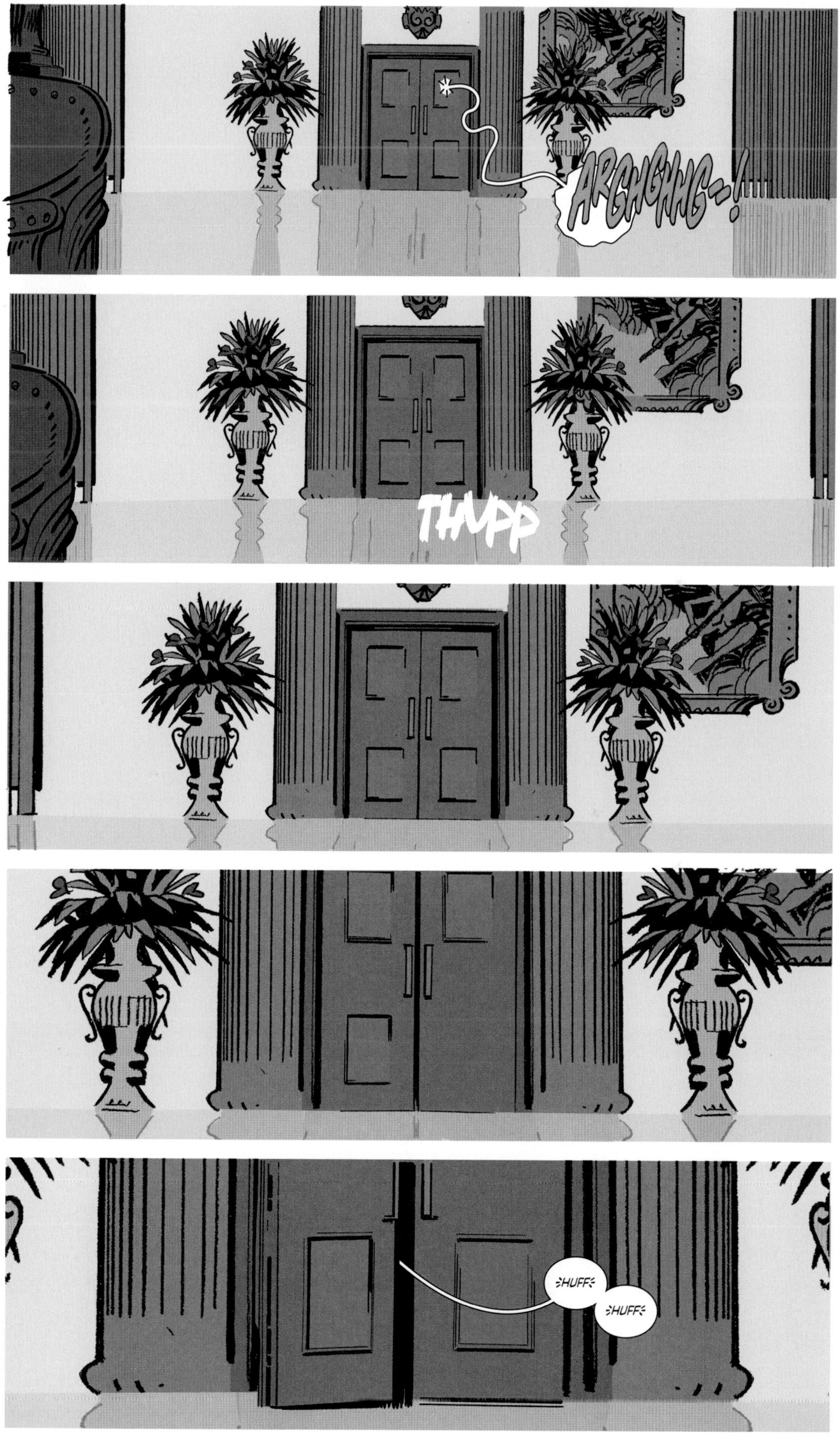
ARGHGHHG--!
THUPP
HUFF
HUFF

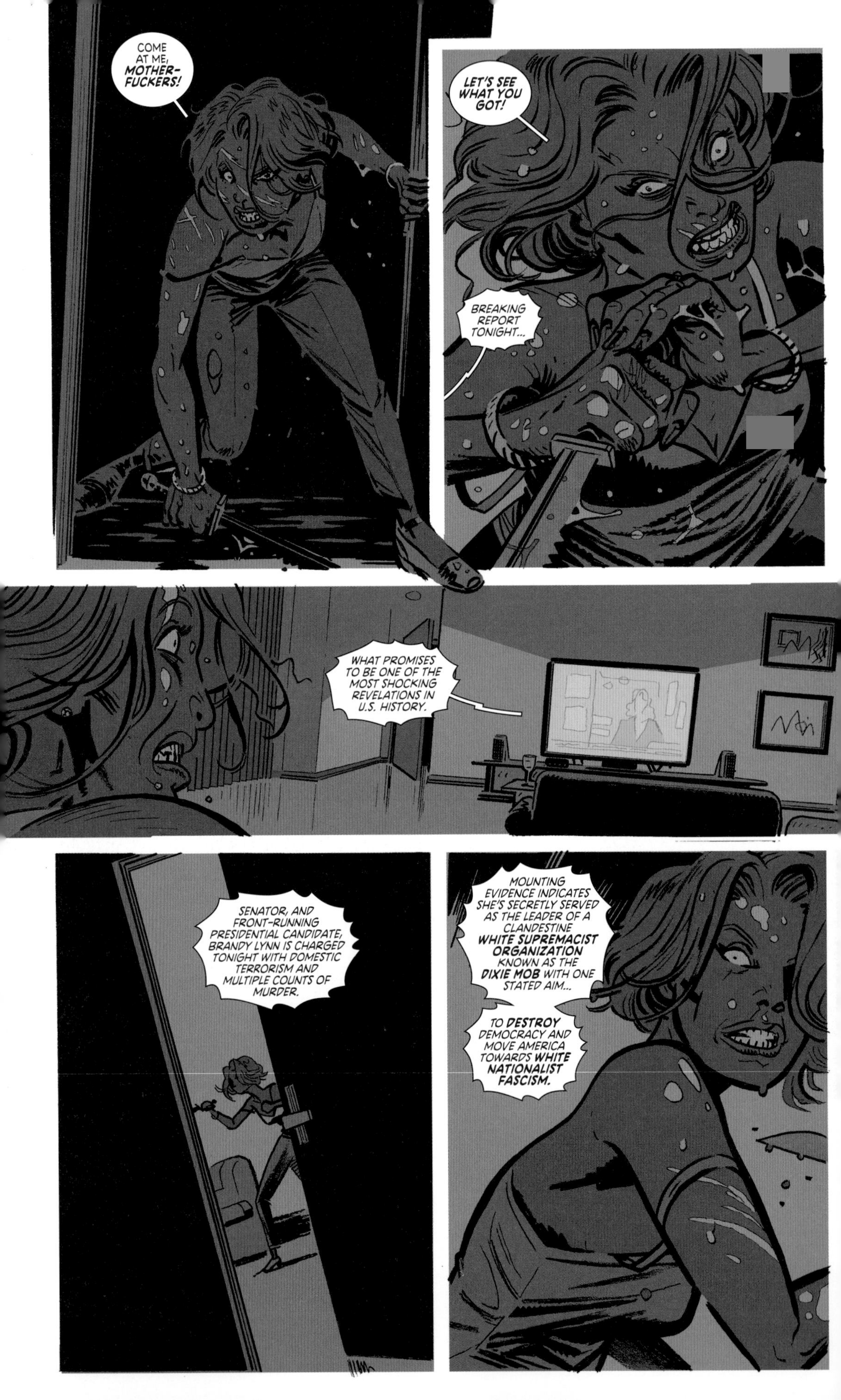
COME AT ME, MOTHER-FUCKERS!
LET'S SEE WHAT YOU GOT!
BREAKING REPORT TONIGHT...
WHAT PROMISES TO BE ONE OF THE MOST SHOCKING REVELATIONS IN U.S. HISTORY.
SENATOR, AND FRONT-RUNNING PRESIDENTIAL CANDIDATE, BRANDY LYNN IS CHARGED TONIGHT WITH DOMESTIC TERRORISM AND MULTIPLE COUNTS OF MURDER.
MOUNTING EVIDENCE INDICATES SHE'S SECRETLY SERVED AS THE LEADER OF A CLANDESTINE WHITE SUPREMACIST ORGANIZATION KNOWN AS THE DIXIE MOB WITH ONE STATED AIM...
TO DESTROY DEMOCRACY AND MOVE AMERICA TOWARDS WHITE NATIONALIST FASCISM.

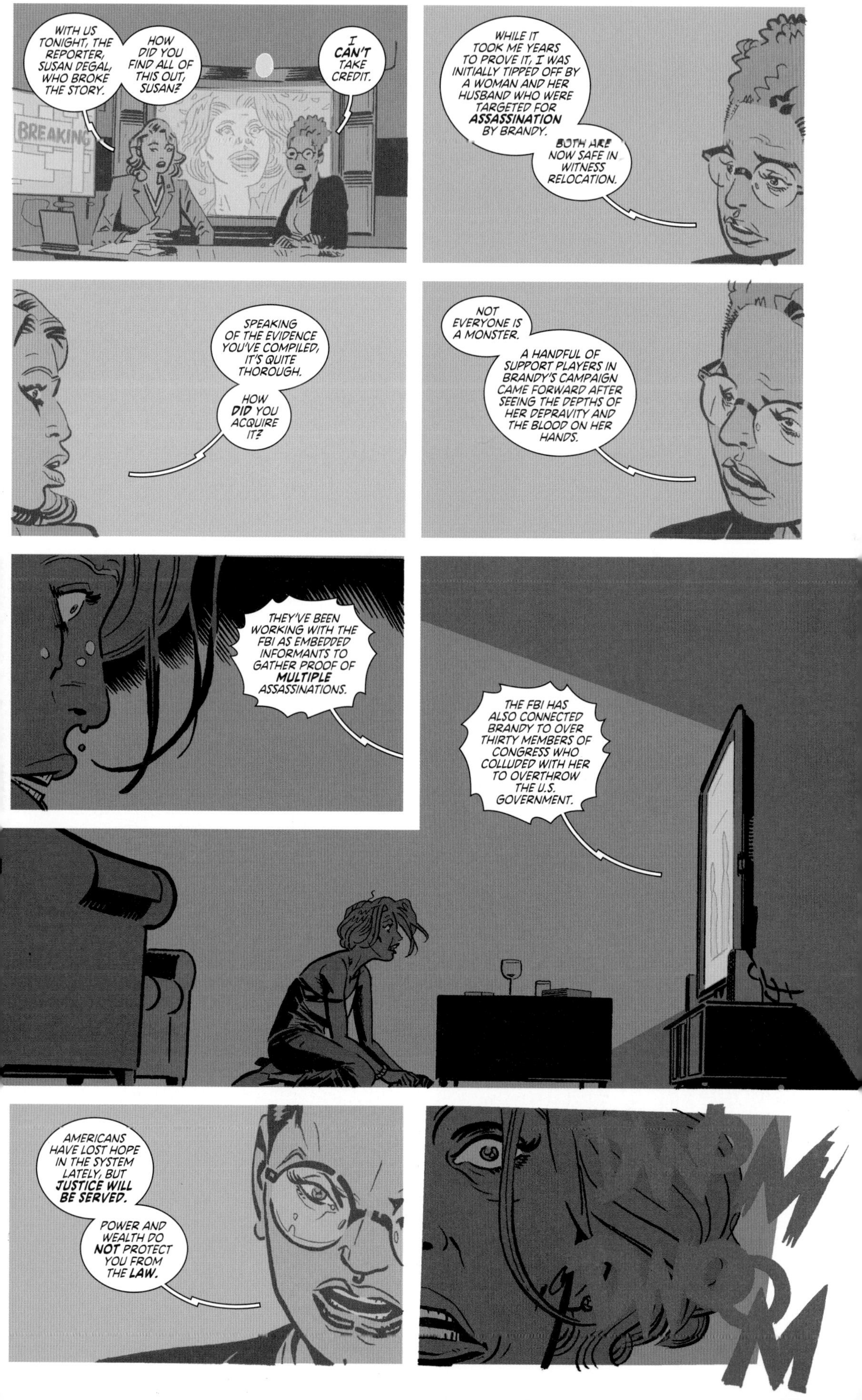

BREAKING
WITH US TONIGHT, THE REPORTER, SUSAN DEGAL, WHO BROKE THE STORY.
HOW DID YOU FIND ALL OF THIS OUT, SUSAN?
I CAN'T TAKE CREDIT.
WHILE IT TOOK ME YEARS TO PROVE IT, I WAS INITIALLY TIPPED OFF BY A WOMAN AND HER HUSBAND WHO WERE TARGETED FOR ASSASSINATION BY BRANDY.
BOTH ARE NOW SAFE IN WITNESS RELOCATION.
SPEAKING OF THE EVIDENCE YOU'VE COMPILED, IT'S QUITE THOROUGH.
HOW DID YOU ACQUIRE IT?
NOT EVERYONE IS A MONSTER.
A HANDFUL OF SUPPORT PLAYERS IN BRANDY'S CAMPAIGN CAME FORWARD AFTER SEEING THE DEPTHS OF HER DEPRAVITY AND THE BLOOD ON HER HANDS.
THEY'VE BEEN WORKING WITH THE FBI AS EMBEDDED INFORMANTS TO GATHER PROOF OF MULTIPLE ASSASSINATIONS.
THE FBI HAS ALSO CONNECTED BRANDY TO OVER THIRTY MEMBERS OF CONGRESS WHO COLLUDED WITH HER TO OVERTHROW THE U.S. GOVERNMENT.
AMERICANS HAVE LOST HOPE IN THE SYSTEM LATELY, BUT JUSTICE WILL BE SERVED.
POWER AND WEALTH DO NOT PROTECT YOU FROM THE LAW.

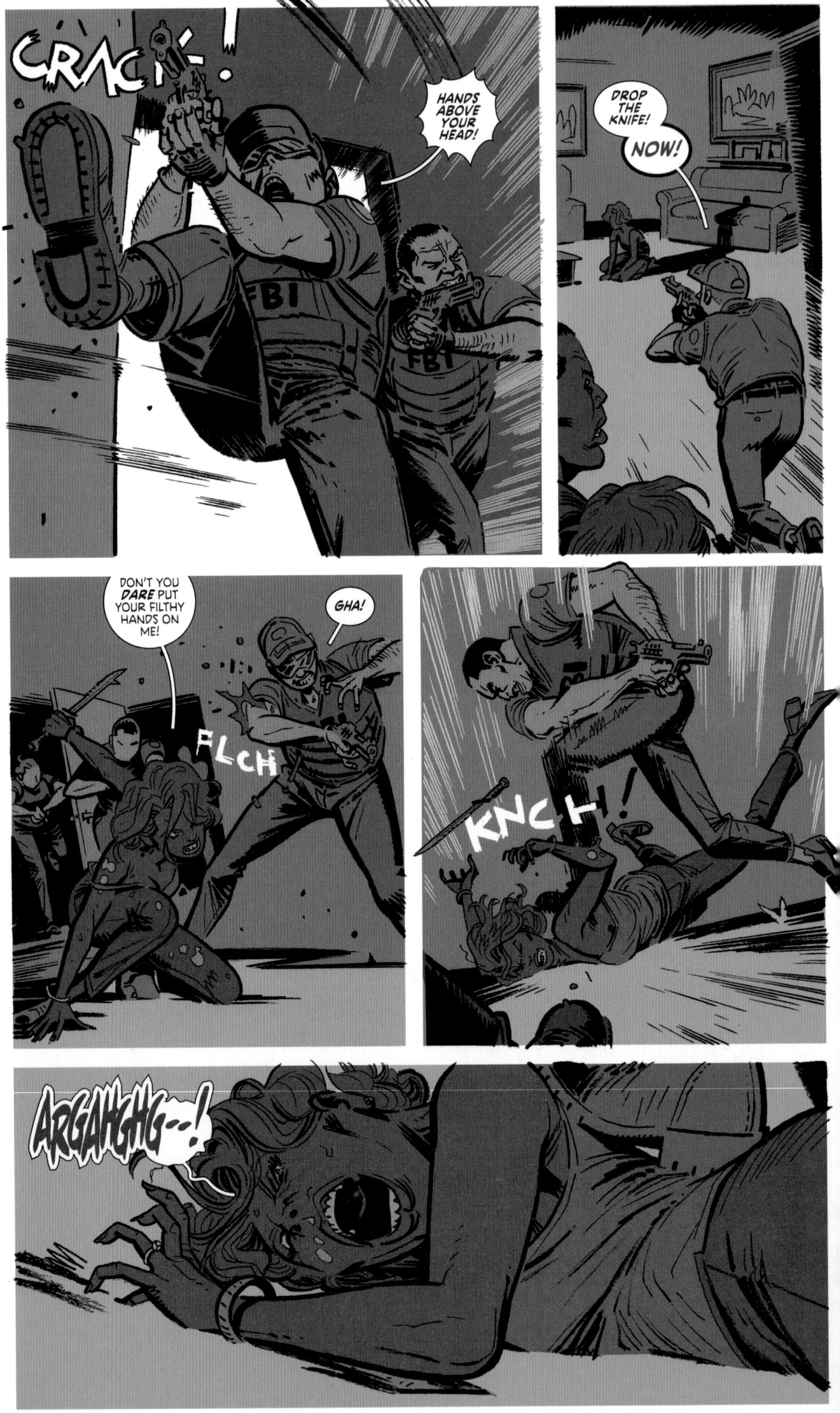

CRACK!
HANDS ABOVE YOUR HEAD!
DROP THE KNIFE!
NOW!
DON'T YOU DARE PUT YOUR FILTHY HANDS ON ME!
GHA!
FLCH
KNCH!
ARGAHGHG--!

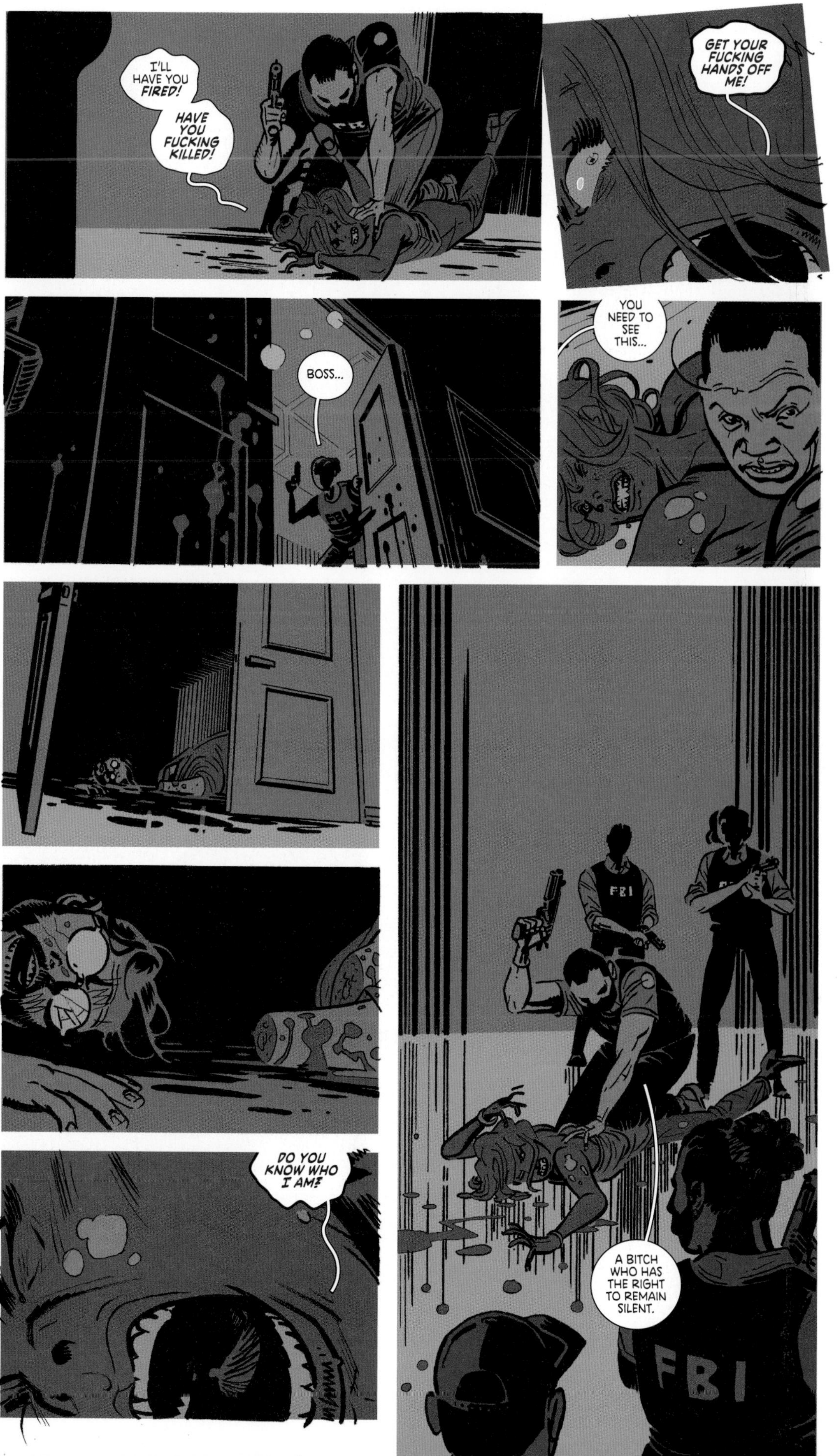
I'LL HAVE YOU FIRED!
HAVE YOU FUCKING KILLED!
GET YOUR FUCKING HANDS OFF ME!
BOSS...
YOU NEED TO SEE THIS...
DO YOU KNOW WHO I AM?
A BITCH WHO HAS THE RIGHT TO REMAIN SILENT.
FBI

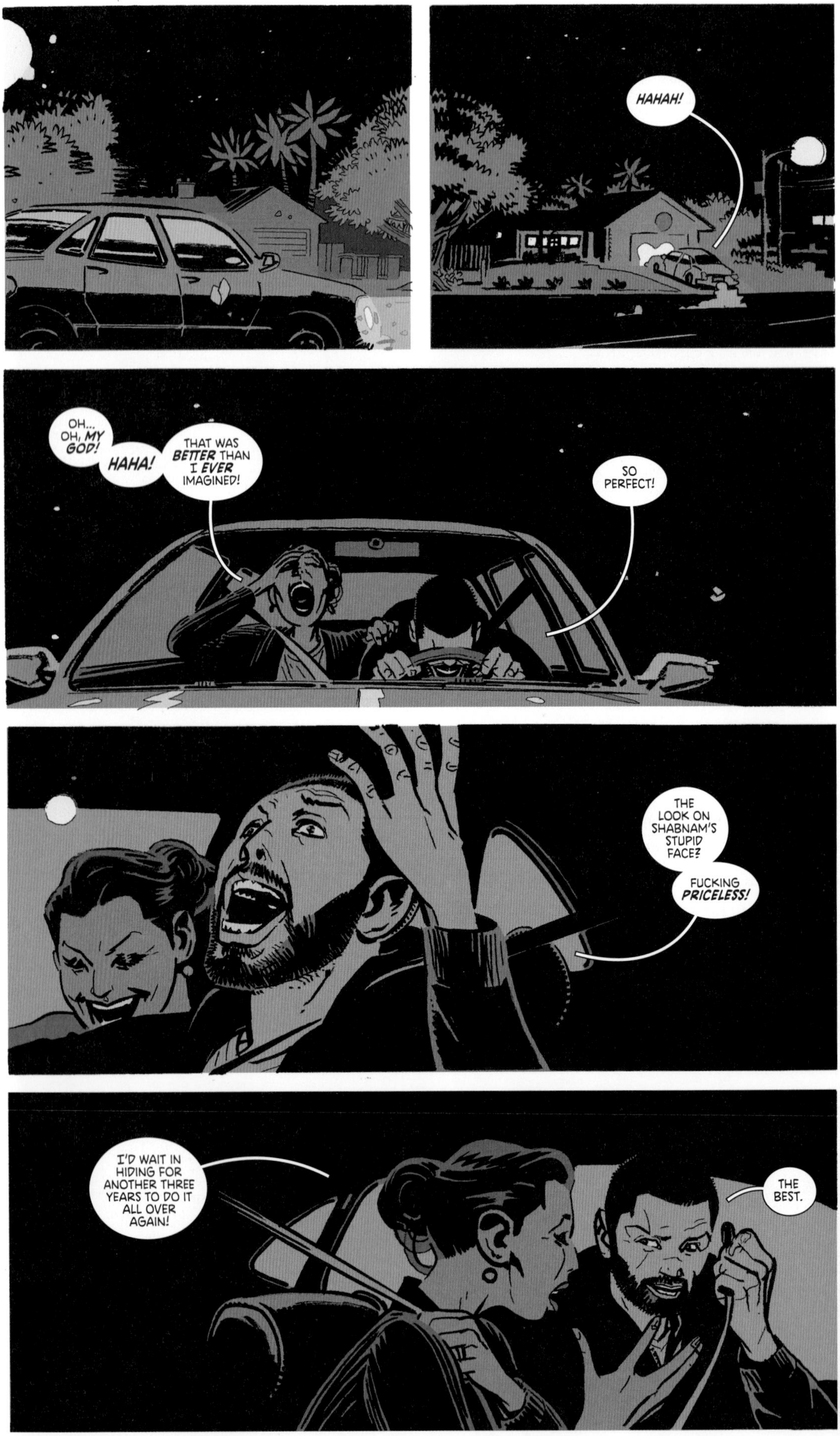

HAHAH!
OH... OH, MY GOD!
HAHA!
THAT WAS BETTER THAN I EVER IMAGINED!
SO PERFECT!
THE LOOK ON SHABNAM'S STUPID FACE?
FUCKING PRICELESS!
I'D WAIT IN HIDING FOR ANOTHER THREE YEARS TO DO IT ALL OVER AGAIN!
THE BEST.

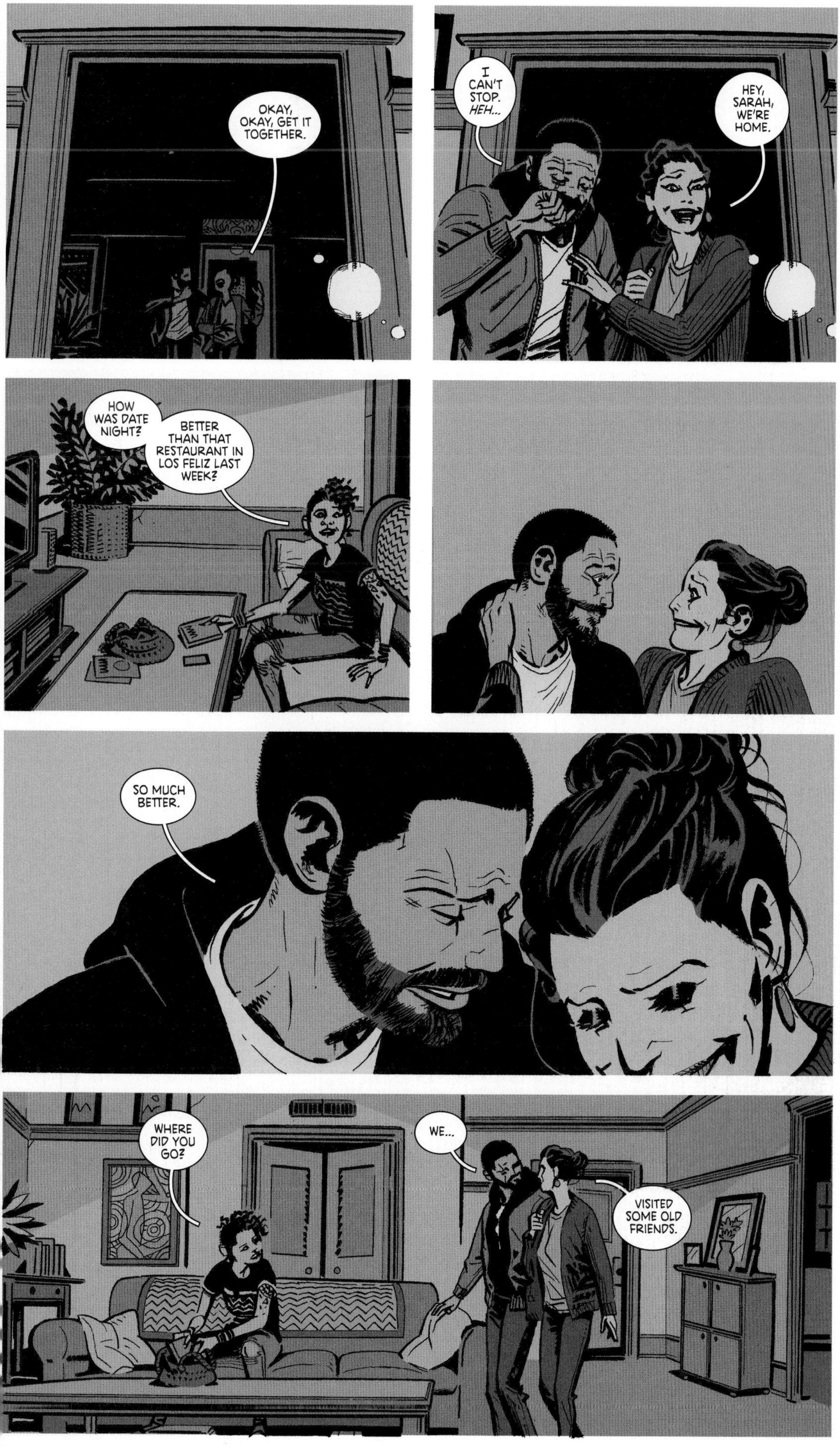
OKAY, OKAY, GET IT TOGETHER.
I CAN'T STOP. HEH...
HEY, SARAH, WE'RE HOME.
HOW WAS DATE NIGHT?
BETTER THAN THAT RESTAURANT IN LOS FELIZ LAST WEEK?
SO MUCH BETTER.
WHERE DID YOU GO?
WE...
VISITED SOME OLD FRIENDS.

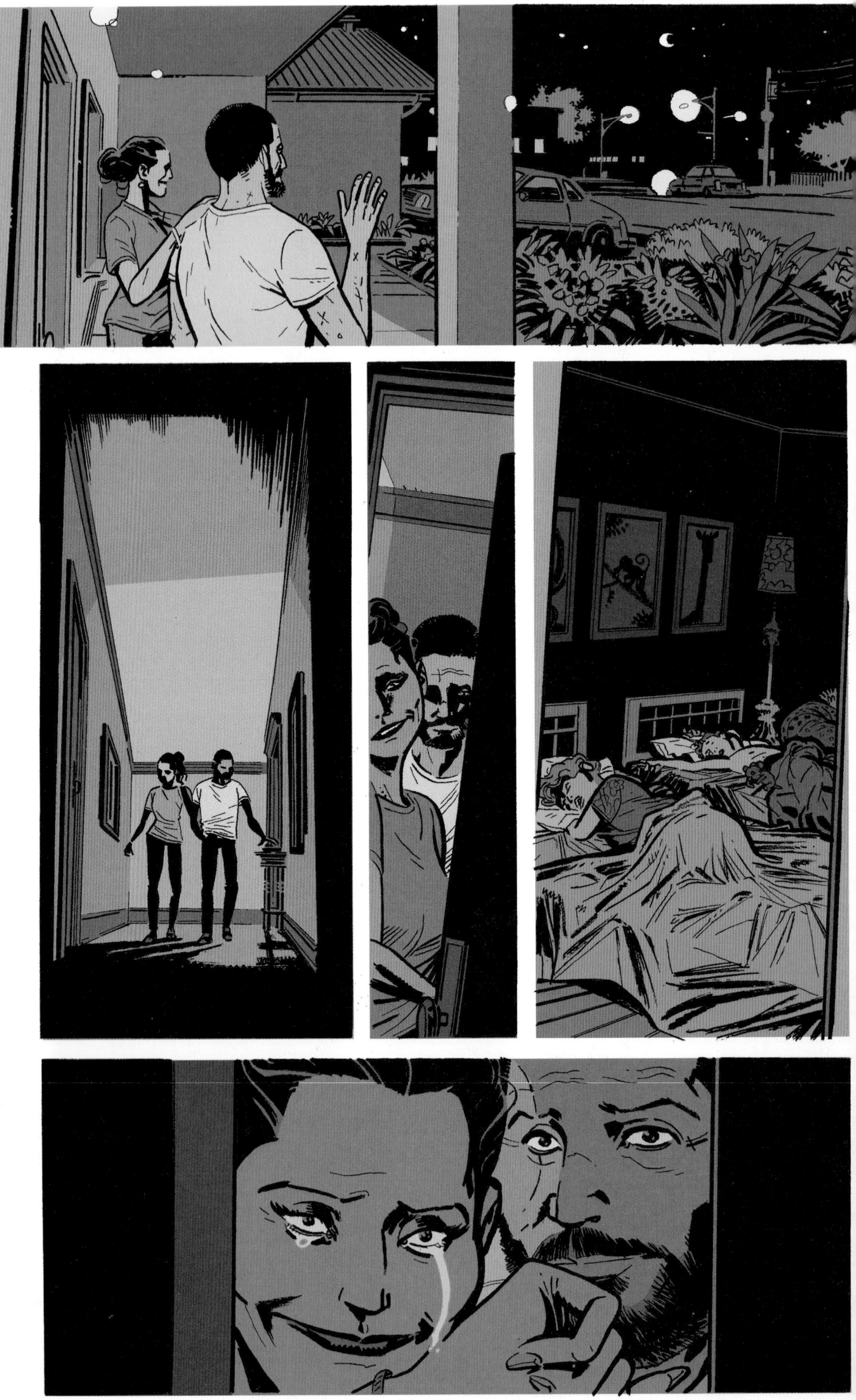

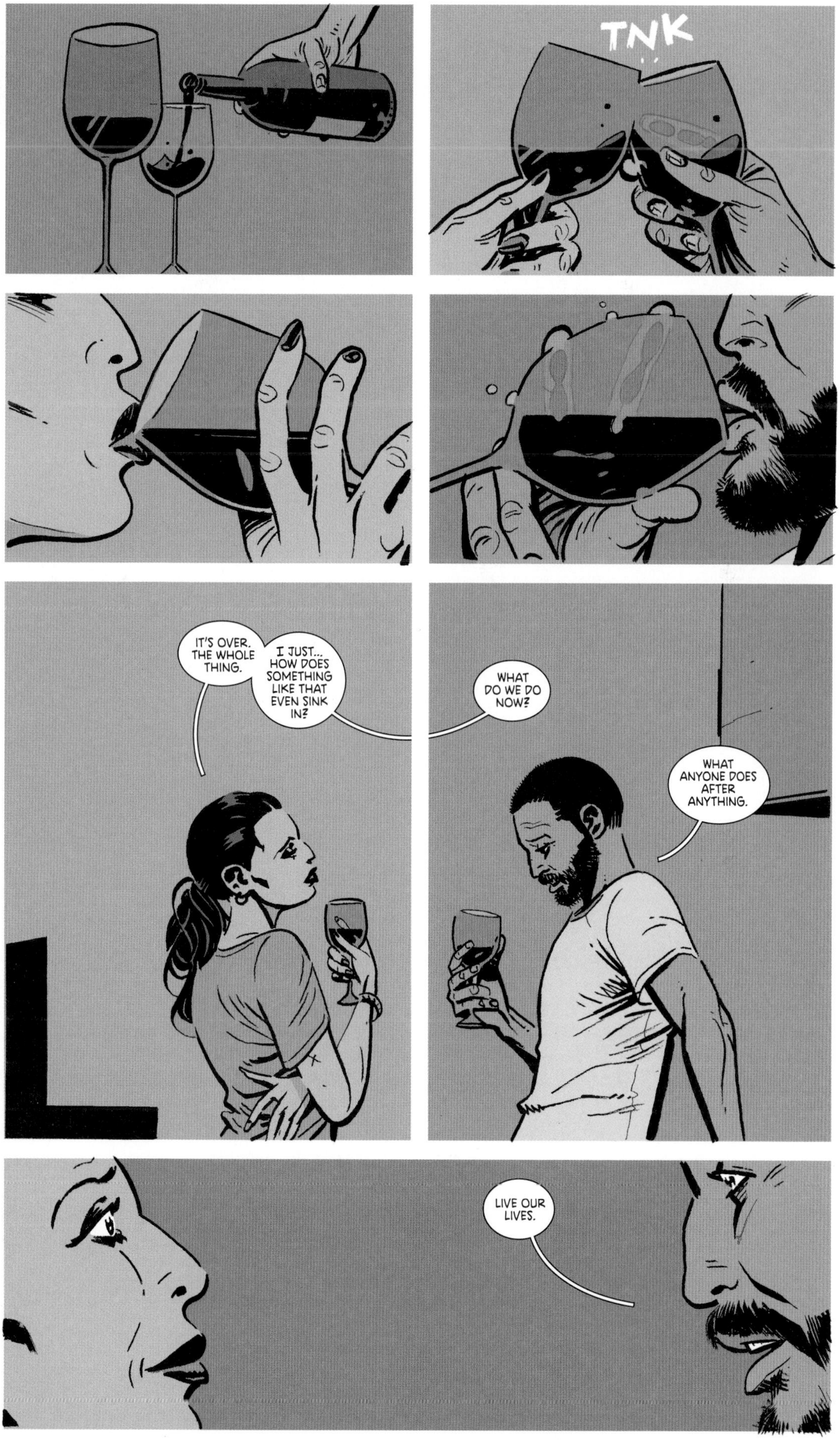
TNK
IT'S OVER. THE WHOLE THING.
I JUST... HOW DOES SOMETHING LIKE THAT EVEN SINK IN?
WHAT DO WE DO NOW?
WHAT ANYONE DOES AFTER ANYTHING.
LIVE OUR LIVES.

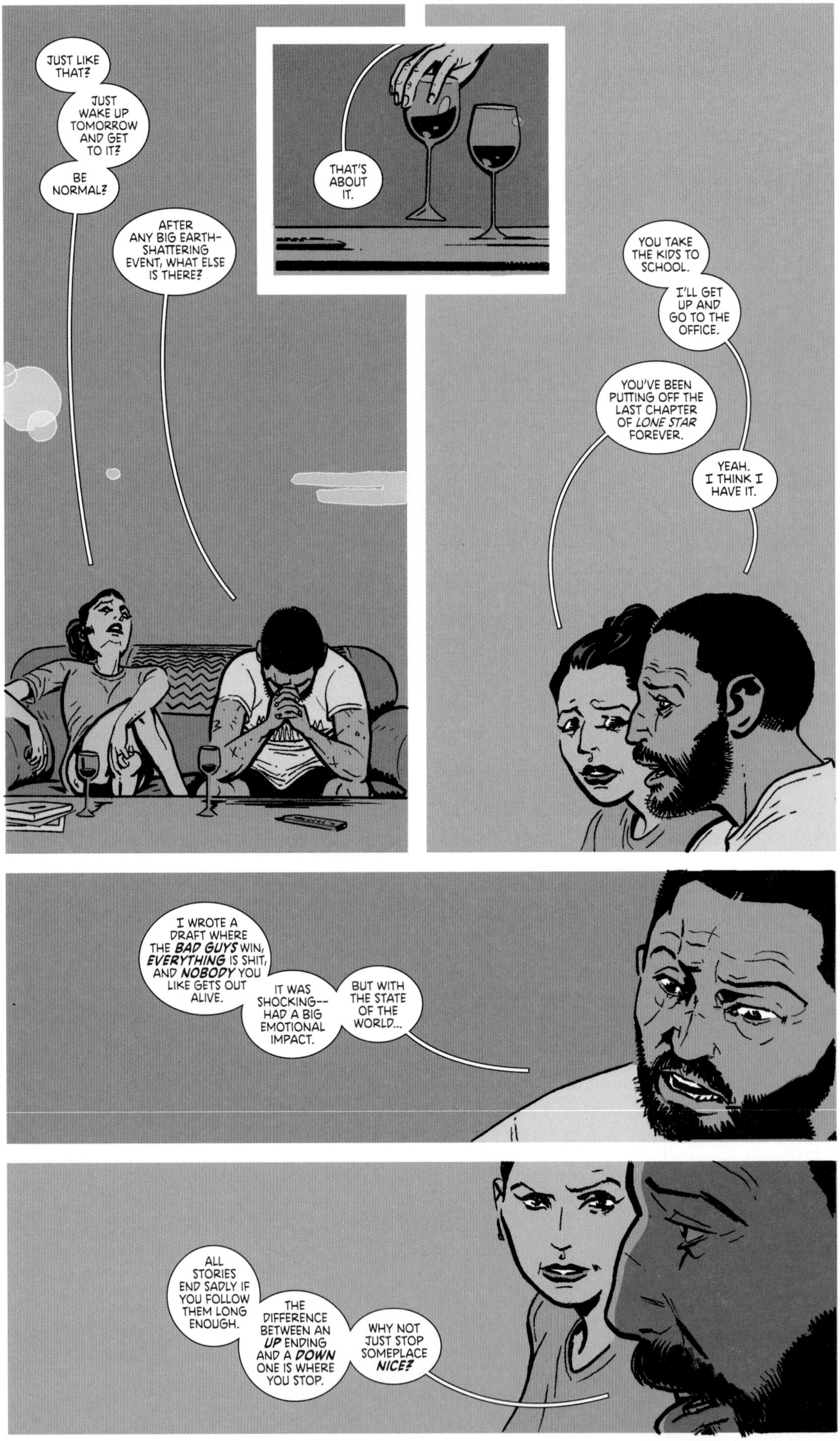
JUST LIKE THAT?
JUST WAKE UP TOMORROW AND GET TO IT?
BE NORMAL?
AFTER ANY BIG EARTH-SHATTERING EVENT, WHAT ELSE IS THERE?
THAT'S ABOUT IT.
YOU TAKE THE KIDS TO SCHOOL.
I'LL GET UP AND GO TO THE OFFICE.
YOU'VE BEEN PUTTING OFF THE LAST CHAPTER OF *LONE STAR* FOREVER.
YEAH. I THINK I HAVE IT.
I WROTE A DRAFT WHERE THE ***BAD GUYS*** WIN, ***EVERYTHING*** IS SHIT, AND ***NOBODY*** YOU LIKE GETS OUT ALIVE.
IT WAS SHOCKING-- HAD A BIG EMOTIONAL IMPACT.
BUT WITH THE STATE OF THE WORLD...
ALL STORIES END SADLY IF YOU FOLLOW THEM LONG ENOUGH.
THE DIFFERENCE BETWEEN AN ***UP*** ENDING AND A ***DOWN*** ONE IS WHERE YOU STOP.
WHY NOT JUST STOP SOMEPLACE ***NICE?***

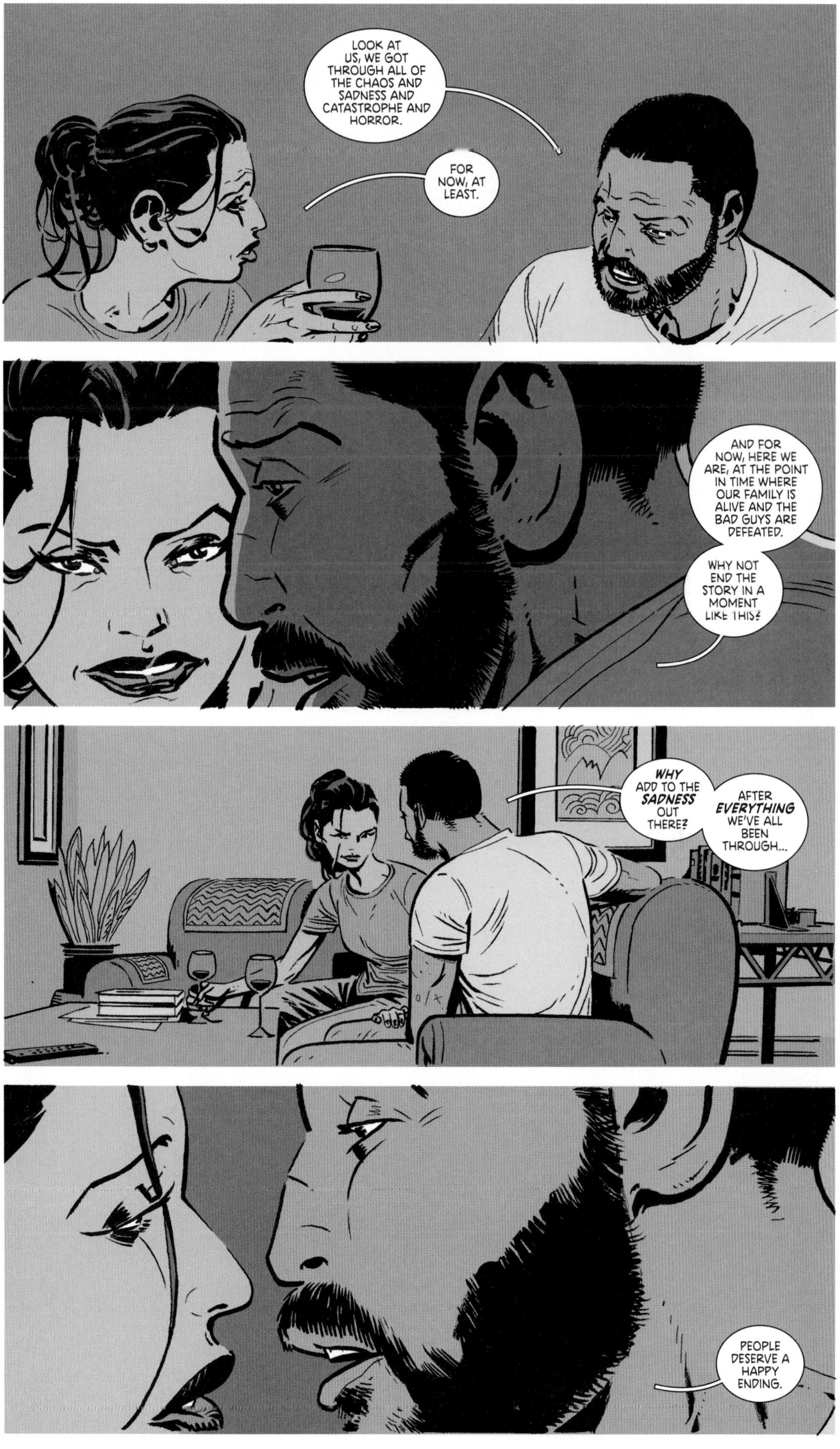
LOOK AT US, WE GOT THROUGH ALL OF THE CHAOS AND SADNESS AND CATASTROPHE AND HORROR.
FOR NOW, AT LEAST.
AND FOR NOW, HERE WE ARE, AT THE POINT IN TIME WHERE OUR FAMILY IS ALIVE AND THE BAD GUYS ARE DEFEATED.
WHY NOT END THE STORY IN A MOMENT LIKE THIS?
WHY ADD TO THE SADNESS OUT THERE?
AFTER EVERYTHING WE'VE ALL BEEN THROUGH...
PEOPLE DESERVE A HAPPY ENDING.

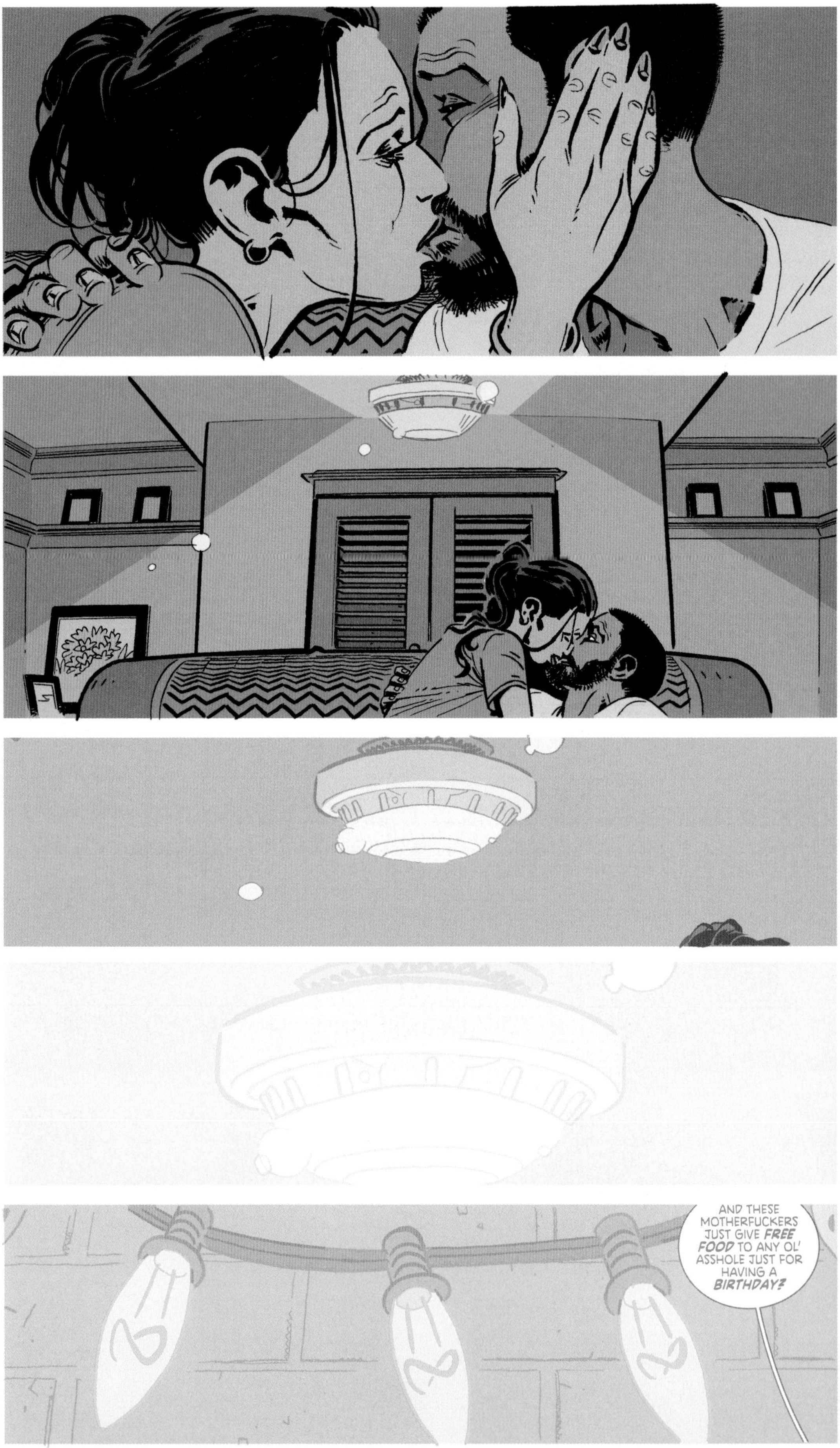
AND THESE MOTHERFUCKERS JUST GIVE *FREE FOOD* TO ANY OL' ASSHOLE JUST FOR HAVING A *BIRTHDAY?*

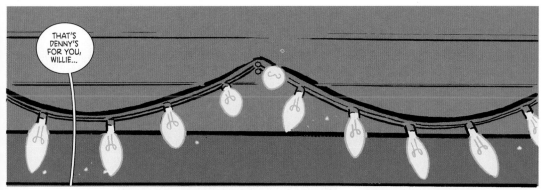

THAT'S DENNY'S FOR YOU, WILLIE...

A FAMILY BUSINESS OUT TO BUILD COMMUNITY THROUGH DILIGENT SERVICE TO THE UNDERCLASS.

A REAL MOM-AND-POP TYPE ESTABLISHMENT.

AN AMERICAN INSTITUTION.

RIGHT. BUT IT'S PETRA'S BIRTHDAY... WHAT ABOUT THE REST OF US?

SHE ORDERS THE FOOD, WE SPLIT IT.

ONE GRAND SLAM BREAKFAST *AIN'T* GONNA FEED US ALL, BILLY.

THEN WE WALK TO THE NEXT DENNY'S.

FOR A FREE EIGHT-DOLLAR PLATE OF FOOD?

AND *CAMARADERIE.*

TO TAKE ADVANTAGE OF SUCH A *NICE* THING THIS RESTAURANT DOES, IT FEELS... *GROSS.*

I MEAN, IT'S *CHRISTMAS*-TIME.

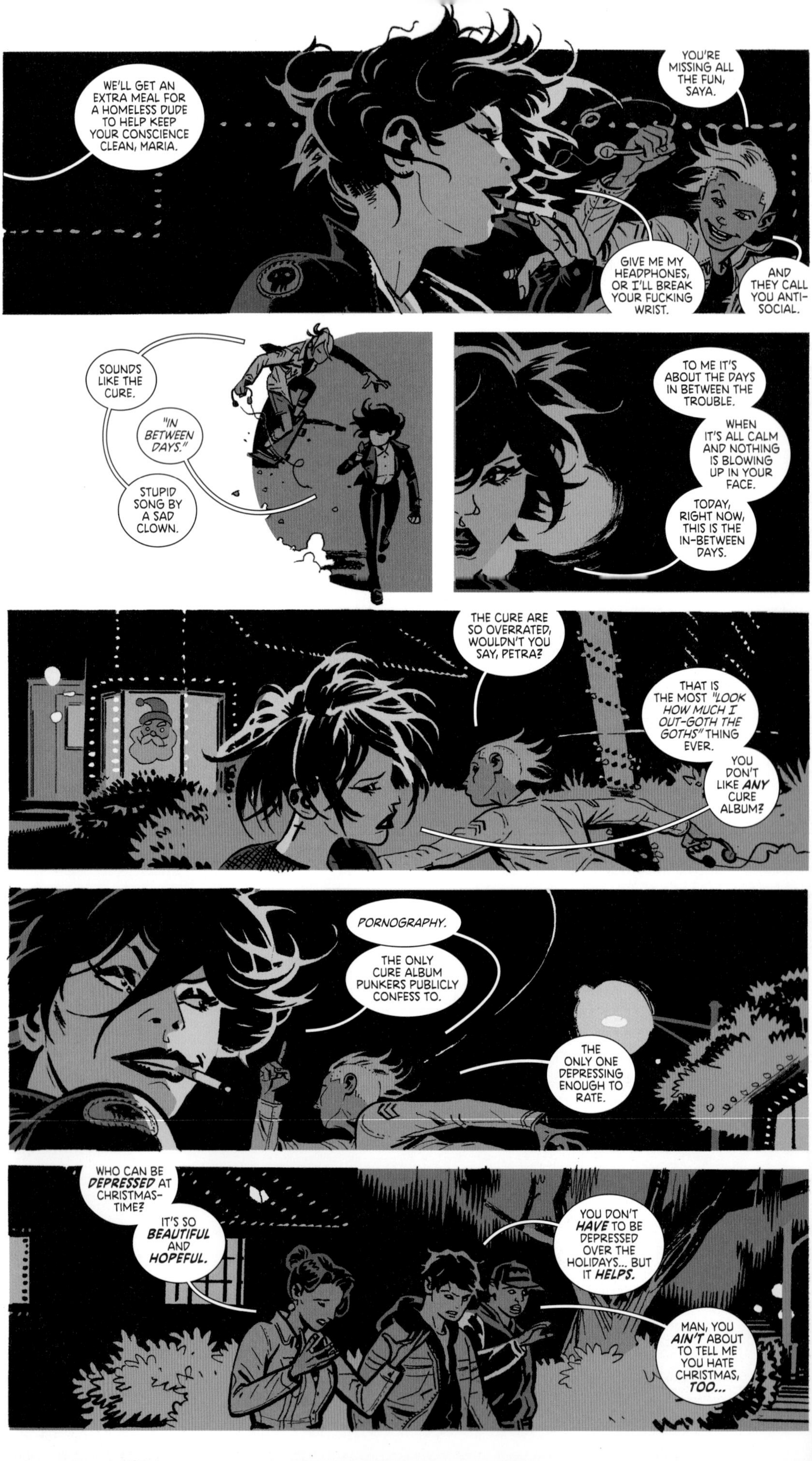
WE'LL GET AN EXTRA MEAL FOR A HOMELESS DUDE TO HELP KEEP YOUR CONSCIENCE CLEAN, MARIA.
YOU'RE MISSING ALL THE FUN, SAYA.
GIVE ME MY HEADPHONES, OR I'LL BREAK YOUR FUCKING WRIST.
AND THEY CALL YOU ANTI-SOCIAL.
SOUNDS LIKE THE CURE.
"IN BETWEEN DAYS."
STUPID SONG BY A SAD CLOWN.
TO ME IT'S ABOUT THE DAYS IN BETWEEN THE TROUBLE.
WHEN IT'S ALL CALM AND NOTHING IS BLOWING UP IN YOUR FACE.
TODAY, RIGHT NOW, THIS IS THE IN-BETWEEN DAYS.
THE CURE ARE SO OVERRATED, WOULDN'T YOU SAY, PETRA?
THAT IS THE MOST "LOOK HOW MUCH I OUT-GOTH THE GOTHS" THING EVER.
YOU DON'T LIKE ANY CURE ALBUM?
PORNOGRAPHY.
THE ONLY CURE ALBUM PUNKERS PUBLICLY CONFESS TO.
THE ONLY ONE DEPRESSING ENOUGH TO RATE.
WHO CAN BE DEPRESSED AT CHRISTMAS-TIME?
IT'S SO BEAUTIFUL AND HOPEFUL.
YOU DON'T HAVE TO BE DEPRESSED OVER THE HOLIDAYS... BUT IT HELPS.
MAN, YOU AIN'T ABOUT TO TELL ME YOU HATE CHRISTMAS, TOO...

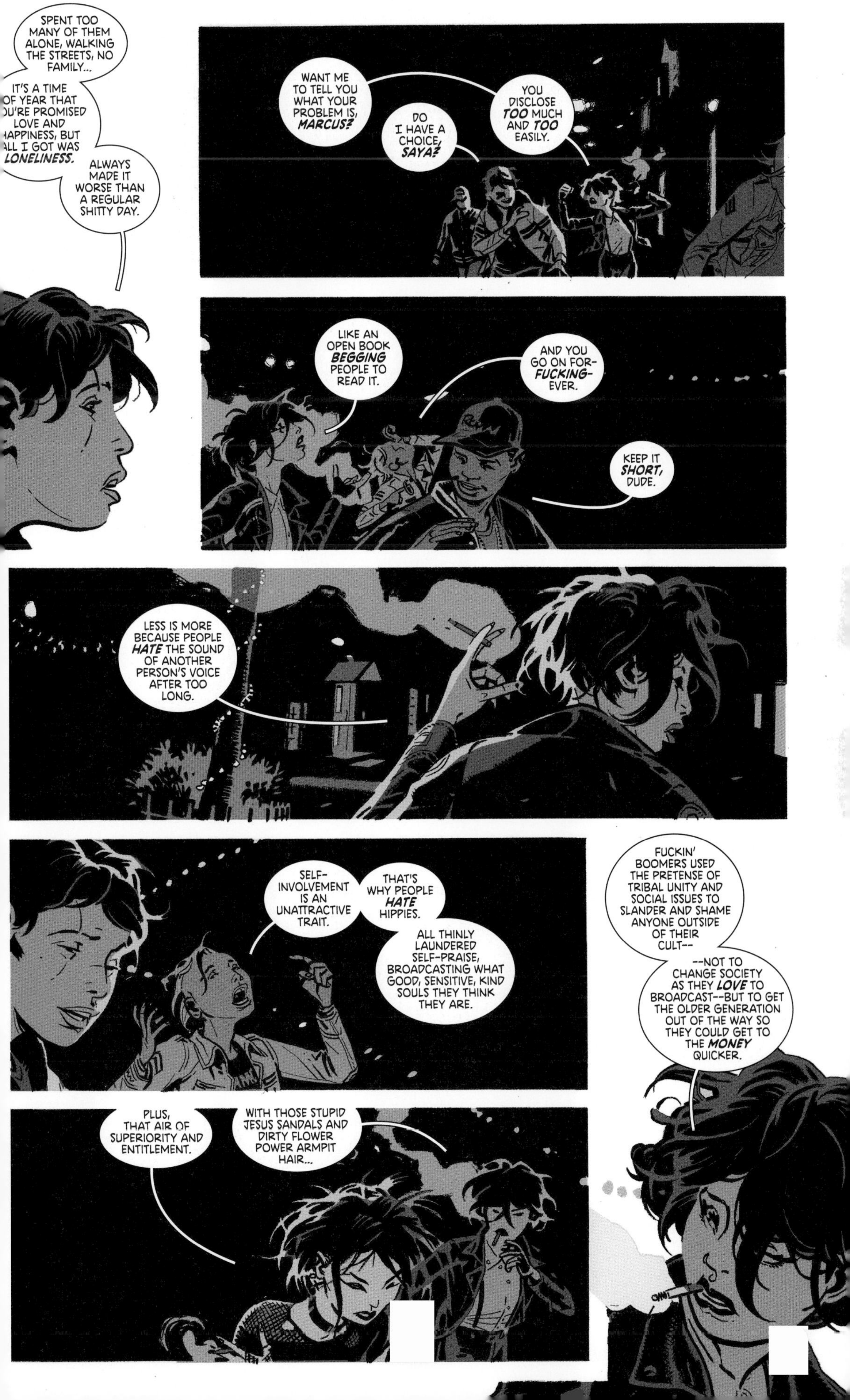
SPENT TOO MANY OF THEM ALONE, WALKING THE STREETS, NO FAMILY...
IT'S A TIME OF YEAR THAT YOU'RE PROMISED LOVE AND HAPPINESS, BUT ALL I GOT WAS LONELINESS.
ALWAYS MADE IT WORSE THAN A REGULAR SHITTY DAY.
WANT ME TO TELL YOU WHAT YOUR PROBLEM IS, MARCUS?
DO I HAVE A CHOICE, SAYA?
YOU DISCLOSE TOO MUCH AND TOO EASILY.
LIKE AN OPEN BOOK BEGGING PEOPLE TO READ IT.
AND YOU GO ON FOR-FUCKING-EVER.
KEEP IT SHORT, DUDE.
LESS IS MORE BECAUSE PEOPLE HATE THE SOUND OF ANOTHER PERSON'S VOICE AFTER TOO LONG.
SELF-INVOLVEMENT IS AN UNATTRACTIVE TRAIT.
THAT'S WHY PEOPLE HATE HIPPIES.
ALL THINLY LAUNDERED SELF-PRAISE, BROADCASTING WHAT GOOD, SENSITIVE, KIND SOULS THEY THINK THEY ARE.
FUCKIN' BOOMERS USED THE PRETENSE OF TRIBAL UNITY AND SOCIAL ISSUES TO SLANDER AND SHAME ANYONE OUTSIDE OF THEIR CULT--
--NOT TO CHANGE SOCIETY AS THEY LOVE TO BROADCAST--BUT TO GET THE OLDER GENERATION OUT OF THE WAY SO THEY COULD GET TO THE MONEY QUICKER.
PLUS, THAT AIR OF SUPERIORITY AND ENTITLEMENT.
WITH THOSE STUPID JESUS SANDALS AND DIRTY FLOWER POWER ARMPIT HAIR...

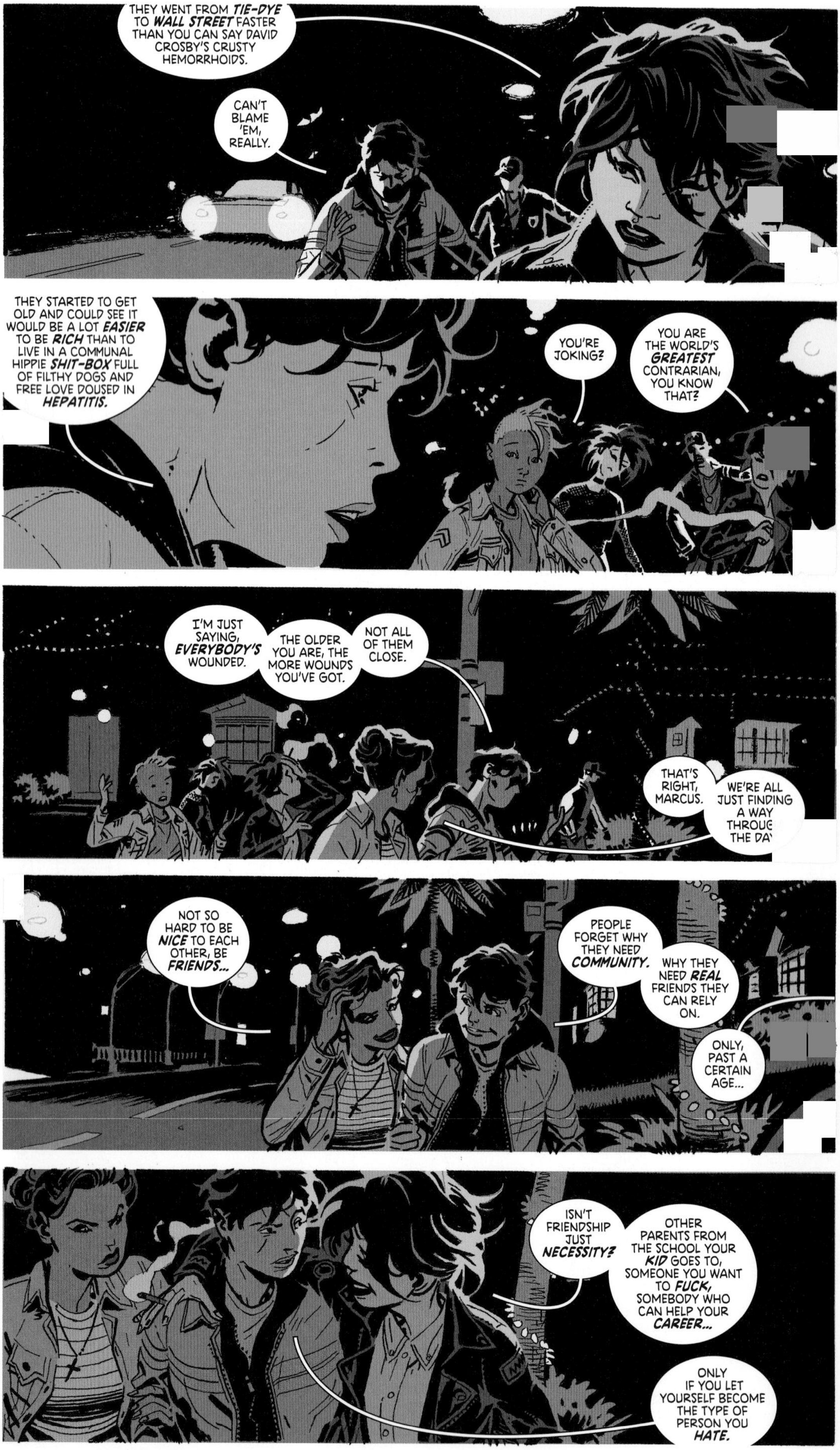

THEY WENT FROM TIE-DYE TO WALL STREET FASTER THAN YOU CAN SAY DAVID CROSBY'S CRUSTY HEMORRHOIDS.
CAN'T BLAME 'EM, REALLY.
THEY STARTED TO GET OLD AND COULD SEE IT WOULD BE A LOT EASIER TO BE RICH THAN TO LIVE IN A COMMUNAL HIPPIE SHIT-BOX FULL OF FILTHY DOGS AND FREE LOVE DOUSED IN HEPATITIS.
YOU'RE JOKING?
YOU ARE THE WORLD'S GREATEST CONTRARIAN, YOU KNOW THAT?
I'M JUST SAYING, EVERYBODY'S WOUNDED.
THE OLDER YOU ARE, THE MORE WOUNDS YOU'VE GOT.
NOT ALL OF THEM CLOSE.
THAT'S RIGHT, MARCUS.
NOT SO HARD TO BE NICE TO EACH OTHER, BE FRIENDS...
PEOPLE FORGET WHY THEY NEED COMMUNITY.
WHY THEY NEED REAL FRIENDS THEY CAN RELY ON.
ONLY, PAST A CERTAIN AGE...
ISN'T FRIENDSHIP JUST NECESSITY?
OTHER PARENTS FROM THE SCHOOL YOUR KID GOES TO, SOMEONE YOU WANT TO FUCK, SOMEBODY WHO CAN HELP YOUR CAREER...
ONLY IF YOU LET YOURSELF BECOME THE TYPE OF PERSON YOU HATE.

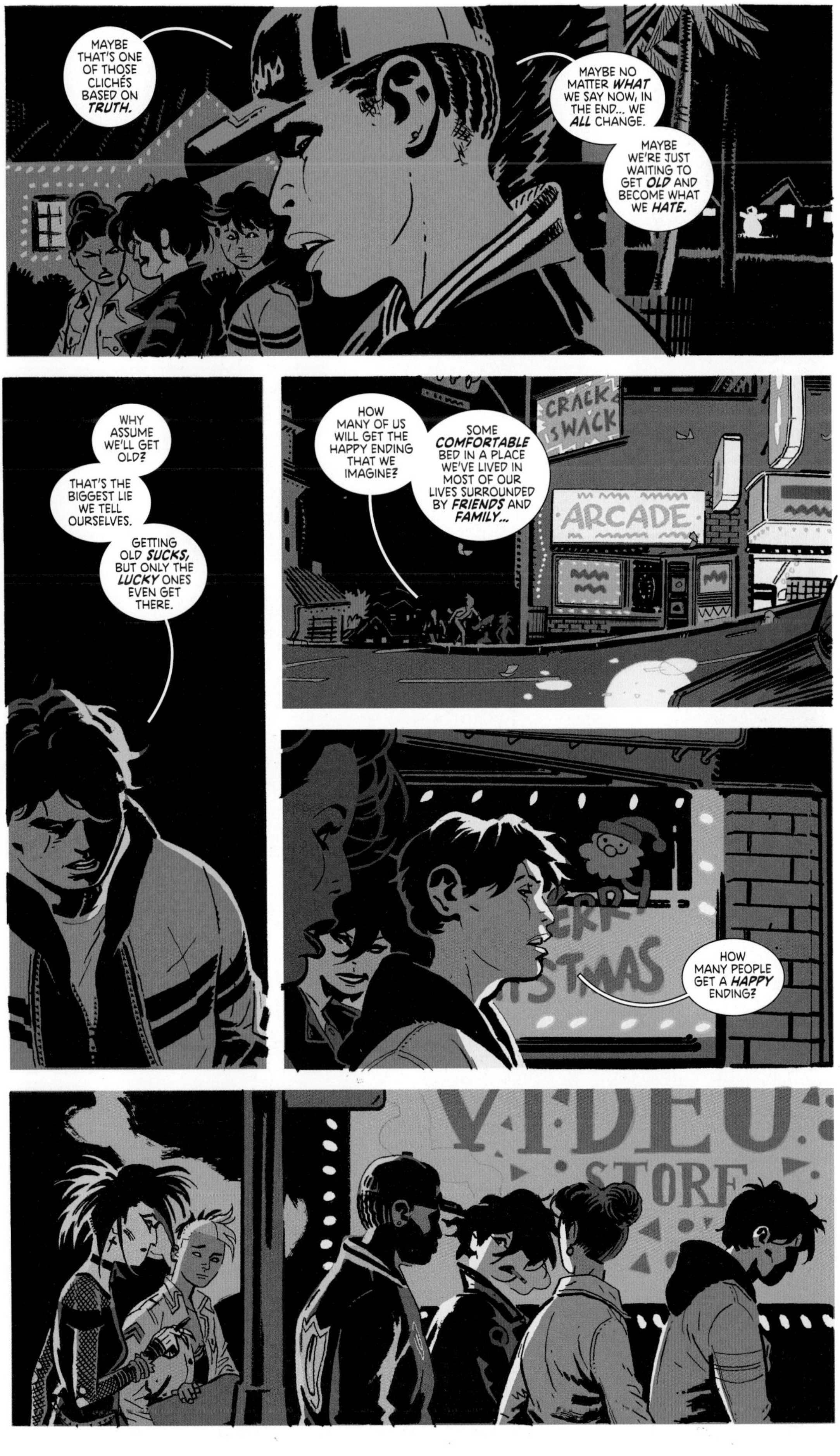
MAYBE THAT'S ONE OF THOSE CLICHÉS BASED ON *TRUTH.*
MAYBE NO MATTER *WHAT* WE SAY NOW, IN THE END... WE *ALL* CHANGE.
MAYBE WE'RE JUST WAITING TO GET *OLD* AND BECOME WHAT WE *HATE.*
WHY ASSUME WE'LL GET OLD?
THAT'S THE BIGGEST LIE WE TELL OURSELVES.
GETTING OLD *SUCKS,* BUT ONLY THE *LUCKY* ONES EVEN GET THERE.
CRACK IS WACK
HOW MANY OF US WILL GET THE HAPPY ENDING THAT WE IMAGINE?
SOME *COMFORTABLE* BED IN A PLACE WE'VE LIVED IN MOST OF OUR LIVES SURROUNDED BY *FRIENDS* AND *FAMILY...*
ARCADE
HOW MANY PEOPLE GET A *HAPPY* ENDING?
VIDEO
STORE

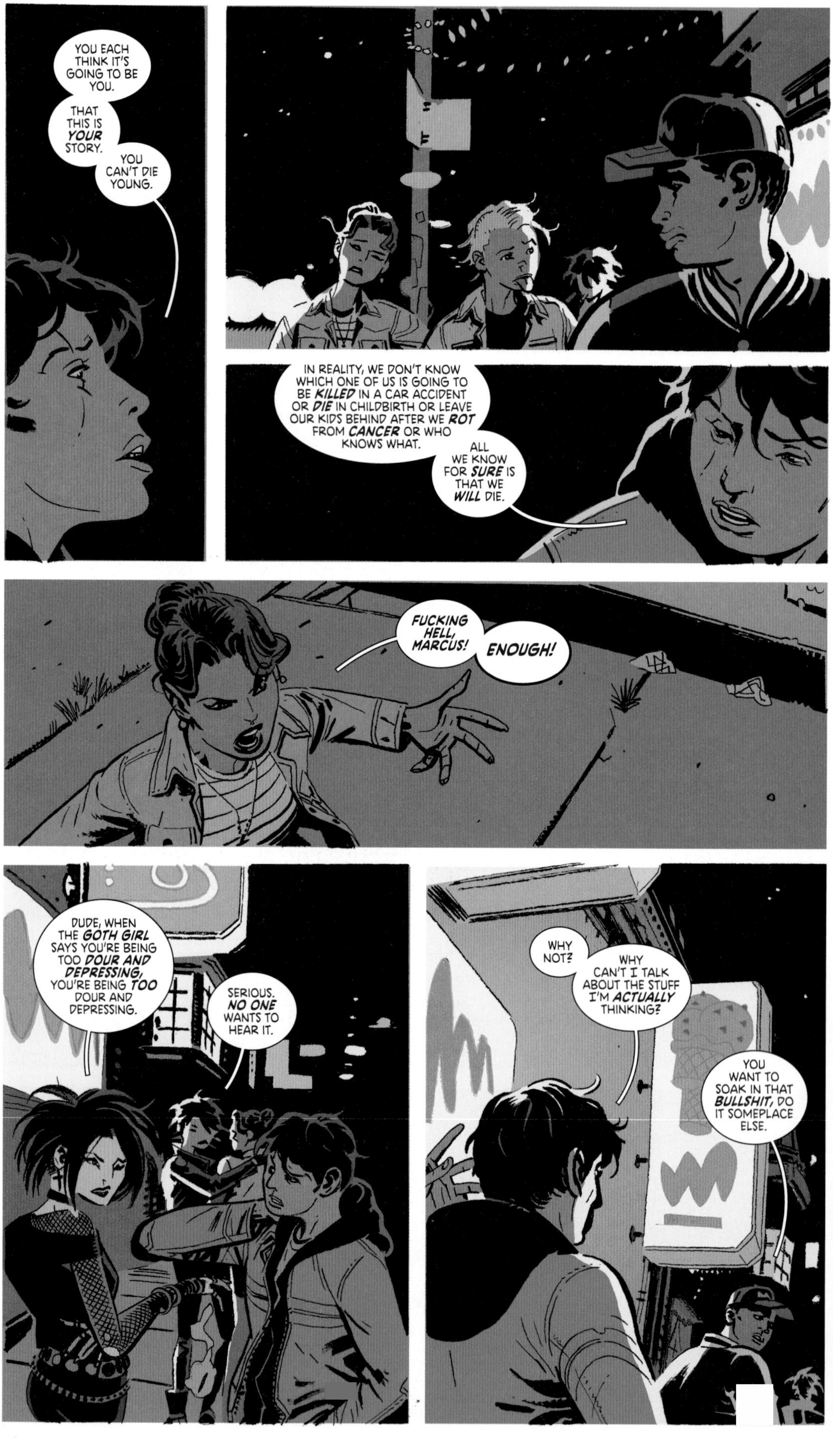
YOU EACH THINK IT'S GOING TO BE YOU.
THAT THIS IS *YOUR* STORY.
YOU CAN'T DIE YOUNG.
IN REALITY, WE DON'T KNOW WHICH ONE OF US IS GOING TO BE *KILLED* IN A CAR ACCIDENT OR *DIE* IN CHILDBIRTH OR LEAVE OUR KIDS BEHIND AFTER WE *ROT* FROM *CANCER* OR WHO KNOWS WHAT.
ALL WE KNOW FOR *SURE* IS THAT WE *WILL* DIE.
FUCKING HELL, MARCUS!
ENOUGH!
DUDE, WHEN THE *GOTH GIRL* SAYS YOU'RE BEING TOO *DOUR AND DEPRESSING,* YOU'RE BEING *TOO* DOUR AND DEPRESSING.
SERIOUS. *NO ONE* WANTS TO HEAR IT.
WHY NOT?
WHY CAN'T I TALK ABOUT THE STUFF I'M *ACTUALLY* THINKING?
YOU WANT TO SOAK IN THAT *BULLSHIT,* DO IT SOMEPLACE ELSE.

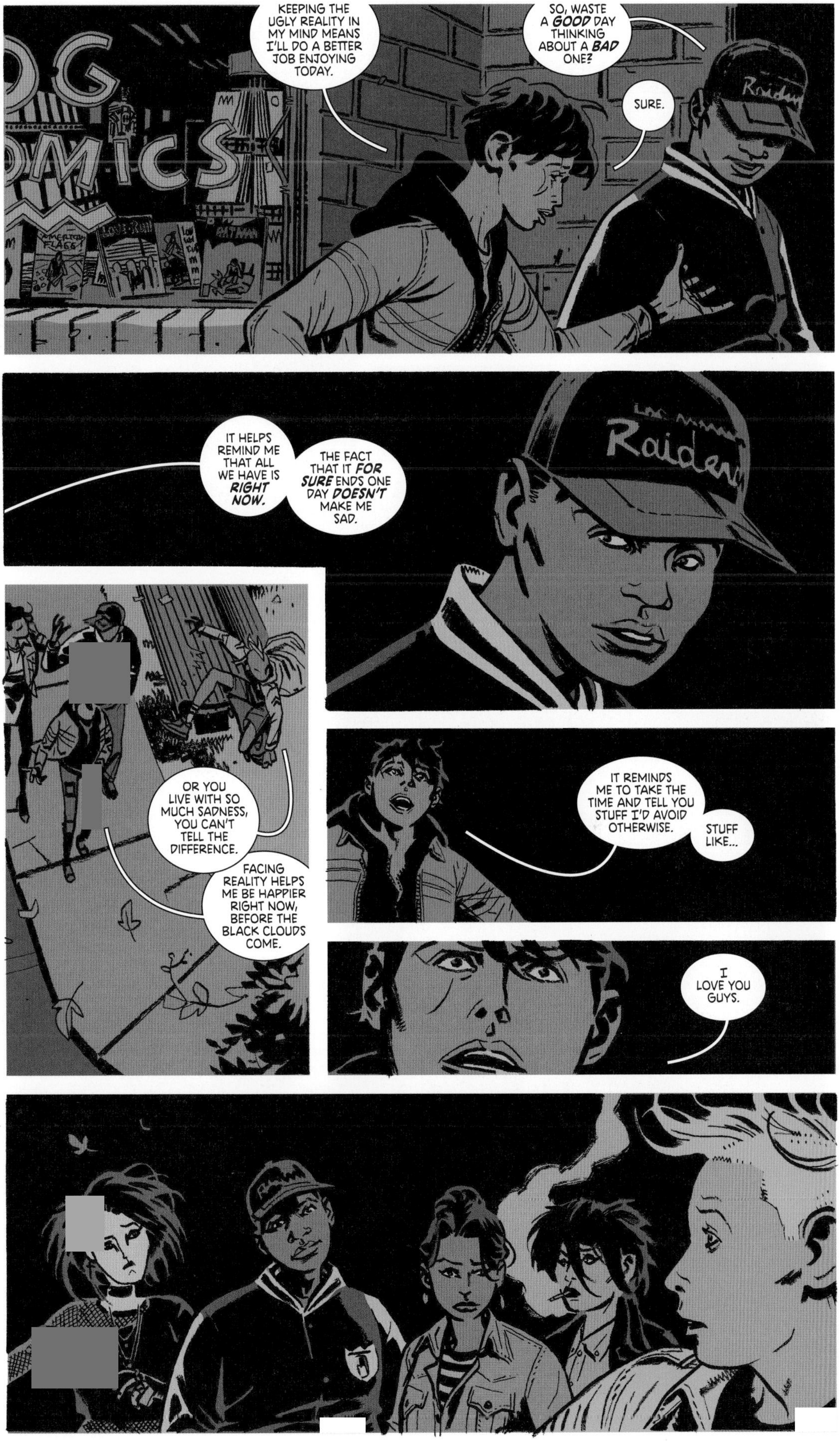
KEEPING THE UGLY REALITY IN MY MIND MEANS I'LL DO A BETTER JOB ENJOYING TODAY.
SO, WASTE A **GOOD** DAY THINKING ABOUT A **BAD** ONE?
SURE.
IT HELPS REMIND ME THAT ALL WE HAVE IS **RIGHT NOW.**
THE FACT THAT IT **FOR SURE** ENDS ONE DAY **DOESN'T** MAKE ME SAD.
OR YOU LIVE WITH SO MUCH SADNESS, YOU CAN'T TELL THE DIFFERENCE.
FACING REALITY HELPS ME BE HAPPIER RIGHT NOW, BEFORE THE BLACK CLOUDS COME.
IT REMINDS ME TO TAKE THE TIME AND TELL YOU STUFF I'D AVOID OTHERWISE.
STUFF LIKE...
I LOVE YOU GUYS.

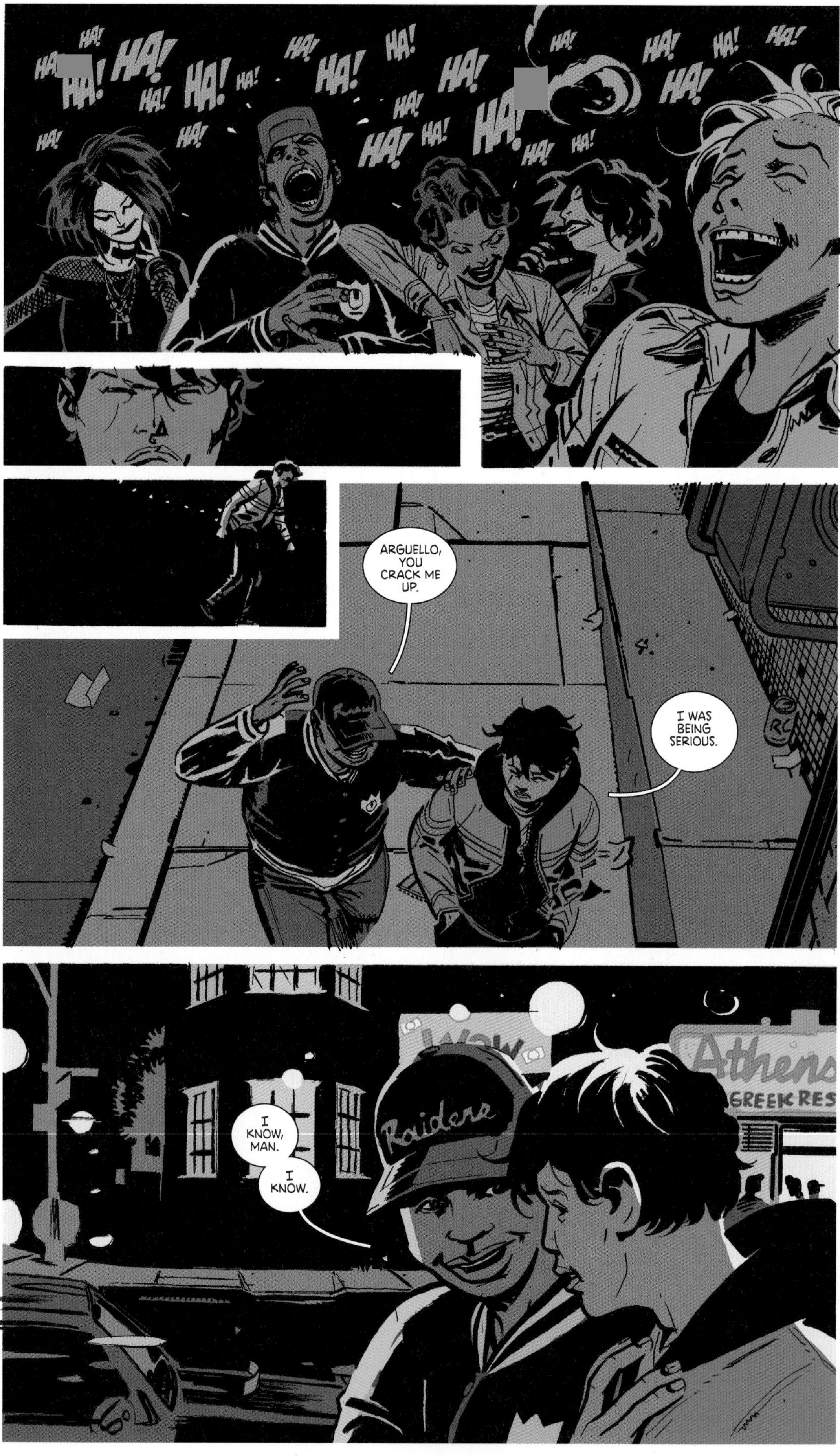

HA! HA! HA! HA! HA! HA! HA! HA! HA! HA! HA! HA! HA! HA! HA! HA! HA! HA! HA! HA! HA! HA! HA!
ARGUELLO, YOU CRACK ME UP.
I WAS BEING SERIOUS.
Raiders
Athens
GREEK RES
I KNOW, MAN.
I KNOW.

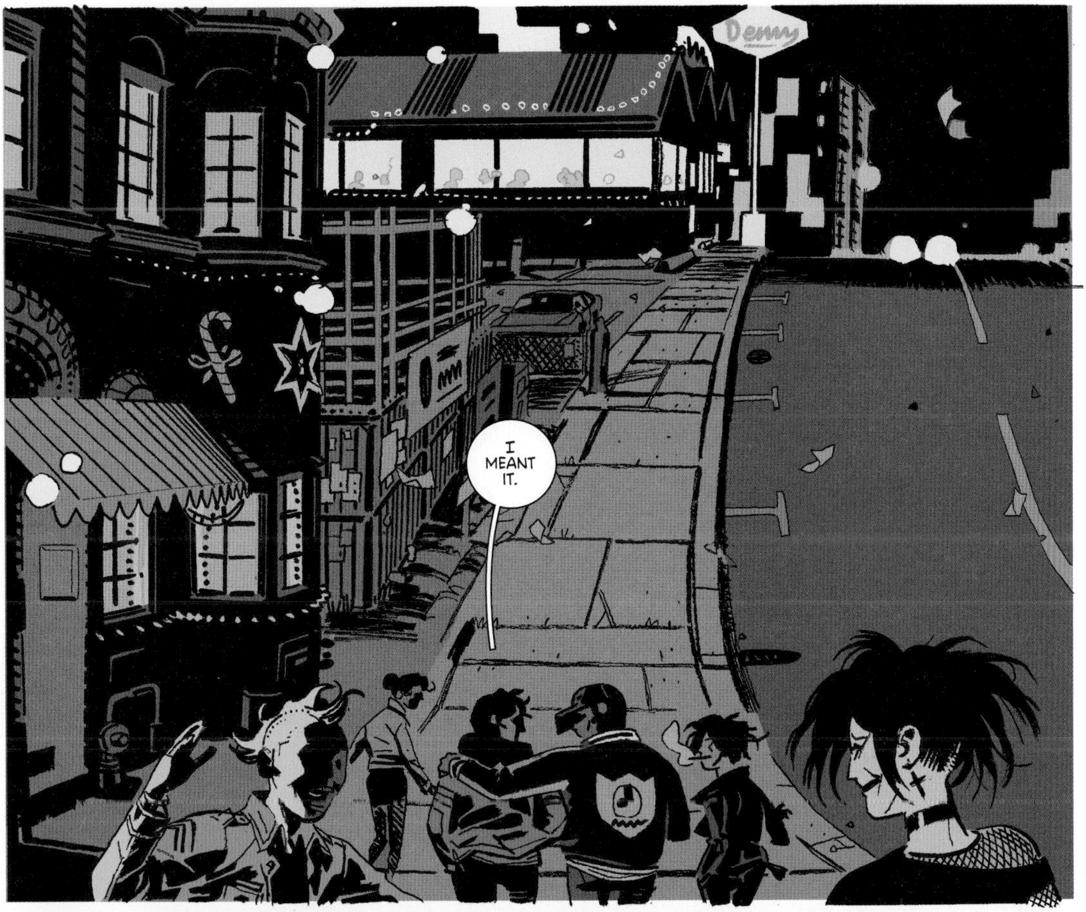
I MEANT IT.

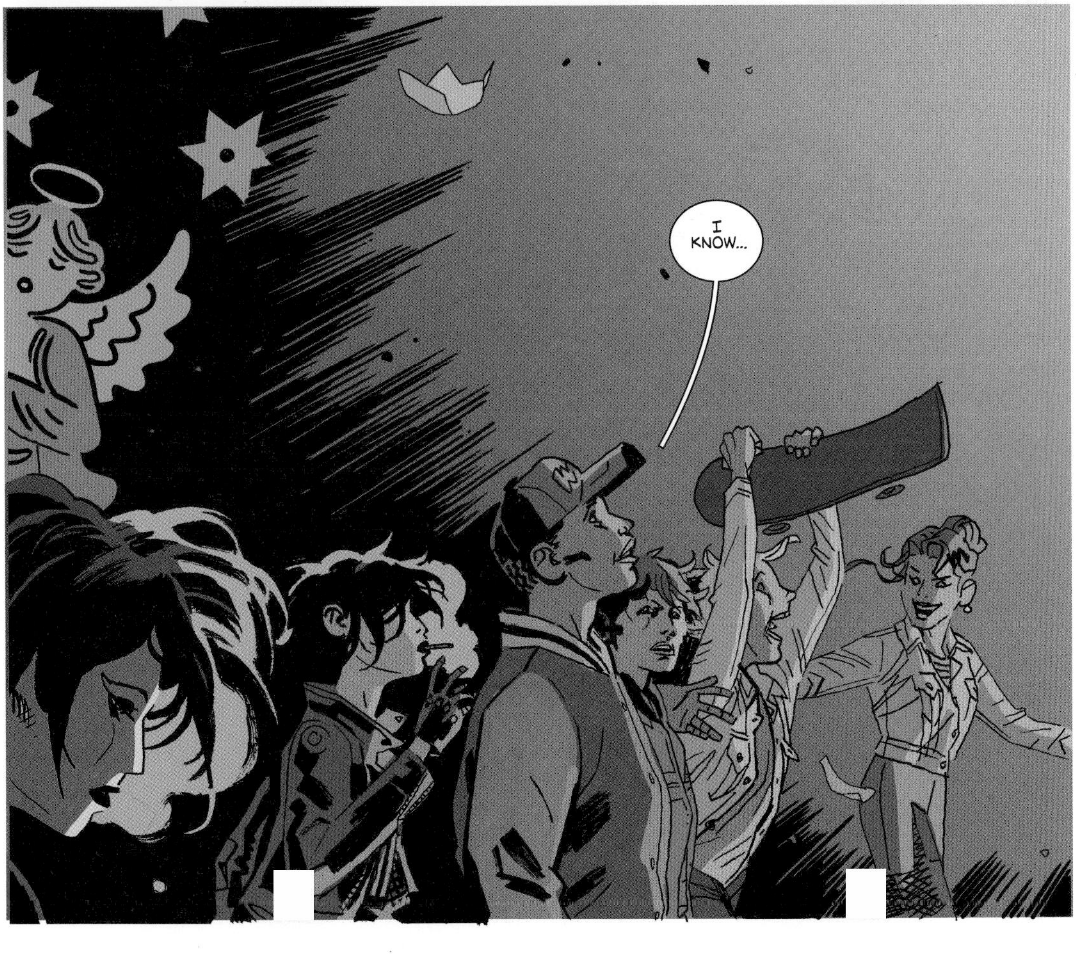
I KNOW...

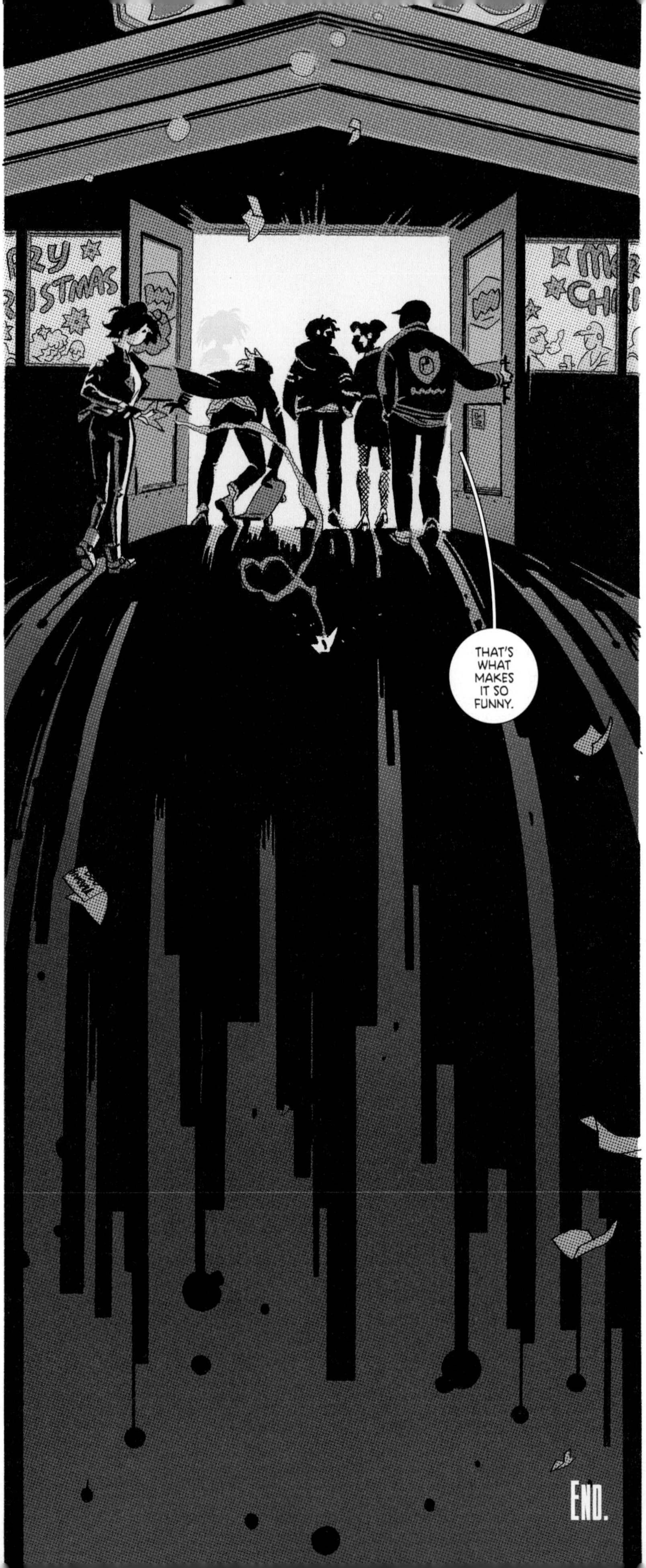
THAT'S WHAT MAKES IT SO FUNNY.
END.

EST 1637

IN VITAM MORTEM

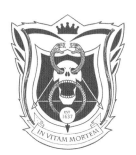

COVER GALLERY

#53 COVER BY **WES CRAIG**

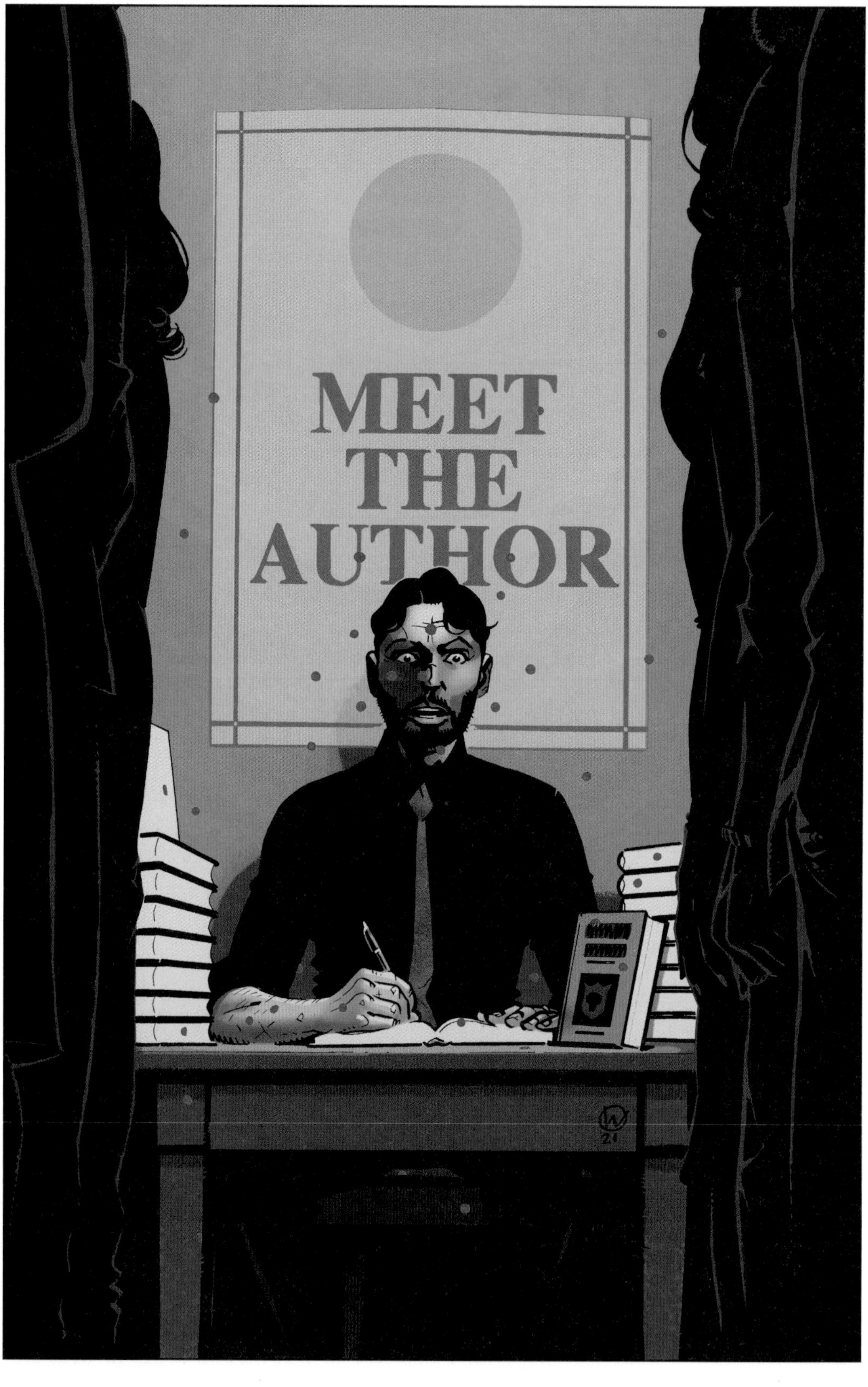
MEET
THE
AUTHOR

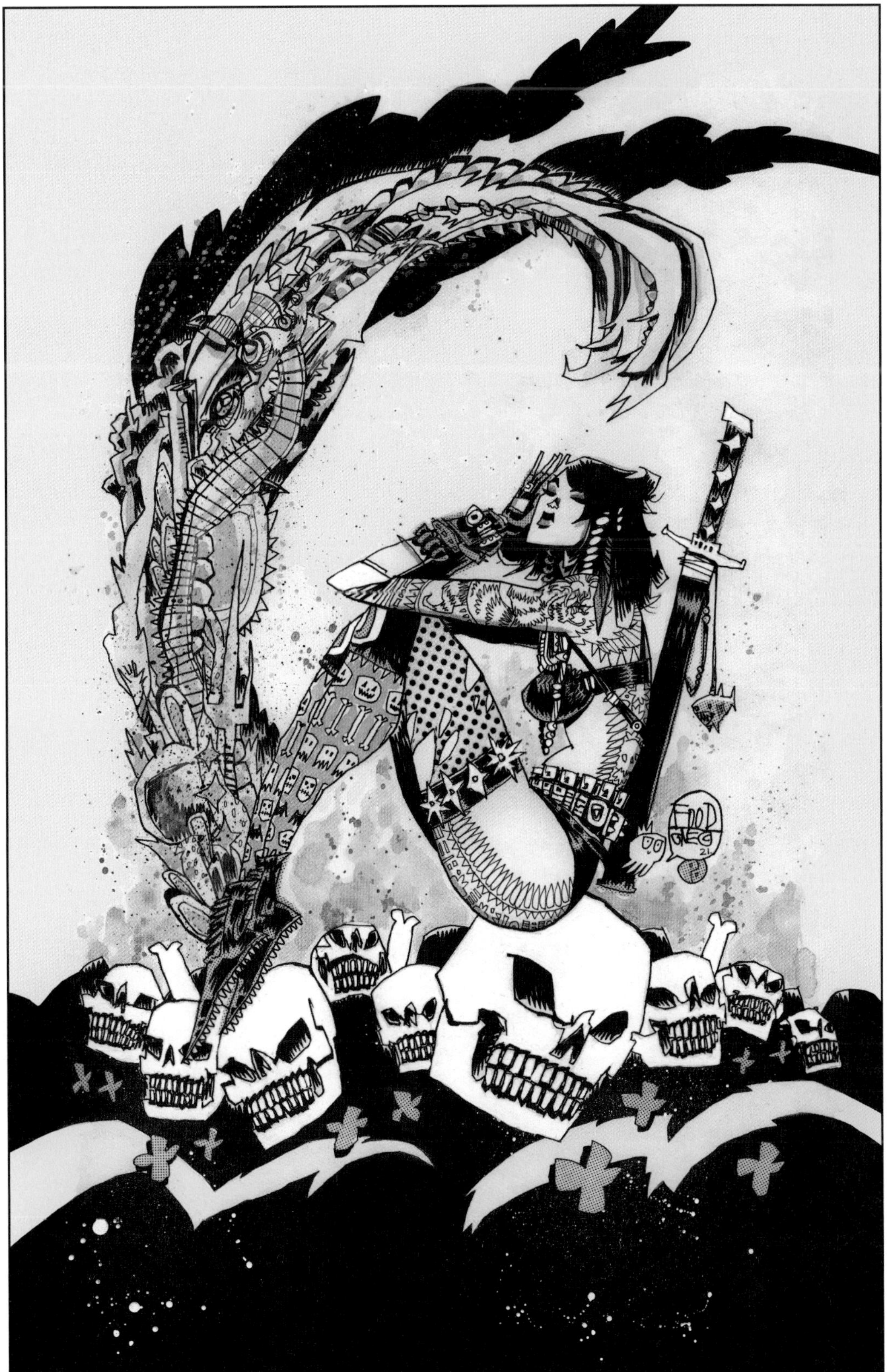

#53 VARIANT BY **JIM MAHFOOD**

#54 COVER BY **WES CRAIG**

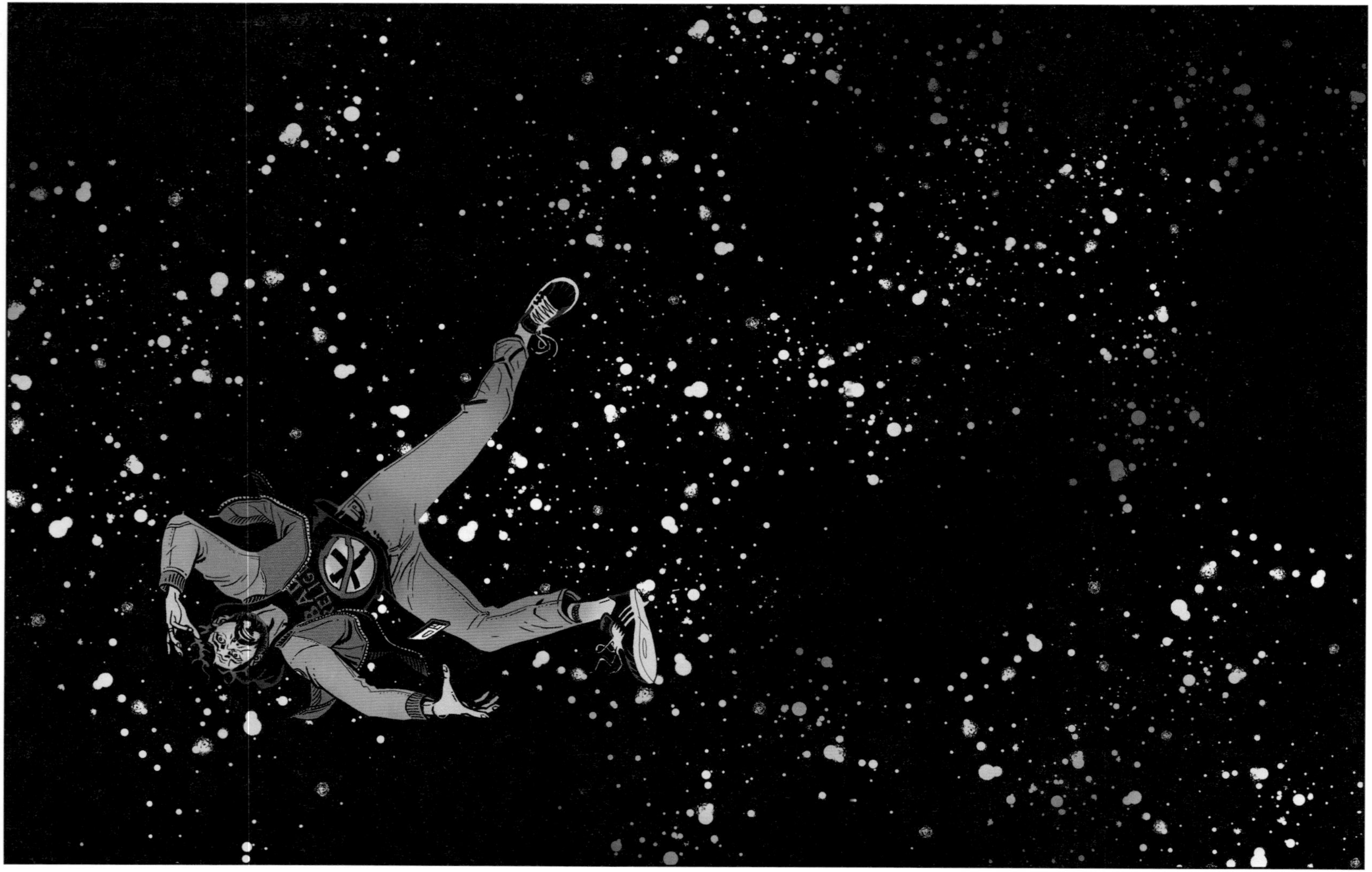

#54 VARIANT BY **MAX FIUMARA**

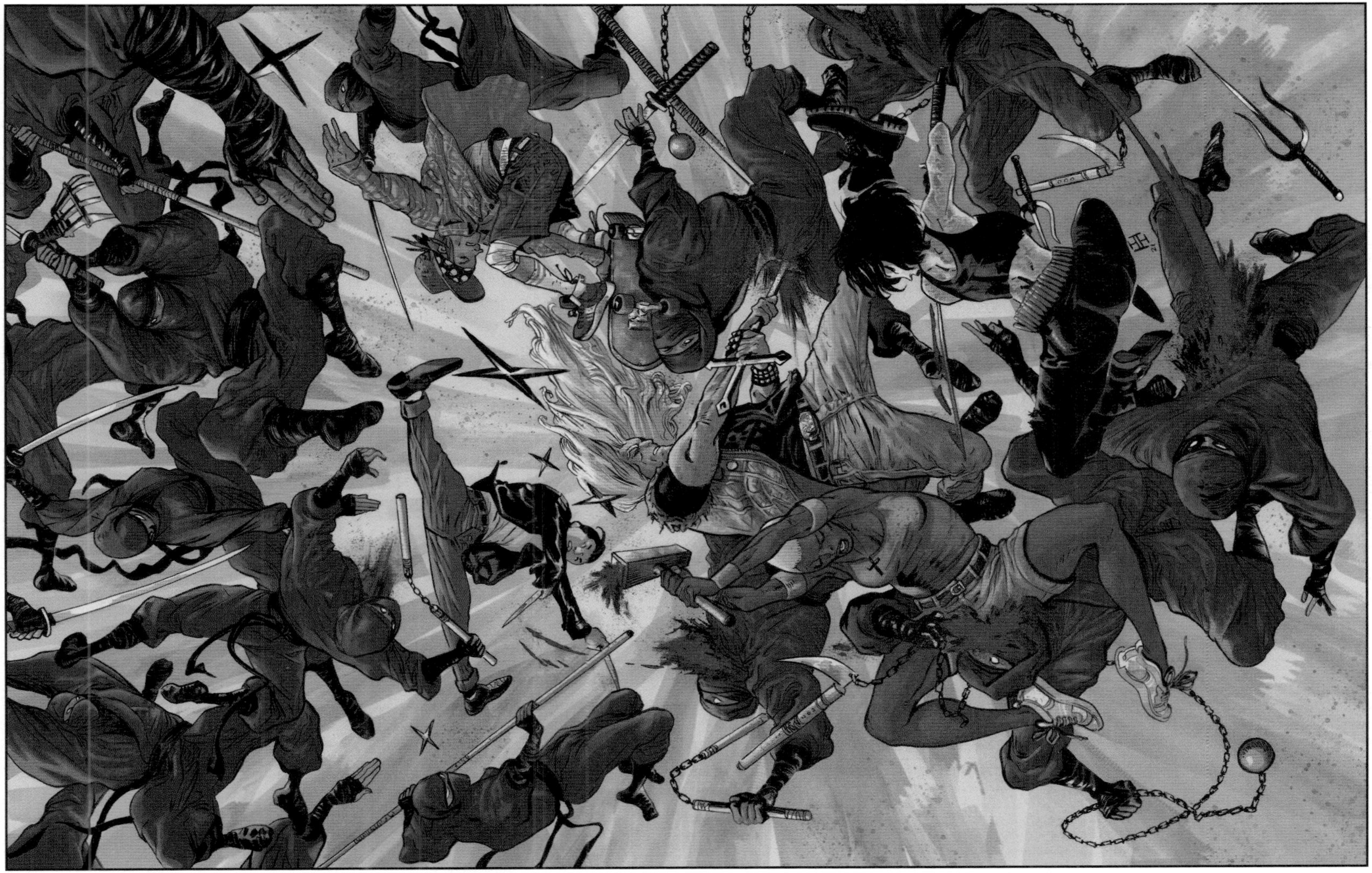

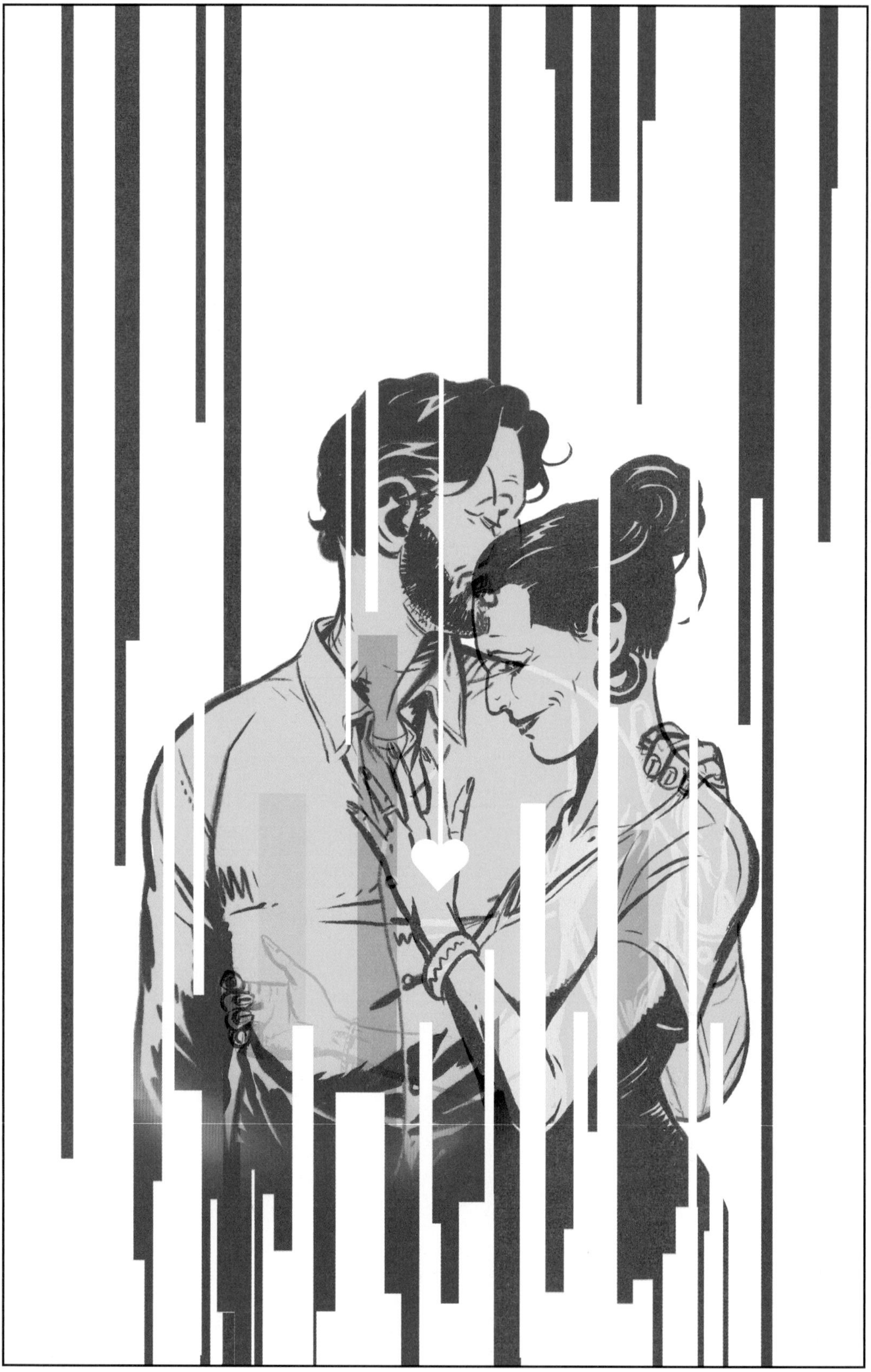

#55 COVER BY **WES CRAIG**

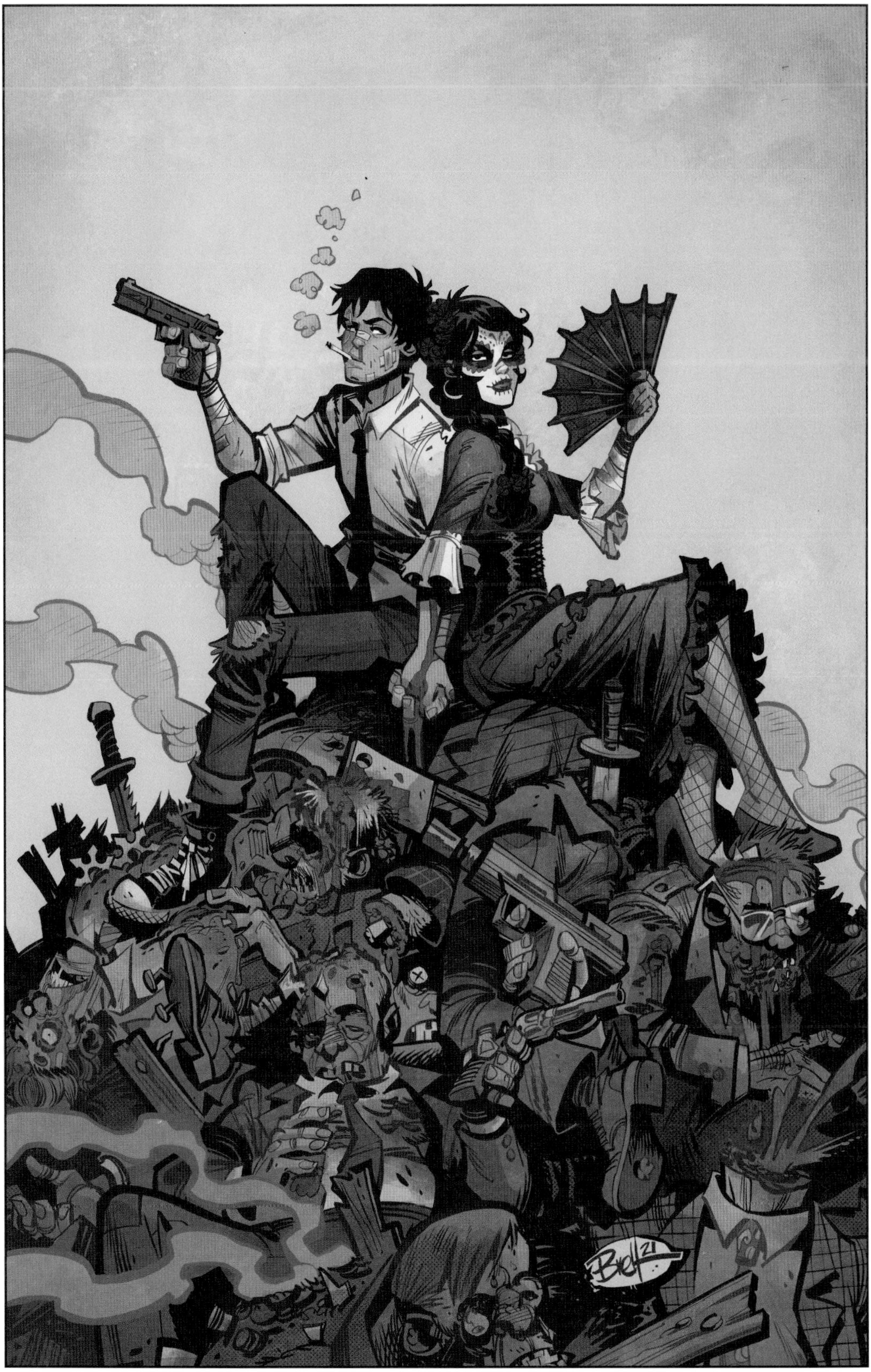

#55 VARIANT BY **BRETT PARSON**

#56 COVER BY **WES CRAIG**

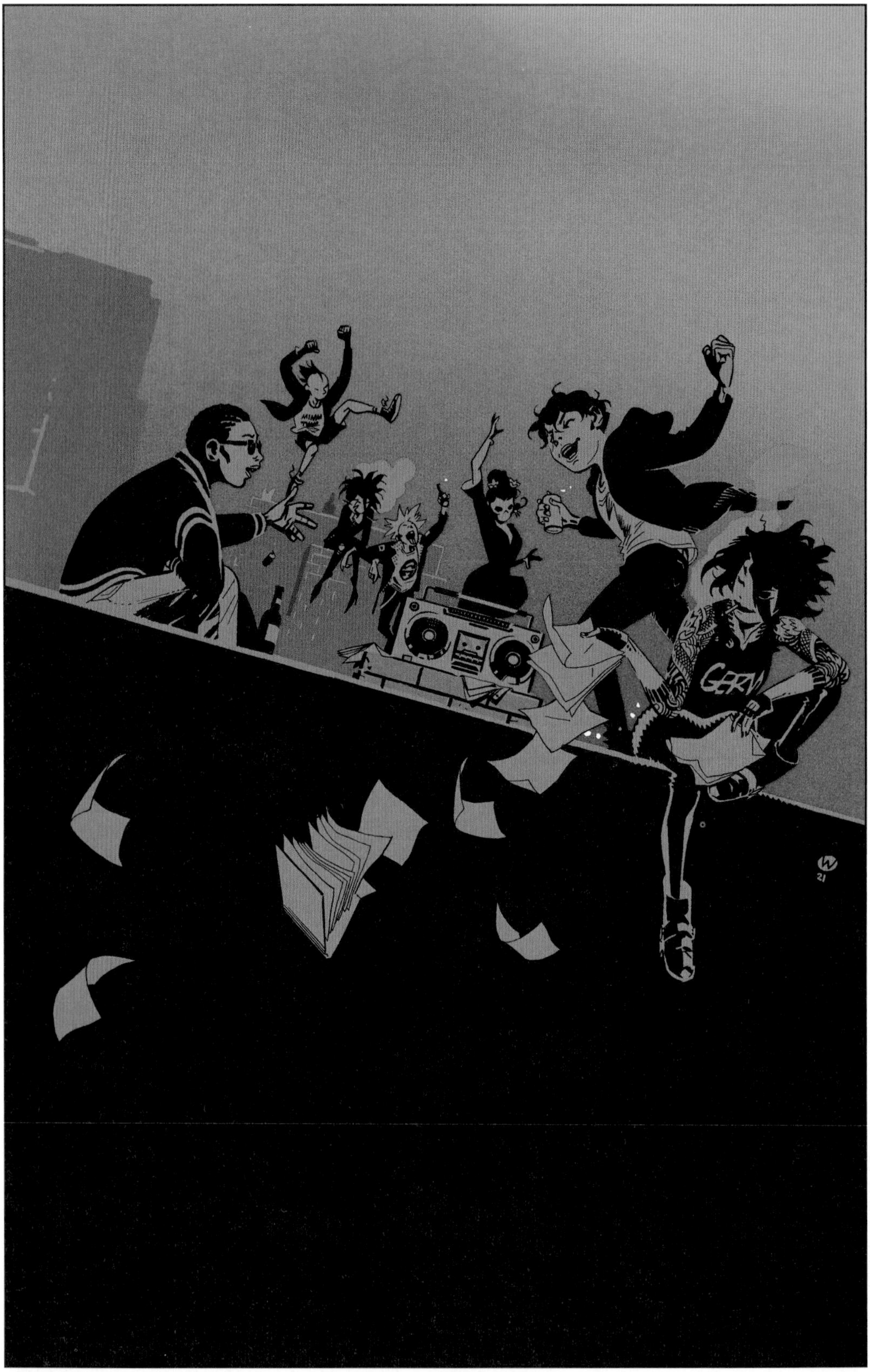

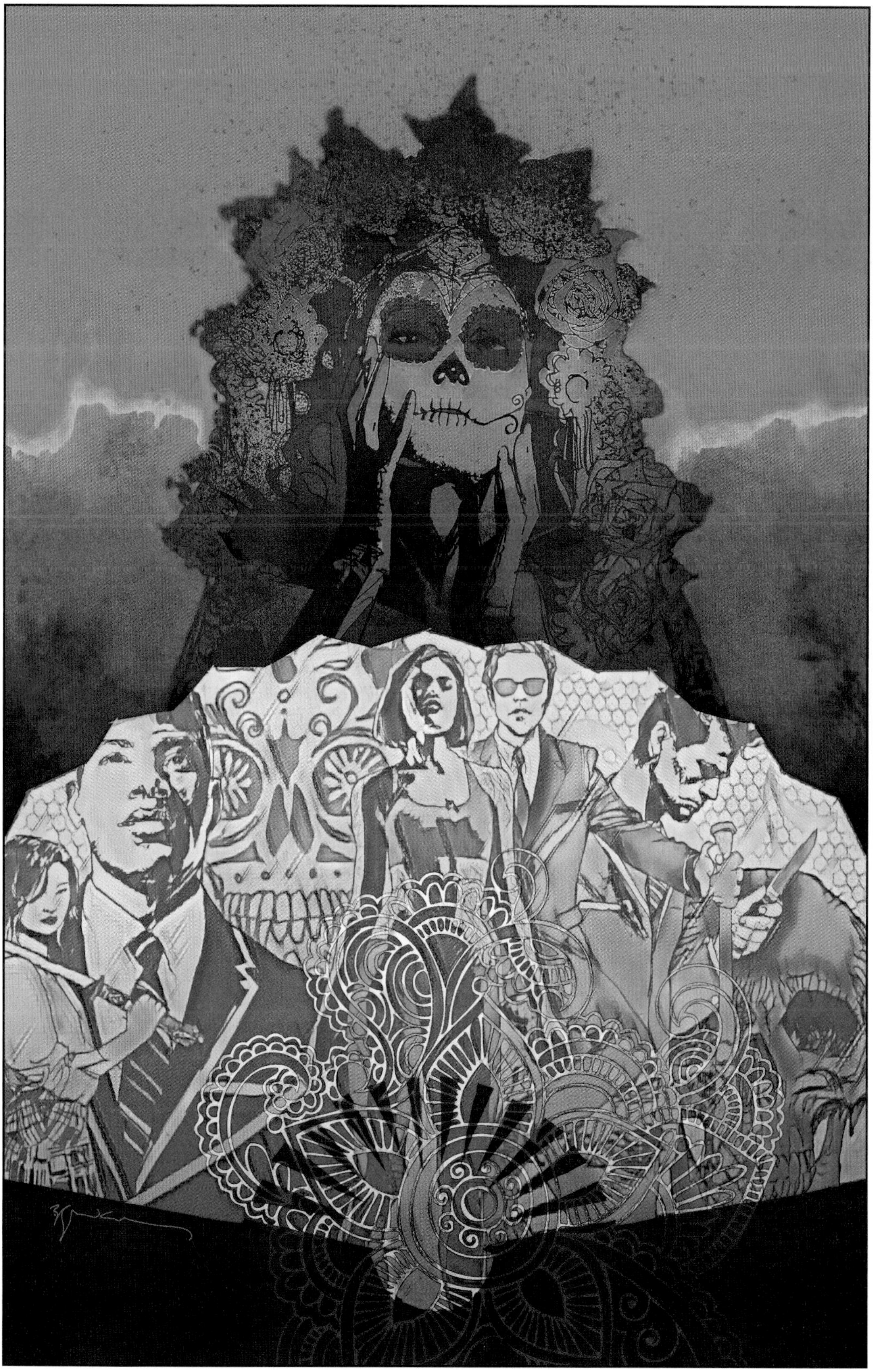

#56 VARIANT BY **BILL SIENKIEWICZ**

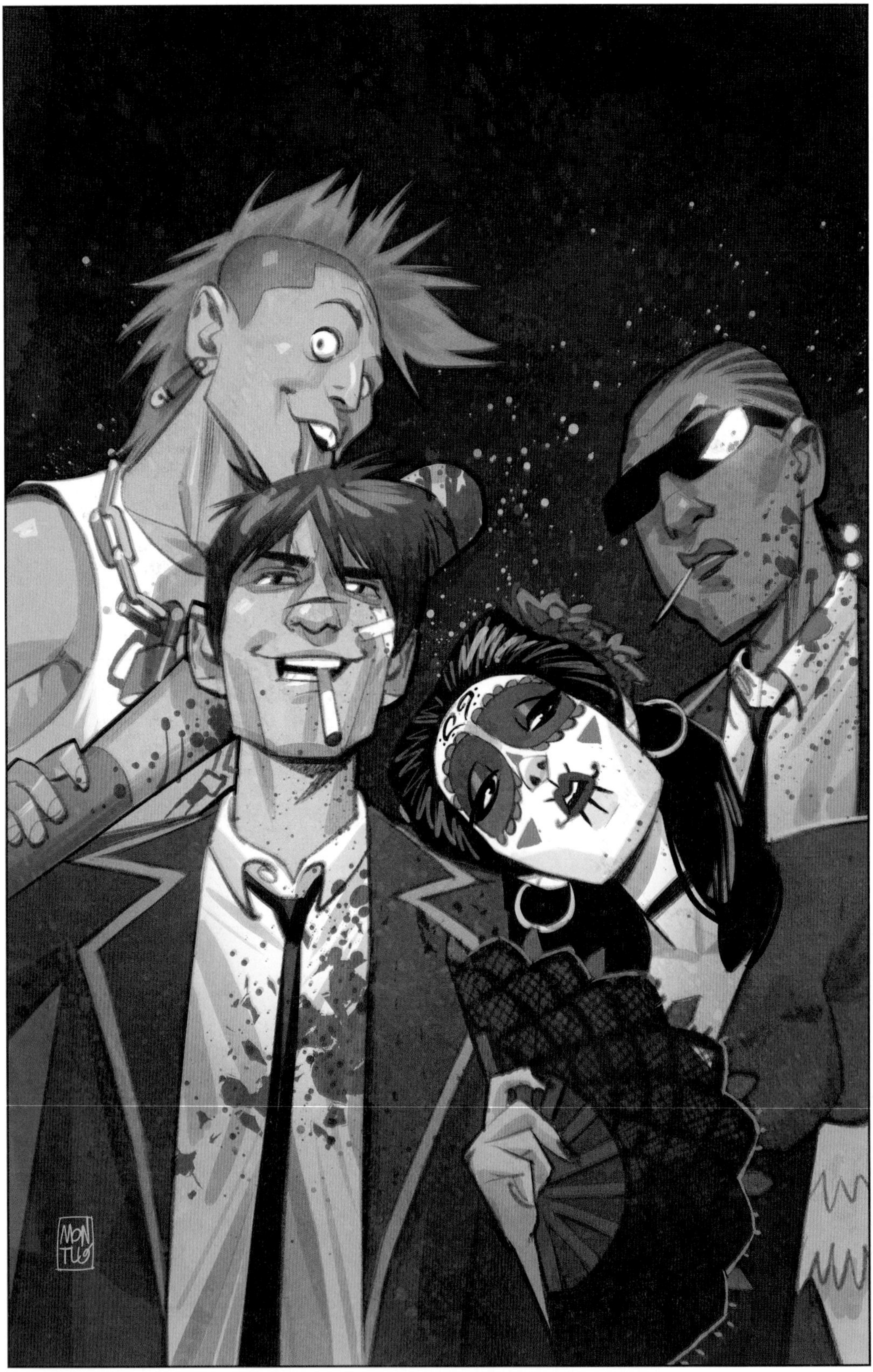

#56 VARIANT BY **MIKI MONTLLÓ**

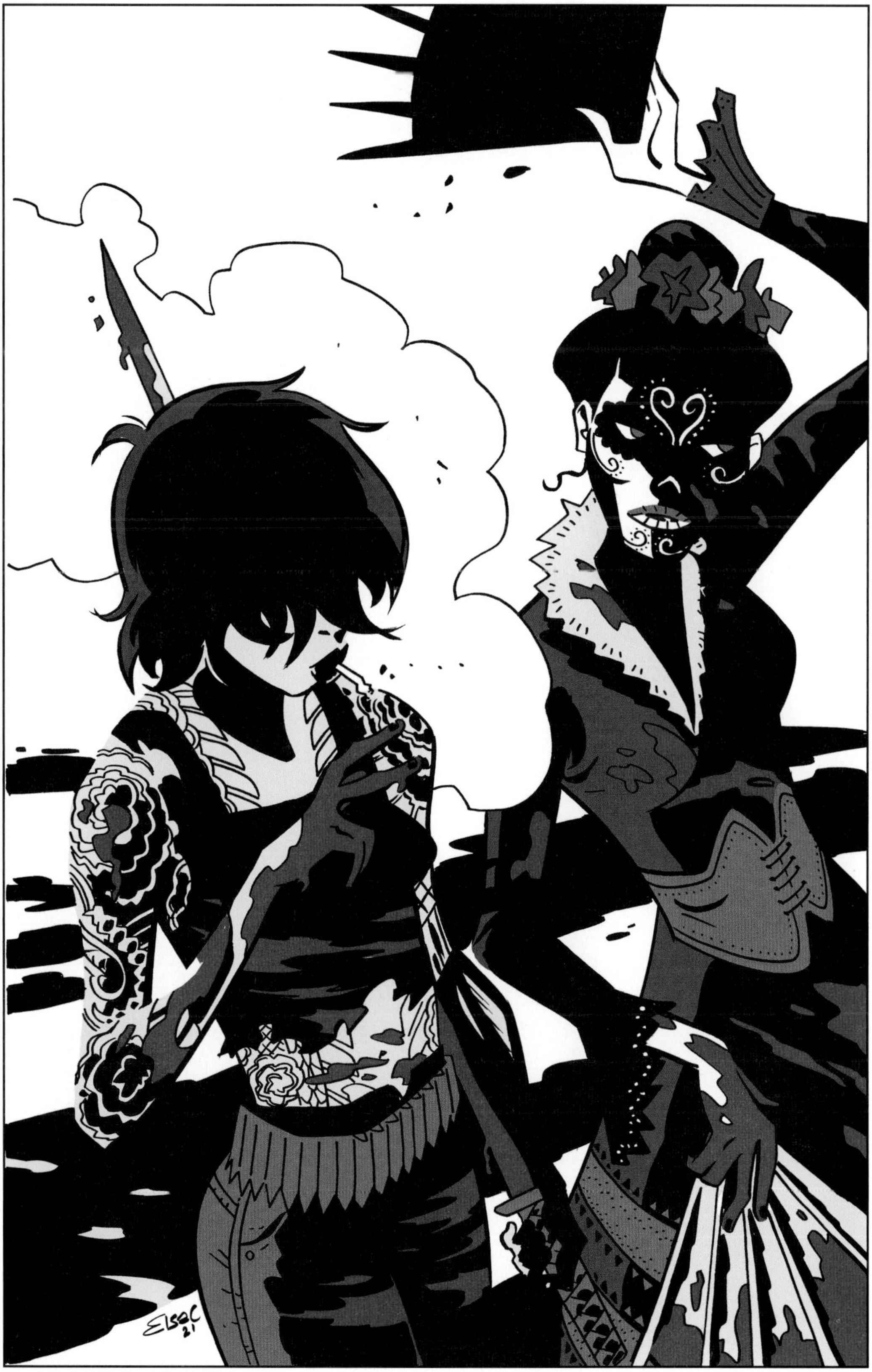

#56 VARIANT BY **ELSA CHARRETIER**

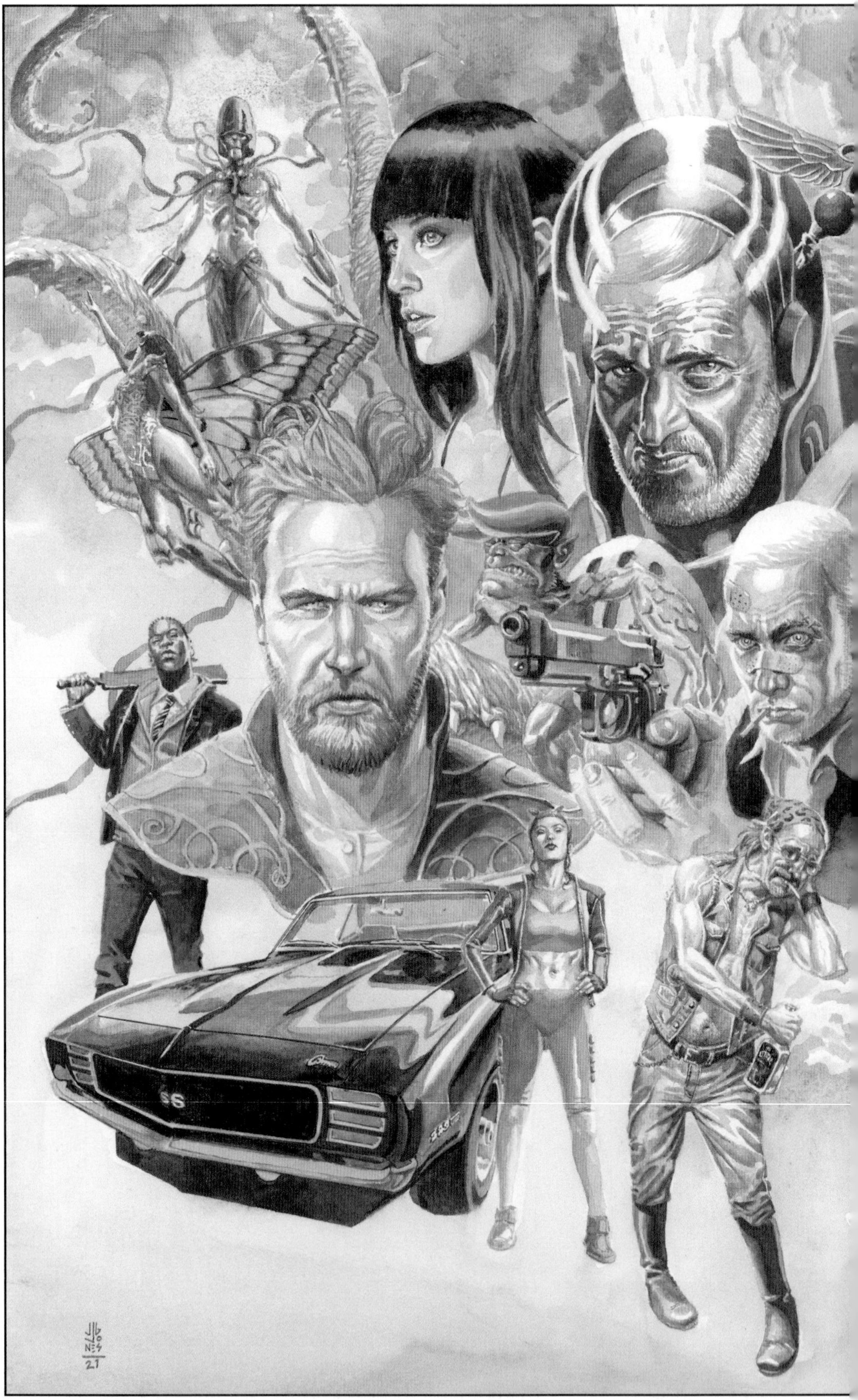

#56 VARIANT BY **J.G. JONES**

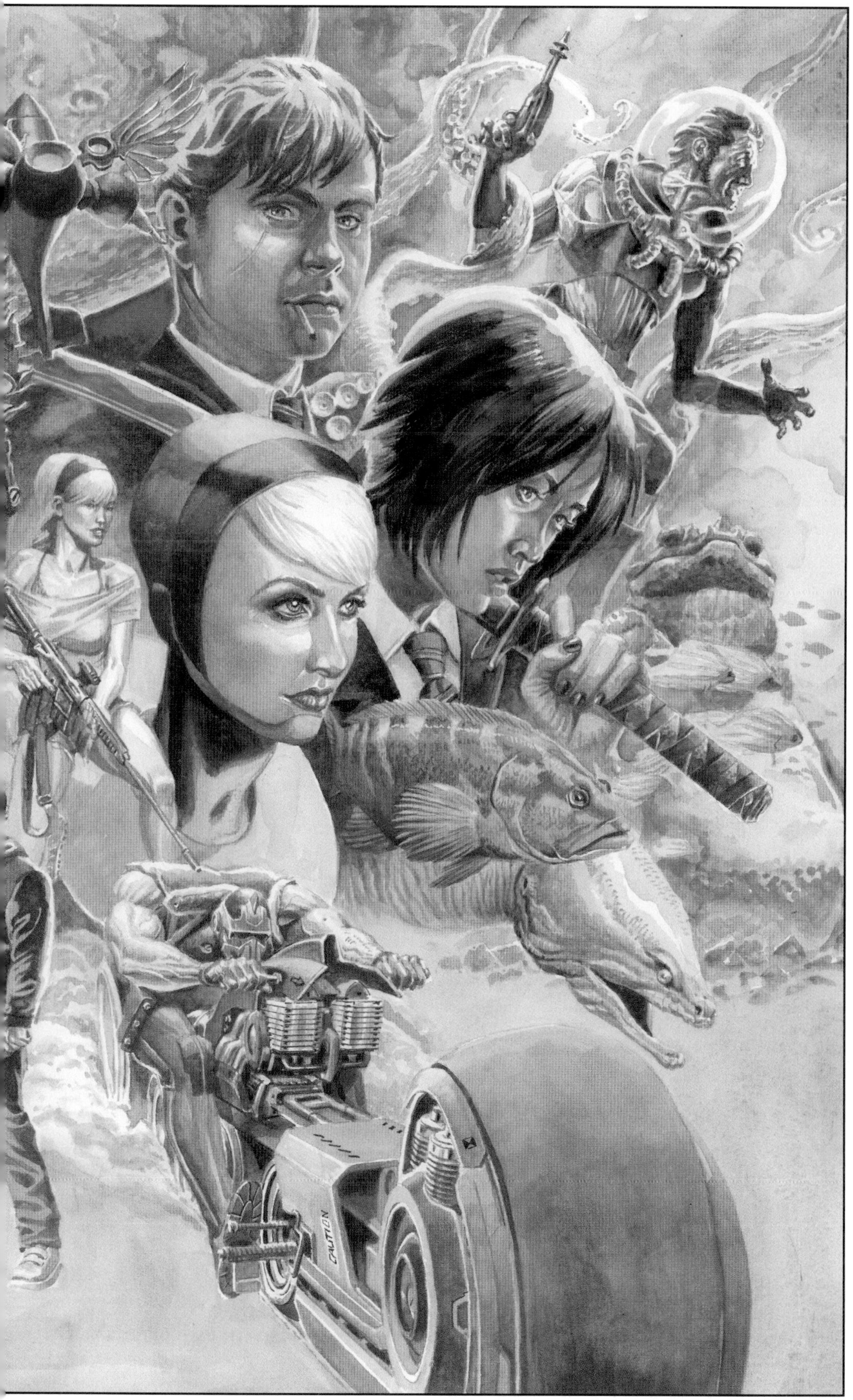
CAUTION

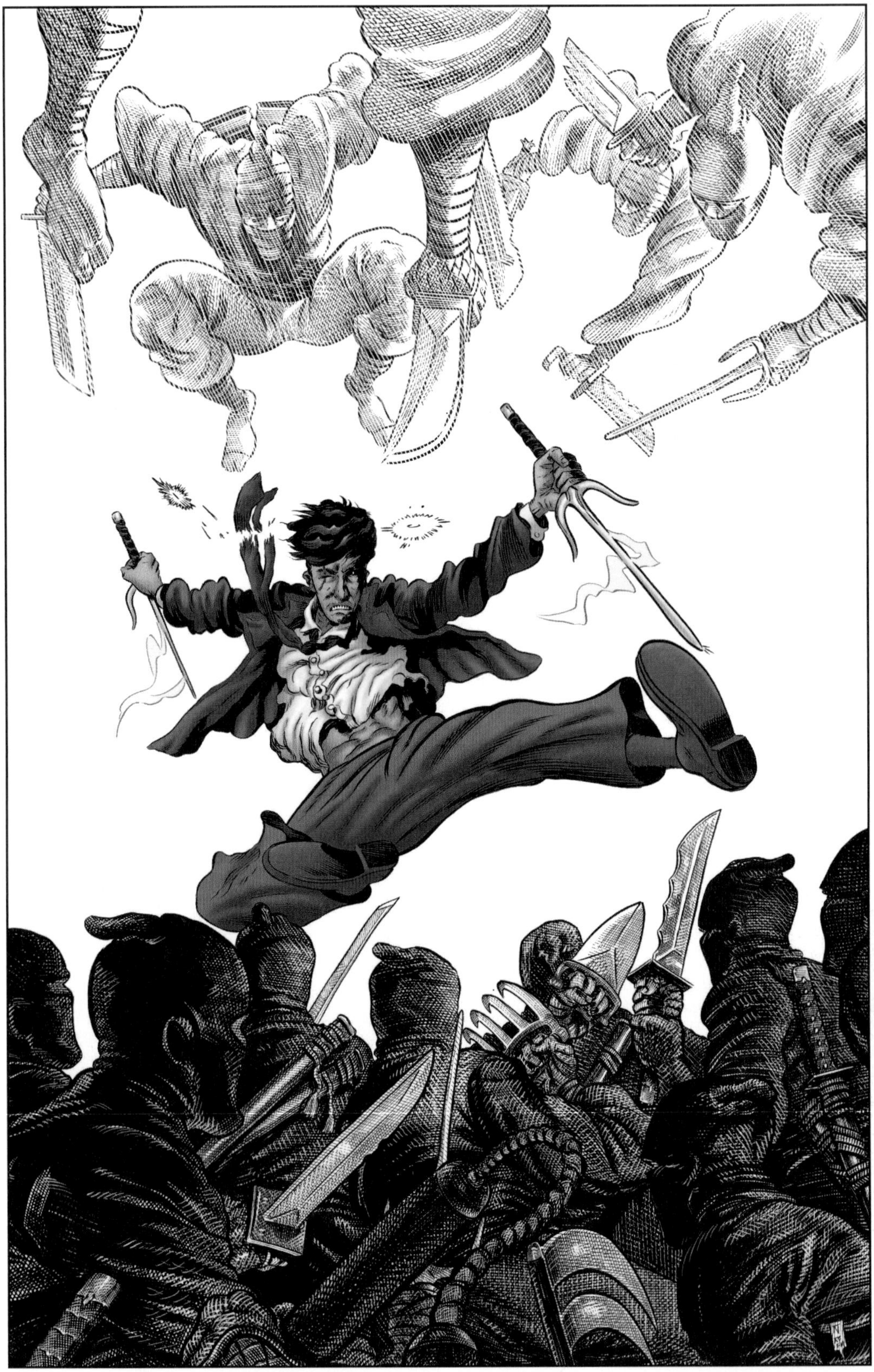

#56 VARIANT BY **TROY NIXEY & MICHELLE MADSEN**

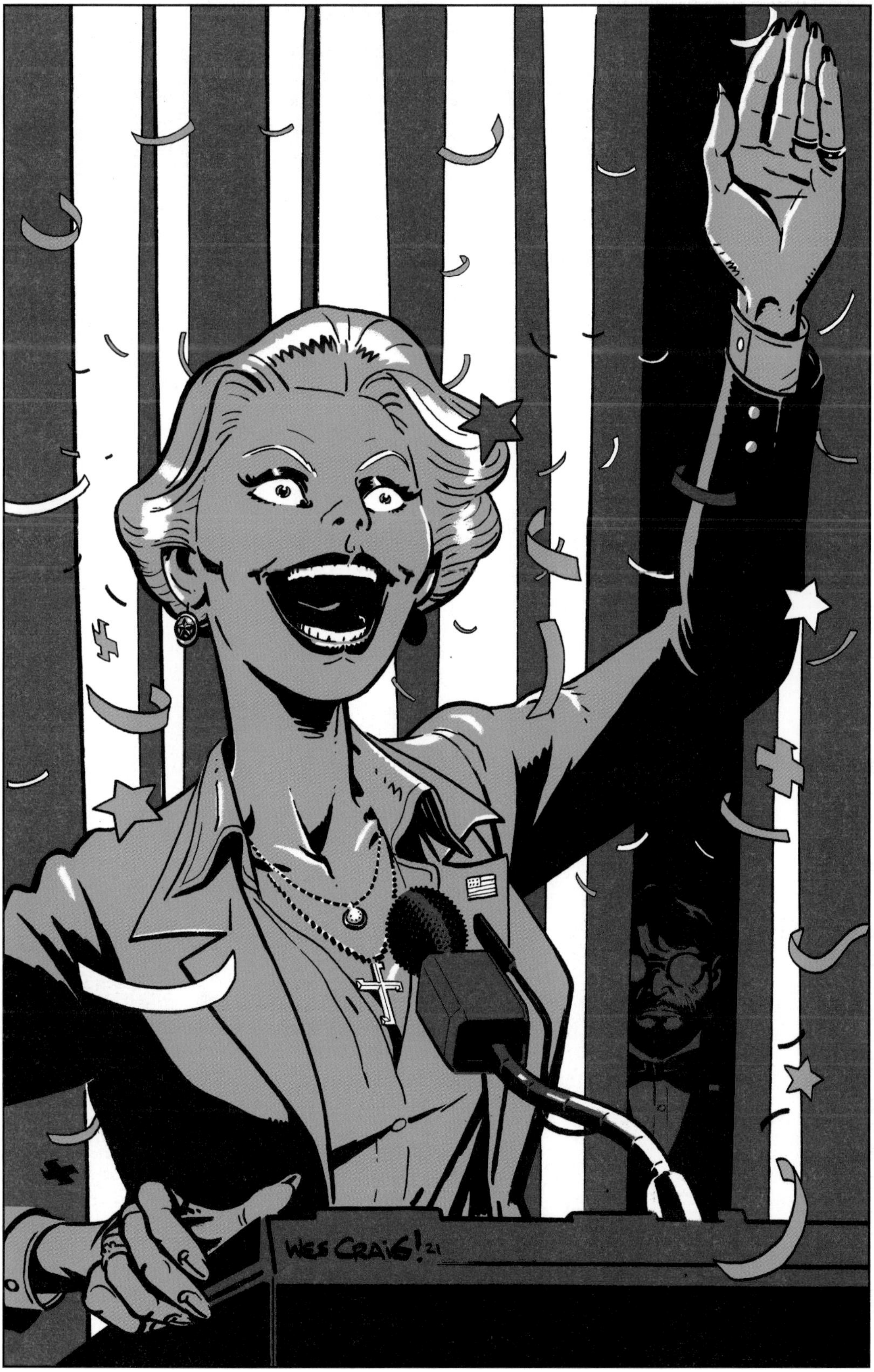
WES CRAIG!'21

#56 VARIANT BY **WES CRAIG**

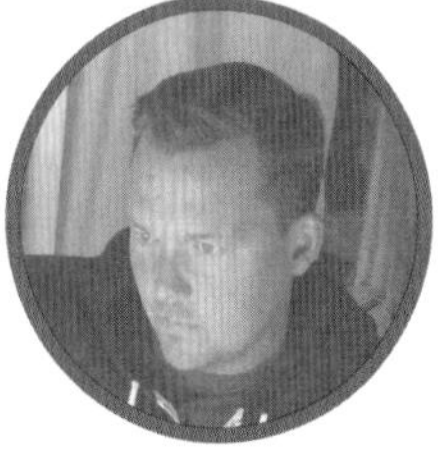

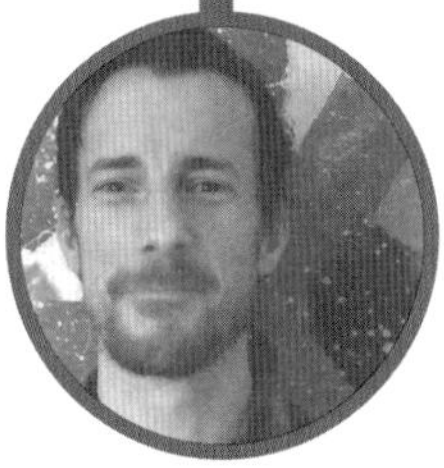

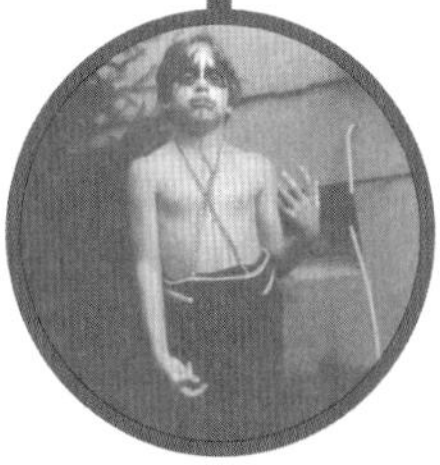

RICK REMENDER is the co-creator of *Deadly Class*, *Black Science*, *Seven to Eternity*, *LOW*, *The Scumbag*, *Fear Agent*, *Tokyo Ghost*, and more for Image Comics. His work at Marvel Comics is the basis for major elements of *Avengers: Endgame*, *The Falcon and the Winter Soldier*, and *Deadpool 2*. He's written and developed several sci-fi games for Electronic Arts, including the universally acclaimed survival horror title *Dead Space*, and he has worked alongside the Russo brothers as co-showrunner of *Deadly Class*'s Sony Pictures television adaptation. Currently, he's writing the film adaptation of *Tokyo Ghost* for Cary Fukunaga and Legendary Entertainment and curating his publishing imprint, Giant Generator.

WES CRAIG is the co-creator of *Deadly Class* and *The Gravediggers Union*, and writer-artist of *Kaya*, all from Image Comics. He has worked on such titles as *Batman*, *Superman*, *The Flash*, *Texas Chainsaw Massacre*, and *Guardians of the Galaxy* for DC and Marvel Comics. He currently lives in Montreal with his family.

LEE LOUGHRIDGE has been in the comic industry for over 20 years working on hundreds of titles. Lee is far more handsome than any other member of the *Deadly Class* team. The last fact was the basis for his previous departure from the book. He resides in Southern California longing for the days when his testosterone count was considerably higher.